Darkfall

M.L. Spencer

Stoneguard Publications

This is a work of fiction. All of the characters, organizations, and events portrayed in this novel are either products of the author's imagination or are used fictitiously.

DARKFALL

Cover by J Caleb Design
Edited by Morgan Smith

ISBN: 978-0-9997825-2-1

Printed in the United States of America

The Southern Continent

Malikar

ISHARA

BRYN
CALAZAR

GREYSTONE
KEEP

WOLDEN

Desert of
Maridur

FALBROOK

GANNET

CASSA
HOLLOW

AERYSIUS

Vale of Amberlie

AMBERLIE

Orien's Finger

GLEN
FARQUIST

AUBERDALE

The River Nerium

ROTHSCARD

The
Rhen

COVENDREY

ISLE
OF
TITHERRY

MERIDAN

SOUTHWARK

DARKFALL

M.L. Spencer

THE RHENWARS SAGA

Darkstorm (Prequel)
Darkmage
Darklands
Darkrise
Darkfall

Chapter One
Dawnbreak

Pass of Lor-Gamorth, The Front

Not all fires burn hot. The fires in Darien's heart raged like a cataclysm of ice, consuming everything he was, everything he'd been. All that he'd ever hoped to be.

He stood at the edge of the Black Lands, at the furthest extremity of the Rhen. A place where the sea of darkness behind him lapped against the promise of sunlight. As he gazed out across rolling foothills garbed in shadow, he realized the only thing left ahead of him was an end. He wasn't sure what that end would entail, or what it would look like. He only knew it would be final. And he looked forward to that finality.

Winding behind him through the Pass snaked a ragtag collection of survivors. Survivors who had, for a thousand years, forged an existence beneath the oppression of everlasting night. He wondered how they would endure under the glaring judgment of the sun. The thought bothered him, crippling his mind until it ground to a halt. He put the question aside, focusing instead on the vast, empty darkness below, a plain that stretched to the distant horizon, broader than eternity. And the spatters of light that glowed like fireflies, creeping out across the sprawling night.

The campfires of two armies awaited them below.

Darien sat down on a boulder. He looked up into the brilliant face of a full moon gliding toward the zenith of the sky, a sky more wondrous than any he remembered. No longer did the savage clouds rage and rush toward the horizon. High above stretched a starry grandeur he'd failed to appreciate until those pinpoint lights had flickered out, shadowed by the cursed darkness that plagued the world he'd left behind.

Below, the glow of campfires danced and taunted, beckoning like a siren's song. He knew better than to heed that call. It was what his enemy wanted: to lure them out from the protective walls of the canyon, to rush blindly into defeat. The Rhen's commanders had chosen their positions with slaughter in mind. Darien couldn't usher his own forces onto the plain without sacrificing the whole of his vanguard. Perhaps most of his army. Looking down, he could easily envision the mounded corpses that would collect and obstruct the mouth of the Pass. They would be forced to scale that gruesome wall. Then the enemy archers could pick them off at will.

It wouldn't even be a fight. It would be a massacre.

No, a sortie into the thick of the encampment was not an option. Without a miracle, they were pinned.

Perhaps he could provide that miracle.

The gravelly sounds of footsteps approached from behind. Darien didn't need to look to know that it was Sayeed; he had the distinct sound of the man's stride memorized. No other could replicate it; Darien would know the difference. When the officer drew up behind him, he turned and gazed up into the bearded face of his friend, his brother. The careworn look in Sayeed's eyes should have given Darien pause. But it didn't. He turned back around, looking out across the plain, considering the myriad campfires and their dire implications.

Sayeed bowed. "They have combined the armies of two nations into a single defensive force," he reported. "They have positioned archers and infantry to guard the mouth of the Pass."

"What do you need?" Darien sat gazing downward at the plain, his long hair stirring in the breeze.

There was a crunching noise as Sayeed shifted his weight. "We need a way of punching through their front ranks. Of creating a breach."

Darien nodded. He'd been thinking the same thing.

"I'll do it," he decided. With a sigh, he pushed himself up and turned to face his senior officer.

The man instantly threw his hands up as if trying to ward him off. "No, Brother. It is too dangerous—"

Darien shook his head, already moving past him. "No. It's not."

Sayeed rushed to catch up, but before he could protest further, Darien said, "I'll push their line back away from the mouth of the Pass. Send the infantry in after me. For every man that falls, have another ready to replace him."

He expected the Zakai officer to protest, but to his surprise, Sayeed didn't respond. He fell in beside Darien, matching him stride for stride as they descended the trail toward the bottom of the Pass. To where his forces huddled in the cold without enough fuel to build fires of their own, with empty bellies and determined minds, and a tenacious faith that remained unfaltering.

They reached the trail that meandered along the river bottom. On this side of the mountain divide, the flagging river trickled downhill toward the plain ahead. They followed the path along the watercourse past lines of hunkering soldiers, toward the forefront of the ranks. There Darien paused, gazing out through the narrow gap in the cliffs that formed the gateway to the Rhen. A gateway that now stood barred by forty thousand soldiers eager to deliver them to their deaths.

He pulled on his threadbare gloves, flexing his fingers. He drew the scimitar he wore at his waist, offering it to Sayeed, who received the blade gravely with both hands. Then he turned and, squaring his shoulders, strode forward.

"Husband."

Darien stopped with a sigh, closing his eyes. He didn't turn around. Instead, he bowed his head in defeat, waiting as Azár approached from behind.

"You promised. Never again." Her voice was as cold and flat as lead.

"So I did."

He turned and looked at her. His wife stood with her hands at her sides, her expression resentful. She had every right to be angry. He had betrayed Azár's trust and left her behind. It had been for her protection, but that hardly mattered. She'd made it abundantly clear that he would never repeat the mistake.

Darien had been born and raised a fighting man. He knew when he was beaten.

"Very well," he said. "I've been meaning to teach you some lessons. Perhaps now's the time for it."

He offered his hand. Azár stepped forward and took it, gazing upward into his face. The look in her eyes was fierce, daunting.

"Where you go, I go," she reminded him.

Darien nodded, internalizing her words. Turning back toward the mouth of the Pass, he started forward, hand in hand with his wife.

"Lord! Your armor!" Sayeed rushed forward.

Darien waved him away. "I don't need it. Have the infantry ready. This won't take long."

Behind him, the men were already rising to their feet, reaching for their weapons. He could feel their eyes on his back. He ignored them and kept walking. He raised his wife's soft hand to his lips, pressing a kiss against her skin.

"Feel through me," he said. "You'll have only a short while, and there's an awful lot to learn. Besides, I might need your help."

Azár looked at him and smiled, her eyes brimming with pride. "You won't need my help. My husband is the most dangerous man ever to walk the world."

"No," Darien said, softly, surely. "I'm not."

Hoyte Griswalt shivered in the cold. The small fire he'd built wasn't nearly enough to overcome the wintry chill that stiffened his joints and numbed his bones. His breath clouded the air before his face, his toes aching like open sores in his boots. It wasn't supposed to be this cold, not so far north or this late in the season. He understood weather; he'd plowed a field far more years than he'd taken coin to serve in the royal army. Weather was something he considered himself attuned to, something predictable most of the time. But this weather…it wasn't natural. Hoyte could swear there was something wrong with the wind. Or wrong with the world.

He leaned forward to warm his fingers over the dying coals of the fire, careful not to stress the longbow lying across his lap. He grimaced as feeling shot back into his hands along with a bone-throbbing ache. The fingerless gloves he wore did precious little good. He rubbed his hands together and brought his palms up to his face, blowing warmth into them.

"Fuck, it's cold," said Moss. He sat across the fire from Hoyte, hunched forward with a tattered blanket slung over his shoulders, warming his hands.

Hoyte envied Moss that blanket, just as he envied the man's thick beard. His own cheeks would only sprout a few patches of sparse whiskers, a family trait that never failed to rankle him. His boyish face had gotten him teased aplenty in his youth. It was even more of a curse now. A right good beard like Moss sported would go a long way toward warming his face. He reached up, running aching fingers over the pathetic growth on his chin.

"Damn fuckin' cold," Pinkston agreed, and spat into the fire. The glob of spittle hissed when it hit the coals. It was one of Pinkston's many talents. He could spit farther than any man in their company, and with acute precision every time. He was also the best bowman Hoyte knew. He had arms like an oak, and a calm steadiness Hoyte envied more than Moss' blanket.

"How long do you think we're gonna sit here?" Flem asked, worrying at a strip of jerky with perfect yellow teeth. He was the only man Hoyte knew with straight teeth. Even if the two front ones were big enough to remind him of a jackrabbit's grin. Flem finally tore off a bite, his jaw working slowly in a circular motion, popping as he chewed. Hoyte hated that sound. A man's jaw shouldn't pop like that. It wasn't right.

"We'll sit here however long it takes." Hoyte picked up a thatch of dry grass from a pile behind him and tossed it into the fire. The flames flared up for a moment with a puff of white smoke.

"Why'd you fuckin' do that?" Pinkston said, sitting up. "You know I fuckin' hate it."

Hoyte shrugged. He couldn't care less what Pinkston hated. He thought about tossing another handful of grass just to piss him off. Instead he turned to Moss and said, "Any more of those beans left?"

"Naw. All that's left's a few strips of meat."

"I'll take it, then. Give here."

"Tastes like dog," Flem warned, still chewing his mouthful like a cud, jaw popping with every bite.

Hoyte shot him a glare, leaning forward to snatch the leathery strip from Moss' hand. He tore off a bite and started chewing.

"I'm gonna take a piss," Pinkston said and stood up. He dusted off his pants then started walking away from the glow of the campfire. Hoyte listened to the sound of his footsteps trudging away.

The footsteps stopped abruptly.

"The fuck is that?"

Moss and Flem rose, clutching their bows. Hoyte frowned, wondering if it was worth getting up. He supposed it might be. With a groan, he pushed his stiff body off the ground, his joints popping like Flem's jaw. He worked his shoulders, trying to stretch some of the stiffness out of them. Holding his bow at his side, he walked over to where Pinkston stood staring out across the prairie with a slack mouth. He followed the man's gaze into the shadowy night. He didn't see a damn thing.

"What?"

Pinkston raised a gloved hand, pointing in the direction of the mountains. *"That."*

Moss and Flem drew up next to them, Flem swallowing his meat noisily. Hoyte stared across the grassland, which glowed like a silver sea under the full moon. Ahead, the foothills of the Shadowspears rolled away toward a jagged wall of darkness. The mountains towered over them as if holding up the sky. Hoyte's eyes traced the slopes of the foothills before focusing on the prairie. At the forms moving toward them through the night.

"What the hell?"

A man and a woman walked through the high grass, holding hands as if out for a moonlight stroll. A stroll through a kill zone.

"The fuck," observed Moss.

He exchanged a flummoxed glance with Pinkston, who shrugged hugely, shaking his head. All around, soldiers surged to their feet, fumbled for their weapons. Hoyte calmly looped his bowstring around the notch at the end of the shaft. Then he withdrew a handful of clothyard arrows, thrusting them into the ground at his feet.

"Ready your bows!" the captain bellowed from behind them.

Hoyte grabbed an arrow and raised his bow, angling it upward as his eyes fixed on the approaching man and woman. Neither wore armor, and they didn't appear to be armed.

What the hell?

"Hold!"

Hoyte froze, eyes fixed on the two people closing the gap of prairie toward their ranks. No, they weren't people, he chided himself. They were the Enemy.

"Emissaries?" Moss guessed.

Hoyte figured he might be right, though neither held a token of parley. It was possible they had come to negotiate. Apparently, the generals felt the same. Hoyte awaited the order to loose his shaft, but it didn't come.

The ranks bowed inward and opened up, admitting the man and woman into their midst. Archers swiveled to track their advance. Hoyte growled, realizing he now stood with his missile aimed at the company of bowmen across the gap. If the envoys proved treacherous, he was more likely to hit his own men than either of his marks. It was a bad situation, and he didn't like it.

"Hold!" the order came again.

Pinkston cursed under his breath, bow sagging at his side. Hoyte glared sidelong at him. "What?"

"It's him," Pinkston gasped, his eyes going wide. "Oh, gods, it's fucking him!"

"Who the fuck's *'him?'*" Moss demanded.

Hoyte felt his bowels loosen as he realized what Pinkston was trying to tell them. *"Lauchlin?"*

Pinkston stood there, head bobbing on his neck. Then he jerked into action, nocking an arrow as Hoyte had done. Flem stared ahead dumbly, his bow hanging slack at his waist.

"Draw!"

The shout confirmed Hoyte's worst fear. His eyes narrowed at the black-haired demon that had inserted himself into their midst. The man was still walking, deep inside their spreading ranks, holding the hand of a small woman whose eyes blazed with eager flames. Hoyte drew his bowstring back.

"*Loose!*"

Hoyte let the bowstring sing. He had another arrow nocked before the first had time to reach its target. He let the second missile fly as the first grouping of arrows shattered in a whiplash blast of air.

Screams and shouts drowned out bellowing orders as the ranks collapsed backward. Hoyte stooped to snatch up his remaining arrows, backing away as quickly as he could. From every side, men jostled and bumped against him in their eagerness to retreat.

A raging firestorm erupted behind them, followed by the awful sound of screams. Hoyte glanced behind to see an inferno gushing toward them from the center of the camp.

The men at his back scrambled forward in terror, shoving Hoyte against the men in front of him. Pinned on all sides, Hoyte dropped his bow and used his elbows to batter his way through the frantic mob. He glanced about desperately for Moss and Pinkston, but they were lost in the surging mass.

Another firestorm exploded only a short distance away. Hoyte felt the heat of it sear his face. Men and parts of men shot high into the air, raining down on those still fighting to escape. The roaring of flames drowned out the sound of screams, as more explosions erupted all around, guts and gore and severed limbs pelting down like battering hail.

Hoyte fought to keep his feet, terror driving him away from the exploding horror. He was shoved, punched, clawed, squeezed, and bludgeoned at every step. He fought his way forward, every inch of ground seeming a mile, as men on every side tried to push past or climb over the struggling mass ahead. Hoyte stumbled over corpses that lay trampled beneath the rage of feet. Soon he couldn't move. He couldn't breathe. The weight of soldiers around him crushed his arms against his ribs.

Hoyte would have howled in pain, but he couldn't suck enough air into his lungs to do it. He felt his ribs cracking. His legs gave out from under him. He should have fallen, but he was held upright by the sheer force of the surging masses.

A roiling furnace blasted him full in the face, ripping him out of the crowd and flinging him backward and up. He hit the ground hard, screaming in shock and pain. His arms scrambled feebly as he tried to lift himself up, but he couldn't get any traction with his legs.

He fought to raise his head from the ground and looked down at his body. At first, he couldn't understand what he was seeing. Then came understanding, along with horror. The last thing Hoyte saw as his vision dimmed was his charred backbone protruding from under his ribs, where his middle used to be.

Chapter Two
Aftermath

Pass of Lor-Gamorth, The Front

Darien glanced up at the star-scattered night that stretched on forever overhead. There were no clouds to darken the sky; it hadn't rained anytime recently. And yet, everywhere he stepped, the ground was slick with mud. He scraped the toe of his boot across the mucky soil and watched the furrow he'd created fill quickly with blood.

The smell was the worst. It rose from the mounds of smoldering corpses, borne across the battlefield by the smoke-fed air. Everywhere he looked, he saw the charred remains of fallen soldiers and horses. Some whole. Most not. The stench was nauseating. The smell of charred human was growing all too familiar. He'd smelled too much of it, too recently. It had a distinctive, sweet aroma. Roasted human smelled like roasted pork, except on a battlefield. There, mingled with the stench of blood and bowel, it was horrifically worse.

Especially when the burnt corpses were of his own making. And his own kinfolk.

The sounds of dying came from every direction and no direction, carried toward him on the air. Anguished moans and desperate weeping. All punctuated by raw, staccato shrieks, as knives worked tirelessly to open throats. His men ranged across the battlefield, sifting and prying through heaps of flesh in search of wounded. Those mortally injured were freed from their pain. Those who stood a chance of surviving were carried back to the encampment. Wounded soldiers of the Rhen were put to the knife, without exception.

Another ghastly shriek cut sharply through the smoke and stench. The sound made Darien's stomach tighten. He stood staring out across the carnage, contemplating the atrocity he had committed. He'd massacred thousands in just minutes, as he had done at Orien's Finger. Only, this time, he had slaughtered the same people he'd once sworn to defend. The thought dredged up waves of guilt he couldn't afford to feel. Guilt served no strategic purpose on a battlefield.

Azár squeezed his hand. Glancing sideways at her, he saw that his wife seemed to be weathering the carnage better than himself. She caught his stare and fixed him with a look of concern.

"This is difficult for you," she observed.

He ignored her and knelt beside a Rhenic soldier who lay moaning pitifully, clawing at his own spilled entrails as if trying to stuff them back inside. Darien stopped the man's heart then rose again. He strode forward, eyes scouring the field for other signs of life.

His gaze fell on one of his own men who lay groaning at the bottom of a heap of smoldering flesh. Darien tugged the first corpse off the top of the pile, rolling it wetly aside. Azár helped him shift the others. By the time they dug down to the wounded man, he was already dead. Frustrated, Darien cursed and whirled away.

He got only a couple of steps before he caught sight of Sayeed winding toward them through scattered piles of remains. The officer stopped in front of him, sweat mottling his brow despite the chill night air. He held his helmet tucked in the crook of his arm. His wet hair was plastered against his head, and there was a distinct line of blood around the edge of his face that resembled war paint.

He acknowledged Darien with a nod. "Lord—"

"Brother," Darien corrected.

Sayeed took a deep breath then started over. "Brother, the last of their infantry has been routed. Their officers fled on horseback at the onset of battle. We lost a little over two hundred warriors and estimate thirty-two thousand enemy casualties. We have taken over a thousand prisoners. What would you have done with them?"

Darien swept his gaze across the smoldering battlefield. There had already been too much death, and too little reason for it. At his feet lay the burnt remains of a fallen officer who wore the insignia of Chamsbrey. Two years before, he would have mourned the same man's death. Now, the only emotion he felt was anger. He despised the Rhen's generals for forcing him to resort to atrocity. Because of his past loyalties, they'd expected him to feel conflicted, to be weak. To soften the blows.

Which meant that anything short of ruthlessness would just prolong the slaughter.

Darien looked back up at Sayeed. "Spare ten prisoners and execute the remainder. Make certain those ten watch. Slay their wounded and scavenge what you can: weapons, arrows, supplies. Especially food. We need food. Slaughter any horses you find, living or dead. We need the meat."

Sayeed paled at his words. Darien could gauge the man's horror from the pallor of his complexion, which confused him. He hadn't expected such a reaction from an officer with Sayeed's discipline or experience. He shot a questioning glare at the man.

"Brother, what you ask is forbidden…"

"It doesn't matter," Darien snapped. "We can't afford to show mercy."

"I meant the horses," Sayeed corrected. "It is forbidden to eat the flesh of animals. Or to slay an animal—"

Darien barked an incredulous laugh. He'd just ordered the execution of hundreds of prisoners who had surrendered willingly. But his second-in-command was balking at the lives of a few horses. He glanced at Azár to find her nodding in agreement with Sayeed. He took a deep breath, struggling for patience. Then he fixed his gaze on both of them.

"We're not in the Black Lands anymore. We can afford to eat meat." Scoffing, he added, "Hell, we can't afford not to." He stalked away from the gaping officer, stepping over a Rhenic soldier who lay whimpering in agony. Without pausing, Darien willed the man dead.

He heard the sound of Azár's footsteps behind him, hurrying

to catch up. He slowed his pace and waited for her. Together, they waded side by side through a swampy sea of blood, charred bones, and charcoaled meat.

On impulse, Darien took his wife's hand and knelt over a wounded soldier with a shattered leg. He wanted her to feel the healing process through him. The techniques he used were well beyond her ability, but he hoped she would find something in the experience that might be useful. He was surprised to see only a look of frustration on her face.

"What did you do?" Azár demanded. "I could not tell. It was too fast, and you did too much all at once."

He shrugged. "Healing's probably the hardest skill to master. That's why not every mage was trained to it."

Azár dismissed his words with a wave of her hand. "I will learn. Next time go slower."

Reaching up, Darien rubbed his eyes in weariness. "I can't heal slower. It has to happen fast, or I'll just do more damage than I'm mending. Healing's not something that can be taught overnight. It takes years."

He knelt beside a woman with a hole in her chest and lungs drowning in fluid. Taking Azár's hand, he let her feel through him as he staunched the blood flow. He worked slowly to reweave arteries and capillary beds, building the flesh around them as they grew. He drained the fluid from her lungs and engorged them with air. When it was done, he rose and left behind a soldier who lay gasping and moaning in pain. But alive.

Darien soothed the woman to sleep. Then he glared at Azár. "That's as slow as I can work. It wasn't easy on her. I won't do it again."

Azár stared at him with a hurtful look. Ripping her hand out of his grasp, she rose and stalked away. She didn't get far before she whirled back around and snarled at him angrily, "You treat me like a child!"

Darien reminded her, "That's because you are a child. At least in this." He stood up but staggered, reeling from a surge of vertigo. He closed his eyes and took a moment to steady himself. The vast amount of power he'd handled was starting to take its toll. He was exhausted, and in no shape to be arguing with his wife in the midst of a battlefield.

Rubbing his eyes, Darien said wearily, "Given enough time, I could teach you to heal. It's the time part we don't have." Seeking to mollify her, he added, "Even if I had a thousand years, I could never weave your light."

Arms crossed, Azár looked at him with an unforgiving stare. Without another word, she turned and stalked ahead of him toward the next pile of corpses. Darien stood still for a moment, watching her go. Then he forced himself to move wearily after her.

He woke up groggy. Staring up into darkness, Darien felt a moment of disorientation. He didn't know where he was. He came to the slow conclusion that he must be back in his tent. Only, he didn't remember getting there. Confused, he pushed himself upright, the motion making him groan. His head throbbed with the familiar pain that came with overexertion.

A light appeared, brightening the canvas walls of the tent. At first, he thought it was lamplight. It took him a moment to realize it was magelight.

Azár's silhouette knelt beside him and pressed a cup of tea into his hand. It was hot and minty, and felt good on his throat. Darien relaxed and drank the warm liquid slowly, hoping it would help the ache in his head that throbbed to the rhythm of his pulse.

"What happened?" he asked.

Azár looked at him flatly. "You were stupid. You killed too many, then healed too many. It was too much."

He took another sip of tea. "I didn't heal enough."

"You cannot save the world," she growled.

Darien shrugged. "Maybe not. But I need to try." He set the cup down by his side and rose from his blankets. It was dim in the tent, even with her magelight. He stared around, looking for his clothes.

"Arrogance is the hallmark of fools," his wife muttered at his back.

"Then I suppose I'm an arrogant fool." Darien rummaged through the shadows until he found a shirt. Pulling it on, he asked, "What time is it?"

"It's night. You slept through an entire day. And part of the next night. Here. Eat something, fool."

Darien smiled as he accepted a bowl from her hand. The porridge inside was a tasteless mixture of grain and something he didn't recognize. Regardless, he swallowed it thankfully. Most of the men and women in his army had nothing to eat. Their rations had been used up before the battle for the Pass, and their supply lines were becoming stretched and strained.

Azár handed him his trousers. "Get dressed. Sayeed has a report you need to hear."

Darien stabbed a glare at her even as he obeyed. "You're my wife, not my mother," he grumbled. "Why didn't you tell me about Sayeed?"

"Because you needed to eat." Her voice was matter-of-fact.

Irritated, Darien struggled into his armor. Pulling on his boots, he grabbed his sword and threw back the tent flaps. A score of officers rose to their feet at the sight of him. In deference to his authority, they had made their small camp outside his tent. Sayeed came forward through the press of men, halting in front of him.

"Lord, it is good to see you hale," he said by way of greeting.

Darien only nodded in response. "You have something to tell me?"

"Your commands were carried out. We left the bodies where they lay." Sayeed shifted uneasily. "Lord, a scout returned from the ruins of the keep. You must hear what he has to say."

Turning, Sayeed gestured behind him. A soldier scrambled forward, dropping to kneel at Darien's feet.

Darien waved his hand dismissively. "Rise. Say what you came to say."

The scout climbed to his feet. "All glory to you, Lord. I was separated from my squad during the battle. I wandered the slopes of the mountains, looking for a path down. I found myself at the ruins of the old fortress. There, I saw three corpses."

Darien frowned. "Go on."

"Lord, one of the dead was Warden Connell."

Darien stiffened, the news catching him off-guard. Byron Connell had been missing since the battle for the keep. But Darien had just assumed he had returned to his own forces, which were camped behind them in the Pass. Cold dread crept over him as the implications of the scout's words sank in.

"Are you certain?"

"I am certain, Lord."

Darien's mind went silent. He stood grappling with his frozen thoughts, uncertain what to do about them.

The soldier continued, "There was another man lying dead, and there was also a woman. The woman…Lord, I have seen her before. She was the woman imprisoned with you in Tokashi Palace."

Darien's shock crystallized. His thoughts froze, then fractured like glass.

"Meiran…?"

He felt a hand rest softly on his shoulder. The sensation jolted him, making him flinch. Turning, Darien saw that Azár had come up behind him. Ignoring her, he turned back to the soldier.

"Take me there."

It took hours on horseback to gain the trail that led to the old keep. Sayeed rode at the front of their small party. He was mounted on the back of a skittish charger whose previous rider had attempted to desert during the battle. Azár rode behind, surrounded by a capable retinue of Zakai, the only men who had any experience on horseback.

When they reached the stairs that led to the ruins, Darien dismounted and handed his reins to a soldier. Accompanied by Azár and Sayeed, he mounted the same granite steps he'd climbed hundreds of times during the two long years he'd been stationed in the Pass. His feet still remembered the path, even though the stairs were cracked and crumbling away. The wind was up, whipping his hair and stinging his cheeks. It let up as they rounded the last switchback.

There, at the top of the steps, Darien halted. He stood staring at the naked foundation of the fortress that had, for over five hundred years, guarded the Pass of Lor-Gamorth. Now only a crumble of fallen walls and charred beams remained. Darien took a step toward a scattered pile of rubble that lay ahead—all that was left of the keep's high turret. The sight of the ruin brought with it a dull ache of sentiment. Darien's thoughts turned to Devlin Craig and Sutton Royce, his brothers in arms during the two years he had served at the Front. Craig and Royce had been the best friends he'd ever known, although they had both betrayed that friendship. So many friends fallen. Most because they had the misfortune of sharing his fate.

Darien turned away from the rubble and strode over to where Sayeed waited alongside the beardless scout who served as their guide.

"Where are they?" he asked.

The soldier effected a curt bow. "Lord, I found them over there." He nodded toward a half-collapsed wall jutting up from the ground.

Darien started in the direction the man indicated. He followed a narrow trail that turned into a precipitous path leading down behind the ruin. When Darien reached the crumbled rear wall, he froze, one hand lingering on the hilt of his sword. He couldn't press himself to go any further.

Two forlorn shapes lay sprawled before him in the dirt. One was Meiran. Darien stopped breathing, overcome by emotion. But it wasn't grief he felt. Neither was it anger. Whatever it was, it was incapacitating. He drew a breath, sucking it hard into his chest. It took long seconds before he could manage another.

On legs as rigid as logs, he stumbled over to Meiran's body and sank down at her side. She had been dead awhile. Her corpse stank of rot. Darien found himself looking down at a gray face that was caked with dried blood. Sunken, milky eyes returned his stare with a look of accusation. He lifted a hand and traced Meiran's bloated face.

"Darien."

He could feel Azár lingering over him, could hear the concern in her voice. He ignored her. Staring down at Meiran, Darien didn't know what to feel. So he decided not to. He climbed to his feet and walked away, leaving Meiran in the dirt.

He went to the corpse that lay just a short distance away. The broken, gaping face looked familiar to him. It took him a moment to remember the man's name: *Traver Larsen*. He'd been Kyel Archer's friend. Darien tucked that piece of information away, saving it for later. He wandered up the slope, his eyes scanning the ground.

"The Warden is over here, Lord."

Darien turned in the direction of the scout's voice. The man stood beside the guts of a shattered wall that had disgorged its blocks over the black soil of the mountain. Darien walked to where the scout indicated, taking in the sight of Byron Connel lying face down on the path. Stooping, he rolled the man over. The stench that action provoked was nauseating. Darien winced away, fighting to keep the contents of his stomach down. It took a moment for the air to thin out enough to properly examine the corpse.

The cause of death wasn't hard to figure out. An ebony hilt protruded from Connel's eye socket. Darien gripped the handle and withdrew the blade. He held it in his hand and turned it slowly. It was the same knife that had once belonged to Garret Proctor, the Force Commander of Greystone Keep. He wiped the blade clean in the dirt, then gazed down at the corpse, speculating. Byron Connell had been one of the greatest military commanders known to history. And yet, he'd been brought down by a fragile, thin-bladed knife. It defied credulity.

But who had wielded it?

Another thought occurred to him, one far more alarming: *Thar'gon.*

Darien bolted to his feet and searched the ground around Connel. The Warden's talisman would have fallen somewhere close by. But, disturbingly, he didn't see it. Darien began pacing in a slow circle. His gaze roved over every rock, every grain of soil, every shadowed depression in the dirt.

The morning star wasn't there.

"Husband. What are you looking for?"

He'd forgotten Azár was following him. "Connel's weapon," he mumbled without pausing in his search.

A look of troubled understanding grew on Azár's face. She took a cursory glance around. "Perhaps it was looted."

Darien shook his head, growing agitated. He raked a hand through his hair. His eyes continued scouring every inch of soil. "It's designed to be wielded only by the Warden of Battlemages. I'm the only Battlemage left."

"Well, someone took it." Azár looked at him blandly. "Perhaps the weapon allowed another to carry it, someone who could pass it on to you."

Darien almost dismissed her comment as absurd…but then he realized she might be right. He stopped his pacing and halted, staring dully at the ground.

"Kyel…" he whispered, shaking his head slowly in confusion. "I don't understand. Why him?"

Sayeed strode forward to stand beside him. "Pardon, Brother," he said, looking apprehensive. "Perhaps it is because this Sentinel Kyel is alive. And you are not."

Darien hadn't thought of that. It was easy to forget that the flesh he clung to was only temporary, that he was merely a ghost in human clothing.

But even that didn't make sense. Byron Connel had been just as dead as himself. The more he thought about it, the more Azár's theory made sense. Thar'gon could have allowed the first mage who touched it to pick it up, on the chance it would be passed to its rightful master. Frustrated, Darien glared down at Connel's corpse.

"We should bury them. Help me get some rocks."

They spent the remainder of the night piling rocks to make a single burial cairn. When the last stone was laid in place, Darien stood back and bowed his head in troubled silence, battling the same conflicted emotions he'd fought earlier. He didn't know what he felt, or what he should be feeling. For so many years, Meiran had been the one thing in the world that mattered to him most. Her betrayal was like a raw wound that had never fully healed. He couldn't help the grief he felt over her death. And he also couldn't help the satisfaction.

Reaching up, he unstrapped the baldric that crossed his chest and removed his sword's harness. He drew the blade from its sheath then flung both harness and scabbard to the ground. Reversing his grip on the hilt, he used all the strength of his anger to drive the blade deeply into the ground.

He left the weapon there and walked away.

Chapter Three
The Warden's Promise

Pass of Lor-Gamorth, The Front

They rode in uneasy silence down the mountainside.

The sky rumbled and raged overhead, echoing Darien's mood. He glanced up as a streak of lightning stabbed a nearby slope, the air erupting in crackling thunder. The horse beneath him jumped sideways and tried to bolt. He pulled the reins close, fighting to calm the animal. With a defiant snort, the stallion yielded control back to him.

He was in a black mood. Too many thoughts raged in his head, warring for dominance. Each fleeting thought bubbled to the surface and then sank, tumbling back down. First Meiran's blood-crusted face gaped up at him, accompanied by an upwelling of grief and loathing. Then Kyel flashed before his mind, wielding Thar'gon in his hand—a thought so dreadful it made Darien flinch. He'd made a tremendous mistake, leaving Kyel alive. He regretted that decision now. He suspected he'd regret it even more later.

Below, the fog in the river bottom parted, and their encampment came into view. There were no lights of cookfires; there was no coal to burn. The camp was almost completely broken down. His own tent was one of the few that remained intact.

Looking at Sayeed, he asked, "How long until we march?"

"The forward camp is not yet prepared," Sayeed informed him.

"Good. That'll give me time to rest."

When they attained the camp, Darien tied his horse to the picket and returned to his tent. He threw his boots into a corner, his mail shirt following them to the ground. Feeling exhausted, he cast himself down on his pallet. He sat there until he heard Azár enter after him. She paused in the tent's entrance, one hand holding back the flap. She took a step inside, letting the canvas sway closed.

"My husband does not look well," she observed, taking another step toward him.

Darien kept his stare angled at the floor. "I'm fine."

She sat beside him and looked into his eyes. "Do you wish to speak of it?"

"No."

There was a long pause that conveyed the weight of her hesitation. After a moment, she said, "I know Meiran mattered very much to you. I know it must be hard for you to—"

"Stop." Darien jerked away from her. "You have no idea how I feel."

Azár's face hardened. She stood up, scowling. "You're right. I do not. That is because you are like a wall to me. How am I supposed to walk beside my husband, if he will not speak his heart?"

Darien glared at her through several layers of irritation. "That's your problem to figure out. When it comes to Meiran, you *will* respect my privacy. What I feel—or felt—for her is none of your damn concern. Understand?" She had no business in his feelings. His feelings were his own.

A troubled silence settled between them.

"I understand," she said at last, though he knew she didn't.

But it didn't matter. All that mattered was that she was done trying to drag his emotions out to dissect on the floor.

"I'm going to get some sleep." He lay back, tugging the blankets up, and turned away from her.

He awoke to a slobbering tongue wetting the side of his face. The sensation was accompanied by a putrid stench that was fondly familiar. Groaning, Darien reached up and pushed the weight of the demon-hound off him. The grisly thing moved back, its tail drumming against the floor.

"Theanoch."

The thanacryst obeyed with a whine, its jaw snapping shut. It stared at him dejectedly.

He rubbed his eyes. Groping at the pallet next to his, Darien found the covers empty. Azár had either awakened before him or had never slept at all. He summoned a blue glow of magelight, enough to look around. The tent was empty. Even his possessions had been packed up and carried out. Only his clothing and armor remained, piled where he'd left them in the corner.

Darien donned his boots and his mail shirt, strapping on the scimitar Sayeed had given him for a wedding gift. *Valdivora*. It had once been carried by Khoresh Kateem, the notorious conqueror who had united the tribes of Caladorn into the largest empire in history. The sword had such an important role in deciding events that had shaken the world, that Darien had been hesitant to wear it. But he didn't have a choice now. It was the only sword he had left.

He emerged from the tent and found his men forming up for the march. Frustrated, Darien wondered why no one had thought to wake him. He set out toward the horse pickets, where he found Azár untethering her mare. She saw him approaching and mounted up, kicking her horse forward and angling away from him. Darien watched her go.

He crossed the camp toward his own stallion, the demon-hound keeping pace with his strides. The soldiers paid the thanacryst no mind as he wove through their midst. It had long ago stopped being an anomaly.

Darien untied his horse and mounted up. He kicked the stallion to a canter, riding toward the front of the column. Sayeed and Azár were already there. His wife glanced his way as he drew up at her side. The anger on her face was still there, looking permanently etched into her skin. She turned away and made a conspicuous effort to avoid eye contact.

As the column moved forward, Darien found himself wondering how long his wife was going to shun him. He didn't have an answer. He didn't understand her any better than he understood himself.

＊

As they rode out of the Pass, the clouds slowly loosened their grip on the sky. Streaks of sunlight broke through the layers, blinding rays that slanted down and dappled the slopes of the foothills. Eventually, the clouds yielded altogether, revealing a sky more furiously blue than Darien remembered. He squinted, his vision overwhelmed by the brilliant glare of sunlight. He brought a hand up to shield his face, his eyes watering. He heard gasps and cries from the soldiers behind him, many of whom had never seen the miracle of daylight.

Their joy came to a nauseating end.

Before them, stretched out across the plain, was a thick black scar where the battle had been waged. The carnage had been left untouched for two days, the dead left where they'd fallen. The air was filled with the consistent cries of birds: black ravens whose sheer numbers carpeted the battlefield and thickened the skies. Darien's stomach twisted at the sight of the birds, at the vast number of dead sprawled across the ground or collected in decomposing hummocks.

When they waded into the sea of rot, the stench became unbearable. Darien held his cloak over his face, though the thick fabric did little good. Hordes of flies bloomed up from the ground, the sound a loud, consistent drone. The stench and the noise set Darien's horse on edge. The stallion laid back its ears and tugged its head, fighting for control of the bit. Darien steadied it with a firm grip on the reins.

The sounds of their passage startled great mobs of birds, which took wing in squalling protest. They swirled in the sky, a bulbous and writhing mass, before settling back down. Looking out across the roiling sea of decay, Darien felt enraged. There was no reason for this waste. No reason why he'd had to resort to such savagery. All of this blood wasn't on his hands. It was on theirs. The commanders of the Rhen could have withdrawn their forces and let them pass. Instead, they'd ordered their soldiers to stand their ground against impossible odds. It was unsettling. And infuriating.

Clucking at his horse, Darien urged the stallion faster.

They reached the forward camp just as the sun's red disc sank beneath the grassland. The sky was a hostile red streaked with gold, an expansive display of beauty that captured Darien's gaze. It had been years since he'd last seen a sunset. He'd forgotten how powerful they were.

As they rode into the encampment, he saw that the command tent had already been raised. It was another testament to the ingenuity of the Tanisars when they were on campaign: they had a way of leapfrogging campsites to hasten the march. As the rear camp was broken down, the forward camp was already being pitched. There were actually two command tents. The one left behind in the Pass would be packed up and moved ahead of them and readied for the next day.

Sayeed set their course toward the pavilion. Darien balked, drawing back his horse's reins. He was too drained to want to deal with the clamor and challenge of the war chiefs. His emotions were too rough, too brittle. He needed time to find some clarity.

"No." He shook his head. "Not tonight. I just want to find my own tent."

Sayeed turned back to him with a confused expression. "This is your tent."

Darien opened his mouth to object, then realized he had no objection to make. With Byron Connel dead, it made sense that he would assume the Warden's command. And his tent. Darien wondered what the elders of the tribes would think about that; he was only blood of their blood through marriage. He didn't want to fight another challenge to his legitimacy.

He dismounted alongside the pavilion and handed his horse's reins to a waiting soldier. Sayeed at his side, Darien walked toward the tent on stiff legs. He stopped at the entrance, not wanting to go in. It didn't seem right. None of it felt right, like it didn't fit.

Sayeed patted his shoulder. "Go in, Brother. I will have your possessions brought to you."

Darien asked, "What about Connel's things?"

The officer shrugged. "Do with them what you will. They are yours now."

Darien followed the man's suggestion and entered the tent. The smell of incense filled his nostrils. It took a moment for his eyes to adjust to the ambient light of the interior. Hanging fabric cordoned off several rooms, and the floor was layered with over-lapping rugs. Through a gap between curtains, he saw that a large table had been set up in one of the partitions. A few men were already seated on the floor in the gathering area. They looked up and frowned at the sight of him.

Darien leaned his sword against the canvas wall. Then he made his way through the cloth partition that cordoned off Byron Connel's personal quarters. Inside was a large four-poster bed with a matching wardrobe, along with cushioned chairs and an iron rack made to hold armor. Bright fabric hung from the walls and the ceiling, the floor layered with sumptuous rugs. For a mo-ment, Darien stood staring incredulously. It all looked so surreal in the midst of a military encampment. It defied reason.

His attention was drawn to the far end of the room, where a book rested on a pedestal. The sight was so peculiar that he couldn't keep himself from wandering over to it. The tome was open, a blue silk ribbon marking the page. Darien gave the text a cursory glance, enough to see that the words were some type of poetry, perhaps an epic ballad. He read a few stanzas before deciding it was not a work he was familiar with.

He heard Azár enter and pause to stand behind him. Darien supposed he couldn't keep avoiding her. But he also didn't know what to say. So he stood there waiting, staring at everything in the tent but her. Preparing himself to weather another barrage of questions he didn't want to answer.

But instead of speaking, Azár simply drew near and wrapped her arms around him. Surprised, Darien hugged her back, won-dering at her change of heart. Azár's touch felt good, comforting. Gradually, he felt the rage of emotions in his head dwindle to a manageable fury. She held him for a long time then pulled back to look into his face, her gaze wandering over his features.

Darien took her by the hand and guided her toward the bed. This time, she let him.

He woke from sleep to a loud blur of conversation. Guessing the cause, Darien rose and dressed. Azár still slumbered in their oversized bed, one hand lingering on a pillow, fingers outstretched. The covers pulled over her body rose and fell in a gentle, consistent tide. Darien lingered for a moment, composing his thoughts, then slipped through the partition into the main gathering area of the tent.

The pavilion was crowded with people. They sat scattered in small groups across the floor. Food was arranged on long drapes of cloth that had been rolled out, covered with bowls and communal platters. There was a constant buzz of discussion, broken only by abrupt spikes of laughter. Darien looked around at the spread of food, wondering what the soldiers in the camp were eating.

The conversation died as people took notice of him. Sayeed sat close by, surrounded by a small group of Zakai. Darien recognized many of the other faces as the warlords and elders of the various clans. They were all staring at him expectantly, as if waiting for him to speak. By the wary looks he was receiving, he gathered his newfound authority was not universally accepted.

Darien decided it was time to formalize the position he'd inherited from Connel. If the war chiefs wanted to challenge him, it would be better if they did so now instead of later. He couldn't afford his orders to be questioned, and the last thing he needed was a power struggle.

Looking at the men and women seated before him, Darien said, "I'll accept your pledges of loyalty now."

Many of the faces darkened with anger. A few of the younger men threw their bowls to the floor and stood up. He knew several of them, and he also knew their temperaments. They were warriors and did not yield easily. They respected authority only when it was wielded over them like a hammer.

The leader of the Jenn Kadeesh rose and stood towering over him, looking Darien up and down as if assessing a bad piece of meat. With a heavy frown, he grumbled, "You might be a Battlemage, Darien Nach'tier. But you are not Warden. Only Zavier Renquist can name you so."

Sounds of collective agreement echoed from all around the tent. Even the elders sat nodding. Darien fumed. Apparently, nothing came without a struggle, even actions that seemed obvious and logical. He was getting tired of people pushing him further than he wanted to go. He hoped the tribal leaders would relent before things went that far.

"Zavier Renquist isn't here," he informed them. "I'm taking Byron Connel's place as Warden of the Combined Legions of Malikar. If you wish to argue, go ahead—but I'll win that argument. I have a goal. And I'll not be deterred from it."

The men stared at him with defiant faces.

Sayeed rose from the floor and whispered in his ear, "They will not give you their loyalty. You must take it."

Darien understood. He would have to prove he had the fortitude and resolve to lead Malikar's armies. In order to lead, he would first have to conquer.

He closed his eyes and reached out from within, taking hold of the magic field. Shadows bloomed within the tent as the light of the lanterns faded to darkness. He concentrated harder, feeding the air with just a trickle of power. After a moment, quiet, uncomfortable noises reached his ears. He drew harder on the magic field, applying more heat and pressure to the air, feeling it thicken around him, until the tent was filled with cries and moans.

Darien held the tormented air in the tent for a minute longer. At last, he let the light return and willed the air to cool and thin. He opened his eyes to find men and women sprawled across the floor, groaning in pain. Shaken elders, pale and trembling, turned to confer with their war chiefs.

Darien didn't wait for them to decide their positions. Stepping forward, he growled to every man and woman gathered in the tent, "Now kneel and pledge me fealty!"

There was a moment's hesitation. Then every elder in the room went to their knees, bowing forward. They were followed by the officers and then, eventually, the war chiefs.

Darien stood staring down at their backs in fury. He made them wait in the position of prostration a long time, each man and woman frozen as if carved from stone. After minutes, he walked to the back of the pavilion and claimed the bench-like chair Connel had ruled from.

One by one, the war chiefs came forward to offer their pledge. When the last man had kissed his hand, Sayeed rose and retrieved Darien's sword. In one graceful motion, the officer bared *Valdivora* from its sheath and dropped to his knees. He bowed his head deeply and, cradling the blade in both hands, offered it to Darien.

Loudly, Sayeed proclaimed, "His Excellency, Darien Lauchlin Nach'tier, Warden of Battlemages, Last Sentinel of Aerysius, and Xerys' Shadow on Earth!"

Darien rose and accepted the sword, sweeping it around and down, parting the air with a hiss. He looked down at Sayeed.

"Sayeed son of Alborz, I name you First Among Many."

Sayeed remained frozen on his knees, absorbing his elevation in silence. But another man surged up behind him, face set in lines of outrage. Darien recognized him as Byron Connel's second-in-command.

"Warden!" the warrior cried. "By tradition, the office of the First is reserved for the general of Bryn Calazar's legions!"

"No longer." Darien glared the man back to his knees.

A cold and heavy stillness settled over the pavilion, encasing them all in silence. Long seconds wore away, each seeming to bear the weight of eternity. At last, Darien surrendered his sword into Sayeed's keeping and sank back down on the bench. He leaned back, spreading his arms as if assuming a throne. The men and women remained on their knees, eyes still fixed upon the ground.

"You may rise," Darrien allowed.

As the warlords settled back to their respective places, Darien turned his gaze to the man who had challenged him. "Make your report then leave my presence."

The general rose and, raising a hand to his chest, bowed stiffly. "Warden, the way ahead lies open and undefended before us."

Darien waved a dismissal, hastening the man out of the tent. He turned to the commanders who remained. "Advise."

There was a low murmur as the war chiefs conferred quietly. Eventually, the warlord of the Beyads rose to his feet. "Warden, we must apply our minds to the problem of logistics. As we move deeper into this land, it will become more difficult to maintain our supply lines."

"Agreed." Darien nodded. "What do you suggest?"

"We need to take care how quickly we move our civilians south of the Pass. It would not be wise to stretch our baggage train thin until we gain control of this region's food production."

Darien nodded. The words were an echo of his own thoughts. "That would be wise. What else?"

The men before him broke out in a chorus of suggestions and requests. Darien raised his hand, silencing the gathering.

"Stop. We need to provide food for our people. Until that's taken care of, no other problem exists. These are my orders: further restrict rationing. Allocate less resources to the civilians— we need our warriors strong enough to fight. We'll advance southward through the plains and scavenge food as we go."

An old woman who wore the mantle of a war chief stood and spread her arms expansively. "Forgive me, Warden, but this region appears unpopulated. Will there be food enough to sustain us all?"

Darien leaned forward in his seat, addressing not just the woman, but every chief and elder gathered in the pavilion. "We won't find enough food in the grasslands. Which is why we'll have to advance quickly. We'll go town by town, filling our stomachs as we go. Once we reach the population centers, we'll have more food than we can eat."

He paused for a moment, letting his resolve solidify. "We need more than just food. We need our own land. Our own borders. Our own sovereignty. We need everything they have, and there's only one way we'll get it. We'll take this land from them and make it our own. We'll drive them from the North."

Chapter Four
Creek Hollow

Kyel Archer didn't like the looks of Creek Hollow. The windows of the town reflected the sunset's orange glare, a harsh intrusion into the tranquility of the forest. Craggy rooftops poked out from behind a palisade that spiked like jagged teeth out of the ridge ahead. The strong odor of wood smoke drifted toward them on the air, overwhelming the clean fragrance of the pines.

He rode alongside Cadmus on a trail that meandered through the dappled shadows of a forest. Kyel concentrated on the stillness of the grove: the faint stirring of leaves, the steady creak of his saddle, the dull plodding of his horse's hooves. The insistent hammering of a woodpecker echoed through the trees, along with the faint scampering of squirrels rummaging in the branches overhead.

"I really hope there's an inn," he commented. His voice sounded louder than he'd intended, interrupting the stillness of the grove.

"If you'd wanted an inn, then we should have taken the Northern Road," Cadmus grumbled, not for the first time.

Kyel ignored him and closed his eyes, savoring the quiet. The cleric had been complaining about his choice of route ever since they'd bypassed Wolden and headed west toward the Vale of Amberlie. Kyel had avoided the usual trade routes, desiring their passage to go as unnoticed as possible. He wanted to arrive in Glen Farquist alive, not delivered on a bier.

He reached down to grip the haft of the morning star affixed to his saddle. Instantly, he felt a soothing wash of magic flood into him from the talisman. It was as though the weapon wanted to be held and was discontent at merely riding at his side. Whenever he touched it, the artifact brought him a feeling of contentment he hadn't felt in years. It was the only thing that relieved the tension of his nerves. They had been stretched to razor-thinness ever since he'd absorbed Meiran's gift from her dying body.

Kyel shuddered, thinking of the awful amount of power contained within him. It was quiescent at the moment, though sometimes it made his blood rage as if boiling. He wondered how much longer he could stand it; he had a full eleven tiers of power ravaging his mind. Which, Kyel figured, was tantamount to a death sentence. He just didn't know how long it would take.

When they reached Creek Hollow's unguarded gate, his horse balked and tossed its head, stubbornly refusing to enter. Kyel had to dismount and lead the gelding through the gate, which seemed more than peculiar. Within the perimeter of the palisade, the town looked even more unnerving than it had from the forest below the ridge. He remounted and directed his horse down an empty boulevard lined with decrepit storefronts made of logs that seemed to sag with weariness. Many of the buildings were boarded up; some looked ready to just give up and die. There were very few people about—all men—who stopped and stared as they rode past.

A breeze kicked up, chasing leaves around the street. A faded sign creaked above a door, swaying back and forth on rusted chains. The daylight had faded to dusk by the time they drew their horses up in the center of town. Kyel looped his gelding's reins around the pommel of his saddle then climbed down, stretching his legs. He stood dusting his shirt off, staring at the one building in town that seemed intact: a river-rock inn with windows that glowed an eerie, death-pale light.

Part of him wanted to climb back on his horse and ride out of town. The last time he'd stepped foot in an inn had been with Traver. The thought brought a sharp pang of sadness along with it. Traver was dead now. And, like everything else, his death had been Kyel's fault.

He looked up at the wan light glowing through the inn's mottled glass. Leading his horse by the bridle, he followed Cadmus across the yard toward the livery stable. They handed the horses over to the hostler then made their way back toward the inn.

Kyel paused in the doorway, letting his eyes adjust to the dim interior. The common room was mostly empty, with only a few customers huddled around an enormous rock hearth. Kyel found that curious—it wasn't all that cold out. He took a step forward. A board creaked beneath his weight. Conversation died. Every stare in the room turned to fix on him.

Cadmus looked at him and shrugged. To Kyel, the reactions of the locals seemed off. They couldn't know he was a mage; the black cloak that identified him was shoved deep in the dusty saddlebag thrown over his shoulder. Kyel took another step then froze, his eyes snapping wide open.

He'd forgotten he was wearing Thar'gon strapped to his hip.

Self-conscious, Kyel reached down protectively and grasped the weapon's haft. He met the gaze of one of the men standing by the hearth, a stare that seemed absent any presence of thought. The fellow paused in the action of raising his tankard to his lips. His expression never changed.

A man behind Kyel made a gurgling sound, like a throat drowning in old phlegm. He turned to find the inn's proprietor staring at them from behind a plank bar. Kyel motioned Cadmus forward to arrange their room and meals, while he claimed a seat at a table tucked away in a corner.

Cadmus returned shortly after haggling with the innkeeper, carrying two tankards of ale. He threw his portly body down on the bench opposite Kyel, sliding a tankard across the table with a grin just as dilapidated as the town. He glanced over his shoulder at the men by the hearth.

Kyel whispered, "Why do you suppose they're staring at us?"

The cleric shrugged, taking a large swallow of ale. "Who could say? I doubt they get many wayfarers through here."

Kyel shifted uncomfortably in his seat, taking a sip from his tankard. As he did, the sight of his bare arm made him choke. His shirtsleeves had pulled back, exposing the markings of the chains on his wrists.

He looked over to the men by the fire and saw them staring at him. Kyel gave a long, troubled sigh, looking down at the rough-hewn wood of the table. He'd left his cloak off in an effort to avoid this kind of attention. He'd attracted it nonetheless.

The men by the hearth exchanged glances then turned away. Kyel settled back into his seat, frowning into his tankard as he awaited more problems. But only the sound of Cadmus slurping his ale disturbed the quiet.

Their supper was brought by a pretty serving girl with warm brown hair and a shy smile. Kyel nodded his thanks at her, noting that she was the only woman he'd seen so far in town. As she slipped away, he turned his attention to the roasted squab she'd set down in front of them.

Cadmus wasted no time tearing into his bird, pulling the flesh off the bones. He talked while he chewed. "You need to stop overthinking things. I understand—you've found yourself in an unenviable situation. But, the way I figure it, you have two choices. First, you can worry yourself into inaction trying to make sense of the senseless. Or you can accept your fate and make the most of the time you have left."

Kyel frowned. "That's not what worries me."

Cadmus harrumphed. He shoved a small wing into his mouth and stripped the meat off. "I know. You're terrified you're going to go mad, like your former master." He took a heavy sip from his tankard. "You won't. To be blunt, you're not going to have time to deteriorate that far."

"You can't know that," Kyel said. "I'm eleventh tier. Darien was only eighth tier and look how fast he declined."

"It's hard to say how much of that was power and how much was pressure. Or personality." Cadmus shrugged. "I'll let you know if I think there's a problem. We'll worry about it when we have to."

"Can I get you more ale?"

Kyel looked up into the doll-like face of the serving girl. She stood gaping down at the chains on his wrists with moonstruck eyes. He did a double-take, eventually coming to the conclusion that she was, in fact, real. Dumbly, he offered his spent tankard to her. She accepted it with the slightest grin then set off, meandering back toward the kitchen.

"That's opportunity there."

Kyel fixed Cadmus with an irritated look. "She saw the chains. I'm surprised she wasn't terrified."

"What did I just say about making sense of the senseless?"

Kyel scoffed, pushing his platter away even though it still contained a half-eaten squab. When Cadmus raised his eyebrows and gestured at it, Kyel waved him on.

Cadmus slid the dish toward himself and picked the carcass up whole, tearing into it. Kyel's eyes roamed to the group of men by the hearth. He wondered if they were locals or just travelers passing through. Whichever, they were still shooting him glances when they thought he wasn't looking.

"Here you go."

The serving girl was back with her sweet face and starry eyes, scooting his filled tankard across the table toward him. Kyel managed to yank his gaze from her cleavage only by a heroic feat of will.

"Are you really a mage?"

Kyel gulped. "I am." He had to force himself to look at her face. From the corner of his eye, he saw Cadmus' mouth screw into a grimace of barely contained laughter. Frustrated, Kyel stabbed him a glare.

"Are you a good mage or a bad mage?"

Such an odd question, especially in light of the animosity he received anywhere else in the Rhen. This tucked-away little hamlet seemed to have missed the more condemning rumors that circulated the North. Though not all, apparently.

"I'm a good mage," he responded carefully.

The girl brightened. "That's what I thought. You look nice."

Kyel felt his ego swell with the compliment. He took a drink of ale, reminded of Cadmus' mention of opportunity. She did seem rather sweet. Her shoulder-length brown hair and pale eyes were especially to his liking. But he wasn't the type to take advantage of a mage-smitten girl he'd never see again. It just wouldn't be right.

The smile fell away from her lips, replaced by a fretful expression. "You're sworn to help people, aren't you?"

To Kyel, the question sounded like trouble. He answered guardedly, "Something like that."

"Can you help me?"

Suddenly wary, Kyel opened his mouth to discourage her, but was drowned out by a shout from the inn's proprietor. Red-faced, the girl knelt beside the table and, running nervous fingers through her hair, whispered, "Meet me out back in an hour? In the barn?"

It had sounded like a question, but she was gone before Kyel could refuse. He turned back to Cadmus, who was chuckling and shaking his head. With a frown, Kyel knocked back a large swig of ale.

"What do you think that was all about?" he asked in irritation.

Cadmus shrugged, a leering grin on his face. "If you want to know, you'd better go find out."

"'Spose she's in trouble?"

"Perhaps." Cadmus tossed the spent carcass down on the platter. "Maybe she has a sick child or a souse for a husband. Or maybe you'll get lucky, and she's just out for a romp. Whichever it is, just remember one thing: we don't have time to pick up strays. Understood?"

"Understood." Kyel felt affronted that Cadmus would even point out something so obvious. What did the man think, that he was going to fall for some starry-eyed village girl and drag her along after them? He'd never do that to any girl. Not when he had less than two months to live.

They finished their meal in silence. When Cadmus retired to their room, Kyel remained at the table, deep in thought and nursing his tankard. He'd stopped paying attention to the group by the hearth. Every once in a while, he chanced a glance at the serving girl. She was conspicuously ignoring him, taking great care to avoid eye contact. He wondered if it was because she regretted their conversation. Or an attempt to hide her interest in him from her employer.

When he'd figured about an hour had passed, Kyel slid a couple coppers to the center of the table and scooped up his saddle bags. He trudged up to the second level and left his things with a snoring Cadmus, then stole downstairs and out the front door.

The wind was up, blustery. Thankful for his coat, Kyel hugged himself as he made his way across the yard toward the stable. A tumbleweed skittered by, making him wonder what business a tumbleweed even had in a pine-forest hamlet. There were many such inconsistencies about Creek Hollow that just didn't set right with him.

He had to fight with the stable door to get it open. Then he had to struggle with it to get it closed, as if the wind was determined to rip the door from his hand. Inside, Kyel found himself accosted by the acute odor of horse manure. The only light came from a slatted window on the far wall. Kyel felt along with his hands as he made his way down the central aisle between stalls. Razor-thin streaks of moonlight slanted in through the window slats—not enough to do his vision any good. Nickers and snorts greeted him from both sides. A velvet nose shoved into him, breathing a gush of warm air against his neck.

The aisle ended at a slivery plank wall. No serving girl, for which Kyel wasn't sure he was grateful or disappointed. But then a gust of wind and moonlight erupted from a side door, startling the horses. Kyel whirled toward a hooded figure carrying a lantern who stepped inside then stopped to fight with the door. Striding forward, Kyel took the lantern, shielding its flame against the wind as he helped the girl get the door closed. Throwing off her hood, the serving girl turned and smiled at him shyly.

"You came." She beamed at him with the same starry eyes she'd had in the inn.

Kyel didn't know what to say, so he just nodded. With her hair in disarray, her cheeks reddened by the wind, she looked even prettier than before. He felt his pulse kick up as his eyes wandered over her.

"Are you really a mage?" she pressed. "Why aren't you wearing a black cloak?"

"It's in my pack."

She accepted his answer with a smile, then turned her back on him and walked away a few steps toward the nearest box stall. There, she reached her hand up and caressed a soft black nose poking out above the door.

Kyel asked, "So...why'd you ask me out here?"

She dropped her hand and turned to face him.

"I'm pregnant," she whispered.

Kyel blinked. That certainly wasn't what he'd expected to hear. "Um...aren't you supposed to tell me that *after* we've been intimate?"

She fixed him with the closest thing to a pout her pretty face could manage. "It's not like that. If my father finds out...he'll kill me."

"Well, I'm sure he won't be happy. But that's not a—"

She cut him off. "I don't think you understand. He really *will* kill me."

Kyel frowned. "You're serious."

"I am. You don't know what it's like here."

He halfway believed her. The entire town had an odd feel to it. The whole place just wasn't right. And this girl...oddly, she seemed to be the only normal person he'd seen.

Kyel's frown deepened. "So, what do you want from me?"

Emboldened, the girl took a step toward him. Looking up into his eyes, she said, "I want you to take me with you."

Kyel was already shaking his head before she got the words out. Cadmus had been right. Again. Just like he usually was about everything. "Oh, no," he muttered. "Where I'm going...no. Look, there's a war. You don't want to be anywhere near me. I can't—"

"Please! You don't understand—"

Kyel started backing away, stepping around her toward the door. "I'm sorry. There must be someone else who can help you. Where's the father?"

"He's gone! He was a patron, only here for a week. Look, you said you swore to help people!"

"It's not like that. I'd like to help you, but there's a bigger problem—"

To his horror, the girl started crying. Kyel closed his eyes, feeling his resolve washed away by the sight of her tears. He flung his hands up in frustration. "Stop! Just stop. Look, maybe we can take you as far as Amberlie. But that's it. No farther."

She gasped. "You will? You mean it?" Radiant hope beamed from her face, sparkled in her eyes.

Kyel groaned, already regretting his words. "I can't believe I'm doing this." He rubbed his brow. "Meet us outside the gate on the morrow. An hour before dawn. You've got a horse?"

She nodded eagerly. "I can take my father's."

Before he could blink, she careened into him, catching him up in an exuberant hug as her lantern bounced against his back. He hugged her stiffly, only too aware of the feel of her breasts against him. He let her go, suddenly flustered, his hands racing to smooth his shirt.

"Thank you!" she gasped. She reached up and kissed his cheek, then was gone in a flurry of wind, fluttering hair, and moonlight.

Chapter Five
The Purge of Wolden

Wolden, The Rhen

The sound of a tolling bell woke Blake Pratson from sleep. At first, the mayor of Wolden just incorporated the sound into his dream: a distant, insignificant noise that barely registered. But the noise was insistent. He tried his best to ignore it, to fall back into the dream again. He was exasperated when it continued. He rolled over in bed, irritated that the sound wasn't going away.

He snapped awake, recognizing the warning bell for what it was.

Pratson sat up in bed, heart pounding in his chest. His brain labored to process the bell's significance. It could be a false alarm. It could be something much less dire than the horrors his mind was trying to leap to. It could be one of the town's many drunkards pulling the rope, or a scorned lover or…

The sound of distant screams shred his hopes. Pratson turned toward the window, only then noticing the dull orange glow streaming in through the tatted curtains, making the shadows dance across the walls.

Fire…

It could be a stable. An inn. It could be anything. It didn't have to be *them*.

They weren't supposed to come. Two great armies stood between Wolden and the Pass of Lor-Gamorth.

Pratson swung his feet over the side of the bed and rushed to the window. Ripping the dusty curtains aside, he pressed his palms against the cold glass and stared out into the night. He could see the outline of jagged rooftops silhouetted by the glow of fires in the distance. The sounds of screams were clearer now, heard through the glass. The scent of smoke finally reached his nostrils.

Cold terror gripped Pratson's throat. He whirled away from the window and made for the chair where he'd laid his clothes. He stumbled into his trousers then strapped his belt around his waist. He picked up his shirt, thrusting an arm into the sleeve—

The bedroom door burst open with a *crack* of shattering wood.

Pratson cried out, backing away from the lone man advancing toward him. The man shot out a hand and slammed him roughly against the wall. He started to struggle.

"They're here!" growled a low and familiar voice.

The glow of the flames revealed Broden's jagged features. The guardsman gripped Pratson by the arm and spun him around, saying, "The gate's been breached—we're overwhelmed. I'm getting you out of here."

Pratson didn't argue. He was too busy trying to keep his feet moving as the guardsman steered him out of the bed chamber. He followed Broden down a dark hallway toward a set of stairs that descended into the basement. There, they could gain access to tunnels that had been dug decades ago to escape this very threat.

As they crossed the foyer, the great double doors burst open. Armored men spilled into the room, blocking both escape and retreat. Broden shoved Pratson back and stepped in front of him, raising his blade into a warding stance.

Black-mailed soldiers fanned out from the door, shields and weapons raised. Broden stood his ground, looking determined to take down as many as he could before meeting his own end. Terrified, Pratson clung to the wall, his eyes sliding over the fearsome helms of the Enemy soldiers who confronted them.

The soldiers parted to create an opening. Pratson's eyes were drawn toward the door, then stuck there as if glued. A cold wash of air blew in, scattering leaves across the floor. The leaves whorled and fluttered, collecting in the corners.

The wind gasped its last breath and went still.

Another warrior entered, taller than the rest, all in black plate with a thick cloak furling about him. He halted in front of Broden, as if immune to the threat of the blademaster's sword. He stood there a long moment as all motion in the room ground to a halt, freezing like jammed gears. The warrior reached up and removed his helm, shaking out a dark mass of sweat-greased hair. Pratson gaped, recognition slamming into him with the force of a hammer blow.

Lauchlin.

The mage was almost unrecognizable. He'd only seen Darien Lauchlin once before, when he'd been a new Sentinel passing through town with dire warnings of invasion. Pratson had been wary of the man even then. There had been something about him. Something *tainted.* Broden had sensed it too. Even after he'd seen the markings of the chains on the man's wrists, Pratson still hadn't trusted him.

Now he understood why.

The same man stood before him. Only, now, the taint of corruption had grown too great to be bodily contained. It bled off him in waves, darkening the air around him like a vile penumbra. The eyes that locked on Broden went far beyond cold. It was as though Lauchlin's mere presence sucked all hope from the room.

Pratson's breath hitched. He stood with his back pressed against the wall, heart lurching in fear. His limbs trembled as he felt the air stagnate around him.

"Stand down," the darkmage ordered Broden. He didn't raise his voice; there was no need. Dire threat was implicit in his tone.

Pratson gaped at him in revulsion. "You were a Sentinel," he gasped. "How do you stand your own existence?"

The demon's eyes bored into him. Calmly, Lauchlin responded, "I swore to serve the land and its people. *All of its people.* I'm doing my duty—*now you do yours.* Tell the residents of Wolden to flee. Or I swear by Xerys, I'll put them all to the sword."

Adjusting his grip on his hilt, Broden growled, "I remember you. I also remember you're helpless within a vortex."

Lauchlin shook his head. "Not anymore."

Broden stood unmoving, staring into the demon's eyes as if

gauging his intent.

"Ah, fuck," he whispered.

His knees buckled. Broden's sword dropped from his hands as he folded over, dead. Pratson gaped at the darkmage in horror, realizing there was nothing between him and death.

"Go do your duty," Lauchlin ordered.

Pratson bolted forward, slipping past the man out the door of the manor. He sprinted for the road, drawing up only when he reached the chaos in the street.

He gaped around in terror.

Wolden was burning. Crackling fires scorched the night, feeding roiling clouds of smoke that blotted out the stars. Screams ripped through the air as people were chased from their homes and stampeded through the streets. It took Pratson only a moment to figure out what was going on: Wolden's inhabitants were being rounded up, herded into the town square, where they were ringed by black-mailed savages brandishing torches and weapons. Women clung to their children, their men shouting in fear or defiance or both. While their homes burned behind them.

Pratson ran right up to the edge of the square and scrambled onto the back of a cart. He stood waving his hands and shouting, desperately trying to get his peoples' attention.

"Take your families and evacuate!" he bellowed. "Leave everything behind! *Run!*"

The ring of soldiers opened to allow the crowd to spill between them. Pratson jumped down from the cart and started after, but the threat of a scimitar stopped him short. He looked slowly up, his eyes meeting Darien Lauchlin's shadowed stare.

"Not you," the darkmage said, holding his blade steady.

Pratson felt all the blood leak out of his face. He whispered, "What are you going to do?"

The demon nodded at the ground. "Kneel, and I'll make it quick."

Gripped in the claws of terror, Pratson couldn't move. A warm wetness dribbled down his leg, scarcely noticed. "No," he gasped, taking a step back and shaking his head. "No, no, please!"

"Kneel or suffer."

He didn't understand his options. They flowed over him like water. He didn't react fast enough.

Pratson screamed as his skin erupted in indescribable pain. Looking down at his hands, he saw his flesh melting, running like hot wax.

The scream that tore from his throat died just as violently as the rest of him.

Chapter Six
The Price of Arrogance

Wolden, The Rhen

Darien turned away from the gelatinous mass that had, just moments before, been Wolden's mayor. It took him a moment to realize he was surrounded by a circle of Zakai who stood staring at him warily. He hadn't bothered explaining to them about the Hellpower.

"How…?" Sayeed gasped.

Looking around for Azár, Darien answered, "I can't use the magic field in a vortex. But I can still use the Onslaught. It's ugly, but it's effective. The one drawback is, I can't heal with it."

He found Azár walking toward them, wielding a double-edged qama in her hand. He wished she had something more substantial than a short sword. She couldn't use magic in a vortex. The torrential power would kill her, just as it would kill him.

Across the street, a building gutted by fire collapsed on itself, showering glowing embers into the air. Screams came from every direction, echoing over the roar of the flames. A lone Tanisar jogged up the road and gave a concise report to Sayeed. Darien's new commander sent him off with a series of barked orders.

"The town is mostly cleared, and the fires are contained," Sayeed relayed the report. "There is only a small pocket of resistance left down by the mill."

Darien donned his helm, tightening the strap. "I'll take care of it. Round up any remaining civilians you can find—if they don't want to leave, take their heads off. Mop up, then loot what you can."

Sayeed bowed and set off with a small group of Zakai. Darien waited until Azár reached his side, then started off in the direction of the mill, surrounded by a small but formidable guard. Screaming townsfolk fled before them, some with babes in arms and children in tow. Darien took in the scene impassively, his concentration pinned on the next objective. Inflicting brutality was much easier if he didn't think about it.

They walked through the emptied streets in the direction of the flames. He had ordered the most impoverished section of Wolden put to the torch, for shock value. There were far less resources there to burn, and the housing was well-separated from the rest of town. But apparently, the tactic hadn't driven out everyone.

They found a large group of men collected in the square around the mill. Some held swords, while others were armed with axes or makeshift weapons. They stood as if guarding the mill—a pointless endeavor. They were a far inferior force than the scores of Tanisars that ringed them. The entire scene made little sense.

With a gesture of his hand, Darien ordered his guard of Zakai to stay behind. He removed his helm and strode forward, intent on a big man holding a mace who stood in front of the others, no doubt the mob's ringleader. He didn't object when Azár took his hand. She was still insistent that her place was at his side, and it wasn't worth the effort to try keeping her away from it.

He stopped in the middle of the square and confronted the ringleader.

"Tell your men to surrender," Darien advised. "If they do, I'll let them keep their lives."

Instead of complying, the bearded man spat on the ground.

His action gave Darien pause. Defiance was one thing, but the mob's behavior was suicidal. Something didn't feel right. He ran his gaze over the crowd, seeing the same confidence in the eyes of every man gathered. None of them looked prepared to die protecting a town mill.

"Go back," he ordered Azár under his breath. For once, his wife obeyed without question. She released his hand and started back across the square toward the Zakai.

He heard her fall.

All at once, a barrage of arrows rained down all around him, ricocheting off his armor. Darien dove forward and threw himself on top of Azár. He looked up to face a charging wall of men rushing toward them with weapons raised, more streaming into the square from the surrounding buildings.

Shielding his wife, Darien lashed out blindly with the Onslaught.

Ghastly screams tore through the air as the square erupted in a roiling explosion of hellish green flames. The screams didn't last long. The arrows ceased their barrage. Darien looked up to find the square covered in bodies that lay strewn like fallen trees, half-melted into the cobbles. Something—either smoke or steam—rose from the corpses.

Some of the fallen were Zakai.

Darien rolled Azár over, loosening the straps that held her breastplate, then ripped it off, casting it aside. He let out a growl at the sight of a crossbow quarrel that had slipped through a gap in Azár's armor to shatter her collar bone. His wife lay gazing up at him, eyes narrowed in pain. The bolt had penetrated deep, narrowly missing the main artery in her neck. If the shaft was jostled, even just a bit, the head might still nick it.

There was nothing Darien could do for her—he couldn't use the Onslaught to heal.

He had to get her out of the vortex.

Darien lurched to his feet, glancing around. Chaos and confusion surrounded him as some soldiers swarmed toward him while others fled back.

"I need my horse!" he bellowed.

He dropped back to Azár's side, wishing there was something, anything, he could do. As it was, he was afraid to even try stanching the flow of blood, for fear of moving the shaft. He gazed down at his wife helplessly, taking her hand. Azár stared up at him, remarkably calm.

Minutes passed. Reinforcements arrived, bolstering his guard of Zakai. All around, fires consumed the surrounding buildings. The square was eerily bright and just as eerily quiet.

From a distance, Darien heard approaching hoofbeats. He jolted to his feet, feeling infinite relief at the sight of Sayeed on his red charger, galloping across the square to draw up beside him. The officer slid from the horse's back and held the reins as Darien mounted. Two Zakai rushed forward, lifting Azár delicately and helping to settle her in his arms.

"Go, Brother!" Sayeed gasped, and swatted the horse on its flank to send it bolting forward.

Darien clutched Azár against him, clinging to the stallion with his legs. The horse raced through the streets, spurred faster by its instinctual fear of fire. Soldiers and fleeing townsfolk leaped out of their path, the sound of charging hoofbeats parting the crowd ahead.

The horse cleared the town walls and broke for the open road. But after galloping only a couple of miles, his mount began to flag. Darien pulled the stallion back to a walk, cursing the horse and cursing his luck. He shifted Azár's weight in his arms, trying to make her more comfortable. She sagged against him, her head lolling against his shoulder.

Panicked, Darien fought the urge to run the horse to death. But doing so wouldn't serve Azár, so he kept the lathered stallion alternating between a walk and a trot as they followed the road ever northward. It was still another ten or so miles before they would be clear of the vortex. And he had no idea how many of those miles Azár would last.

Darien clenched his fists in anxiety. Every minute, he felt his wife sinking lower and lower against his chest. It was a constant struggle to keep her sitting upright, keep her from slipping off the horse. Her eyes were closed, her face pale in the moonlight. He kept checking her pulse, unable to resist the compulsion. Every time he did, he was surprised to find her heart still beating. Dark blood saturated the front of her shirt. His arms were slick with it.

Darien started measuring the minutes in heartbeats, dreading the moment her pulse stopped. He felt certain that moment was coming. He didn't have the power or the luck to stop the inevitable.

He rode on, gritting his teeth and holding his dying wife against his chest.

Eventually, the vortex above them thinned. Darien checked Azár's pulse again. It was thready and rapid, almost too weak to feel. The magic field was still too hot to handle, but he couldn't wait any longer.

Desperate, Darien pulled the horse up and slid off its back. Carrying Azár in his arms, he laid her out on the grass. He could feel the vortex still battering against the shield he'd thrown up to protect his mind from its raging torrent. It was weaker than it had been. He wasn't sure if it was weak enough.

Regardless, he had to try.

Setting his hands on Azár's chest, Darien opened his mind to the vortex. The raging cyclone of power tore through him, slamming into Azár. Every muscle in his body contracted at once, ripping a scream from his throat. He worked through the agony as fast as he could, as long as he could, throwing every effort of will into healing his wife and leaving nothing for himself.

Darien awoke hours later to the feeling of something shaking him, over and over. He groaned and shook his head, trying to rid himself of the sensation. It was more than irritating. But it continued, relentless.

"Husband!"

He gazed blearily into Azár's face. She was leaning over him, fear widening her eyes. He didn't know where he was, didn't understand why she was there.

Then he remembered.

Rage filled him.

Darien scooted away from her and staggered to his feet, fighting waves of vertigo that almost took him to his knees. Azár reached out and tried to stabilize him, but Darien jerked away. He trudged forward a few steps, fighting to contain his fury.

"What is wrong?" Azár shouted at his back. "Are you angry?"

Darien brought his hands up to clutch his throbbing temples. "Yes, I'm angry!"

She stared at him. "Why are you angry?"

Her voice was suffused with hurt and confusion. She didn't understand. How could she not understand? Her ignorance infuriated him all the more.

He whirled back to her. "Because you almost *died!*"

She stood her ground.

He moved forward and raged into her face, "Don't you understand? I couldn't heal you! *The only thing I could do was watch you die!*"

She gazed at him with mute understanding in her eyes. The look did something to him. His anger liquified, draining right out of him. He turned away.

He heard a quiet noise that sounded like a sob. Looking back, he saw that his fierce wife had tears in her eyes.

Confused, Darien gaped at her. "Why are you crying?"

She muttered something in a voice too soft to hear.

"What?"

Softly, she said, "Thank you."

Darien shook his head, baffled by her answer. "Thank you for what?"

Her eyes glistening, Azár whispered, "Thank you for caring."

It was too much. Her words tore him wide open.

He lifted Azár and lay her down on the dew-wet grass, then collapsed on top of her. His lips scoured her face, her neck, her chest. Her body moved beneath him, her lips seeking his. She wrapped her legs around him.

For one brief moment, the entire world paused and held its breath.

Chapter Seven
The Good Mage

The Vale of Amberlie, The Rhen

They left Creek Hollow as the predawn light just barely grayed the eastern horizon. The town was silent and still, its shadowed streets haunted by absence. Kyel's eyes roamed the side of the road nervously as they slipped out the gate. He hadn't liked the feel of the place the previous night. He liked it even less the next day.

There was no sign of the serving girl, for which he was grateful. He hadn't mentioned his agreement with her to Cadmus. Part of him hoped they could slip out of town ahead of her. In the fresh light of morning, he found himself doubting her story. But another part of him hoped she'd catch up. He wanted to believe her. It had been a long time since he'd met a sincerely good person. He wanted very badly for her to be as nice as she seemed.

As they rounded a switchback in the trail that led down from the ridge, he heard hoofbeats. Turning, he saw a dark horse trotting toward them up the slope, the girl on its back, her hood pulled up and cloak flapping.

Cadmus took one look at the girl then shook a finger at Kyel. "No, no, no! I told you we don't have time to take in strays. Now send her back where she came from!"

The girl reined in, a troubled frown on her face as her eyes flicked back and forth between the two of them. Exasperated, Kyel let out a heaving sigh. He'd known it would come to an argument. Only, this argument he intended to win. He was getting tired of being led around by the nose.

"I told her she could come," he stated firmly.

Cadmus snorted. "Then you can tell her she can go."

"No." Kyel felt his temper heating. "I gave my word we'd take her with us as far as Amberlie. I'm not going back on my word."

Cadmus gave a loud *harrumph* and turned to the girl. "What did you tell him? That your husband beats you? You're running away from an arranged marriage? Whichever, it must have been convincing. You play the victim well."

The girl glanced at Kyel with hurt in her eyes.

"She's pregnant," Kyel snapped. "And her life—and the child's life—are in danger. She's coming with us."

Cadmus chortled. "And what do we do when her family comes tracking us down? Or do you think they're just going to let her go? The last thing we need is a herd of fools with bent noses chasing after us."

"That won't be a problem."

"Oh, it won't? How exactly do you plan to deter them?"

Kyel glared at him. Then he reached down and patted Thar'gon's haft. "With this."

The cleric lifted a skeptical eyebrow. "What about your Oath of Harmony?"

"I'm a Sentinel." Kyel shrugged. "There's a hell of a lot I can do without breaking Oath."

Cadmus stared hard at him for a long moment, a world of skepticism in his eyes. Then he blew out a loud snort. "Let's hope so, boy. For our sake. And the world's."

"I'm not a boy," Kyel growled at him. "And I'm getting sick of being treated like one. You're not even a priest—all you are is a mouthpiece. So tell His Eminence from now on, I'll be taking his advice under consideration, and not the other way around."

Red-faced, Cadmus glared at him. Then he wheeled his horse around, kicking it forward down the path. Kyel watched him bump along, jolting in his saddle as his stirrups flapped in time to his horse's strides.

He glanced at the girl in apology.

They rode in silence through the grove as the day dawned overhead. The chatter of birdsong filled the forest, a sound Kyel had all but forgotten during his long months in the Pass. The girl's horse plodded along behind his own, fully content to follow. She had to give it a few good kicks to make it move forward alongside his gelding.

"I'm sorry I upset your friend," she said in a lowered tone.

"He's not my friend. So don't worry." Kyel glared ahead at Cadmus.

The girl found her shy smile. "My name is Alexa. Alexa Newell."

"Kyel Archer."

Her eyebrows pinched together in a frown of confusion. "You have a longer name than that, don't you? Being a mage, and all?"

Kyel shrugged. "I have a title. But I don't like to use it." Feeling awkward, he cast his gaze back down at the road.

"Thank you for helping me, Kyel," she said after a moment. "I was right. You really are a good mage."

He managed a wan smile. "Well, I'm not a very good mage. But I'd like to think I'm a good person."

She brightened at that, gifting him with a smile that eclipsed the daylight. He couldn't help grinning back. It had been a long time since he'd been able to make a girl smile like that.

"What is that?" She pointed at the silver morning star affixed to his saddle.

"Oh, this?" He drew Thar'gon from its saddle holster, holding it up for her to see. "It's my weapon."

Alexa's brow furrowed. "I thought mages didn't carry weapons."

Feeling deflated, Kyel hung Thar'gon back in place. "Well, it's more like a talisman."

"A talisman? What does it do?" She sat up straight, her eyes teeming with interest.

It was the one question he'd rather she hadn't asked. "I haven't actually figured it out," he admitted. "I just came by it recently and haven't had a lot of time to fiddle with it."

She stared at him flatly for a moment, then turned back to the road. They rode in silence for a while. After uncomfortable minutes, Kyel glanced at Alexa and caught her staring at him. She looked away quickly. Suddenly self-conscious, he searched for something to say. The only line of conversation that came to mind was the obvious.

"I don't mean to pry," he said, "but I'd appreciate you telling me more about your …situation."

"My situation?" She looked at him with confusion on her face.

Embarrassed, Kyel motioned toward her middle. "You know…your…"

"Oh…" Slow realization seeped onto her face. Her eyes slipped to the side, and she looked lost in thought. "There was a man who passed through town. We took a liking to each other. He said he'd take me with him, but he didn't. He left in the night and didn't come back for me."

Kyel frowned. "And what about your father?"

She pressed a finger against her lips, as if mired in deep thought. "That's just the kind of man he is. Merciless. Heartless. He has no soul…" Her voice trailed off into silence.

Ahead of them, Cadmus had drawn his horse up. When they neared, he threw a glowering stare their way. "If you two love-birds would stop yammering for a moment, we might be able to hear if anyone's following us."

Kyel scowled, knowing the cleric was right, but nevertheless hating to admit it.

After that, they rode in silence for long hours as the gloom of the woodland creeped over them. The canopy thickened, becoming crowded by maple and birch. The grove darkened, the smell of pine replaced by the musty-damp scent of moss and detritus. All around, an eerie silence descended around them, disturbed only by the plodding of hoofbeats and the distant, trickling sounds of water.

Kyel breathed in the cold, moist air, for once wishing he'd worn his cloak. His stomach rumbled, reminding him he'd skipped breakfast. Clucking to his horse, he angled it off the road in the direction of a moss-encrusted tree that had fallen over at an angle.

"Where, pray tell, are you going?" Cadmus called at his back.

"I'm going to eat."

Ignoring the sounds of grumbling behind him, Kyel swung off

his horse and tethered it to a branch. He snatched up his saddle bags then turned—

—to find himself standing nose-to-nose with Alexa. He jerked back, reflexively reaching for the magic field. He hadn't heard her coming up behind him. He held onto the field tighter as he fought to calm his racing pulse.

"How did you…" he shook his head. Staring into her doll-like face, his thoughts melted and oozed away. He let go of the field, allowing it to seep out of him slowly. He took a step back, staring questioningly into her face.

"Aren't you hungry?" she asked.

Before he could respond, she reached into her pack and removed a small burlap sack. With an angelic smile, she produced two apples, offering one to Kyel in her open palm. He accepted the apple and, lifting it to his mouth, took a bite. It was perfectly crisp and ripe, perhaps the best apple he'd ever had.

"It's delicious," he said, taking another crunching bite.

She smiled at him dearly, but instead of eating the fruit in her hand, she tucked it back away in the sack. She stood watching him with a smile on her face while Kyel finished his apple, core and all. He took a swig from his water skin and, looking up, saw her smiling at him.

Cadmus grimaced his disapproval. Turning away, he called over his shoulder, "I'm going to go find a tall bush. Don't do anything that'll get her more pregnant."

Kyel could feel himself blushing. As Cadmus' heavy footsteps retreated into the forest, he hurried toward his horse. He rifled through his saddlebags in a clumsy attempt to keep Alexa from seeing his heated cheeks. He dug his hand around, trying to find just one possession he could use to justify his action.

He felt a hand on his shoulder. He froze, uncertain what to do. He wasn't sure what to say to a pretty girl whose smile lit up the day. He turned toward her—

—and was flung backward, the forest exploding in dazzling brilliance. His body slapped hard against the ground. Kyel cried out, his mind reflexively scrambling for the magic field. He caught ahold of it and used all eleven tiers of power to strike back against the threat. Opening his eyes, he blinked against an overwhelming light that dazzled his senses. He wiped his eyes, struggling to clear his vision, then looked around.

Alexa lay on the ground in front of him, unmoving. Kyel froze halfway between breaths. Time stopped. Everything stopped.

She's dead.

Then: *I killed her...*

He scrambled forward to the girl's side, reaching out—

—another brilliant burst of light lifted him up and threw him backward. Kyel reached for Thar'gon, his hand closing on the haft—

His vision cleared. Time lurched forward. The dazzling whiteness fell away. Kyel stood up, wielding the talisman over his head as his adversary came into focus.

He gasped. Then he swung.

Thar'gon's magical strike threw the dead man away from him. Kyel swept the talisman back in an arc, repulsing the remainder of the dead things that surrounded him. Limbs flew, and corpses tumbled in a rain of decayed body parts. He felt the energy released by the morning star, an incredible surge of force. It was indomitable, unfathomable. Nothing could survive that.

But something did.

One of the corpses started crawling toward him, clawing itself over the ground, dragging the snaking ropes of its entrails behind it. Repulsed, Kyel leveled the talisman at the thing, watching it burst into pieces that showered gore all over the forest bracken.

He stood quivering, panting, his eyes ticking over the grisly scene. When he was sure the rest of the dead weren't going to get up again, he scrambled back to Alexa's side.

She was alive, but barely. He healed her injuries expertly, instantly, sucking glorious power through the talisman. He didn't have to think about what he was doing. It was as though Thar'gon sensed his need and acted of its own accord, using him as a mere conduit. When Kyel opened his eyes, Alexa lay sleeping on a bed of ferns, her head cradled in his lap. He dropped the morning star, gazing around with wide and horrified eyes.

They were surrounded by corpses and parts of corpses. He'd

killed them all.

Crying out, Kyel raked back his shirtsleeve. The chain of his Oath was still intact. He looked around, taking in scattered body parts. He hadn't killed them, he decided. They weren't alive. He let out a deep, relieved, sigh.

He hadn't broken Oath.

Chapter Eight
No Mercy

The Cerulean Plains, The Rhen

Darien climbed onto his horse and, wrapping an arm around Azár, sent the animal forward at a walk, wading knee-deep through the prairie's tall grass.

To the east, the sun broke over the mountains, streaking the sky with lines of gold. Sunrise had once been his favorite time of day. The hues of the colors were different: warmer, rarer. But he could no longer take comfort in the wakening sky. Not since Orien's Finger, when he had immolated thousands and shattered the break of dawn. Now the sunrise, like everything else, was ruined for him.

"My father," he said softly, turning his face away from the sun's reproving glare.

"What?" Azár glanced back at him.

"When we first met, you asked me what I was thinking about the moment I died." He felt her body stiffen against his. The breeze chased dark strands of her hair. "I was thinking of my father."

A long silence followed his words. Darien's stare remained fixed on the sprawling prairie ahead. He remembered this place. Somewhere close by was the shrine he had entered with Naia, the one that contained an entrance to the Catacombs. There, somewhere deep in those warrens, was the chamber of souls where he'd encountered his father's spirit. Darien knew he would never see him again. His own soul was destined for a different place.

He tightened his grip around Azár, pulling her closer. He savored the scent of her hair, knowing that he didn't have much time left with her. Very soon, he'd be losing her, too.

Forever.

She said, "Tell me about your father."

Her words yanked him out of his thoughts. "His name was Gerald. He was a good Sentinel. And a great man."

Her hand found his, stroking it tenderly. "What is your best memory of him?"

Darien thumbed through his recollections, searching for the right one. Eventually, he found it. "It was the day I passed Consideration. When I became an acolyte. Instead of taking me directly up the mountain, my father led me out into the forest near Amberlie. We walked until we found a stream, then we sat down on the rocks beside it. That's all we did. For hours. We didn't talk. He never said a word to me, but I sensed he was sad. I didn't understand why at the time. Now I do. I'd never want a son of mine to follow my path."

Azár glanced back at him. "That does not sound happy. So why is it the best memory you have of him?"

Darien hung his head, ashamed to admit his feelings. He didn't like thinking about them, much less feeling them. "Because it was the last time I ever saw him."

She lifted his hand to her lips, pressing a kiss against his skin. Then she fell quiet. The horse carried them southward with a steady gait. Eventually, they came to a place he recognized.

It was the shrine.

The lone building rose out of the grassland ahead, forlorn and isolated. Darien turned the horse away from it. His memories of this place were far from comforting. The shrine led to the Catacombs. Which had led him to breaking his Oath. To his mistreatment of Naia. To the sacrifice of his soul. It led to everything that had gone wrong. He wanted nothing more to do with it.

The shrine, like his past, slipped behind him and disappeared in the distance.

It wasn't long until they came upon the encampment. They were greeted by a party of scouts, who rode out toward them on captured mounts, most looking unstable in the saddle. Darien gazed sadly at the approaching men. These were a people descended from the greatest horse culture the world had ever known. Yet they were so far removed from their origins that their blood had lost all trace of its memory.

Sayeed galloped toward them on a horse as red as Darien's, scattering soldiers out of his way. He drew his mount up and leaped to the ground, falling to his knees. He stared down at the trampled grass and, drawing his sword, offered it up.

"Lord, I have failed you twice. Please take my life."

Darien dismounted, handing the stallion's reins to Azár. He walked forward until he was standing over Sayeed. He wasn't sure what to do. This was a matter of *sharaq*, he felt certain. And he had no idea what the proper response should be that would preserve both Sayeed's life and honor. He remembered the promise he had made back at Kajiri flats, that if the Zakai ever failed him again, they would forfeit their lives. Gazing down at Sayeed, Darien now regretted those words. He would lose every drop of *sharaq* he possessed if he didn't follow through with that threat.

He had no choice. A wrong had been committed, and it would have to be redressed. Or his command—and Sayeed's life— would end here today.

Accepting the sword, he set the edge of the blade across the officer's neck. Sayeed remained motionless, frozen in his bow. He suffered the blade's touch without so much as a flinch. Darien's mind scrambled through options, finding none that were certain and safe. He decided to settle for the uncertain. And the unsafe. He widened his stance, adjusting his grip on the hilt.

"Sayeed son of Alborz, you have now failed me twice," he pronounced. "But I failed you first."

He retracted the sword and cast it to the ground. Gasps of dismay issued from the soldiers gathered around.

"I put myself in harm's way, leaving you and your men without recourse." He drew his own blade. "I dishonored you and all the Zakai. My life is yours. Take it."

He fell to his knees, offering the weapon out before him.

Sayeed raised his head to gape at Darien's sword with horrified eyes. All around, soldiers looked on with faces frozen by shock.

Azár leapt from the horse with a strangled cry.

Time froze. Not a soul moved.

Sayeed lurched to his feet.

Darien felt his sword leave his hands. There was a moment's pause. Then the sharp edge of the blade kissed the skin of his neck. He closed his eyes and hoped. There was no other way. Not if he wanted to preserve Sayeed's life and honor. He hoped that by putting him in an impossible position, the soldiers couldn't blame Sayeed if he failed to strike.

Darien felt the blade's edge trembling against his neck, sending shivers down his nerves. Sayeed was Zakai—a paragon of discipline. He'd been molded from birth to remain steadfast, even in the direst of circumstances. That Sayeed couldn't maintain a steady grip on his hilt warned Darien of his danger.

In a voice fraught with dread, the officer proclaimed, "Warden Darien Lauchlin, you have failed me and all the Zakai. For that, your life is forfeit."

The pressure of the blade eased. Then it settled back down again as Sayeed adjusted his aim. Darien felt a terrible chill wash over him. He realized he'd made a fatal mistake. He had underestimated the rigidity of the Zakai's honor code.

He would have to kill Sayeed.

Darien's vision exploded as a body plowed into him, hurling him to the ground. Another soldier collapsed on top of him, knocking the wind from his lungs. Pinned to the dirt, Darien struggled as another man added his weight. Soldier after soldier fell on top of him, shielding him from Sayeed's strike with their own bodies and lives. He lay prone on the ground, gasping for air, his ribs crushing his lungs.

The weight pinning him shifted, then released.

He was jerked to his feet and held there by Sayeed. Dazed, Darien looked around to see every soldier kneeling in a great circle. Only Sayeed remained standing, his face a mask of outrage.

He let go of Darien, shoving him backward. Then he threw the sword on the ground and stormed away.

"You are stupid!" Azár raged, pacing away from him.

Darien scooped up a jug then sat down on the floor, pouring himself a cup of water. His gaze tracked his wife's motion as she stalked away from him across the length of the tent.

"Stupid!"

Azár paced back toward him. She stopped, looming, her hands planted firmly on her hips. "What were you *thinking?!*"

She whirled and paced away.

"Stupid!"

She made a growling sound deep in her throat. Then she jerked back the tent's partition and tore through it. Darien listened to the sound of her footsteps stalking off, followed by one last *"Stupid!"*

He let out a sigh and leaned back against a tent post, closing his eyes in weariness. Azár was right—he had acted stupidly. He should have never confronted the townsfolk without a guard. He'd let his command of the Onslaught go to his head. And, because he had, he'd almost lost his head. He brought his hands up to rub his face, cursing his own arrogance.

"Brother."

He looked up to find Sayeed holding back the cloth partition. His commander's face had lost some of its anger, though not all of it. Darien sighed, feeling defeated. Figuring that he was due another scolding, he beckoned the man in. Sayeed claimed one of the cushions against the wall, sitting back and crossing his legs. Scowling, he dug the cushion out from under him and tossed it in front of Darien, then scrambled forward to sit on it.

Sayeed lifted a finger and opened his mouth to say something. But then he snapped his jaw shut, closing his eyes as if reconsidering his words. Then, with renewed conviction, he leaned forward and shook his finger in Darien's face.

"I would have killed you to preserve your honor!" His voice was strained with rage. "Do you understand? That is the position you put me in!"

Darien gazed at the man he had named First Among Many. He

took a sip of water. "No. That's the position you put yourself in. I'm not going to murder you just because you've got a sick sense of honor. So don't ever ask me that again—or neither one of us is going to come out of it with any amount of *sharaq* left." He tossed the water out of his cup onto the rug, grumbling, "I need something stronger."

He rose and went to select one of the jugs that lined the walls of the tent: all gifts from the various clan chiefs. Unstoppering one, he took a drink that burned his throat and made his eyes water.

"This'll do."

He filled his cup and offered another to Sayeed, returning to his seat. He took another drink, making a face as the liquor went down. "What *is* this?" he gasped. It was horrifically strong—exactly what he needed.

Sayeed smelled the liquor without tasting it. "It is rika. It is served during times of celebration. Or times of woe."

Darien grunted, taking his cup back and raising it to his lips.

"Stop. Rika must be served a certain way." Before Darien could object, the man snatched the drink from his hand. "This is too much," he snapped. Sayeed returned most of the liquid back to the jug. "First, you must pour your cup into my cup," he said, performing the act. "This shares your troubles with me. Then I pour my rika back into your cup. This gives your troubles back to you, but also my understanding. Now we drink together. You must drink it all at once."

He raised his cup, gesturing for Darien to follow suit. Darien stared at the beverage warily. There was a lot more rika left in the cup than just a sip. But he followed Sayeed's prompt and drank it down, grimacing at the fire igniting in his gut.

"Now you must speak of your troubles," Sayeed said, refilling their cups.

Darien felt the magic field waver as a fiery warmth spread throughout his body. He drank the second cup that was offered, then quickly received a third.

"That is all until you speak," Sayeed told him.

Darien stared into his cup, searching for words. He was not

even sure if he could put a label on his feelings. They were too muddled, too rampant. It was like mixing different textures of sand in one vessel: impossible to separate and identify. And, he had to admit, he was nervous about what the man might think of him.

He took a breath, admitting finally, "I've slain a lot of people in the past week. People who were my kin. People I'd sworn to protect."

Sayeed shrugged. "You are allowed feelings. You are allowed guilt."

"That's good, because I've a hell of a lot of it."

"Are you losing resolve?" Sayeed mixed his cup of rika with Darien's. His voice was conversational, but Darien knew better. He could sense the man's hesitance.

"No." He couldn't afford to lose resolve. Too much depended on him.

Sayeed said, "Your orders and actions have been without mercy. You have nothing to prove, Brother. You can afford to show compassion to those you have defeated."

Darien shook his head. "No. I don't want to kill any more people than I have to—killing isn't my goal. To take the North, we'll need to drive them southward. We can do that either by the sword or by fear. I choose fear. That's why I have to be ruthless. 'Compassion is like a dull blade: it might seem kinder in the moment. But in the end, it often deals more cruelty,'" he said, quoting a maxim of the Arms Guild.

He swallowed his rika, then reached up to rub his eyes. He felt enormously weary. It went much further than just the effects of the liquor. He was weary all the way to his bones.

"Be warned, Brother," Sayeed said, leaning forward. "There is no mercy for the merciless."

"Is that another one of your proverbs?"

"Perhaps. Or perhaps it is prophecy." Sayeed climbed to his feet. "You'd better find your bed, Brother."

Chapter Nine
Alexa

The Vale of Amberlie, The Rhen

Kyel lay Alexa down on a bed of oak leaves and covered her with his black cloak. He sat there for a while, making sure she was going to be all right. Then he stood up, dusted off his pants, and set off into the forest to find Cadmus.

He wandered through the dense bracken with a heavy heart. The cleric hadn't returned after the attack, which wasn't a hopeful sign. So it wasn't a surprise when he found Cadmus lying pantsless and bloodless in a ditch. Kyel stopped yet a ways back from the cleric's body, knowing there was no sense in going any further. Out of respect for the man who had helped raise his son and had followed him half the length of the continent, Kyel paused and bowed his head. He stood for a moment listening to wind whispering through the pines, his thoughts turned inward, his eyes averted.

Then he did what Cadmus would have wanted. Gripping Thar'gon's hilt, he fed energy into the corpse until the flesh ignited. He fished a rag out of his pocket and held it to his face as the smoke and stench hit him. The smell was repugnant. It brought back the vivid horror of the time he'd spent locked in a cage with Myria Anassis' charred remains. He closed his eyes, breathing through the rag's dirty fabric, until the sound of the fire died in his ears.

When he opened his eyes, Cadmus was gone. There was nothing left of him but scorched earth and gray ashes. Kyel hooked Thar'gon to his belt and turned away, walking slowly and sadly back through the thicket.

He tethered Alexa's horse to his own and climbed into the saddle, cradling her against his chest as he jabbed his heels into the gelding's flanks. She somehow remained asleep through it all. He directed his horse toward the south, deeper into the Vale of Amberlie, sticking to the lowlands and the darker thickets of trees. Always, he kept his eyes open for the reappearance of the dead.

The forest darkened as the sun sank behind the Craghorns. The shadows thickened, the birds silenced. The insects began their nightly chants. He pulled back on his horse's reins and climbed down from the saddle, carrying Alexa to a spot of ground sheltered by a rocky outcrop not too far from a small brook. There, he built a fire and tended to the horses. Then he cast his tired body down beside hers and sat worrying a strip of jerky, not really tasting it. His eyes scanned the night, not trusting it. The smallest noises set him on edge.

The shadows of the trees revolved around him, lengthening. He let the fire burn and then die a slow death.

It was morning. A new fire now crackled atop the ashes of the old. Beside Kyel, Alexa stirred. She opened her eyes and gazed loosely up at him. Stretching, she asked, "What happened?"

Kyel didn't look at her. Instead, he picked up a stick and poked a log back toward the heart of the flames. "We were attacked. By dead people." His tone conveyed the anger he felt.

Alexa sat up, drawing her knees against her chest and wrapping her arms around them. She didn't respond to his statement. To Kyel, her silence was more honest than anything she could have said.

"You're not pregnant."

She looked away into the forest. Again, her lack of response was answer enough. Kyel nodded. He'd hoped she would have an explanation he could accept. But she was damned by her own silence.

He threw the stick down. "Cadmus is dead. I almost died, too. I *would* be dead, if not for this." He brandished Thar'gon as if ready to strike her with it.

She stared at the weapon in silence. Any normal girl would have cowered in fear. Alexa didn't.

Lowering the talisman, Kyel said, "You've got one chance to convince me not to take both horses and leave you behind."

She turned away from him and fixed her gaze on the fire. He waited. She said nothing. A log popped, flinging sparks onto the ground. Alexa didn't flinch.

In a flat voice, she mumbled, "They're all dead."

"Who? Who's dead?"

"The people of Creek Hollow. They're all dead."

Kyel stared at her, digesting that information. It was the first thing she'd said that he knew he could believe. Everything about Creek Hollow had seemed wrong. Everything but Alexa.

"What about you?" he said at last.

"I was their prisoner."

He doubted that. None of her actions had seemed unwilling.

Alexa's face crumbled into a grimace of sorrow. Shaking her head, she said, "I'm so sorry Kyel. I like you. I really do. I'm sorry…"

Kyel shot to his feet, eyes scouring the shadows of the forest. He took a step back away from her, reaching out for the magic field. He dragged it into him through the talisman.

"What are you sorry about?" he demanded.

Alexa shook her head and gazed up at him sadly. "It's a trap. *I'm* a trap. He wants you. Alive or dead, he doesn't care which."

Kyel took another step back. "Who? Who wants me?"

She gazed at him flatly. "Zavier Renquist."

Kyel's eyes widened. He whirled away, striding quickly toward his horse. Behind him, he heard Alexa rushing to catch up. She caught him by the collar, tugging him around.

"He took my baby!" she shrieked, pulling on him even as he fought her off. "I didn't want to do it! He took my baby!"

Kyel tore her hand off his shoulder, flinging it away. He tied her horse to his own then turned back to her. "If Zavier Renquist took your baby, then it's already dead."

He put his foot in the stirrup and swung himself over his horse's back, kicking it forward.

"What are you doing?" Alexa screeched. "Don't leave me here!"

Kyel ignored her. He kicked his horse to a trot.

"I know how to use that talisman!"

Filled with startled rage, Kyel jerked back on the reins. He turned and cast a glare back over his shoulder. "How could you know that?"

She stood there quivering, arms folded, shaking her head.

"Answer me!"

She lowered her gaze, as if in shame.

"Because I'm a mage," she whispered.

Chapter Ten
Well of Mystery

Isle of Titherry, The Rhen

Quinlan Reis stared down from the balcony that overlooked Athera's Crescent, watching the Crescent's surface swirl and roil in patterns that looked like a boiling cauldron of quicksilver. It was mesmerizing. The dark places that had been there were now gone, the curve of its surface unbroken. A beautiful dance of energy swarmed across it, free and unconstrained.

The Crescent's power had been restored. But not without sacrifice.

Quin raised a hand to his head, massaging his temple. Ever since his near-death in the nodal chamber, his head ached from time to time. Sometimes the pain was terrible, forcing him to lie in bed in the dark, for hours at a time. It was like a migraine, only different. This pain was self-inflicted.

It was the price he paid for turning against his Master.

He had defied Xerys when he'd repaired the conduit, an act in direct contradiction with his Master's objectives. In retaliation, his connection with the Netherworld had been severed. The Onslaught was denied him now. The Soulstone was the only reason his soul hadn't been banished to Oblivion. The medallion had returned the Gift to him. He was truly alive, now, and beyond Xerys' reach.

Quin felt Naia's fingers tighten around his own. She stood next to him on the balcony, clothed in a blue gown. Her auburn hair spilled down her back, ruffled by a breeze that moved over the bowl-shaped valley. The air was warm. The curse of winter had been lifted from the isle. Athera's Crescent was sustained by its conduits now. It no longer needed to harvest energy directly from the air.

"How are you feeling?" Naia asked.

Quin smiled, turning his attention to her. "Better. I feel alive. *Really* alive."

"Which is unfortunate."

He whirled to find Tsula behind them. The Harbinger wore the same affectless look she always had. She stood with her hands clasped in front of her, a feathered turban on her head. Quin was mildly surprised to see her. She had been missing from the castle for nine days, ever since the conduits had been repaired.

"What an unpleasant thing to say," he remarked. "Does this mean you wish me to leave your ungracious hospitality?"

"It means that hope for the world has just been reduced significantly," she said.

Quin turned to Naia. "Did you hear that, darling? My very existence saps hope from the world. I believe that's rather an accomplishment, don't you think?"

The Harbinger stamped her foot on the flagstones. "It is no time for sarcasm, Quinlan Reis! There is still opportunity to recover, but it will take much sacrifice on both our parts."

"Would you rather I just jumped off the balcony?"

"If you are so inclined." Her cat-like eyes gazed at him impassively.

Letting go of his hand, Naia stepped between Quin and the Harbinger. "This is what you feared from the beginning," she accused. "Why you wanted to leave me frozen. You knew I could bring him back—and you feared that possibility."

The woman's eyebrows flicked upward in confirmation of Naia's guess. "That is part of the reason, yes."

"What's the other part?" Quin asked.

Turning to him, the Harbinger said flatly, "There is a great chance Naia will destroy the rule of the gods."

Quin blinked. That wasn't the answer he'd been expecting. He looked to Naia and smiled apologetically. "I'm sorry, darling. My penchant for disaster seems to be rubbing off."

Naia shook her head. "I don't understand."

"It is but one possibility." Tsula beckoned them toward the stairs. "Come. We have much to speak of. And you have much to learn."

Quin wasn't certain he wanted to hear anything the woman had to say. It seemed that every conversation he had with Tsula was becoming progressively grimmer. It was getting to the point he feared anything that came out of her mouth, especially now that the Crescent was fully operational. He wondered what information Tsula had managed to garner during the nine days of her absence.

She led them to the vast chamber that occupied the entire bottom floor of the castle and invited them to sit with her in a small cluster of chairs with over-stuffed cushions. Quin gazed around the enormous hall, at its hundreds of empty chairs, and felt a pang of sadness. The castle had once been bustling with mages and their attendant staff, all gathered here to serve the Crescent. All gone now. All gone because of him.

"Please, take a seat." Tsula extended her hand. "There is much for us to discuss."

With the slightest narrowing of her eyes, she ignited a fire in the hearth behind them, even though the room didn't need the warmth. Rays of sunlight glistened down from windows high above, lighting the hall and warming the air.

Quin took a seat beside Naia, holding her hand. Tsula stared down at their hands, her face darkening in irritation. It was the first emotion Quin remembered seeing on her face. He found himself enjoying it. Just to provoke her, he raised Naia's hand to his lips and kissed it, grinning in triumph at the seething look on Tsula's face.

She went deliberately about smoothing her gown, as if using the action to compose herself. Then she looked up with a flat expression and told them, "For nine days, I have been analyzing the information harvested by the Crescent. There has been much to take in."

"And what did you discover?" he asked.

"There are many things going wrong in the world, and very

few going right. There are too many variables in play to guess the outcome of it all. But one thing is for certain: we must destroy the magic field. It is the only way to break the Curse over the Black Lands. And it is the only way to destroy the Well of Tears."

Quin looked at her sideways. "*Destroy* the Well of Tears. I thought that wasn't possible."

"It is possible. Difficult, but possible."

"How?" he demanded. Naia squeezed his fingers. She looked just as confused as Quin felt.

Tsula crossed her legs, folding her hands over her knees. "For you to understand, we must discuss the nature of the Well itself."

"I'm listening." Quin glanced at Naia, seeing the intense frown on her face that had to mirror his own.

The Harbinger nodded. "The Well of Tears unlocks the Gateway between worlds. Think of it as a tunnel between two realms: our realm, and the realm of Xerys."

Quin frowned. "You mean hell."

Tsula waved her hand dismissively. "Hell is a religious concept. I do not speak of religion. What you know of as the Netherworld is simply one facet of an infinite number of realms that define existence. It is the realm most closely associated with our own plane."

Her concept of the universe was so far removed from anything in Quin's experience, that her statements seemed preposterous. "I've been to the Netherworld," he reminded her. "For a thousand years, I existed there in torment. Now you're telling me I wasn't damned?"

Tsula shrugged. "Damnation is simply the consignment of a soul to the realm of Xerys. Your soul, unfortunately, was imprisoned there and subjected to torture."

He demanded, "Why? Why was I tortured?"

"Because you defied the will of Xerys."

Quin felt the heat of outrage flush his cheeks. Stewing in bitterness, he asked, "So what is the Gateway, exactly?"

Tsula crossed her arms. "The Gateway is like a tunnel with two openings: one in our own realm, and the other in the Netherworld. It is a rip in the fabric which separates those two planes."

"How was the tunnel created?" Naia asked.

"It was created by harvesting an extraordinary amount of vitrus in the eye of a vortex, then focusing that vitrus on Xerys' plane."

Quin frowned as he thought about it. Vitrus was an archaic term used to describe the Gift that was passed from a dying mage to their successor—a mage's life force. The creation of the Well of Tears must have required the slaughter of dozens of mages.

Tsula continued, "This act opened the mouth of the tunnel in our world. The other end was bored by Xerys using the Hell-power. The manipulation of the Gateway requires tremendous amounts of vitrus. That is why a Grand Master must be sacrificed to seal the Well of Tears—the sacrifice has to be great enough; elsewise, it will fail."

"So a thousand years ago, I was the sacrifice," Quin concluded.

"Yes." Tsula nodded. "Just as Darien Lauchlin sealed it more recently."

Quin exchanged looks with Naia. Despite his reservations, he believed Tsula. She came from a perspective that contradicted every religious doctrine he had ever heard. But her explanations were too rational to deny. If she was correct, then Xerys was not necessarily a god of evil. He was merely the ruler of his own domain.

Baffled, Quin asked, "So how do we destroy the Gateway?"

"The Gateway is unstable. Its natural tendency is to collapse. It is maintained by the Well of Tears, which draws its power from the magic field. In the Netherworld, there is another Well that is powered by the Onslaught."

Tsula leaned forward, her black eyes taking in both of them with a look of grave portent. "To collapse the Gateway, we must destroy the stabilizer that holds it open: we must destroy the Well of Tears. And the only way to do that is to destroy the power that feeds it."

Quin understood. He understood completely. "Destroy the magic field," he concluded in a whisper.

"Yes."

His head spun. He felt the dizzying sensation of his headache returning. He asked, "And there's no other way?"

The Harbinger nodded. "There is no other way."

Chapter Eleven
The Naturalist

The Vale of Amberlie, The Rhen

Kyel gestured at Alexa, demanding, "Let me see your arm."
She pulled her right sleeve back, exposing the glistening
mark of the Mage's Oath. Kyel glared down at the emblem, not trusting it. Perhaps Renquist had found a way to replicate it. His hand lingered on the talisman's haft while Alexa tugged her sleeve back down.

Kyel looked at her. "Start talking. Right now."

Alexa nodded, her gaze dropping to the ground. "I was away when Aerysius fell. But I returned…and I was captured."

"By Zavier Renquist?" he asked skeptically.

"No. By Cyrus Krane." She reached up and brushed a lock of hair out of her face. "They took me to Bryn Calazar and made me a slave. I was there for two years…" Her voice shook. She looked like she was close to crying.

He didn't care; she was lying to him again. "You're a mage. How could they keep you as a slave?"

She cast an injured pout his way. "They took me into the vortex. There was nothing I could do." The look on her face begged him to believe her.

He didn't. Kyel paced away, one hand on his hip, the other on Thar'gon. "So how did you end up in Creek Hollow?"

"Cyrus Krane came back. He took my baby." Her voice shook harder. "He told me he'd kill her if I didn't do what he said."

Kyel gritted his teeth. That was a lie. She couldn't possibly have a baby if she'd been a slave in the Black Lands for two years—

The thought staggered to a halt. It suddenly occurred to him how such a child could have been conceived. He turned back to her, hoping for her sake she was lying. More gently, he asked, "And what did Krane tell you to do?"

"Krane told me you were Darien's acolyte. And that Renquist wanted you. He didn't say why, but I can guess."

"Then guess!" Kyel's voice was harsher than he'd intended.

She pointed at the weapon hanging from his belt. "You're carrying the most powerful talisman in the world. I'm sure Renquist wants it. And there's only one way he can get it."

"By killing me," Kyel concluded, feeling his anger rising. Not specifically at Alexa, but at the whole situation. Almost, he thought he could believe her. Almost. But not quite. He glanced down at the ground, at the shadows of the pine trees laced with sunlight. A cool breeze swayed the branches overhead and moved the fronds of the bracken around them.

"Thar'gon binds to only one person at a time," Alexa explained. "Right now, it's bound to you. There's only two ways it could ever abandon you. First, you could die. Or if the Warden of Battlemages ever touches it, then Thar'gon will transfer to his hand."

"Byron Connel's dead," Kyel said, feeling relieved.

"Who took his place?"

Jarred, Kyel stared unblinking at Alexa. He hadn't thought of that. "There's only four Servants left. Renquist, Krane, Quin Reis…and Darien."

Alexa spread her hands. "Then you have your answer. Darien Lauchlin is the new Warden of Battlemages. And if he ever gets his hands on that weapon—"

"Oh, gods…" Kyel let out a slow sigh, realizing the likelihood of that danger. He remembered the atrocious means Darien had used to escape the dungeon of Greystone Keep. And the implacable ease with which he'd killed.

"I can't let him get it," Kyel said. No matter what. He looked at Alexa, realizing it didn't matter whether or not he trusted her. He couldn't take the risk of bringing her along. "I'm going to leave you with your horse. Don't follow me."

"I thought you—"

Kyel shook his head. "I can't trust you." He went to his mount and threw the saddle blanket over the animal's back. Alexa dashed after him, shaking her head, her eyes wide and desperate.

"I made my bargain with Krane before I ever knew you had Thar'gon!" she gasped. "Now...the stakes are too high." Her eyes fill with tears. "I'll teach you how to use it!"

Kyel paused in the action of lifting his saddle off the ground. He set it back down. "You know how it works?"

"I'm a Naturalist...pushing the boundaries of Natural Law is my area of expertise. And that talisman you're holding bends Natural Law far beyond the limits of what should ever be possible. Thar'gon is every Naturalist's dream. We studied it exhaustively, at least as much as we could from historical records."

Kyel's eyes narrowed in distrust. "Then show me something. Show me something I can do with it."

Alexa spread her hands. "What do you want to know?"

"I don't care!" He flung his arms up in frustration. "Show me anything!"

"All right." She walked away from him a few paces. Then she lifted her hand, gesturing around at the forest and the rocky outcrop behind them. "First, get a good look at your surroundings. Notice things like the horses, the rocks, these particular trees. Are you doing it?"

Kyel nodded, following her directions sourly, even though he didn't understand why he was doing any of it. For all he knew, Alexa could be tricking him into killing himself.

"Now think of somewhere nearby. Somewhere you've been and can easily visualize."

Curious now, Kyel forgot his reservations. The campsite where they'd left the remains of the dead leapt into mind. The fallen tree. The rotting body parts. Cadmus' ashes. He remembered all of it.

"Now what?" he grumbled.

Alexa approached him slowly. "Try to see it in your mind. Every detail that you can remember, as clearly as you can."

"I am." It wasn't difficult.

She stopped beside him. "I'm going to hold your hand."

He felt her fingers clasp his own. He almost flinched away. But he gripped her hand, far too curious to stop now.

"Hold your weapon," she instructed softly. "Bring it up. There. Now, say this word: *Vergis.*"

"*Vergis,*" Kyel echoed.

The forest shivered and disappeared…and another appeared. Startled, Kyel broke away from Alexa's grip and spun in a slow circle, taking in the sight of the grove complete with its rotting smell and decomposing flesh. Lowering Thar'gon to his side, Kyel blinked, feeling dizzy.

"How is that possible?" he gasped.

"It's called transferring," Alexa informed him with a smile. "Thar'gon is imbued with several motive characters. That's one." She gestured around expansively. "Do you trust me now?"

"No."

The smile collapsed, replaced by a scowl of frustration. She stalked away through the bracken then whirled back, planting her hands on her hips.

"Use logic," she snapped. "If I was trying to hurt you, why would I be showing you how to use the most powerful talisman in the world?"

"I don't know, but I'm sure there's a reason."

Kyel moved to the nearest corpse, nudging it with his boot. Flies swarmed up to buzz him angrily before settling back down again. The stench that rose from the rotting tissue made him gag. He moved away quickly.

"What else can it do?" He set off through the trees toward the little brook he knew was there.

Alexa rushed to keep up. "Thar'gon was crafted to enhance a war mage's effectiveness in battle. Mobility. Communication. Defense. It anticipates its master's needs and reacts accordingly."

"What else?" Kyel paused, looking around for familiar landmarks.

Alexa said to his back, "Several of its motive characters are powerful offensive strikes. It also has an amplification character I'm sure you've discovered."

"I have."

He stopped by the brook and looked down sadly at Cadmus' ashes. He turned to Alexa, gesturing with the talisman as anger tightened his throat. "This is your fault. If it wasn't for you, he'd be alive now. I needed him. And now he's dead."

A look of regret filled the woman's eyes. "I'm sorry, Kyel. It wasn't my intent to get him killed."

"No. Your intent was to get *me* killed." He glared at her. "What were those things back there? The dead people?"

She clasped her hands together. "They are the men of Creek Hollow. Or what's left of them. The women and children were carried off. I don't know what happened to them."

"They didn't look like rotten meat in Creek Hollow." The men of the town had been alive. Awkward and strange, but definitely not decomposing. But she was right; there'd been no sign of women or children. He'd thought that odd at the time.

Alexa explained, "The ward of preservation ended the moment they left the town." She lifted her arm, offering her hand out to him. "Please. Take us back."

Grudgingly, he took her hand. He looked back at Cadmus' ashes. *"Vergis."*

The world spun and lurched. Kyel staggered as the ground stabilized beneath his feet. The horses tossed their heads, rolling their eyes at their sudden appearance. Kyel released his grip on Alexa's hand and moved to reclaim his mount. He tossed the saddle over the animal's back, then bent to tighten the girth strap.

Alexa rushed up behind him, grabbing his arm. "Please, Kyel! Take me with you! *I'm the only chance you have!"*

Kyel ripped his arm out of the woman's grasp and swung around to shout at her, *"Why?* Why are you my only chance?!"

She looked at him coldly. "Because that weapon wants to return to its rightful master. And you're not him."

Kyel held her gaze. "And what can you do about it?"

"Darien Lauchlin commands a host of necrators. They will shut you down in a heartbeat. But as you see, I have some experience with the undead." Alexa smiled slowly. "If you take me with you, we'll shut him down, instead."

Chapter Twelve
Blood Kin

The Cerulean Plains, The Rhen

Darien woke to darkness. For a moment, he thought he was back in the Black Lands. But the ubiquitous flickers of cloud-light were absent, not ribboning across the fabric of his tent. Then he remembered: he was in the Rhen, where the night sky had never been tortured by Malikar's Curse.

He put out a hand, searching next to him, but felt only empty blankets. Azár hadn't returned.

He climbed out of the covers and walked naked across the rugs to the water jug. He took a gulp of water and swished it around in his mouth. The taste was foul. Grimacing, he picked up a bristled tooth-stick and used it to scrub his teeth as he pulled on his clothes. He gathered his weapons then walked out into the gathering area.

A dozen or more men lay sleeping within, sprawled across the rugs. Darien had to pick his way carefully as he wound his way toward the door. He found his boots and pulled them on by the straps. He left the tent and walked out into the cool night, spitting the film from his teeth and pocketing the tooth-stick.

The air smelled robustly of woodsmoke. Darien breathed in deeply, filling his nostrils with the scent of it. After so many months breathing the harsh stench of burning coal, Darien relished the scent of woodfire. All across the encampment, his soldiers leaned over fires of wood and prairie dung, a first of the many bounties the Rhen had to offer.

Darien looked around for sight of his wife, wondering where she could have fled to. Azár had no immediate family to take her in. She also didn't seem to have any friends—at least, none that he was aware of. The life of a Lightweaver was a solitary existence. Searching the camp, Darien finally remembered that not all friends walked on two legs.

He found Azár by the horse pickets. She was rubbing down her mare's glossy coat, moving her hands in slow circles over the animal's neck. The horse followed her movements with its head, brushing its nose against her back. Smiling, Azár caught hold of the bridle and focused her attention on the mare's head.

A twig snapped under Darien's boot. Azár flinched then twisted around to look back at him. Her hands ceased their motion, and a scowl of anger twisted her face.

Darien halted, raising his hands. "I'm sorry. I know you're angry—"

She turned and stalked toward him, glaring at him with an alarming fury. She raised her hand as if to strike him. But instead of landing a blow, she lurched into his arms, growling, "Don't ever do something so stupid again."

Instead of responding, Darien picked her up and carried her into the shadows of the tall grass.

He woke to the sound of distant thunder. The sun was already up, its glaring light stabbing darts into his eyes. Darien sat up from the bed of grass he shared with Azár. He squinted against the light, his pulse kicking up as he recognized the earth-shaking rumble that was growing louder by the second.

Horses. Hundreds of horses. Perhaps thousands.

In the distance, he heard the encampment stirring.

At his side, Azár roused from sleep.

"Get back to the pavilion," he told her.

She glared at him reproachfully, looking ready to protest.

"We're in a *vortex,*" Darien snapped, reminding her of her vulnerability.

Azár's face softened, and she nodded. She rose and pulled on her clothes, muttering, "Don't do anything—"

"Stupid," Darien finished for her. "I know."

Confident she was on her way back, he dressed and strapped his sword on. By the time he returned to camp, the forward scouts had already reported in, and the encampment was in a state of readiness, waiting to receive an attack. The forward defenses had positioned themselves along the camp's western edge, taking cover behind earthworks and long lines of pickets. Darien looked out across the prairie in the direction of the rolling thunder, wondering what kind of horse lord would dare challenge an army of the size and capability of his own.

Seeing a cluster of Zakai, Darien sprinted toward them. He caught sight of Sayeed among their number. Halting in their midst, he demanded, "Report!"

Sayeed gestured toward the horizon. "A great many horse warriors approach from the west. They do not appear hostile, but their numbers are concerning."

Darien looked to the west and saw a brown plume of churned-up dust rising hugely into the sky. Sayeed was right to be concerned. The Jenn of the Cerulean Plains were fierce warriors who had little patience for outsiders infringing on their grazing territories. Gesturing for the demon-hound to remain behind, Darien made his way up the slope of a berm mounded to create a defiladed position. He halted on the top of the mound and gazed out across the sprawling sea of grass.

Dominating the prairie was a dark tide of horses carrying riders with dusky brown skin garbed in furs and hide. They were armed with arsenals of spears and hornbows, and their horses' blankets jingled with beads and bells. Darien stood motionless, astounded by the swirling sea of brutal weapons and flowing manes arrayed before him across the grassland.

He abandoned the berm and made his way back to Sayeed. "It's the Jenn," he said. "I don't think they'll attack."

"Why not?" The officer frowned.

"I know these people," Darien said, then corrected himself, "I don't *know* them, but I know a lot about them. I think they're here to negotiate." He glanced back over his shoulder.

"Negotiate what?" Sayeed's frown deepened.

"Our passage."

Darien started forward, ignoring Sayeed's look of incomprehension. Followed by the Zakai, he rounded the berm and strode toward a plank bridge that spanned a trench dug into the ground on the other side. He could hear the loud clatter of the officers' boots as they kept pace with him. Stepping off the planks, he made his way out across the mud-slathered kill zone.

Sayeed walked at his side, while the rest of the Zakai fanned out to stalk around them. Darien glanced around, seeing nothing but flat horizons and swarming horses in every direction.

"I thought you were going to stay out of harm's way," Sayeed growled under his breath.

"I'm not in harm's way."

Darien waded into the knee-high grass of the open prairie. Spread before him were thousands of horses clustered together in a great herd that spanned miles. They roved in circulating patterns, never still. There were men and women, even children. Horses and foals. An entire culture loomed before him.

Ahead, three horses broke off from the massive herd and trotted toward them. Darien halted, holding his ground, waiting for the riders to approach.

The man who rode in front had long black hair pulled back and tied in a topknot. He was dressed in furs and tanned leather and wore his full beard groomed to a tapering point. All three men rode without saddle or tack, using only the pressure of their legs to guide their mounts.

The strangers drew up only paces away. They didn't dismount, but sat staring down at Darien and Sayeed from their horses' backs. A tense silence clotted the air between them. Only the twitching of tails and the rippling of grass marked the passage of time. Eventually, the darkly bearded horselord nodded as if satisfied.

"Darius dreoch," he said in a rumbling voice.

Darien stood stunned at hearing those words. At his side, Sayeed issued a sharp gasp. The man had spoken the ancient greeting of the Khazahar. Darien's brain fumbled to make connections that should have been obvious from the start. The man's olive skin. The bareback riding style. The horse blankets tinkling with tassels and bells.

The Jenn. These people call themselves the Jenn…

Stiffly, Darien returned the greeting. *"Darius dreoch,"* he said, then added, *"Sulimu kadreesh."*

The man glanced back and forth between Darien and Sayeed, his eyes widening. *"Akadreesh issulim,"* he responded, and jumped down from his horse. He strode forward with a wide smile to grasp Darien's arm in a two-handed grip. "I am Ranoch son of Tellat, warlord of the Jenn."

Sayeed stood speechless as the man clapped his arm in greeting.

Darien's mind scrambled as he realized the vast opportunity Ranoch and his people afforded them. The Jenn had been devoted allies of the Sentinels for hundreds of years. If he could harness that allegiance, the horse clans would be a formidable asset. Darien drew in a deep, steadying breath, wondering how far he dare go. With the Jenn, there could be no halfway.

"I am Grand Master Darien Lauchlin of the Order of Sentinels," he announced, claiming the title he had not worn since his death. "Warden of Battlemages and Overlord of the Khazahar."

"You are *him*," Ranoch gasped, backing away. His men jumped off their mounts and surged forward, reaching for their weapons. Ranoch raised his hand, halting them.

Darien spread his arms, indicating the vast Malikari encampment behind him. "I've come to reunite you with your brethren."

The horse lord frowned. "I do not understand."

"What is the name of your tribe?"

Ranoch shook his head in incomprehension. "Once long ago, the Jenn were divided by clans. No longer. Now we are one tribe. One people."

"Do you know which tribe your people descend from?" Darien pressed.

The man answered slowly, "Once, my ancestors called themselves the Omeyan Jenn. But that was long ago. Now we are simply the Jenn."

It was Darien's turned to be astounded. These people were

more than just a lost tribe—they were *his* tribe. His own blood. Quietly, he said, "Then you are my kin."

Ranoch shook his head. "That is not possible."

"My ancestor was Braden son of Marthax, of the Omeyan Clan of the Dur ul-Jenn."

Ranoch stared at him flatly. "You are a son of the Omeyans?"

Darien nodded.

The warlord crossed his arms, appearing greatly troubled as his eyes slipped slowly over the vast Malikari encampment. At last, he nodded.

"Then we are kin," Ranoch decided. He turned and shouted back over his shoulder, "Ride forward and welcome your lost brothers to our home!"

A deafening cry resounded across the plain. The horses of the Jenn broke forward as if sprinting into the charge. When they closed the gap, their riders abandoned their mounts and leaped to the ground. They dashed forward and embraced the Malikari soldiers like long-lost brothers in a surreal scene that transcended anything in Darien's broad experience.

"You never told me Braden Reis was your ancestor."

Darien glanced sideways at Sayeed. The man was frowning as he walked, his fingers stroking his sword's hooked pommel. It was obvious the omission hadn't pleased him. Darien glanced back to where the rest of the Zakai were clustered in the lee of the command tent. He wondered how the others would take the news.

"You never asked," Darien said, then admitted, "I figured it wouldn't go over very well."

The man nodded. Some of the tension eased from his face, though he still looked as though he held a fair bit of resentment. Darien berated himself for not being more honest from the start.

"I'm sorry, Brother," he said. "When we started down this road, I wasn't certain how far I could trust you. And I had reason not to."

Sayeed nodded thoughtfully. "It is probably for the best you kept that information to yourself. The name Braden Reis is cursed. It was he who brought about the Desecration. It is very unfortunate that this man's blood runs in your veins."

Darien was mildly surprised Sayeed didn't already know of his relation to the First Sentinel. When he'd been forced to provide his lineage to the elders of the clans, Sayeed had made him sit down and scribe a complete list of his pedigree. Braden Reis had been the last name on that long list. Apparently, the tribal elders hadn't shared that information with the Zakai.

"You have it wrong," Darien said. "It was Braden's brother who caused the Desecration. And it wasn't his fault. Braden and Quin were trying to save the people of Caladorn from the rule of Xerys. But they failed."

Sayeed looked at him, confusion carving deep furrows into his brow. "That is not the story that has been passed down."

"Then your story is wrong." Darien turned from him and shrugged. "It happens. Stories can change. Especially the stories of those who have suffered defeat. I had never heard of Braden's brother until I met him. His name had been erased entirely from our records."

Darien halted and stood looking around at the bustling encampment. To every side, soldiers were going about the labors of the day: honing weapons, repairing armor, cooking meals. At almost every fire stood men and women of the Jenn, watching the Tanisars as they worked, offering knowledge and answering questions. There were many facets of living in the land of sunlight that the Malikari people were ignorant of. He was glad to see them learning from their new allies.

Sayeed followed his gaze, his face darkening. "This man, Quin Reis—how did you meet a man who died a thousand years ago?"

"Because he is also a Servant of Xerys."

His answer appeared to have a great effect on Sayeed, who drew his pack from his shoulder and turned to Darien with concern in his eyes. "So this cursed man is a Servant? How can that be?"

Softly, Darien answered, "We are all cursed, Brother."

A long silence fell between them. Sayeed stood staring past

him into the distance. At first, Darien couldn't tell what the man was looking at. Then it occurred to him: he was looking at the sun. Turning, he followed Sayeed's gaze. The sun had risen well above the Craghorns, burning fiercely in the brilliant sky. Before his death, he'd always taken the sun for granted. No longer. Darien realized that, for the rest of his time in this world, he should be thankful for every sunrise. He could only imagine what the Malikari must be feeling.

"We keep calling ourselves brothers," Sayeed said in a gruff voice. "Perhaps it is time to formalize this bond we claim to share."

Darien glanced at him sharply. "What do you mean?"

Sayeed's reply was measured and emotionless. "Among my people, there is a ritual that unites two men as kin."

"How does that work?" Darien had never heard of such a thing, although it didn't surprise him. The Malikari seemed to have a ritual for everything. For a people whose very existence was defined by chaos, such a highly methodized culture added an element of structure to their lives.

Sayeed took Darien by the arm and drew two fingers across the palm of his right hand. "Your blood and my blood would be mixed, as though we had been born of the same father."

"A blood rite," Darien concluded, not liking the sound of it. The only other blood ritual he'd experienced had ended with the chains of his Oath cleaved from his wrists. The day he'd pledged himself to the goddess of Death to become her hand of vengeance. Which brought Darien to another thought equally disturbing: he had sworn his life to a goddess and sworn his afterlife to a god. He wasn't sure how much was left of him to pledge to Sayeed.

"And what would that mean for us?" Darien asked warily.

Sayeed retracted his hand. "We would become family, in every sense of the word. Our fates and fortunes would be joined. I would support you—and your wife, and any children you might have—in all ways. I would fight at your side in every battle. I would second you in any feud. And upon your death, I would put you in your grave, and provide for your family as though they were my own. Just as you would do the same for me."

Darien dropped his gaze, feeling overwhelmed. What Sayeed was offering…it went beyond natural bonds of blood. True brothers were seldom so dedicated to each other. He felt unworthy of receiving such a commitment from another human. He couldn't fathom it.

He struggled to find words. It took him a moment. "I had a brother once. I didn't get to choose him; I never would have. But if I'd had a choice, I would have chosen you instead." He knew his response wasn't eloquent, or even sufficient, but it was as close as he could manage.

Sayeed's smile was jubilant. He clapped Darien on the back. "We need your wife. And we need witnesses!"

Before Darien could respond, the man scooped up his pack and hauled him forward by the arm in the direction of the command tent. Darien was pressed to keep up, pulled along by Sayeed's enthusiasm. He was a little taken aback—he hadn't expected Sayeed to act on the agreement immediately.

"Can't this wait?" he gasped, thinking of the scores of other things he should be doing at the moment. He had a war council to convene, the Jenn to attend to, a land to conquer—

"These things do not wait!" his First exclaimed in a reproving tone. "We are at war, and neither one of us is guaranteed to live another day."

Darien grunted an acknowledgement. There was logic to that reasoning, he supposed. He followed Sayeed into camp along the main road that bisected the grid of tents, separating the Khazahari side of the encampment from the Calazi and Mariduri armies. Banners of different colors fluttered above the tents, each emblazoned with the symbols and emblems of their units.

When they arrived at the pavilion, Darien lurched to a halt. He stood in a patch of trampled grass, staring at the sight of Azár armed with a wooden sword facing off against one of Sayeed's Zakai. They were slowly circling each other, blades poised and ready to strike. Azár lunged first, the waster in her hand parried by the officer's wooden blade. She pulled back, raising her practice sword to block the man's attack. But she moved a second too slow—the officer's wood blade connected with her chest. Azár jerked away with a growl, moving her waster back to highward.

Darien exchanged glances with Sayeed. Azár's movements were halting, her footwork clumsy. But her focus was intense. He had no doubt that, with time and practice, she could be quite competent with a sword. He came up behind her and grasped her sword arm, gently lowering her blade to mid-ward, and adjusted her grip.

"That's better," he said. "Otherwise, he'll just come in under your guard. Unless you're trying to feint. But I wouldn't worry about that just now."

Azár turned to him, lowering her waster to her side. She flashed him a confident smile.

"Warden." Her Zakai opponent saluted with his sword and then backed away.

Darien nodded in acknowledgement. To Azár, he said, "If you wanted to learn the dance of the blade, you could have asked me."

Azár's smile grew mischievous. "I wished to surprise my husband."

"I'm not surprised at all." His wife was the most competent woman he'd ever known. Azár had the heart and spirit of a warrior, traits he found captivating. He took her by the hand, drawing her away. "Come. I need you as a witness."

She glanced at him with a bewildered expression, then turned to look suspiciously at Sayeed. The officer walked toward them carrying a large bowl in his hands, flanked by a grave-faced group of Zakai.

"What is this?" Azár asked, tossing her practice sword on the ground.

"Sayeed asked me to become his brother by blood," Darien admitted. "I told him I'd be honored."

Azár beamed at him and kissed his cheek. "I am glad for you. You are too alone in this world."

Perhaps she was right. She usually was.

"I need your dagger," Sayeed said. He handed the bowl to a

soldier at his side, then waited as his men spread out to encircle them. Darien glanced around at the ring of witnesses, feeling suddenly uncomfortable. The officers stood at attention, their faces expressionless, as if they were witnessing some formal and weighty ceremony. He hadn't realized Sayeed's ritual would amount to such a solemn ordeal.

Darien drew his dagger from its sheath and handed it to his First. Sayeed caught his forearm and forced his sleeve back to his elbow. Without hesitation, the officer drew a wide cut across Darien's palm, slicing his skin. The wound didn't bleed at first. But when the blood started, it flowed liberally down his arm.

Sayeed handed Darien back his dagger then drew his own, pressing it into his hand. Without hesitation, Darien made a similar incision in Sayeed's flesh. The officer sheathed his dagger and retrieved the bowl, which he used to collect their spilled blood. Another man stepped forward to add some wine to the pooling liquid. Darien's stomach roiled, seeing the blood swirling around in the wine. To his disgust, Sayeed raised the bowl to his lips and took a great swallow, wiping his mouth.

In a voice rigid with formality, Sayeed proclaimed, "Before the gods, I pledge my loyalty to this man, Darien Lauchlin of Amberlie, and take him into my heart as blood of my blood."

He passed the bowl to Darien. Darien stared down at the ghastly concoction, feeling his stomach tighten with nausea. Naia had forced him to drink from a chalice of his own blood to consummate his vow to her goddess. He still remembered the awful taste of it in his mouth.

Holding his breath, Darien raised the bowl and let the thick, warm liquid run into his mouth. Gagging, he forced himself to swallow it down. The wine did little to cut the sharp metallic taste of the blood.

Swallowing back bile, Darien stated gruffly, "Before the gods, I pledge my loyalty to this man, Sayeed son of Alborz, and take him into my heart as blood of my blood."

Hearing his words, the soldiers standing around finally let their discipline slip and let out a bellowing war cry. Sayeed swept forward and clapped Darien against his chest in an exuberant hug.

At first, Darien recoiled from the touch. But he steadied himself and drew his wife in to include her in the embrace.

For the first time in his life, Darien felt grateful to have a family. And for the first time in a long while, he knew true happiness.

But the moment expired quickly, as he was struck by the harsh slap of reason. He pulled away, suddenly regretting his decision. He had forgotten who he was. And what he was. He hadn't been brought back into the world to form ties of kinship. He'd been brought back for a singular purpose. And when that purpose was fulfilled, any bonds he'd made along the way would shatter painfully.

Especially for those he left behind.

Chapter Thirteen
Tendrils of Portent

Isle of Titherry, The Rhen

I t had been another five days with no sign of Tsula.

The Harbinger had disappeared again without warning. Naia had no idea where she had gone, though she had some idea what the woman was doing. Tsula was undoubtedly taking readings from Athera's Crescent. But where she went to do that—and how she went about it— remained a mystery. So Naia had been forced to content herself with waiting, not knowing how long that wait would last or what would come from it.

She had spent the past few days in the castle's vast library, which occupied the upper three floors. The walls were painted white, and the ceiling was a massive series of vaults covered in bright frescoes. Shelves filled with books lined the walls—all three stories—accessible by colonnaded walkways. It was the most beautiful library Naia had ever beheld, and it contained more information than she had ever seen gathered in one place.

Naia walked the long hallway back to her room with her arms full of books. She deposited her findings on the desk and then went looking for Quin. He wasn't hard to find; he'd barely ventured out of his own room in days. He'd been carving a staff out of core wood from one of the castle's many trees. It was a dark and knobby thing, roughly his own height, unadorned. Some kind of artifact, he insisted, and she believed him. She had witnessed the scope of his talents with both the Soulstone and the Crescent's conduit. Naia had no doubt he could accomplish any task he set his mind to.

She didn't bother to knock—he'd told her not to. She entered and found Quin sitting on his bed, sprawled back in a tall cushion of pillows with the staff laid across his body. He had his glasses on and was fiddling with some instrument that looked like a needle-thin probe. His roll of tools lay next to him on the bed, and an assortment of small vials was arranged beside him on a table. The vials contained a diverse collection of tiny crystals attuned to different characters of the magic field.

Lingering in the doorway, Naia asked, "How is it coming along?"

Quin raised the staff and looked down the length of it. Naia wasn't sure what he could possibly be checking for; the shaft was warped and gnarled, hardly straight.

Setting it back down, Quin shrugged and looked up at her. "Certainly not my best work, but it will have to suffice. I won't be able to give it enough time to properly season. Here, take a feel of it and tell me what you think."

He sat up and offered her the staff. Naia took it and held it vertically. The staff was taller than she was, and lighter than expected. It didn't feel like core wood.

Almost immediately, she felt the power imbued in the staff creep up her arm. It felt cold, like a reptile in the morning shade. The feel of it was unnerving, unnatural. Naia handed the staff back quickly, rubbing her hand to rid herself of the disturbing sensation.

"What's wrong with it?"

Quin grinned, obviously amused by her reaction. "It's a shadow staff," he said, laying the artifact across the bed and standing up. "Working with shadow is difficult. It's contrary to human nature."

"I should say so!" Naia thought of the times she had seen Darien weave shadow. She shivered. "I didn't realize it was so evil."

"It's not." Quin smirked. "Ever since we were children, we've learned to be afraid of the dark. It's a very primal fear. To work with shadow, you have to conquer that fear. Which is difficult, because it's very ingrained. Most mages can't tolerate it."

"I'll leave you to it." Changing the subject, she said, "I was just up in the library again. There's an awful lot of knowledge amassed there."

Quin strolled around the bed to scoop up a small cup of coffee from a bureau against the wall. "I should imagine," he said, taking a sip. "Once they were identified, apprentice Harbingers never studied in the Lyceum or Aerysius. They learned everything here."

"Why was that?"

"It was always a very secretive Order." Quin shrugged as he sat back down on the bed. "Because there is only one Crescent, it had to be shared by both the Lyceum *and* Aerysius. So the Harbingers had to go to great lengths to make certain readings from the Crescent couldn't be used for political or military gain."

He reached over to the table and picked up a leaf-wrapped cigar. He bit off the end and sent it flying across the room. He touched the other end to the shadow staff and smiled when a thin tendril of smoke appeared. Bringing the cigar up, Quin closed his eyes and drew in a long mouthful of smoke.

"I see you've been tinkering again," stated a low voice.

Naia turned to find Tsula standing in the doorway.

"Good," the Harbinger said. "We will be in need of your skills, so hone them well."

Quin puffed harder on the cigar, breathing out a great cloud of smoke. "You're assuming I still want to help you."

Tsula folded her arms, looking down the length of her nose at him. "You do not have a choice. If we destroy the magic field, then the Curse shall be lifted. Magic and mages will be gone— but our civilizations will be restored."

Quin appeared to mull over her words. "It's not going to be that easy. Even if the Curse was lifted today, there haven't been any plants growing in the Black Lands for a thousand years. There's no seeds in the dirt, and nothing to fertilize them. I don't imagine everything will come bounding back just the same as before."

"No," Tsula confirmed darkly. "It will take hundreds of years before the affected lands can be resettled. But it's the only option we have."

Quin looked sideways at her. "What if there's another option you don't know about?"

"There are no other options, Quinlan Reis. Or I would have foreseen them."

Quin's eyes narrowed. "Prove it."

Naia looked back and forth between Quin and the Harbinger, wondering who the victor of the exchange would be. Both participants seemed equally matched.

Tsula made a *tsk*ing noise with her tongue. "My readings do not work that way. You will have to trust my word."

Quin smiled sardonically around his cigar. "I learned a long time ago not to trust the word of people who tell me I have to trust their word."

Tsula paced deeper into the room. Naia moved out of her way as the Harbinger strode across the patterned rugs to stand towering before Quin, arms crossed and eyes narrowed, glaring down at him.

"The only way I could show proof of my claims is to teach you to read the Crescent yourself. Which is impossible. You are not a Harbinger."

"So make me a Harbinger."

"You know I can't do that. You are already sealed to your Order."

Quin's eyes shot to Naia. Holding his cigar between his fingers, he said, "But Naia isn't. You can teach her."

Before Naia could protest, Tsula snapped in a tone of disgust, "The magic field will reverse in two months' time. I could not possibly teach her all she would need to know in only two months."

"Who said anything about two months?" Quin ashed his cigar. "I'll be magnanimous and give you a week. After that, I'm afraid you'll have to make other arrangements, because Naia and I will be leaving."

Tsula gritted her teeth, her eyes narrowing in anger. She wrinkled her nose at a puff of smoke that drifted her way. "You cannot leave. I cannot destroy the magic field by myself!"

"Then I suppose you'd better get started." Quin smiled triumphantly, popping the cigar back into his mouth.

Naia stared at him, wide-eyed and appalled. She did not want to be trained as a Harbinger. She couldn't imagine living a life of seclusion in the castle. She had other, much more pressing things to do—

"You are a fool, Quinlan Reis," Tsula growled.

Quin blew a long trail of smoke out the side of his mouth. It curled toward Tsula's face. "Not just any fool, but a *persistent* fool. And believe me—there is no more dangerous creature on this earth."

Tsula backed away, making a face. She whirled around, snapping over her shoulder, "Come, child. Leave the fool to his foolishness."

Naia shot a glare at Quin, who responded by raising his eyebrows. She moved quickly to follow Tsula out the door and into the hallway, their steps resounding sharply off the walls.

Naia walked in silence, following Tsula through the echoing emptiness of the castle's ground floor, then out onto the long balcony that overlooked the Crescent. The air was cool but not cold, the sky clear, the surrounding mountains gleaming white. Even though the island had been freed from winter's reign, snow still lingered at the higher elevations. Tsula walked across the balcony to the stone-carved balustrade. Gripping it with her hands, she turned back to Naia.

"What I'm about to divulge to you is a secret known only to Harbingers. Think very carefully before we proceed another step. Once we start down this path, there is no turning back." She stood waiting for an answer, her eyes daring Naia to change her mind.

Naia wanted none of it. But she had a duty to the people of the Rhen. Even the people of Malikar. She had no choice but to blindly follow the woman down a road she would likely regret.

Squaring her shoulders, Naia said, "Show me what I need to know."

With one last, disparaging glance, the woman let go of the balustrade and walked *through* it. Standing on the air above the Crescent, Tsula turned and beckoned. "Then walk the path, if you dare."

Naia gazed down at Athera's Crescent then looked back up at the Harbinger. No stranger to mysteries, she wasn't disturbed by the odd circumstance of the woman standing in midair. It could be a trick, she realized. It was possible Tsula was suspended by magic, and there really was nothing beneath her feet to hold her up. Perhaps she was lingering there, taunting, hoping Naia would step off the balcony and plunge to her death.

But Naia didn't think so.

She had no reason in the world to trust Tsula.

And yet, for some reason, she did. Naia walked forward, passing through the balustrade as if it were made of gauze. She took a step off the balcony and jolted to a halt. Ahead of her appeared an arching path of glass stepping stones, carefully placed with small gaps between. Feeling a sharp twist of fear, Naia cast an accusing glare at Tsula. The woman could have warned her about the broken nature of the path. The Harbinger turned back around with a gloating smile and continued up toward what appeared to be a floating glass orb that hovered over the crescent, opalescent and gleaming in the sunlight.

"What is that?" Naia asked, staring up at their destination. A cool breeze tossed her hair about her shoulders.

Without looking back, the woman informed her, "It is the Nexus. It is where the infinite versions of the Story are read."

Naia lowered her eyes from the gleaming Nexus, taking great care in the placement of her feet. "How is it possible that I didn't notice this was here?"

"Your eyes see the Nexus," Tsula informed her, stepping onto a thin and invisible ledge that ringed the orb. "But your mind has been instructed to ignore what your eyes are telling it. It is the effect of a ward. It is a last resort, should all other means fail to protect the Crescent."

Naia stepped off the path and onto what appeared to be a glass shelf that sank slightly beneath her weight. Looking back over her shoulder, she saw the castle far below them. The path had taken them much further than it had seemed. They were hovering suspended in the air hundreds of feet above the liquid surface of the Crescent.

Gesturing for her to follow, Tsula stepped through the crystalline wall of the Nexus. Naia followed hesitantly, closing her eyes as she moved through what seemed like the thin membrane of a bubble.

She found herself standing within a spherical chamber made of shadow, interrupted by twisting tendrils of silver. The ambient light came from nowhere and everywhere. The curving walls absorbed every last drop of that light, sucking it out of the air as if feeding their hunger. Only the fine filaments of silver were visible, writhing over the curving texture of the walls. Naia realized they moved as if living things, branching and unbranching, weaving and unweaving, ambling over the walls like a living tangle of silver vines.

Tsula stopped in the center of the chamber and turned back to Naia. "The Crescent detects fluctuations in the magic field. Any disturbance of the field creates ripples in the patterns. The Crescent magnifies those ripples and interprets them. It separates the probable from the possible. We use the information it collects to read the myriad versions of the Everlasting Story."

"That is an interesting way of putting it," Naia said, moving toward Tsula and the heart of the spherical chamber.

The Harbinger opened her hands in an expansive gesture. "Every life is a chapter in the Book of All Things that tells the Everlasting Story. As a person lives their life, it is as though the mightiest of all pens is scribing their own personal Story. As long as a Story is not yet complete, it can have any number of possible endings. We call these possibilities versions. But when a Story is complete, the ending has already been written, and cannot be changed. The final version has been penned."

Naia concluded, "So a person can only see the possible versions of their own Story?"

"That is correct." The Harbinger nodded. She clasped her hands in front of her.

"But not other people's Stories?" Naia's eyes scanned the dark, curving walls, watching the thin silver vines tangle and untangle, twist and untwist. It was dizzying, mesmerizing. It made her stomach edge toward nausea.

"No," Tsula answered. "A Harbinger can only read the possible versions of their own Story. That is why Harbingers always lived apart from other mages. To read the versions of the Book of All Things, a Harbinger must be exposed to the world: living it, experiencing it. But no other person should ever know a Harbinger for what she or he is. Such would influence the versions and therefore influence the Story as it is being penned."

Naia frowned, reassessing everything she knew about the Order of Harbingers. Or thought she knew. Never was there an order of mages so cloaked in secrets and mystery. And outright misinformation. "So the Harbingers were not isolated, after all. They would have to come and go from the island frequently."

"Correct."

"But you haven't left the island in a thousand years," she protested. "Surely that must affect your Story. How much could you possibly know about the state of the world?"

Tsula narrowed her eyes, raising her chin. "Nothing about the Reversal or the magic field has changed in a thousand years. The solutions I have seen are still valid."

The silver vines twined and untwined, wove and unwove.

"How can I read my own Story?"

"When you are ready, the Crescent will show you all possible versions of your Story and separate the likely from the unlikely."

"That's all there is to it?" It was too simple. Naia's eyes wandered over the scrolling tendrils.

"Yes. The Crescent interprets the ripples in the magic field and uses those ripples to present your versions. As a Harbinger, you would merely read your own Story."

Naia turned all the way around, her mind echoing the confusion of the tendrils. "That's ridiculously simple. Why, then, would it take years of training to produce a Harbinger?"

Tsula explained, "It is not reading the Story that is difficult. What is difficult is knowing which knowledge to divulge, and which to hold back—no matter the cost. If used without wisdom and restraint, the Crescent could be made to work great evil. And a Harbinger must learn how to digest the information that is revealed without internalizing it."

"That makes sense." Naia yawned. She was becoming tired. The vines were beginning to blur and run together, weeping silver tears down the length of the curving walls. It seemed the world wept with them.

Tsula announced, "That is your lesson for the day. I want you to think very long and very hard on all I have revealed."

Naia didn't respond. She stared transfixed at the writhing tendrils.

"You have taken your first steps down the path that will make you a Harbinger. You still do not have a good understanding of which knowledge is safe to share, and which knowledge is necessary to hold back. At this point in your training, you shall share nothing. A Harbinger must remain absolutely neutral in all things. You must understand that anything you tell Quinlan Reis could have dire and everlasting consequences."

"I understand," Naia whispered.

Tsula barked, "'I understand, *Warden Renquist.'*"

Naia's attention snapped into acute focus. "I beg your pardon?"

The vines flinched all around the walls, then twinged away into nothingness. The Nexus darkened. Naia's pulse throbbed, shuddering in her ears. She stared aghast at the woman who stood before her with all the power and dignity of an empress.

The Harbinger took a step forward then informed her with a graceful sweep of her hand, "You are now my apprentice, so I expect you to address me by my proper title. I am Tsula Renquist, Warden of the Order of Harbingers. When the two of us are alone, you will address me as Warden Renquist. But when we are not alone, you are to address me simply as Tsula. Am I understood?"

Naia nodded, feeling her face whiten and her extremities go numb. She whispered, "Warden Renquist…if I may ask…?"

The woman lifted her chin and answered Naia's unspoken question, "I am the wife of Prime Warden Zavier Renquist."

Naia shook her head in confusion. It was impossible.

It is possible, the silver tendrils whispered at her from wherever they had twined away to. Or perhaps it was her own mind vining around the thought. Her heart, like the walls, wept mercurial blood.

"But how could that be?" she gasped. "Weren't you just lecturing me about the importance of neutrality? How could you be both a Harbinger and the wife of a demon?"

Tsula walked toward her until she stood only inches away, her black eyes as harsh and cold as obsidian. Folding her arms, she said carefully, "That is indeed a very important question, especially for you. I suggest you spend some time searching your own soul for the answer to it. Good day."

Naia fled the chamber of darkness and tendrils and secrets, to emerge shaken into the cruel glare of sunlight. Shielding her eyes, she hurried down the glass footpath that sloped toward the castle's balcony. Her mind reeled with an overload of information, trying to forage through tumbling thoughts and twisting fears. Nothing seemed to make sense, and yet everything did. Her footsteps rang off the walls of the castle's corridors.

As she walked, she could feel the silvery tendrils groping within her mind.

Throwing open the door to Quin's room, Naia hesitated, feeling conflicted. The Harbinger was right; she would have to be careful. She would not reveal more than she had to. Whether she liked it or not, secrets had been entrusted to her. Secrets that were dangerous to share.

But some secrets were too dangerous not to share.

Quin looked up at her, startled, and laid down his staff. He rose halfway from the bed.

"We have to kill Tsula," Naia gasped.

Quin paused in the action of standing up, straightening only slowly. His face darkened in confusion. "Why?"

Because she is Zavier Renquist's wife! The silvery tendrils in Naia's head constricted at the thought. She brought her hands up to clutch her temples.

"Because she sees only two options!" She felt the vines relax a bit. "If any other options exist, then we won't know about them unless she's dead."

Quin frowned, stroking the whiskers on his chin. "Why not?"

The tendrils tightened just a bit. Naia closed her eyes and forced the words out. "Because if any other option was part of *her* Story, she would have seen it already."

"I don't understand."

"You're not meant to understand." Naia shook her head. She was starting to feel panicked. It was as though her mind were being ripped away from her control. As if she were losing herself.

"Please trust me," she gasped. "You're an assassin—*and I need you to kill Tsula.*"

Quin regarded her a long, silent moment. His eyes roamed her face the way the harshest critic might study the work of an amateur. At last he nodded. "All right, then. I'll kill Tsula. But only because it's you doing the asking."

Chapter Fourteen
Ruthless

Acold fog descended, roiling like billowing clouds of smoke. Darien's armor was frigid, sapping the heat right out of him, and the mist collecting on his face felt like pinpricks of ice. He reined in, looking out at the muffled lights of a town visible through a tangled windbreak of trees. His horse stood on the edge of a field of winter wheat ready for the harvest: a bounty his people needed desperately.

He was determined to claim it for them.

He glanced to his right, at a mounted wedge of Zakai, their armor gleaming orange in the light of the torches they held. To his left, Azár sat mounted on a fresh courser she had claimed from the Jenn's vast herd. She looked ferocious in her black armor, her gleaming short sword in her hand. The look of eagerness on her face was chilling, and yet beautiful to behold.

"What town is this?" Sayeed asked him.

"Gannet."

The man grunted. "What kind of people live here?"

"It doesn't matter."

There came the dull thrumming of hoofbeats pounding against damp, compacted soil: their scouts returning from the town. The riders broke through the billowing mist, loping toward them across the dark field of grain. When the men drew up, they removed their helms and ducked their heads. The nearest scout, long-haired and bearded, was having a hard time holding his mount in check. It shied away from the light of the torches, dancing sideways and tugging at the reins. Of the six men who rode with him, only Sayeed was a proficient rider. That should change, though. There were many long leagues between Gannet and Rothscard.

"Warden, the town stands mostly unguarded. There are a few outlying farms, but most are empty. There is some type of festivity. Many people are gathered in a large structure on the far side of town."

"Good." Darien jerked his head, signaling the scout to join the line of men spread out at his sides. It was helpful that the townsfolk would be clustered together. That meant a more direct confrontation and less chasing about.

"Let's go."

He donned his helm then stabbed his heals into his horse's flanks. The stallion sprinted forward, the Zakai following behind. They gained the edge of the field and plunged into a snarl of willows. Whipping branches lashed at Darien's helm, reaching out for him, as if eager to tear him off his horse. The stallion hurled onto a wide road within earshot of the town's barred gate. Shouts rang out over the mist as the townsfolk responded to their attack, too late. A group of men spilled out to ward the gate, swords and shields in their hands.

Darien reined in as the Zakai charged past him, rushing the defenders. They made short work of the townsmen with their spears then pulled back from the barred gate.

Darien drew on the Hellpower. It was all he could resort to. Orien's vortex still spun the lines of the magic field into a deadly cyclone of power, so he was forced to keep his mind walled away from it. The Onslaught was slipperier than the magic field, but far more comforting, filling him with a tingling euphoria. He narrowed his eyes and focused his will on the gate.

The gate imploded, spiraling in on itself in a whirlwind of splinters, until it disappeared with a mortal groan. On the other side of the opening, a group of townsfolk stood with eyes wide and horrified. They looked up from the fallen bodies in the road, at the smoldering hole in the air that had swallowed the gate. They backed away slowly, lowering their weapons, then turned to bolt.

Darien let the Zakai enter first. They whipped their horses forward, charging down the center of the street, driving the fleeing townsfolk before them. Men and women fell beneath the thundering hooves of horses. Many fled into doorways or bolted down alleys. The charging Zakai followed in pursuit, their swords and spears inspiring panic.

The soldiers pulled up and, leaping from their mounts, began ranging house to house. They kicked in doors and shattered windows, flushing the occupants out into the streets. A few townsfolk offered resistance, only to be trampled by horses or gored by spears. The dead collected in the dirt, littering the street. The sounds of screams and the clatter of hooves grew distant as the population was herded toward the far side of town.

Darien slid from his horse's back. He stalked down the center of the road, blade drawn, stepping over bodies lying in dark pools of blood. Some still breathed. With a thought, he stopped their breathing. Fires crackled in the distance, their glows whipping the shadows. The demon-hound paced at his side, eyes gleaming with the taint of the Netherworld. Azár patrolled the side of the road, her sword bared and threatening.

The sound of a crying babe came from one of the houses. Darien started toward it, finding the door barred. He kicked it open. The wood splintered, giving way with a crack. He stepped into the gloomy interior, preceded by the haunting glow of fires. Looking around, he made out the forms of a family huddled under a table in a corner.

At his side, the thanacryst bared its teeth and emitted a low growl. A child shrieked over the sound of a baby whimpering. With a glare, Darien sent the demon-hound back outside then gestured at the doorway with his sword.

"Get out."

The woman leaped for the doorway, clutching her baby and dragging the older child behind her into the street. The man rose slowly, holding his hands up. He edged toward the door, keeping his eyes fixed on Darien's blade. When he reached the threshold, he stopped and glanced back.

Darien stepped sideways, avoiding the dagger that swept out

at him. He brought his blade up in a sharp motion. The man groaned, clutching his gut as his entrails slithered out of him. He sank to his knees then collapsed to the floor.

Darien kicked the dying man out of his way and sprinted back into the street, scanning the shadows for Azár. He found her pressed up against a wall, stalking two men armed with swords who stood guarding the entrance to an alley. Darien wasn't certain she could take them both. He wasn't going to stand aside and find out.

"Visea," he whispered.

From the ground rose two living shadows that glided hellishly forward through the night. The necrators were noticed too late. The men's screams ended in sobs. The sobs ended in silence. His minions moved away, roving in a search pattern across the street. They would reap their own dark reward, ridding Gannet of any living that remained.

Darien strode to Azár and caught her by the hand. Fingers laced with hers, he walked at her side in the direction of the fires. A guard of five Zakai moved behind them, swords drawn, eyes warily scanning the rooftops.

A crossbow bolt shot past Darien's face, so close he could feel the wind of its flight. With a cry, Azár released his hand and bolted toward a building on the far side of the street. Taken off-guard, it took Darien a moment to catch up with her. He found his wife in an alley, foot planted on the chest of a man who lay dying on the ground. She twisted her sword and jerked it out of him. A repeating crossbow lay in the dirt with quarrels spilled from the magazine. Azár turned to face him, a ferocious light in her eyes.

Together with their guard of Zakai, Darien walked, holding his wife's hand, down the now-empty streets of Gannet, to a square ringed by stone houses. In the center of the square, Darien found the rest of his men gathered before a two-story inn with a shingle roof and mismatched sides. Seeing their approach, the soldiers parted to admit them into their midst. Darien drew up beside Sayeed in time to hear a report from a torch-bearing Zakai.

"Many of the townspeople have taken refuge in the building," the soldier informed them. "They braced the doors."

Darien looked over to the inn and saw the problem: the windows were set too high to break through, and there didn't seem to be another entrance. It was a problem easily solved. Darien took the torch from the Zakai and walked across the square toward the inn. He tossed the torch onto a second-floor balcony. The planks caught immediately, the fire racing up the sides of the building and across the roof.

"Either they'll come out or they won't," he said.

He made his way back through the crowd of soldiers and set off down the street without looking back. His lengthened shadow strode before him, cast by the crackling fire that consumed the inn. The sounds of screams clawed at the night, echoed through Gannet's empty streets. The demon-hound jogged up and travelled at his side, tail wagging approval, eyes glistening a hellish green.

Darien strode away from the encampment into the open prairie. As he walked, he spread his hands out at his sides, feeling the blades of grass slide over his palms. Well away from the camp, he stopped and stood gazing at the sky. The waxing moon was already making its slow descent toward the horizon. Its light spilled across the prairie, transforming the grassland into a silver ocean, its soft tides stirred by the night air. Above, the stars glittered in a sky devoid of roiling clouds. It ranged enormously above him, a vast reminder of his purpose. Even that did little to comfort him.

When he closed his eyes, he saw fires. Fires that raged within his memory, threatening to engulf him. The inn. Myria. Orien's Finger, Arden Hanna. Aerysius. Despite the cool night air, Darien broke out in a sweat. He clenched his fists at his sides, squeezing his eyes shut, grappling to smother the visions.

A scuffing noise made him flinch. Turning, he saw that Sayeed had come up behind him unnoticed. He hadn't realized the man was there, which was terrifying. So entrenched was he in his thoughts that he'd ignored the basics of self-preservation. He nodded a curt greeting, raking the sweat off his brow with a shirt-sleeve. The fabric came away black with soot.

Darien asked, "Did they come out?"

"No."

He nodded and cast his stare at the ground.

Sayeed said, "What now, Brother? Can you live without mercy for your own people?"

Darien's stared at him, filled with a sudden, terrible anger. "They're not my people any longer! I can't afford to have mercy any longer! If I soften my tactics *one damn bit,* then the next town won't have forty defenders—there'll be eighty. And the next town will have two hundred! *My tactics save lives."*

"Then find your nerve, Brother," Sayeed said. "We can't afford for you to lose resolve."

His First turned and headed back toward the camp while Darien remained behind, struggling with brute self-loathing. With a growl, he raked his shirtsleeve back, exposing the bandage that encircled his palm. He tore it off, revealing the half-healed cut Sayeed had made there. He unsheathed his dagger and drew the edge of the blade across the wound. Beads of blood appeared along the cut, then ran, streaking down his arm. He closed his eyes, relishing the pain. It had an edge to it that diverted his mind from the rage of the fires. He replaced the bandage, using his teeth to pull the knot tight.

He yanked his sleeve down and strode after Sayeed. It took a while to make his way back to the encampment. There, he trudged down ordered pathways between rows of tents, until he found the command pavilion. Tugging his boots off, he tossed them aside. He batted back the flaps and ducked in, instantly confronted by a strong combination of pipe smoke and body odor. He picked his way around sleeping men and women, slipping through the tent's partition.

Azár was already in bed, asleep. He stood gazing at the curve of her body beneath the covers, outlined by the diffuse moonlight filtering through the canvas. The sight of her soothed his fury somewhat. He removed his clothes, tossed them into a corner, then sank down beside her in the bed.

Azár stirred from sleep. "Husband—"

He silenced her with a kiss, driven by a desperate need to smother his rage in her. Darien felt her stiffen beneath him. He stopped and lay unmoving, stroking her hair, until the tension eased from her body.

Kissing her softly, he took what he needed.

Three great bonfires crackled in the center of the camp, tongues of flame whipping at the air. Sparks showered upward, flitting like fireflies, obscured by rolling clouds of smoke. The Malikari soldiers had gathered to one side of the fires. On the other side clustered men and women of the Jenn, clothed in horse skins and dripping with armaments. War drums beat and instruments played, vying for dominance over shouts and chants in a boisterous contortion of noise.

Darien stood beside Ranoch in the center of the gathering. The war chief raised both hands above his head, calling for silence. It took a moment. But, gradually, the drums halted and the instruments tapered off. The shouts quieted to a blur of conversation. The conversation ceased. The only sound that remained was the crackle of flames. Darien turned, his eyes skimming over the hundreds of people gathered before him.

Ranoch stepped forward, raising his voice as he announced, "Darien Lauchlin, the men and women of the Jenn have gathered to hear you speak. Say what you have come to say."

Darien nodded, stepping forward. Raising his voice, he address all those gathered around. "*Darius dreoch.* My name is Grand Master Darien Lauchlin of the Order of Sentinels. I am here to ask you to lend your aid to your brothers and sisters from the north. We flee a land that has known only darkness for a thousand years. Our situation has become desperate—we have reached a crux. Either we flee the Black Lands, or we die of starvation. We no longer have a choice."

He paused, sweeping his eyes over the gathered crowd. "The monarchies of the Rhen have decided that we should perish in darkness. No people deserve that. We don't deserve that. We ask that you help us make a place for ourselves at your sides, where we can build homes and harvest food. A place where our children can grow to adulthood knowing the light of the sun.

"A thousand years ago, the horse tribes of the Khazahar formed the cavalry of Caladorn's combined legions. Today, those same legions ask that you ride with us again. Help us claim this land for ourselves. Help us *survive*. We ask this of you, not only in the name of blood, but also in the name of decency."

He backed away from the glow of the fires, while Ranoch moved forward to take his place. The war chief raised his voice and addressed his gathered people:

"The call of a Sentinel must be answered! It is our sacred duty to ride at his side! People of the Jenn, what say you?"

A thunderous cry went up as men and women surged to their feet, waving their arms and armaments in support of Ranoch's request. The war horns and drums racketed back to life, booming above the commotion. The war chief turned back to Darien with a triumphant smile on his face.

"Warden Lauchlin, your request has been heard. Your people are welcome to our food, our fires, and our protection. We will ride by your side, and your enemies shall be our enemies. Together, we will conquer the North!"

Ranoch took him by the arm and led him away from the fires and the cacophony of the celebration. Darien followed him a little ways out into the dark shadows and cool air of the grassland. They paused under a stand of oak trees.

Looking back at the fires of the gathering, Darien told the war chief, "You have my thanks. Without you, we wouldn't have received that kind of support."

The man nodded, smiling wryly. "You owe me. Someday, I'll ask you to return the favor."

"Gladly." Darien answered Ranoch's smile with his own. Then he grew serious. Now that the treaty was secured, he could waste no time in ironing out the details. He said, "I'm going to need to divide our forces. Together, there are too many people for us to feed. If we split our numbers, we split our need for resources."

Ranoch nodded. "That is wise."

Darien continued, "The army of Maridur will remain behind to defend our train. The army of Bryn Calazar will continue southward and lay siege to Rothscard. I'll take a smaller force south through the Vale of Amberlie to assault Glen Farquist. I ask that you divide your riders and travel with our armies."

Ranoch took hold of his arm, clutching it in a two-handed grip. Solemnly, he promised, "We are yours. And you are ours, as it was a thousand years ago. The lost tribes of Caladorn have been reunited. We will always ride where you lead."

Chapter Fifteen
Versions of Calamity

Isle of Titherry, The Rhen

N aia stepped through the swirling colors of the membrane
into the dark inner sphere of the Nexus. The transition
reminded her of entering the Catacombs of Death: there
was just a moment's disorientation, as if the world shuddered
and then stabilized. The curving walls within were the quintes-
sence of black, and they enclosed her like a womb. The silvery
tendrils pulsed once as if welcoming her into their midst, twirling
and untwirling.

Tsula had arrived before her. The Harbinger stood in the dim
nonlight that came from everywhere and cast no shadow. Folded
in a bronze kaftan and absent her signature turban, Tsula looked
like a cast human sculpture, standing bald and daunting in the
center of the chamber. At the sight of Naia, Tsula gestured with
her hand, commanding her forward.

"Today, I will teach you how to read."

Naia knew Tsula wasn't referring to letters or words. Her
stomach twinged its apprehension. The Harbinger set her hands
on Naia's shoulders, turning her gently but firmly around and
moving to stand behind her. Naia could feel Tsula's breath
against the back of her neck as her hands slid from her shoulders
to grip her arms.

"Empty your mind, child."

Naia closed her eyes and pushed her thoughts aside, until the
only thing she saw within was blackness. In the absence of
thought, her breathing became more relevant. Each swell and
release of breath was like waves breaking and then retreating

along a shoreline. She could feel her heartbeat in her temples: a serene and stately rhythm.

"Now, you must read each version of your Story in order." The Harbinger's voice was a low, whispering echo in her ear. "You cannot begin reading another version until the previous is complete. You cannot skip a version that might be painful and simply move on to the next. The Crescent will select the most probable versions first, but there can be thousands of subtle variations of each. You must learn to distinguish between them. Now. Prepare yourself. The first time is always the most difficult. For some, it is unbearable."

Naia clenched her jaw as she felt the stabilizing grip of Tsula's hands leave her arms. In her mind, there was only absence. Even the tides of her breath fell out of reach. Then, a faint glimmer of light slithered out of the blackness of nothing. A vine-like tendril uncurled before her, twisting and twining. It wound through the darkness, winding and coiling, the coils constricting around her. The darkness bled away, and her mind ran like quicksilver.

She groveled within a universe of agony, a downpour of tears raining from her eyes. Her fingers clawed at her scalp, trying to scrape away the infinite pain that seared her head. Quin clutched her tight against him, his hands running frantically over her in a vain attempt to soothe. But any comfort he could give was woefully inadequate. She was dying in agony, in terror. In futility.9

Outside, the epitome of all storms—the storm that every other storm aspired to be—raged and ripped across the atmosphere. Thunder lashed against the windows, and lightning the color of blood sliced wounds in the air. The wind howled a monstrous wail as it rampaged across the earth, terrorizing the tree limbs, which fled wildly before it. The world itself screamed in mortal anguish, and Naia screamed with it.

"I'm here! I've got you!" Quin shouted over the fury of the wind.

But he didn't have her. She was fading. The world was fading. And though it hurt, it didn't matter. All was lost—they had lost—the world was lost. It was her fault. No, Quin's fault. No, Kyel's fault for abandoning them to the violence of the Reversal. Now all the men and women of Malikar would be beaten back into the Black Lands to starve in eternal darkness. Every mage was dying in torment, and every wonder they'd ever created would be erased from the world's long memory. All was fading, all was dying. And she was dying with it.

"I can't stand it!" she shrieked to the absent gods.

She could feel the magic field stretched around her to its thin limit. It cried out in protest, in defiance, in outrage. And then it ripped. Naia screamed her life away, feeling her mind heated to boiling inside her skull.

She opened her eyes, sobbing uncontrollably. A hand reached out and collected her into a cold embrace.

"What was that?" she wailed through terror and shock and inconsolable grief.

Tsula said without emotion, "That was the most likely ending of your Story."

Naia shook her head against the woman's shoulder. "No! That can't happen! We can't let that happen!"

Tsula drew back and, reaching up, wiped Naia's tears from her eyes. Her face was as bland and expressionless as always. "Tell me what you saw."

"The Reversal was happening. All the mages were dying. Magic was ending. And we didn't break the Curse."

The Harbinger simply nodded. "That confirms what I have seen. There are other versions still available to us, but for every second that passes, the more complete our Story becomes. And the more versions will be denied us. Soon, there will be only one version left to pen."

She turned Naia back around. Taking her by the shoulders, Tsula commanded, "Try again."

Drawing a deep breath, Naia closed her eyes.

The epitome of all storms—the storm that every other storm aspired to be— raged and ripped across the atmosphere. Thunder lashed against the cliffs, and lightning the color of blood sliced wounds in the air. The wind howled a monstrous wail as it rampaged through the mountains, terrorizing the clouds, which fled wildly before it. The world screamed in mortal anguish, and Naia screamed with it.

Quin was gone. He couldn't help her anymore.

Sprawled in the center of Aerysius' great Circle of Convergence, Darien lay in an expanding pool of blood. The blood was artery-red and volumi-nous—far more than one human body could possibly contain. It flowed into the gaps and crevices of the Circle's rays, delineating the marble tiles with heightened contrast. The blood continued to advance, as if seeking to saturate the entire Circle. Or the entire world. Or the universe.

Zavier Renquist stood behind Naia and pushed her to her knees. In his hands, he held Quin's scimitar. His face was slicked with blood, and his eyes gleamed with triumph. He drew the sword back over his shoulder, pre-paring to strike the death-blow that would end her life.

"Let the reign of Xerys begin!" he snarled, and cleaved Naia's head off.

Naia opened her eyes, gasping for breath. She whirled back to Tsula. "Oh, gods! Do we have any chance at all?"

"We do," the Harbinger assured her. Reaching up, she stroked a strand of hair back from Naia's cheek. "What did you see?"

"Renquist sacrificed Darien on a Circle of Convergence. Something about his blood…He was trying to bring about the reign of Xerys. I didn't understand any of it."

"I think that is enough for one day," Tsula said and turned away, her dark eyes wandering over the walls. All around the spherical room, silver tendrils curled and uncurled in infinite var-iations.

Naia nodded, feeling defeated. She did not want to read an-other version of her Story. At least, not today.

She fled back to Quin.

He wasn't in his room. She found him in the library, sprawled across one of the sofas. He was leafing through a text with one hand, the other absently flipping a feathered quill.

"What is it?" he asked, seeing her face. He snapped the book closed and sat upright. "Did you see something…?"

Naia drew in a deep, steadying breath. She couldn't tell him, not everything. Practically nothing. The more she thought about it, the more she wondered why she had sought him out at all. Wearily, she sank down beside him on the sofa.

He reached up and gently turned her face toward him. "Tell me what you saw."

Naia pulled back, grimacing. "I can't. If I do, then the things I saw might come to pass. And we can't let that happen."

Quin stared at her a long, hard moment, looking deeply into her eyes. At last, he nodded. "I'll kill Tsula tonight, then."

Naia gasped. "No. Not tonight—I still need her!"

Quin sucked in a cheek, looking uncertain. "But if you want to avoid the options you saw—"

"Give me one more day. I want to make certain I've learned everything I need to know from her."

He looked decisively skeptical. "Do you die in every vision you have?"

"Of course." Naia threw her hands up in exasperation. "That is the only way my own Story can end." All he ever seemed to care about was her safety. Never mind what the stakes were, or that the future of an entire population might be in jeopardy.

"What about me?" he asked. "What do I do in these visions?"

"You know I can't tell you that." Naia bent over and picked up the text Quin had been reading. She glanced down at the title, but it was written in a language of glyphs she'd never seen before. She set the book aside.

Quin grumbled, "You'd better start telling me some of the things you see, before I destroy the world all over again out of ignorance."

"I will when I find the right version for us," Naia promised. She looked at him sadly, still haunted by what she saw. "Until then, there's no sense worrying about futures that might never happen."

"Come here," he said, and pulled her down on the sofa with him. His hand rubbed her back soothingly. "You'll get through this," he assured her. "It might not seem like it now. But you will. And if you need me, I'll be here for you. Like it or not."

Naia rose with the dawn and made her way up the crystalline path to the Nexus. The sun had just started its climb into the sky, casting its light in vibrant hues of gold. The shadows clung to night's chill, but the sunlight felt fierce and warm on her skin. Naia smiled, looking out across the volatile beauty of Athera's Crescent, at the rippling patterns that swirled over its surface.

She wasn't surprised to find Tsula already waiting for her.

"Are you ready to read another version of your Story?" the Harbinger asked. She smiled invitingly, an expression that seemed out of place on her face. Naia was taken aback. She tried to remember another time she had ever seen the woman smile and couldn't think of one.

"I'm ready," she said, adding with a sigh, "It is daunting, though. It seems we are destined to fail."

Tsula shook her head. "There are versions still left to us, and all versions are governed by our choices. We will not run out of options until we run out of choices. And, until then, we cannot run out of hope."

She beckoned Naia closer, her face growing grim. "I was a bit disturbed by one of the versions you read yesterday."

"Which version?"

"You must remember to address me by my title," Tsula reminded her.

She'd forgotten. "Which version, Warden Renquist?"

"The version in which my husband ends your life over a spreading pool of blood. It aligns with a version of my own Story that has always been highly unlikely…until now. Now, the Crescent deems it by far the most probable."

That did worry Naia. Of the two versions she had foreseen, that was the one she feared most. She wasn't sure why. Something about the images of the blood and the sword terrified her. It was almost as though they were symbolic of something much more visceral.

"What do you think it means?" she asked.

Tsula glanced at her sharply. "It means that my husband has found a way to halt the Reversal of the magic field. Just as he tried to do a thousand years ago."

Naia stood shocked. For a moment, she couldn't react. That had never been a possibility before, at least none she had considered. Renquist had attempted such a feat a thousand years ago and had failed then—disastrously. And he no longer had Eight Servants nor eight Circles of Convergence to accomplish the act.

"How is that possible?" she whispered.

Tsula paced away, a frown of concern on her face. "I do not know. It would take the power of eight grand masters combined to stabilize the magic field. I do not know how, but it seems that my husband has found a way around it."

Naia asked, "Pardon, but…Zavier Renquist is your husband. Do you not know his plans?"

The woman looked at her sideways, cocking an eyebrow.

Naia decided to press the issue. "To be blunt, Warden Renquist—I assume you are trying to help him."

"Pfft!" the woman spat, scrunching up her face as if tasting something awful. "Of course not! Zavier Renquist is my husband. But any love I ever had for him died the day he murdered our daughter. Ever since then, I have not once looked upon his face."

Naia gasped. "He murdered your daughter?"

Tsula regarded her flatly. "You do not know?"

"No…" Naia shook her head. "Why would I know?"

"Did Quinlan Reis never mention Amani?"

The name didn't sound familiar. Until it did. Naia blinked, suddenly remembering the story Quin had told her when they'd first met. About a woman he'd loved, who had loved him back. But she had been forced to marry his brother and had died at Braden's hand.

"Oh, gods…" Naia whispered. "Amani was your daughter?"

Tsula nodded. "It took me many years before I was able to admit the truth: that it was my own husband who had conspired to have Amani slain. Quinlan Reis and his brother were both merely pawns in Zavier's many intrigues."

Naia stared at her in horrified incomprehension. "Why would Renquist murder his own daughter?"

Tsula drew in a deep breath, face twisted into a grimace. "Because Zavier needed Braden's strength to complete his Circle of Eight. And, unfortunately for Braden, he was a man of integrity. He would never sink to the moral depths necessary to channel the Onslaught. So Zavier decided to put him in an impossible position to force the issue.

"He sent Quinlan to Aerysius under the pretense he was to assassinate Cyrus Krane. Predictably, Quinlan was captured. My husband made sure Amani knew her lover was slated to be executed unless an appropriate ransom was paid. Krane demanded documents that were in Braden's possession, and Braden was duty-bound to deny him. Amani stole the documents and delivered them to Cyrus Krane herself."

Naia shook her head, feeling sickened.

Tsula continued, "When Amani returned to the Lyceum, Zavier declared our daughter a traitor and sentenced her to death. And, for Amani's executioner, he picked Braden, who was bound by duty to murder his own wife."

The Harbinger drew in a deep, shuddering breath, bowing her head in grief. "All of this horror to corrupt the morals of one honorable mage who would never stand again at Zavier's side." She looked up then, her eyes filled with wrath. "My husband was the most despicable man the world has ever known. And now, fueled by Xerys' vast power, he is the most dangerous demon. So, no. I do not support him."

The weight of her words seemed to drag the whole world down. Naia stared at the floor in silence, respecting the doleful quiet that comes when a mother mourns her child. As a priestess, she had seen it before, many times.

Eventually, Tsula looked up and offered the smallest, strongest smile.

"There's one thing I don't understand," Naia said after a moment. "If you are Amani's mother, how could it be that Quin didn't recognize you?"

Tsula scoffed, turning away. "I never met him. I'm a Harbinger. I exist only in secrets and in shadow. Even my own daughter never knew my face… But I knew hers. I lived my entire life through her. Now, enough of this." Tsula waved her hand. "It is time to read the next possible version of your Story. Close your eyes. Now. Try again."

Naia didn't want to. But, prompted by the unyielding iron in Tsula's gaze, she collected her strength, closed her eyes, and tried again.

The epitome of all storms—the storm that every other storm aspired to be— raged and ripped across the atmosphere. Thunder lashed against the cliffs, and lightning the color of blood sliced wounds in the air. The wind howled a monstrous wail as it rampaged through the mountains, terrorizing the clouds, which fled wildly before it. The world screamed in mortal anguish, and Naia screamed with it.

Quin was below, in the chamber of the Well of Tears. Trying to wrench the portal full open before the Reversal could maximize.

In front of her, Kyel Archer advanced across the Circle of Convergence, wielding a silver morning star in his hand.

In the center of the Circle—in full command of it—Zavier Renquist swept out a fist. A blinding glare of light whiter than bright and brilliantly powerful assaulted Kyel from the sky. He brought the talisman up to deflect it, but the strike was indomitable—it impacted with all the fury of the vortex. It overwhelmed the talisman's power, hurling Kyel backward to the ground, ripping the weapon out of his hands. Another magical assault drilled down from the clouds, stabbing into him.

The blow threw Kyel across the terrace. Another strike lifted him again, slamming him against the cliff. Zavier Renquist raised his arms, summoning the energies of the vortex for one last, mortal strike.

The green pillar above them exploded in fury. A great inferno shot upward, igniting the clouds, roiling the atmosphere. Fire streamed across the sky, cauterizing the air as it scourged the magic field. The field wailed in outrage as it died. And then it went silent, its rhythmic pulse stopped forever.

Naia screamed her life away, feeling the gift inside seared out of her.

Chapter Sixteen
Farbrook

The Vale of Amberlie, The Rhen

"What town is this?"

"Farbrook," Darien responded without looking at Sayeed.

He pulled his helmet down over his head and tightened the strap under his chin. Beside him, Azár did the same, her long braid snaking down her back. Darien turned at the sound of hoofbeats approaching behind them on the road, barely visible in the light cast by the faintest sliver of moon. He turned his mount around as the scouts rode up, horses blowing hot mist into the cold air.

The lead scout, a man named Seljik, made a quick bow from his horse's back. "All appears empty, Warden."

Darien digested that information in silence. It was the fifth town since Gannet and the second they'd found deserted. It was to be expected, he supposed, with the tactics they'd been employing. He still didn't like the feel of it, all the same.

"They are starting to anticipate which towns we will hit, and when," Sayeed commented. "That can go in our favor. Or it can go very badly."

"Agreed," Darien said. He sent Seljik off with a gesture. Looking up the road toward Farbrook's jagged silhouette, he contemplated the tidings. Word had spread far ahead of them. Each town they raided was more prepared than the last.

Reaching out from within, he opened his mind to the magic field and sampled the flow of the field lines. They ran smoothly, like velvet on satin. Following the line of the mountains southward toward Aerysius. It felt good to be out from under the oppression of Orien's vortex. It felt chilling to be so close to the fallen city he'd once called home.

Darien summoned a mist of magelight that trailed out ahead of them, lighting the road with an eerie blue haze. He whistled, then waited. There was a faint rustling in the trees behind them. Then the thanacryst broke out of the shadows and bounded to his horse's side.

He said to Sayeed, "We'll split up. Take your men and go around to the south gate. I'll come in from the north. We'll meet in the middle."

Sayeed nodded and kicked his horse to a canter, followed by four dozen mounted men. Darien held his horse to a walk, following a trail of glowing mist, the remainder of his men following behind. Around them, the night was cold and still as death.

To Azár, Darien said, "Remember what I taught you about fire?"

"I do." She turned toward him, her eyes shadowed by her helm.

Darien lowered his visor. "If something attacks you, burn the hell out of it." He couldn't see the smile on her lips, but he knew it was there.

The demon-hound ranged ahead of them, nose to the ground, ears pricked. As they reached Farbrook's open gate, the beast sprang forward, working the sides of the road like a hunting dog sniffing for a trail. It zigzagged back and forth across the empty street, scenting the sides of the brick-and-lumber buildings. The thanacryst was like a fluid shadow weaving among other shadows, its eyes boring green holes through the darkness.

The sound of their horses' hooves echoed sharply off the walls of the houses, ringing through the streets. The magelight lit the path ahead of them, creeping forward like a trail of blue flames. Darien's horse snorted, shaking its head. He reached down and stroked the animal's neck, seeking to calm it. The stallion flinched at the feel of his hand.

A low growl from the thanacryst made him jerk back on the

reins. His horse whinnied in protest, backing up a few steps before coming to a foot-stomping halt. Darien slid from its back, the Zakai following him to the ground. Azár moved behind him, hand resting on the hilt of her sword. The demon-hound turned back the way they had come. Hackles raised, it bared its teeth and snarled.

Darien slid his sword from its sheath.

A barrage of arrows rained down from the sky, stabbing the ground all around them. His eyes shot up to the roof of the building across the street, to the group of several archers already loosing their next volley. One of Darien's men fell with a cry. More arrows clattered down.

Darien didn't bother with the magic field. He went right to the Hellpower. The men on the rooftop dissolved into a cloud of ash that simply blew away.

He sheathed his sword and dropped to the side of the man who had fallen. An arrow had pierced his thigh. Blood spurted from the wound in time to his heart beat. With a growl, Darien set his hands on him. It took only seconds to mend the severed artery.

"Keep an eye on the rooftops," Darien ordered his men. He led his horse forward by the reins, his wife and the demon-hound stalking at his sides. He let the magelight crawl ahead of them, licking at the shadows.

All at once, a terrified-looking man burst out of an alley. Before Darien could react, the man let out a staccato scream as he erupted in flames. Shocked, Darien turned to find Azár standing beside him, hand outstretched. He could see the pride that glimmered in her eyes beneath the shadow of her helm. She had been practicing the *ruhk* attack for days.

Apparently, she'd mastered it.

Darien nodded his approval then waved his men forward, brightening the intensity of the magelight.

"Search every house," he ordered, then waited in the street as the soldiers began breaking down doors and shattering windows. He stood listening to the sounds of the town's defilement, one hand absently petting the demon-hound's head. The thing tilted its head back and licked his knuckles with a putrescent tongue. He waited for minutes. Then, taking Azár's hand, he walked calmly down the middle of the street.

They met up with Sayeed's band of raiders in the center of town. There was a large, cobbled square housing a font fed by the town's covered well. Darien led his men to where Sayeed sat his horse, scimitar in hand.

"There's nothing," the officer reported, swiping an arm across his brow. "They took everything with them. No food. They burned the granaries and drove away the livestock."

Darien cursed, turning his back on Sayeed. Farbrook was the second town they'd encountered that had either destroyed or carried off all their provisions. The situation with his own resources was becoming dire. He stared down at the ground, pondering options he didn't have.

"We captured three townsmen by an abandoned barn."

That caught Darien's attention. He turned back to Sayeed. "Take me there."

They mounted up and rode out of town, surrounded by a protective ring of Zakai. They rode past empty buildings with shattered windows and out across a harvested field.

Sayeed led them to a dilapidated barn that looked to be standing only by the grace of the gods. The leaning walls were supported by angled beams hammered into the ground. A group of Tanisars holding torches stood in the yard in front of the barn, the wavering light writhing a tortuous dance across the ground.

"They're in there." Sayeed pointed with his sword toward the entrance to the structure.

Darien dismounted and strode forward, spreading his fingers, ordering the men behind him to remain in place. Sayeed and Azár at his side, he strode toward the barn's yawning entrance. Within, a cluster of Zakai stood under the hayloft, guarding three bound men. Darien pulled his helmet off and held it dangling at his side by the chinstrap. He walked in a measured pace toward the prisoners, halting in front of them.

He looked deeply into the eyes of the eldest of the three men— a blacksmith, judging by the soot-stained apron. By his bearing, the man had probably served some time at the Front. There was no fear in his eyes. Just more scornful confidence than any man in his situation had any right to.

"Do you know who I am?" Darien asked quietly.

"I do." The smith stared at him unwaveringly. His hands were bound behind his back, his legs lashed together with strong hemp cord. All around him stood soldiers with crossbows leveled at his chest. Still, the man showed no trace of apprehension.

Darien said, "You knew we were coming. So why stay behind?"

"This is our home."

Darien shook his head. That wasn't a good enough reason to make three men eager to die. He stared harder into the smith's blue eyes, seeking there for explanation. Just in case, he reached out for the magic field and held it close. He said, "You knew you couldn't win this fight. So I'll ask you one last time: why did you remain?"

The man glared back at him with a disdainful, hard-as-stone gaze. "We heard what you did to the people of Gannet."

"That doesn't answer my question."

The smith's stare turned vengeful. "We stayed behind because we wanted to make you pay."

Something detonated in a shower of liquid. An explosion of flames erupted from the floor. Darien lashed out with his mind, beating the fire back into the ground, reversing the combustion. The flames burned back into themselves, until even the smoke curled downward. Steam rose from the fuming ground, condensing out of the now-frigid air. Darien glanced quickly to Azár, relieved to find her unharmed. There was a bitten-off scream as one of his guards shot a quarrel through a man hiding above them in the hayloft.

Darien's stare locked on the smith's.

The man's eyes now contained the fear that should have rightfully been there all along. His face had gone white beneath a thick layer of soot. His two companions stood terrified, trembling in their restraints.

Darien informed them, "You made a mistake."

He turned to Sayeed and ordered, "Let the forger go. Let him live to eat the guilt of his decisions. And tell the tale of what he's seen here tonight." To Azár, he said, "You've been wanting some practice. Go ahead. The other two are yours—make examples of them."

He strode out of the barn, taking half the Zakai with him. He didn't stay to listen to the screams.

"There was no food in all the town," Azár said, removing her helm. She released her sweat-damp hair from its braid, letting it fall in greasy waves down her back. Darien pulled her against him, squeezing her close. She smelled of smoke and sweat and was covered in grime. To Darien, she looked beautiful.

He kissed her damp hair then released her, pulling back. He knelt to rummage through a burlap sack he'd brought with him. From within, he retrieved a parcel wrapped in cloth, the one treasure he'd managed to scavenge from Farbrook. He unwrapped the loaf of bread and handed it to her.

"I saved this for you."

Her eyes widened as she stared down at the loaf hungrily. "We will share it."

Darien smiled, shaking his head. "I already ate," he lied.

He scrubbed a rough cloth over his face, wiping off most of the sooty sweat. He tossed it on the floor, then sat on their pallet watching Azár tear hungrily through the loaf. When she was done, she stood with her eyes squeezed shut in pleasure, licking the last of the crumbs off her fingertips. His own stomach tightened in envy.

"How are you faring with all this?" he asked. He wasn't speaking about hunger.

Azár's face went from blissful to ferocious in a heartbeat. "Those men tried to kill my husband. I wanted them to die slowly."

He nodded. He'd come to expect nothing less from her than cold brutality. But he wanted to be certain. He didn't want to push her past the limits of her morals.

He asked, "Which attack did you use?"

Azár smiled playfully, sitting down beside him on the pallet. "I tried something different."

"Oh?"

She leaned in close and kissed him languidly, her tongue sliding over his lips. She whispered, "It is a surprise."

He returned her kiss. Ignoring the empty ache in his belly, he pulled her on top of him.

They broke camp the next morning and headed southward into the deep forest of the Vale. As they left Farbrook, they passed a hill where a dozen long poles had been driven into the ground. On each pole, one of the town's defenders was impaled groin to neck. Two were still moving, still sobbing and moaning. Darien didn't need Azár to tell him which two they were. He was impressed. That had taken some skill, to impale men in such a way that they would remain alive to suffer the next day. He nodded his approval at his wife. Not because he took any pleasure from watching his enemies squirm on a pole, but because the people of the Vale needed a graphic demonstration of the consequences of opposition.

"Which town is next?" asked Sayeed, his face haggard.

"Kantsby."

"I hope they eat food in Kantsby."

There was nothing left of Kantsby. Just burned-out houses and watered grain—even the livestock had been slaughtered in the fields and left to rot.

There was also nothing left of Torwood.

Or Castleton. Or Glendoe.

Or Summerton.

"That was Ryloch," Darien said, even though Sayeed had stopped asking several towns and several days back.

His legs trembled as he dismounted and stood exhausted, leaning against his horse's heaving side. The wind breathed a sigh, stirring the branches of the oaks that folded over them, blocking out the starlight. He looked wearily up at Sayeed and shook his head.

"That's it, then."

Sayeed looked at him with eyes glazed and weary. He'd had that look ever since Farbrook, ever since the food had run out. Hunger had sunken his cheeks, making his angular features even more jagged. He turned and glared into the shadows of the grove, where the rest of their band had taken refuge. A form of silent protest, Darien was sure. He scuffed the leaf-laden soil with his boot, struggling to think through the fog that mired his brain.

"We can't go back," Darien grumbled. "And we can't stay here. The only thing we can do is go forward."

Sayeed didn't respond. Darien reached up and stroked the delicate head of his red stallion. The soft fur felt like velvet beneath his fingers. The horse's silken coat was the product of a thousand years of crossbreeding followed by another thousand of inbreeding. It was one of only a handful of steppe horses left alive in the entire world. With one last pat, Darien released the tasseled bridle.

"Slaughter the horses," he ordered. "We'll walk from here."

Chapter Seventeen
Tom the Smith

The Vale of Amberlie, The Rhen

A frantic thunder made Kyel twist in his saddle. Behind, three riders galloped toward them, urging their mounts faster with spurs and crops. Kyel kicked his own horse clear of the road as the riders shot past in a jarring clatter of hoofbeats. He glanced sideways at Alexa, who shrugged in reply.

"Wonder what that's about," Kyel grumbled, brushing off the dust kicked up by the galloping horses. He scanned the surrounding forest but saw nothing amiss. There was the same smell of woodfires that had dominated the air for two days, but that was all. The forest was almost unnaturally calm.

They had been riding since dawn, trying to cover as much ground as possible. Glen Farquist wasn't more than a week south of them, and Kyel was anxious. It had been months since he'd last seen his son. He'd left Gil at the Temple of Wisdom, under the tutelage of the clerics. But with recent events, Kyel had begun to fear Glen Farquist might be the most dangerous place his son could be.

Minutes later, another jarring noise disrupted the silence of the trees: this time, the juddering clatter of wagon wheels. Kyel halted his horse along the side of the road as a caravan of carts and wagons passed them by. Many of the carts were overloaded with supplies. Some only contained people. Too many people, who looked far too shocked and grieved.

"Something's wrong," Kyel muttered.

Alexa nodded, saying nothing. After the caravan passed, he nudged his horse back onto the road.

Kyel heard the commotion of the town ahead even before it came into view. The streets were swarming with people rushing in a panicked frenzy to load wagons and mules with whatever they could fit. The entire town had the look of an ant colony after a good kicking, with everyone running frantic with little mind and less direction.

"This is bad," Kyel commented, pulling his horse up.

"What do you think happened?" Alexa raised her voice to be heard over the din of the commotion.

"I think the Enemy broke through." Seeing the congestion in the streets ahead, Kyel decided against trying to wade his horse through the turmoil. He dismounted and tied the animal to a fence, then waited for Alexa to do the same.

"Isn't the Pass guarded by two armies?"

Kyel shot a glance her way. "I guess two armies weren't enough."

That silenced her.

By the time they fought their way through the crowd to the center of town, it became clear he'd been right. Scores of folk had gathered in the town square around a brick house. Two men stood on the steps: one that looked like the mayor, and another man wearing a blacksmith's apron. The smith appeared to be directing the evacuation, while the mayor stood off to the side with his hands stuffed in his pockets

"Take everything!" the blacksmith shouted. "If you can't fit it in a wagon, then burn it!"

Cries rose from the mob of panicked citizens: outrage and terror and everything in between.

The blacksmith's eyes fell on Kyel. At first, he couldn't figure out why the smith was staring at him. Then he realized: he was wearing his mage's cloak. The man raised his hand, pointing at Kyel across the gathered crowd. Glaring him in the eye, the smith beckoned him over with a snap of his head.

Feeling more than a bit unsettled, Kyel fought his way through the jostling crowd with Alexa in tow. He mounted the steps to the porch and halted before the two men. The mayor's eyes fixed on Kyel's cloak, his cracked lips muttering words too low to hear.

It was the blacksmith, though, who commanded Kyel's attention.

"Who are you?" the forger demanded, making it patently clear who wore the authority.

Before Kyel could answer, Alexa announced, "His name is Grand Master Kyel Archer. He is a Sentinel of Aerysius!"

The mayor's face ran through a range of emotions faster than a pianist's fingers flitting through scales. The smith's eyes remained cold and even, fixing Kyel with a look of distrust.

"Show us the marks of the chains," he ordered.

In the space between heartbeats, Kyel became aware that the commotion in the square had halted altogether. Glancing back, he saw that every person in the crowd had stopped moving and now stood frozen, gaping at him with fear in their eyes. With no small amount of apprehension, Kyel held his hands up one at a time, thrusting back his sleeves and baring his wrists for all to see.

The blacksmith stared hard at the markings of the chains. His gaze slid to Kyel's face. He nodded curtly.

A bottomless silence settled over the crowd. Silence and deference. At first, Kyel couldn't understand it. Then, in a flash of insight, the answer became obvious. For hundreds of years, this town had stood in the long shadow of Aerysius. None of the men and women gathered before him would dare disrespect the emblems of the chains. Kyel hadn't counted on that reaction, but that didn't make him any less relieved.

The forger thrust out his hand. "Tom Akins. I'm a smith down from Farbrook."

Kyel accepted the smith's handshake, noting the lingering doubt in the man's eyes.

Tom continued, "I'm here because, well, Farbrook doesn't exist anymore. Neither does Gannet or Castleton, or anything else north of here. The Enemy's been raiding town-to-town. Within the past week, I've witnessed atrocities that will haunt my sleep for the rest of my days. I stood in a barn and looked the demon himself in the eye. I've never seen such inhumanity. He's torched people in their own homes, crucified others. Impaled men on stakes and left them alive for the ravens to eat. He's massacred whole families: mothers, babes. He has no mercy. No respect for life."

The smith fell silent, visibly wrestling with the ghosts of the horrors he'd seen. His eyes fell on Kyel's cloak, staring at it with a peculiar mixture of revulsion and expectation.

Kyel looked at him a long moment. Tom's story was chilling. More so because his account was in line with everything Kyel had always heard about the Enemy, the kind of tales that used to terrify him as a boy. Apparently, the dark stories told to scare children were all based on truth.

The smith puffed out his cheeks in a protracted sigh. "Since Farbrook, I've made it my purpose to destroy that devil and his horde. I've been traveling south, warning the people ahead of him. Town by town, we've left them nothing. What we couldn't take, we burned. What we couldn't burn, we buried." His stare hardened, locking on Kyel's face. "Perhaps you can help us. Redeem the honor of that damn cloak you're wearing."

Kyel glanced sideways at the gathered crowd. Then he returned his stare to the blacksmith. "How hungry are they?"

"His raiders haven't had a good meal in over a week. By now, they're starving and desperate."

Kyel nodded. He'd always heard that starving men didn't think clearly. He hoped starving demons didn't, either.

"I've an idea," he said. "But it's a gamble. And I can't stay to help you pull it off."

Chapter Eighteen
Darien of Amberlie

The Vale of Amberlie, The Rhen

The cold grip of memory wound around him and constricted.

Darien gazed down at the long strip of rutted dirt and felt throttled by remembrance. He tried to maintain his focus on the road ahead, bending all his will into the effort. It was no good. He kept glancing upward. His gaze roamed over the tangle of branches overhead, desperate for just one glimpse of the mountain cliffs above. But the forest canopy refused him. So he forced his gaze back down at the dirt, plagued by emotions he couldn't name.

A town became visible through an opening in the trees. He nodded his head toward it. "That's Amberlie."

Azár and Sayeed exchanged sharp glances. Azár asked, "This is your home?"

Darien shook his head. "No. My home was up there"—he glanced up at the merciless snarl of branches— "but down here's where I grew up."

He stared harder at the road, so he wouldn't have to look up, or ahead, or back. He studied the ruts in the dirt, the pockmarked clay broken with scuffed tracks, both human and animal. At the half-buried stones. He could name most of the rocks; they were common to the area. He stepped over a pebble of gypsum. A lump of quartz protruded from the side of the road, half-covered by grass. A small chunk of granite turned under his foot. The ubiquitous river-rock, round and smooth and polished. Mica. Fool's gold. Feldspar.

"What's up there?" Azár asked softly.

He wanted to ignore her. She already knew what was up there—she had to. Flatly, he responded, "Aerysius."

"I don't see it."

Neither could he. Perhaps the thick branches were protective, like a scab over a wound.

"That's because it's gone," he answered.

Azár walked with her head craned, searching for a break in the trees. Behind them, the rhythmic clatter that accompanied a column of armed men announced their presence to the world.

A broad streak of light shot down, making him squint. Making him stop. Darien took a deep, steadying breath. Then he looked up through the trees at the soaring cliffs overhead. His eyes traveled up the sharp granite wall. And up. And up, until he couldn't tilt his head back any further.

"It was up there," he said. "Where the cliff bows inward. You can see the terraces if you look hard enough. But there's nothing else left."

He glanced back down again and started forward, his boots scuffing the dirt. Azár took his hand. He supposed it was a gesture of comfort. He didn't want it.

Two of Sayeed's scouts jogged toward them from the direction of Amberlie. The first man reported, "The town appears empty, Warden. All of the structures are intact."

"Good," Darien said. "Maybe they left some food behind."

He trained his focus on the town, visible through the trees. Out of the corner of his eye, he saw that Azár and Sayeed were still scanning the cliffs.

"It is so far up," she gasped. "How do you climb that?"

He could hear the awe in her voice. It was the same awe he used to feel as a boy, standing in that same grove, gazing up at the mountain in yearning.

"There was a lift," he said, and didn't elaborate. Ahead, the town was mercifully closer.

"It is said you fell from that mountain." There was a lightness in Sayeed's tone that made Darien realize he was trying to make a jest. Probably an attempt to buoy his mood.

"I did."

The levity melted from Sayeed's face, his eyes widening as his gaze darted back upward.

The town of Amberlie was just as Darien remembered it, only empty. Like every other town they'd come across. He stopped in the middle of the square, his eyes wandering slowly over the littered street, fighting a sharp pang of nostalgia.

Around him, Sayeed's Zakai spread out to search the structures. Darien waited with his eyes pinned on the mountain cliffs overhead. For minutes, that was all he could do. At last, the scouts reported back that the town was completely empty. Not one stubborn holdout had remained behind. Which was good. Darien hadn't wanted to kill people he'd known all his life, had grown up with. Of all the towns they'd captured in the Vale, he'd dreaded taking Amberlie the most. He'd left too many friends there. And too many memories.

"Wait here. I'll be back in a bit," he said to Azár. Ignoring her look of confusion, he walked away from her.

Turning onto a side street, Darien strode past rows of houses he remembered well, following the same old cobbled street he'd taken a thousand times before. His feet remembered where to go. He found a small dirt path just out of town that looked more like an abandoned deer trail than a footpath. He followed it anyway, aware of the crunching sounds of Azár's footsteps following behind, and the eager patter of oversized paws that trailed him everywhere he went.

Darien scowled, irritated that his desire for solitude continued to be ignored. Without looking back at his unwanted companions, he followed the path as it meandered through the trees, finally ending at a dilapidated stone-and-wattle cottage covered by gray, ancient thatch.

He paused, staring for a moment at the outside of the cottage and the glen that surrounded it. Off to the side was the covered well he used to draw water from as a boy. Across from it was the sycamore with the beehive in it. The patch of ground that had once been the widow's vegetable garden. The spot in the corner of the house where he'd buried the squirrel he'd killed with his slingshot. His brother's treehouse in the sprawling oak, now fallen. He hadn't been allowed up there. But he'd gone anyway.

Darien walked the rest of the way up the path and, motioning for the demon-hound to remain outside, entered the dark cottage. The floorboards groaned and cracked beneath his weight. Beams of light, swarming with dust, slanted down through gaping holes in the thatch. The cottage smelled of earth and mildew and abandonment. Everything inside was coated with dust. Old, tattered cobwebs sagged in the corners, looking just as neglected as the rest of the place.

He walked toward the hearth and stood looking down at the remains of the widow's bed. Mice and rats had made nests in what was left of the bedding. Water and rot had claimed the rest. On the floor beside it was a rusted rushlight holder, left behind. Everything else had been either looted or decayed.

A cracking noise told him Azár had entered the space. Without looking back at her, he said, "This is the home of the widow who raised us." He gestured at an empty corner. "We slept over there—me and my brother. She couldn't afford a bed for us, so we gathered straw and threw it down and covered it with a blanket every night. There were chinks in the walls that let the cold in. Every morning, dew collected on the ceiling and fell on us like rain."

Azár laid a hand on his back.

"We never lacked. My father made sure the widow always had food for us. He came to visit from time to time. Mother never did." He stood quietly, eyes loosely focused on the dust swirling in the air as he struggled with the decision of how much he wanted to let himself feel.

"It was a good home," Azár said, looking around.

He silently disagreed.

Footsteps on the path outside broke his attention. Sayeed burst into the cottage with an excited grin, announcing, "There's food, Brother!" He retreated out the door then turned around, beckoning.

Darien led Azár by the hand away from the cottage, taking a shortcut he remembered. It led them under the fresh leaves of a maple grove, and down a small embankment into the outskirts of town.

Reaching the town square, Darien discovered that Sayeed's men hadn't been idle; they'd been cleaning out store houses and root cellars, stacking crates and bags of food in the center of town. Sayeed walked toward them up the main road with a broad smile on his face. "They left behind a bounty of food!" he announced. "We will feast tonight!"

Darien eyed the food stores warily. Every town they'd come to since Farbrook, without exception, had prepared in advance for their arrival. Burned to the ground, gutted. Stores depleted or destroyed. Nothing had been left to sustain a foraging army. All except this one town—a town that had special significance to him.

"No." Darien shook his head. "We can't trust this."

Sayeed's face went serious. He nodded slowly.

Darien said, "Have some of the men try it. Small portions. If they're still standing this time tomorrow, then we'll have your feast."

He looked around at the empty houses that lined the square. "Let's camp here."

They bedded down in town—at least as many as the town would yield grudging space for. The remainder of the Tanisars camped outside in a neat ring of tents. Throughout the next day, Darien paced restlessly up and down the length of Amberlie's streets, accompanied by his ever-slobbering pet. He tried to keep his eyes averted from the cliffs above, but the occasional hawk cry— or just plain distraction—inevitably turned his gaze in that direction. At last he gave in to the compulsion to acknowledge the scars raked across the cliff face above like self-inflicted wounds—and bit down on the instant pang of sorrow that shot up from some forgotten place inside.

He'd stood in this same spot as a boy, gazing up at the cliffs that loomed taller than the sky, staring in over-awed wonder at the city high above on the mountain. Dreaming of a time when he, too, could find his own place among the clouds. When he could become a Sentinel like his father and finally look upon the mother who had borne him, the woman who, for all intents and purposes, ruled the world. A time when he could at last come into his own and forge his own legend and legacy.

How naïve he had been. An ignorant boy, fool enough to hope and dream.

He shielded his eyes from the glare, focusing on a thin stream of water that plunged down the cliff in a tendril-thin cascade, never quite reaching the ground. At a point about halfway down the mountain, the waterfall dwindled to mist that was simply blown away.

He saw Azár turn a corner and angle toward him. She wore her hair unbound, which was a rare thing. It changed her appearance drastically, softening her features. He wasn't used to seeing her with her hair unconstrained outside the privacy of their own tent.

"They are hauling in wood for the fires," she announced with a smile. "It seems we will feast tonight, after all."

Darien grunted. He'd kept an eye on the men who had tested the provisions. None had fallen ill. His mouth started watering at the prospect of a full meal. Azár wrapped an arm around him and glanced upward, using the other to shield her eyes from the sun's glare.

"Tell me about the city in the sky. Speak to me of Aerysius."

He slouched under the heavy weight of the inevitable. He'd known he'd have to confront his feelings at some point. He just hadn't wanted it to be in front of her. Darien took his wife's hand and drew her over to the side of the street, where the view was better and there was a bench they could sit on. Azár lowered herself down at his side and sat looking at him expectantly. Darien didn't say anything for a while. He glanced down at her soft hand and trailed his fingers across her skin.

Indicating the cliffs, he said, "It was beautiful. It was built all on terraces, carved right out of the mountain. The towers were so elegant. It was like they floated in the clouds. The Hall of the Watchers was enormous. It was built around this giant dome. The pillars inside looked like trees. Enormous trees—far bigger than those." He gestured at the old-growth pines lurking over the rooftops. "Row upon row upon row. Scores of them. It was breathtaking. I've never felt so insignificant as I did standing under that dome."

He fell silent. Azár squeezed his hand.

"I am sorry you lost so much," she said. Then she paused. "But I am not sorry your city in the clouds perished."

He looked down regretfully. "No, I don't suppose you would be."

She reached up and turned his face toward her, forcing his eyes to meet hers. She said firmly, "If Aerysius had never fallen, then you would not have fallen. And we would not be here now. All of us—we would still be in Malikar. Waiting to die. So Aerysius had to fall. It had to fall so that we could live."

She kissed him gently, caringly. Then she rose and walked away, leaving him alone with his hound and his memories.

Somehow the anticipated meal had evolved into a full-fledged festivity. The men had found a few casks of cider and rolled them out. A great bonfire was built in the center of the square, fed with items of furniture plundered from nearby homes.

Darien felt a tug on his arm and turned to find a smiling Sayeed carrying a mug of cider. The officer forcibly planted the drink in his hands, then tugged him down the street in the direction of the fire. The odor of searing meat made Darien's stomach spasm. Tumbling smoke and waves of heat rose from the fire, the flames crackling high into the air. The sky was the bleak color of the ocean, and only one faint star braved the twilight, flickering anxiously just above the trees.

Sayeed propelled him to where a tight cluster of men and women sat on rugs thrown across the ground a little way from the fire. Azár was already there, sitting on a cushion under a cloth canopy. She sat in a ring of Zakai gathered around a cluster of dishes and bowls filled with an assortment of foods. She was laughing at a comment or joke.

When Azár looked up at him, her eyes shone joyfully. She

waved him over, patting a cushion by her side. Darien sat next to her, Sayeed following right behind. The men and women acknowledged his presence with reverent bows, not going fully to the ground, but not far from it. He ignored the deference.

Darien lifted the mug to his lips and took a gulp of hard cider. He already knew what it would taste like before it reached his tongue—he'd grown up drinking Koff Tabard's favorite recipe made from local crab apples. It took just a taste to be certain the cider had come from old Koff's hoarded stash. The knowledge came with a sharp pang of guilt that didn't stop him from drinking it. Darien chugged the cider down, setting the empty mug by his side.

"Try the basha!" Azár exclaimed, scooping up some gravied vegetables with a piece of bread. She held it up before his face, grinning as he bit into it.

Immediately, Darien's hunger overrode every other impulse. He dove into the meal, unable to stuff the food into his mouth fast enough. It was a long time before he slowed his chewing enough to even taste what he was eating. Azár laughed delightfully, tearing off a slice of bread and helping herself as Darien went on to explore the numerous other offerings spread out before them.

"Whatever this is, it is very strong," Azár said, making a face and handing him her cup.

Darien accepted it with a grin. Koff's cider had been known and respected throughout the Vale. Gazing into her cup, he wondered where old Koff was now. And Koff's wife. And the rest of his family. He tossed Azár's cider down in a few swallows, feeling the magic field ebb as he did.

He stood up and wandered back through the thick smoke toward the fire, scanning for the cider cask. Night had smothered the town while he wasn't looking. The bonfire crackled at the darkness, its flames snapping at the air. The sounds of laughter and conversation rose in a dull haze of noise, punctuated by the clatter of drums and the erratic blare of a war horn. A cry went up from a ring of soldiers standing nearby—someone had won a game of cross-sticks. A group of men had formed a line beside the fire and, linking arms, began a foot-stomping dance that snaked around the gathering, picking up participants as it went.

He found one of the oak barrels and angled toward it but was intercepted by Sayeed. The officer plucked the empty mug from his hand and replaced it with a fresh one.

"Just ask, Brother," he admonished.

Darien asked, "Have you tried it?"

"Someone must have a clear head." Sayeed smiled and clapped Darien on the back. Then he took him by the arm, guiding him back across the square. Darien had the mug drained by the time he reclaimed his cushion.

"Go dance!" Azár commanded, waving him away.

Darien sat down, staring at her with a look of affronted dignity. "No."

Mischievous intent glittered in her eyes. Azár grinned at Sayeed, then leaned into Darien, nudging him forward. "Go! Just one dance!"

"Battlemages don't dance," Darien said firmly, and meant it. He reached across her for a piece of bread. The next thing he knew, he was being hauled to his feet.

"Tonight, they do!" Sayeed cried and, to Darien's horror, pulled him by the arm toward the bonfire.

He shot an outraged glare over his shoulder at Azár, who flashed him an indulgent grin. He tried to yank his arm out of Sayeed's vice-like grasp but a loud *whoop!* from the gathering stopped his squirming. Soldiers laughed and sprang back to clear a path for him. Men cheered, and women trilled their tongues, urging him forward. Before he knew it, he was standing in the line of dancers, trying to figure out when to kick and when to stomp—the whole while looking like a complete ass, he was certain.

The crowd laughed and clapped and cheered. He hadn't had near enough cider, Darien decided. He missed a step and staggered—and was caught by Sayeed, who threw his head back and burst into hearty laughter. Darien found himself grinning, finally finding some humor in the situation. He stomped and kicked and kicked and stomped, finally figuring out the pattern—and found he was able to laugh at himself when he got it wrong. The crowd roared and cheered.

Hearing the song die around him, Darien twisted out of line and fled back toward the cider cask. He stopped when he was halfway there, feeling suddenly light-headed. For just a moment, his vision blurred. The cider had been stronger than he'd thought. He decided he didn't need any more. The magic field was already a thin filament in the back of his head, scarcely tangible. He changed direction and walked back toward where Azár sat surrounded by Zakai. By the time he reached her, the exhaustion of the day had caught up with him. He sank down next to her with a full stomach and a weary sigh.

Azár threw her arms around him, squeezing him tight. "The Battlemage who dances!" she announced gleefully.

Darien feigned outrage, pulling away, trying hard not to laugh. Azár kissed him on the cheek and took his hand. Her touch sent a strange sensation shooting up his arm, like a fine needling of prickles that started in his fingertips. He let go of his wife's hand and wiggled his fingers, trying to work the sensation out of them. He felt suddenly, uncomfortably warm. A sweat broke out on his forehead.

"What is it?" Azár asked.

Darien shook his head. The prickling feeling retreated back out of his fingers. He dropped his hand to his side. "I'm just tired," he assured her. "I think I'll find my bed."

He pushed himself up off the ground.

She said, "I'll go with you."

He took her by the hand and led her through the hollering revelry back toward the mayor's home. And the mayor's bed.

Chapter Nineteen
The Sentinel's Gambit

"Wake up!"

The voice wasn't sharp enough to cut all the way through the dense fog that smothered him, holding him down.

"Brother, wake up!"

An incessant shaking threatened to break him out of the fog. Darien groaned, willing it to stop. But it didn't. The shaking continued. He grew exasperated. He wanted to sink back down into the comfortable mist and never come up again. He lashed out with an inarticulate groan.

"He will not wake!"

The shaking stopped. A hand slapped his cheek, over and over and over again. It wouldn't let him slide back down where he wanted to go. That made him angry. He swiped out with an arm.

"*Stop!*" he growled and cracked open his eyes.

"Brother!"

Sayeed lifted him upright, a motion that made Darien retch. His stomach convulsed, squeezing bile into his throat. He clamped his mouth shut, trying hard not to vomit. He was still shaking, though no hands were on him. His clothing stuck to his skin, drenched in sweat. The room was dark and infinitely cold.

"What is it?" he mumbled.

"You are sick!" Azár cried. "Many are sick! You must heal yourself!"

Sick. Yes. He was sick. He supposed he could heal himself. The magic field was right there, within easy reach. He caught ahold of it—

—and jerked his mind back away.

"I can't heal myself and stay awake," he rasped. If there were others that were sick, he would have to see to their needs first, before he let the healing sleep overcome him. Gritting his teeth, Darien fought himself fully upright. Doing so made his head reel and his stomach twist. His pulse raced. He felt like he'd run miles in his sleep.

"It is poison!" Azár exclaimed, touching his cheek with the back of her hand. "It is acting fast. You do not have time to delay!"

"Not yet." Darien shook his head. "I have to stay awake. Help me up."

Azár exchanged concerned glances with Sayeed. At last, she relented. Sayeed stood and took hold of him, pulling Darien to his feet. His knees buckled, but the officer's strong grip kept him upright. Darien stood clinging to the man's shoulder until he felt stable enough to stand on his own. He took a spongy step forward. Then another. With Sayeed's help, Darien staggered down the hallway. Azár walked ahead of them, glancing back fretfully.

Darien halted in the doorway and looked out at the square, which had been turned into a makeshift campsite. Men and women lay groaning in their blankets around the still-glowing ashes of the bonfire. Others wandered as if dazed amongst the sick. The air was filled with the sounds of moans and the reek of human waste.

Sayeed shook his head. "We tested the food."

"It wasn't in the food," Darien said, cursing himself. "It was in the cider."

For the first time in a long while, he felt white-cold panic. Staring out across the devastation of his warband, he realized a very cunning mind had planned this assault—planned it well. And it wasn't over yet.

"They're going to attack," he said.

Sayeed looked at him gravely, then nodded. He shifted Darien's weight to Azár. The officer set off across the square, shouting orders at the soldiers still on their feet. All but the sickest ran to form a perimeter. Scores of men poured in from the side streets, supplementing their defenses.

Feeling suddenly weak, Darien sank down and leaned against the doorway, holding his head in his hands. Azár knelt beside him, looking at him in concern. Nothing happened for minutes. And every minute, he felt the poison gnaw a little more of him away. He stared down at the number of men who still lay on the ground, unable to stand with the rest of their comrades. He should be helping them, healing them.

But he'd been a fool. He'd lowered his guard.

"Fall back!"

Darien glanced up, peering intently out across the night. Then he heard it: the clattering sound of arrows pelting the ground, followed by the ragged sounds of his sentries dying somewhere on the outskirts of town. He pushed himself to his feet and staggered down the steps, leaning heavily on Azár. More arrows splattered the ground, this time closer. Across the square, unarmored men and women started dropping by the dozens.

Darien reached out from within and threw his will on the air, struggling to conjure a shield to protect them from the bowmen's long reach. He couldn't do it. His mind was just as feeble as the rest of him. Staggering, he trudged forward.

"What are you doing?" Azár cried. "You cannot—"

He waved her silent. "I have to get closer!"

Another cloud of arrows whispered at them from the darkness. They clattered to the earth, finding purchase in the bodies of the ill and injured. Across the square, his soldiers were dropping at an alarming rate.

Darien knew he was close enough when he felt the wind of an arrow hiss past his ear. He closed his eyes, focusing his mind as best he could. He cast a glowing shield up over the square. Arrows battered against it, ricocheting off. In the distance, he could hear shouts of frustration when the bowmen realized they were neutralized.

Knowing what was coming next, he reached to draw his sword. And cursed when it wasn't there.

"We need to flee. *Now!*" Azár jerked his arm, yanking him

backward.

The shield was costing him. Darien didn't have the strength to maintain it and grapple with his wife at the same time. So he staggered after her, letting the shield thin behind him. Sweat streamed down his face, and his legs trembled beneath him. He couldn't keep up with her.

"Hurry!" Azár cried, tugging him forward.

Darien tripped and landed face down in the dirt. Azár managed to get him back on his feet, to get him moving. He could hear his soldiers engaging an assault force, the clamor of battle ringing across the square, echoing off the walls of the houses. Exhausted, Darien dropped the shield entirely. It wasn't necessary anymore.

"Back in the house!" Azár gasped, hurrying him toward the stairs. But his strength gave out. Darien sank to his knees in the dirt. The world lurched, his vision reeling. He felt like he was going to be violently ill.

"I have to help them," he gasped, trying to make the two Azárs in front of him merge into one image.

Both Azárs raised a fist as if to strike him. "You cannot help anyone dead! You need to heal yourself—*now!*"

Darien closed his eyes. The world sagged, and he sagged with it. He rolled onto his side, clutching his stomach. He felt a growing calmness, a comforting fog drifting up to claim him.

Commotion across the square made him look. A group of Valemen had broken through the perimeter and were charging their position. A few Tanisars streamed in from the alleys to attack their flanks, not fast enough to overcome them.

Azár leaped in front of him and dropped into a fighting crouch, one hand on the ground, as if readying to take them all on by herself.

Darien could do nothing to help her. He lay on his side in the dirt, watching events unfold through a bleary, tilted world. Azár held her ground as the charging men closed the distance between them.

All at once, she screamed and swept out with her hand. A whooshing gush of flames poured forth, engulfing the Valemen's front ranks. Men fled, screaming, through the street, trailing smoke behind them in a fiery wake. Others dropped and rolled in the dirt, enveloped in flames.

The last of the Valemen retreated but didn't get far. A group of Zakai rushed forward, cutting down most with swords and crossbow bolts, routing the rest.

Darien watched the last burning man flail then stop moving. He thought maybe he recognized him. Not that it mattered.

With a cry, Azár dropped back to his side.

"You are safe," she assured him, though the fear in her voice spoke otherwise. She rolled him onto his back.

Darien stared up at her blearily. He fumbled around for the magic field, grabbing the little bit he could. He drew it in and used it to look inward—

—and was horrified by what he found. His organs were shutting down, his tissues dead or dying. His heart stuttered along weakly, his lungs laboring to move air.

He closed his eyes and sucked in as much power as he could with what little he had left. He worked as quickly as he could, racing time against his own flagging consciousness. A wash of peaceful bliss swept over him, calming his heart, soothing the fire in his lungs. The fog came back and rose around him, consuming him, comforting him. Azár's face faded as the mist claimed him entirely, sucking him down. Pulling him under.

Darien awoke comfortable and warm.

The mist was gone, receded back into whatever depths it had roiled up from. Darien blinked it away.

He was back in the bedroom of the mayor's home. The mahogany bed with its over-stuffed mattress contained him, his head supported by down pillows. He was covered by a thick wool blanket that felt warm and scratchy against his skin. A tallow candle glowed from a bronze holder above the bed, the wall behind it darkened by soot.

He felt a hand squeeze his.

Darien turned his head to find Azár sitting at his bedside. She leaned forward, stroking her fingers through his hair. He couldn't tell from the expression on her face whether she was happy or angry at finding him awake.

"How many did we lose?" he asked gruffly.

"Many."

Azár continued to stroke his hair, gazing somberly down at him. Darien closed his eyes, internalizing her answer, using the knowledge to feed his self-loathing.

The deaths were on his hands.

He sat up with a struggle, swinging his legs over the side of the bed. The room wavered for a moment, then stabilized. He cast a glance around, taking in the dull, exhausted look of the bedroom. He wondered who the mayor might have been. Probably someone he knew. A tattered man with a tattered life, judging by his worn possessions.

With Azár's help, Darien rose unsteadily to his feet. He tried a step, making sure his legs could support his weight. Azár peered at him skeptically.

"I'm good," he told her.

He found his clothes draped over a shabby velvet chair. He started pulling on his shirt, but a purring noise behind made him turn. The demon-hound stood in the doorway, slobber stringing from its jowls. Darien tucked in his shirt and laced up his trousers. He walked across the room and offered out his hand. The hound licked his fingers with a festering tongue.

"Where were you last night?" he asked the detestable creature. The thing cocked its head to the side, looking fondly up at him.

"The attack was two nights ago," Azár corrected him sharply.

Darien glanced back at her, hearing the anger in her voice.

"You're unhappy."

She stood with her arms crossed, exuding rage. "You were *stupid!*"

Darien couldn't argue. He nodded in agreement, ruffling the thanacryst's fur. "I agree. I'm stupid. I shouldn't have trusted the cider. I'm sorry."

Azár made a growling noise and spun away. "I am tired of your apologies! Every day, another apology! The problem is not the cider—the problem is *you,* acting as though you are immortal!"

Darien barked a scornful laugh. "Well, I'm not mortal, either, so what does that make me?"

"It makes you a fool!"

With that, she stormed out of the room. Darien stood listening to her loud footfalls echoing down the hallway. The front door opened and slammed shut again, rattling the windows. He let out a lingering sigh, looking down at the hound.

"Never get married," he advised.

The thing looked up at him and yawned. Darien gave it one last scratch, then sat down on the bed and pulled his boots on. He fastened his sword to his waist and followed his wife out of the house.

He walked down the stone steps to the street. There, Darien paused, looking over the debris-filled square. The dead had been cleared away, but evidence of the battle lay everywhere. The dirt was ribboned with blood and scorched by fires. Pieces of armor and bloody rags lay strewn everywhere. He walked slowly across the square, watching soldiers clearing away the remaining debris. They were working hard to return the town back to the state they had found it. Not for their own sakes; their force would be moving on. They were making ready for the civilians who would be following behind to settle in this place.

Darien followed a steady stream of soldiers moving in and out through the town's main gate. He took only a few steps down the road before he slowed to a stop, too disturbed to move any further.

There, lining one of Nat Calway's grain fields, lay a long row of corpses arranged neatly side by side. Sayeed's men were laboring with shovels, digging a long trench along the far side of the field.

Darien's insides twisted up in a knot. He didn't know whether the dead were his own people…or his own people. He squeezed his eyes shut against a deluge of conflicting emotions he couldn't push aside or ignore. The one that dominated, he thought, was an intense feeling of shame.

He forced himself to walk into the field of wheat, wading

through the dew-wet grass. He needed to see their faces, had to know which friends his choices had slain. Starting at the end of the row of corpses, he worked his way slowly down the line, his gaze slipping from familiar face to familiar face. They were a sad, broken mix of men and women, white and brown. He knew the names of each. By the time Darien was halfway down the line, he felt physically ill. He made himself continue, scorching each name and face into his memory. When he reached the end of the row, he stopped and stared out across the grain field, feeling suddenly, inexplicably, numb.

He stood there a good while. Then he turned his back on the people he'd failed and walked away.

He didn't know where he was going. It was almost as though he wasn't the man walking out of that field. He was someone else. And he was somewhere else, looking down at himself from some high vantage. It was all too confusing. And he was too dazed to wonder at it.

He trudged into the forest, his feet snapping twigs, crunching on pine needles and oak leaves. Somehow, he ended up on a dirt path that meandered alongside the scar of a stream. It led him deeper into the forest, through a dusty oak grove. Shadows closed in overhead, the branches thickening. Light streaked down to dapple the ground. The air was filled with the scent of forest loam and leaf litter. For some reason, those details seemed important to him.

Gradually, the forest thinned. Blinking, Darien glanced around and realized where he was. He'd journeyed much deeper into the woodland than he'd thought. He turned slowly around, as if waking from a dream, struggling to get his bearings. If he remembered right, there was another footpath just to the east, past a stand of fir trees. He started toward it as if compelled.

He found the path without difficulty. It wasn't very familiar, but he remembered clearly where it led. It ended at a small clearing surrounded by a grove of sycamores. Ahead of him sat a small cottage made of old, rotted planks and bitter memories.

Darien stopped in the clearing and stood looking at the structure for a moment. Then, with a defeated sigh, he walked toward it. He paused before entering, resting a hand on the doorframe. As though the feel of the rough, splintery pine would make the cottage seem more real.

He pushed the door open, letting it swing, moaning, on its hinges.

Immediately, he was confronted by a great heron hanging low from the ceiling on the other side. He stood still, staring at the bird sadly. It looked half-rotten. Many of its downy feathers were loose and falling out. He reached up to touch it, sending the bird spinning on its string.

He ducked under the heron and entered the cottage.

Dozens of birds hung from the ceiling, no two alike. They spun slowly above him, wings outstretched. Sadly, more than a few had fallen to the floor. The air had a rotten smell to it he didn't remember from before. Soft feathers were scattered everywhere, collecting in the corners and captured in the cobwebs.

His eyes scanned over the Bird Man's bed, coming to rest on a chest pushed up against the far wall. The chest was covered in more birds: some upright, most not. All appeared in various stages of decomposition. Darien felt saddened, remembering how lovingly Master Edric had cared for his collection.

Curiosity impelled his feet toward the chest. He'd been too distraught to open it two years before, when he'd woken from sleep blazing with power, a dead old Master lying next to him on the floor. His only thoughts then had been of escape.

Darien knelt before the chest and lifted the first bird, setting it aside. One by one, he removed the birds from the lid, trying not to disturb the feathers. Despite his best efforts, soft down collected on the floor at his feet. The birds were far too decayed to be handled, even gently.

He removed the last small finch and, using both hands, lifted the cover of the chest. The strong smell of cedarwood jarred his nose. Darien scrubbed his shirtsleeve across his face then reached within. One item at a time, he began removing the chest's contents. An assortment of clothes was soon stacked next to him, all neatly folded. An old leather-bound tome wrapped in cloth and tied shut with hemp cord. A bone-handled knife in a leather sheath. Two chipped ceramic plates. And a folded, age-yellowed note.

Addressed to him.

The feeling left his hands as he picked the note up. He unfolded it carefully, running his fingers over the parchment to smooth out the crease.

Darien,

I hope one day you can forgive me for what I did to you. I knew that one mage could never make a difference in this war, and I was too old and weak to help you. But perhaps my legacy—and my research—can serve you better than they could ever serve me. I am leaving you my journal. Study it well. Perhaps, one day, you can realize what I never could. I did not have enough of the gift in me to bring my dreams to fruition. But now you do. I have every faith and confidence in you, just as your father always had.

Your Friend,

Edric

Darien lowered the note, setting it on the stack of clothing beside him on the floor. He knelt there for a while, staring ahead with a confused, unfocused gaze. He had never understood why Master Edric had forced more of the gift into him than one man could ever endure. It had been a death sentence. One that had never made any sense to him—it was one of the great mysteries of his life. Perhaps, now, he could finally have an explanation for it.

He reached down and lifted the cloth-wrapped tome, holding it in his hand. Delicately, he untied the hemp cord and folded back the fabric. The thick leather cover was old. Very old—far older than the normal lifespan of a man. He opened it carefully and gazed down at the first page. A single date was written there in blue ink: *1621-*.

Darien blinked. The date was over a hundred years ago. And yet it was written in the same flowing script as the Bird Man's letter. Darien turned the page and scanned the first paragraph. He dismissed it quickly—the writing was a reflective piece, nothing of importance. He opened the text to a page marked by a frayed ribbon.

On the page before him was a sketch of one of the many birds that dangled over his head, along with accompanying measurements. The same bird was sketched again at the bottom of the page, only with wings extended and feathers and skin removed— a labeled diagram showing the bird's musculature. Turning the page revealed another diagram, this one of the bird's skeleton. Then another of internal organs. Another of lace-like vascular tissues, rendered painstakingly. The next pages were devoted entirely to mathematical calculations.

He didn't understand any of it, much less why the Bird Man had gone to such lengths to explore the anatomy of a single warbler. As for the calculations…he would have to spend some time with them. Whatever problem they had been applied to solve, he couldn't determine at first glance.

He closed the book and was about ready to wrap it back up in its cloth cover. But then he paused, for the first time noticing the elegant embroidery that had been sewn into the fabric. He traced a finger over it, admiring the minute details that had been worked into the wings, the vibrant colors of the scales—

"What manner of creature is that?"

Darien flinched, almost dropping the journal. He glanced up at Sayeed. He took a deep breath, seeking to steady his nerves. Then he rose to his feet, handing the embroidered cloth to his First.

"It's a dragon," he said. "They breathe fire, slay heroes, and ravage cities."

Sayeed frowned, holding the fabric at various angles, studying the embroidered dragon with a look of grave concern.

He said, "I never knew such monsters existed."

"They don't. Except in heraldry."

Darien took the cloth back and folded it around the journal. He tied it closed then looked around, making sure there was nothing left in the cottage of any importance. He gazed upward at the twirling birds that dangled on their strings: hawks and jays, ducks and woodpeckers. A great horned owl mounted in a corner stared at him accusingly.

"Who lived here?" Sayeed asked, ducking under a peregrine falcon. He reached up and poked the wingtip, sending the bird rocking.

"The man who saved me when I fell from the mountain."

Sayeed touched another bird, making it twirl faster on its string. "A strange man."

"Aye," Darien agreed, remembering the three tiers of power the old Master had forced into him on top of the five he'd already had. "A very strange man."

"I heard you came this way," Sayeed said. He knelt and began replacing the contents of the cedar chest. "The men thought you seemed unsettled. Did you know some of the townsfolk who were slain?" He closed the lid of the chest, then set about returning the scattered birds back to their roost.

Darien nodded, feeling the shame return to clutch his throat. "Aye. Every one of them." He closed his eyes, dredging up their images in his head. "Mace Mullins taught me how to fish. He was an old farmer with six boys. Only three made it to adulthood. Lost his wife in childbirth."

He moved toward the window, looking through the uneven glass in the direction of the grove. "Nat Flannon owned a farm up the road. He was the town chandler. We always did chores for him, and he always gave us treats. Dane Tirrel was the miller's son. We used to set traps together—"

"Stop," Sayeed commanded, standing up. "There is only one man alive who can defeat you, and that man is you. Do not surrender to him."

Darien nodded, understanding. Sayeed was right. Yet he had no idea how to vanquish that particular foe.

Sayeed placed a hand on his shoulder and looked at him

gravely. "Be the dragon, Darien. Breathe fire, slay heroes, and ravage cities."

Staring out the window, Darien muttered, "I told you. Dragons don't exist."

Sayeed assured him, "They do now."

Chapter Twenty
Story's End

Isle of Titherry, The Rhen

Quin inhaled the cigar deeply and, closing his eyes, let the smoke out savoringly. He lifted a cup to his lips, chasing down the taste with anise-flavored arak, swishing it around in his mouth. He smiled as the alcohol scorched his throat. Arak was supposed to be a delicate beverage, well-watered and served over ice. Quin preferred it straight from the bottle, undiluted. He smacked his lips and nestled his head back to stare directly up at a garish blue sky.

He turned at the sound of approaching footsteps, squinting through a wash of sunlight to see Naia moving toward him. Her face was set in the same, flustered scowl she had taken to wearing lately. She paused in front of his chair, hands on her hips, looking down at him with an air of disapproval. Quin adjusted his hat until the brim shielded his eyes from the sun's glare. He could see her features better, now. She was even more agitated than he'd realized.

"Whatever's the matter?" he asked. "You look like someone just pressed the ruffles out of your petticoat."

"Please, Quin." Naia sighed in exasperation. She sank down in the chair next to his. The soft breeze played with a wisp of hair that had fallen out of her braid. He leaned forward and tucked the wayward strands back behind her ear.

"I apologize for my lack of social graces. Here," he said, offering his cup to her. "This should make it all better."

Naia received the cup and brought it to her lips. Immediately, she winced, her face crumpling into a grimace.

"What *is* that?" she gasped, handing it back. "It tastes like medicine!"

Quin smiled, accepting the cup and knocking back a healthy mouthful, grinning devilishly. "Think of it as medicine for the soul."

Naia scowled. "My soul is perfectly fine, thank you. It's your own soul I'm more concerned about."

"As am I." Quin set about replenishing his cup. "Which makes finishing this bottle of paramount importance."

Quick as a snake, Naia's hand shot out and snatched the container from his hand. She turned it on end, pouring the liquor onto the flagstones in a long, thin stream. She shook the bottle to make sure every last drop had been evacuated, then clunked it down on the stones by her feet.

Watching his arak spreading across the ground, Quin sighed morosely. "I take it you have no care for my salvation."

"Please. What I need from you right now is support."

Quin couldn't ignore the weary plea in her eyes. "Come here, darling," he said, and leaned forward to embrace her with one hand, holding his cigar as far as he could away from her face. He gave her a good, tight squeeze, then kissed her forehead. He sat back in his chair, taking a few short puffs.

"More visions?" he asked.

"Versions," she corrected him, rubbing her eyes. "And yes. I mean no."

Quin cocked an eyebrow. "Do you mind clarifying?"

Naia breathed a heavy sigh. "The versions I've been seeing just keep repeating. Over and over and over. With only minor variations in detail. In all the time I've spent reading the Crescent, I've seen only the same three outcomes." She held up a finger. "We destroy the magic field." A second finger: "Renquist halts the Reversal." And a third: "The Reversal happens and kills us all."

Quin reached over and rolled the end of his cigar against the ground to knock some of the ash off. "By 'kill us all,' you mean just us mages?"

"That's correct."

"And which outcome will free the skies over Malikar?"

Naia's gaze slipped to the side. "Destroying the magic field would break the Curse, as Tsula says. Or we could help Zavier Renquist halt the Reversal."

Probably not the best alternative, Quin decided. "I don't understand. A thousand years ago, Renquist said it would take the combined strength of eight Grand Masters to stabilize the magic field. Now he thinks he can do it all by himself?"

Naia's face became grave. "In every version of that Story, Renquist sacrifices either Darien or Kyel on a Circle of Convergence. And then he kills me."

Frowning, Quin took another puff of his cigar, giving himself time to grapple with his emotions. Out of all the terrible outcomes Naia had listed, that was the one he couldn't tolerate. He hadn't meant to fall for Naia. When it came to love, he'd had nothing but terrible experiences. He'd thought he'd learned. But he hadn't been able to help himself. Zavier Renquist had already taken Amani from him. Quin wasn't about to let him take Naia, as well.

He asked, "Is Tsula still alive in all the versions you're seeing?"

Naia paused in thought before nodding. "Yes."

Quin took a few short puffs of his cigar. "So…it's possible there are still other versions of this story that are still out there. Is there some way Tsula could be blocking you from seeing them? You said her death might open up other avenues."

"Possibly."

His brain ticked through a quick checklist of reasons and rationale. When he reached the end of that list, the obvious course of action seemed like a non-decision. There were no more facts to ponder. And there was no reason to hesitate.

Quin leaned over and mashed his cigar against the ground, scrubbing it back and forth, leaving a streak of black soot on the flagstones. Flicking what was left over the side of the balcony, he rose from his chair and kissed Naia's cheek.

"Why don't you go up to the library, darling," he suggested, straightening his hat. "I think I'll go for a walk."

Naia nodded absently, gazing over the edge of the balcony in the direction of the Crescent. She didn't look up as he walked away. He wondered what she was thinking about so hard. A cool breeze came up, stirring his coat. He glanced back at Naia one last time then opened the door to the castle.

Once inside, he focused his concentration on the sound of his feet echoing sharply off the walls. The castle rang eerily, vastly empty, which worked to his advantage. The last thing he needed was distraction. As he walked, his thoughts started drifting. He battered them back into focus. Thinking led to doubt. Doubt led to hesitation.

And that was the one thing he couldn't afford.

In his profession, morality had no relevance. Right or wrong, the world—and Naia's life—depended on his decisiveness.

Quin entered the great hall and wound through the intimate clusters of furniture that filled the sprawling room. It was as though the chamber was a neglected host, waiting eternally for guests who would never arrive. He took great care to step quietly, not wanting the sounds of his footfalls to announce his presence prematurely.

He found the small room Tsula occupied at the far end of the hall.

Quin paused outside her cracked door, taking one last moment to prepare. He checked his boot knife to make sure it was loose in its sheath. He checked his pulse, checked his resolve, then reached up to push the door open.

The sound of Tsula's voice halted his motion. "Stop lurking in the doorway and come inside, Quinlan Reis."

He supposed he should have been startled. But he was unsurprised. The Harbinger seemed to have an endless supply of prescience. Quin pushed the door open and found Tsula sitting in her chair, awaiting him with hands folded on her lap. She wore an elaborate headwrap, her body swallowed by the fabric of an over-sized kaftan. She gazed up at him with eyes as dull as stone and hard as steel. Raising her hand, she indicated the chair opposite her own.

"Have a seat." Her voice was just as level as her expression. "You kept me waiting. I expected you much sooner."

Quin sat in the offered chair and stared around at the screaming colors of the cluttered room. Everywhere he looked were tapestries, knickknacks, baskets, vases, jewelry—a lifetime's worth of possessions all gathered together in one dense, claustrophobic space. It was all so distracting, he almost missed the substance of Tsula's words.

His gaze snapped toward her. "You know why I'm here?"

"Of course." She draped her hands over the armrests of her chair. "I am a Harbinger. Knowing the hour and manner of my death is just one of the many burdens those of my order must bear. At first, we see our death as only one of an infinite number of possibilities—or versions, as we like to call them. But each decision we make turns another page in the Story of our life. The longer we live, the versions of our narrative diminish before our eyes, until there is only one version left to pen. And then our life's chapter is written. I've known how my own Story ends for quite some time. And I know it will end here today."

Her words made Quin feel cold and clammy—a sensation he wasn't used to. He found himself having second thoughts.

Suspiciously, he asked, "Then why aren't you trying to stop me?"

"Because death cannot be avoided." Tsula confronted him with a relentless, deadpan stare. "Far too many times in my life, I have had to stay my hand and watch fate reap its terrible harvest. I foresaw the fall of my nation. And I foresaw my own daughter's death. Yet I could do nothing to prevent either. If I had stopped you from causing the Desecration of Caladorn, then the entire world would now be under Xerys' sway. And if I had stopped my daughter from trading her life to save your own, we would not be sitting here today. You would have never foiled my husband's plans. And now Xerys would be reigning from the throne of Isap, with the world groveling at his feet."

Quin's breath hitched. He sat frozen in his chair, shocked into rigidity. His mouth went dry. His thoughts hung suspended in the air, waiting for impact.

He whispered, "You're Amani's mother?"

"I am."

His heart broke open. Quin lurched from his chair, overcome by mindless rage. He towered over Tsula, fury sweeping away what was left of his rationality.

"And you *knew?* You knew she was going to Aerysius? *You knew she was going to be executed?*"

"I did." Tsula's expression was glacial.

Quin wanted to howl. He clenched and unclenched his fists. "Why didn't you warn her? Why didn't you stop her? *You let her die!*"

"I already told you," Tsula said, calmly. "There is a reason why all Harbingers were trained in seclusion on this isle. We are called upon to make difficult choices. Sometimes, those choices are unbearable. I knew Amani would die. And I knew her death would destroy you. And yet I could do absolutely nothing to save either of you. Otherwise, the reign of Xerys would have already come to pass."

Quin shot forward, planting both hands on the back of her chair, his face an inch away from her own. Gritting his teeth, he growled, "Amani meant everything to me! *Everything!*"

"I know."

"She didn't have to die!" His voice shook just as hard as the rest of him. His vision blurred. He pushed off from the chair, whirling away.

Almost gently, Tsula said, "I hope someday you can forgive me, Quinlan Reis. As I forgive you."

It was too much. He lashed out with the magic field, ending her life in a heartbeat.

Chapter Twenty-One
The False God

Northern Chamsbrey, The Rhen

Darien raised his practice sword, catching Azár's strike on his crossguard.

"Don't let the blade get ahead of you," he instructed. He stepped back, bringing his blade up into a high ward above his shoulder. "Again. Move together with your sword."

Azár took a step back, then repeated the action. This time, her blade impacted solidly with his.

"Like that," Darien said. "Again. This time rotate your left hand. Watch your structure."

Azár stepped back, brought her sword up, then moved forward with a downward cut. Darien moved crisply to block, noting the difference in her blade's impact. There was a lot more power behind her strike than there'd been before.

"Better."

He smiled, lowering his guard. "Why don't you practice that a few times?"

Azár grinned back, resuming her stance. Darien tossed the practice sword down on a rug beside the other dulled blades the Zakai had brought out for morning drills. He stood watching Azár rehearse her cuts, her feet now in time with the rhythm of her blade. Satisfied, he turned and strolled back across the encampment in search of Sayeed. As he walked, he realized he was smiling. He took enormous pride in his wife. He couldn't think of another woman he'd ever admired more.

He crossed the entire encampment in less time than it had

taken him a week ago. The attack in Amberlie had greatly reduced their numbers. There were less soldiers, and therefore less
tents. He'd healed all the men and women he could, making
certain they'd suffer no further losses on the march. Even so, it
had taken them longer to reach Glen Farquist than he'd anticipated.

He found Sayeed conferring with his senior officers. The men
stopped talking as soon as they caught sight of him, their gazes
slipping to the ground. Even after all the time he'd spent
amongst the Tanisars, their eyes had never lost the formal deference that had been there from the outset.

Sayeed left his men to intercept him, guiding him away with a
hand on his arm. Darien still found it peculiar, the lack of personal distance Sayeed and his people were comfortable with.
He'd never liked being touched. He'd liked it less in recent
months. There were only two people in the world he could endure being in close proximity to: Azár and Sayeed. Everyone else
knew better and kept their distance.

At the top of a low rise, Sayeed let go of his arm and gestured
downhill at the valley below. They stood in the shadow of the
Craghorns, the mountain's snowy summits blocking the warm
rays of the morning sun. Below, the forest thinned to grassland.
Beyond the ridge, the grassland thinned to sand. The valley below was a microcosm of desert surrounded by mountains and
rolling, heathered hills, protected by a horseshoe ring of golden
bluffs. Highly defensible geographically. In all of recorded history, Glen Farquist had never fallen.

Sayeed asked, "What are your thoughts?"

Darien stared down at the opening between the cliffs, remembering the last time he had ridden between those sandstone walls.
It had been with Naia, the same day he had forsworn his Oath
of Harmony. He still remembered the harsh face of Naia's father,
the High Priest of Death, who had tried to convince him to abandon his course. Darien wondered how his life would have been
different if he'd listened to the man.

"It'll be well-defended," he said. "They don't have a standing
army, but they can raise a competent force of clergy and laymen.

A few of the temples have monks trained in the martial arts. They're also in possession of several artifacts that might give us problems."

Sayeed's face grew very serious. "And will they yield?"

Darien shook his head. "No."

Sayeed blew out a long sigh, then bit his lip thoughtfully, his gaze travelling over the valley. His face ranged through a variety of emotions, finally settling on trepidation. "If these are men and women of the cloth, it is ill luck to strike them down."

Darien turned his back on the valley. "They struck first."

Glen Farquist, The Rhen

Kyel strode beside Alexa down a narrow tunnel that plunged beneath the cliffs rimming Glen Farquist. The silent cleric who guided them carried a flickering torch in his hand that cast a rippling plume of light. The massive expanse of rock above them seemed to bear down on the roof of the tunnel, so much so that Kyel felt like he had to duck as he walked along. The air was frigid and smelled of wet clay, an odor Kyel found nostalgic.

In the weeks before the Battle of Orien's Finger, Darien had sent him on a mission to find a way to seal the Well of Tears. There was no greater library in the world than the vast warren of Om's temple. Kyel had spent three days leafing through texts and documents in the belly of the temple, only to find out his search had been merely pretense. Darien had already known the text he needed. The search had been just another of the infuriating lessons Darien had contrived for him.

Alexa hadn't spoken a word since they'd entered the tunnels. She walked at Kyel's side looking utterly serene, as if she had been in the warrens of the temple a hundred times before. Perhaps she had. Along their journey south, she'd shared tidbits of her life, like crumbs scattered before him on the floor. But the same way crumbs did a poor job of describing the loaf they'd been broken from, Alexa's scraps of information yielded surprisingly little about her life before Aerysius' fall.

At the bottom of the tunnel, they reached a broad avenue

carved from rock. There, they were passed off to another cleric, who led them along a subterranean highway past a tall water clock. They followed their guide through several corridors filled with silent men and women carrying armloads of scrolls and books. They turned down a whitewashed hallway that led to the High Priest's personal chambers.

Their brown-robed guide knocked on the door then swept it open before them. But when Kyel moved to enter the room, the cleric stepped between Alexa and himself, preventing her from following. The balding old man shook his head.

"It's all right," Kyel assured Alexa. "They're funny like this. I'll catch up with you when I'm done here."

Alexa's eyes clouded with doubt, but at last she nodded and followed their guide back in the direction they'd come from.

Kyel had good reason to trust the clerics. And good reason not to. He'd spent a lot of his time in their warrens during the past two years. They had helped him make the transition from commoner to mage, helping him locate information he so desperately needed to increase his knowledge. And they'd cared for his son and seen to Gil's education, something Kyel hadn't been able to do alone. Even after what had happened to Cadmus, he had every reason to believe the priesthood of Wisdom would still support him.

He hoped.

He entered the High Priest's chambers and found two men waiting for him within. The first was a middle-aged man Kyel had never seen before. He was slender, except for his cheeks, which looked mottled and swollen. He wore a pair of spectacles that hung off-kilter too far down his nose. But it was the man sitting beside him who commanded Kyel's attention.

Kyel moved into the room, nodding formally at the High Priest of Wisdom.

The priest returned the gesture, his long white beard dipping to brush his steepled fingers. He wore elegant robes of rich brown, along with a bronze stole draped over his shoulders. His vibrant blue gaze came to rest on Kyel's cloak.

Kyel turned to the gangly cleric sitting on the stool next to him.

"I'm Kyel Archer," he introduced himself. "Pardon, but I don't believe we've met?"

The cleric's glasses slipped further down his nose. He pushed them back with a finger. "My name is Arvel. I am the Voice of His Eminence."

The man was Cadmus' replacement, Kyel realized. "Your Eminence, where did you have Alexa taken?"

It was Arvel who replied. "Your companion has been escorted to a guest room, where she may recover from her journey." He adjusted his posture on the stool, sliding his bare feet up to rest on the crossbar between the stool's legs. "We are glad you have returned. Events have transpired that—"

"I want to see my son," Kyel cut him off.

The High Priest shook his head.

Arvel stated firmly, "You may see your son after we have spoken. There are many issues that are of paramount importance, and—"

"No."

Kyel shook his head firmly. When he'd first met the High Priest of Wisdom, he had allowed the man to unsettle him, and in doing so, allowed himself to be manipulated easily. No longer. He was done with being controlled.

"Whatever you want to say, it can wait," he told the two men, pushing back his chair and standing up. "I want to see my son first."

Arvel stared at him unblinkingly. Tense moments wore by. At last, the cleric shook his head. "Our warrens extend for miles. A small child could easily get lost within," he said softly, dangerously.

Kyel froze, rooted by fear. They had anticipated his arrival and had prepared for it. He sank back into his seat, glaring at Arvel with a raptor's intensity.

"Be warned," Kyel said. "I've lost any patience I ever had with the temples of Glen Farquist. This temple, in particular. Bring my son to me. Now."

Arvel turned and looked at the High Priest. The two stared at each other a long moment. They were conferring, Kyel knew.

The Vicar of Om had taken a vow of silence and could only express his thoughts through the medium of his Voice. That Voice had once been Cadmus. Apparently, it was now Arvel.

"We are willing to make a compromise," Arvel said at last. "If you address two of the issues we wish to speak of first, then your son will be brought to you. You may spend the remainder of the day in his company. Then tonight after supper, we will gather here again to address the remainder of the issues that confront us."

Kyel glared at him a moment longer, stewing. At last he nodded. The compromise was likely the best offer he'd get. He sat back in his seat and crossed his arms. "Very well."

Arvel looked pleased. He set his hands on the table, knitting his fingers with a smile. "We shall first address the abhorrent amount of power in you."

Kyel blinked. He hadn't expected that. At least, not right away. They had jumped right to the most damning subject they could confront him with. Perhaps it was an attempt to throw him off balance. If so, it was working.

"What about it?" he asked warily.

The man leaned forward in his chair, smiling at Kyel apologetically. His glasses had slipped down his nose again. This time, he didn't bother pushing them back. "Before we begin, we wish to apologize for our lack of sensitivity on these issues. However, it is not possible to discuss—"

"Just get on with it," Kyel growled.

Arvel stared at him in silence for a moment, then said with a flick of his eyebrows, "To be very blunt, you have eleven tiers of power in you. If you were any other mage, and this were any other time, we'd already have your execution prearranged. However…we wish to assure you that is not the case. We have no plans to harm you."

Kyel shrugged dismissively. "That's because you don't think I'll live long enough to be a threat."

Arvel smiled. "I'm glad you understand. Considering the situation, there can be no secrets between us." With one hand, he slid the spectacles from his face and set them on the table. Reaching up, he massaged the bridge of his nose.

When he lowered his hand, Arvel's face had transformed.

Sitting across from Kyel was a different man entirely, one of robust stature and imposing presence. Kyel stared at him in stunned silence as seconds ticked by. His eyes went to the old man. Then back to the man who had just been Arvel.

Kyel didn't know how he knew. He just *knew.*

"You are Om," he whispered.

"No." Arvel shook his head. "Om does not exist. He never has. Like almost every other deity, Om is merely an inception, an archetype of an ideal. Which explains my existence: I am the incarnation of what Om *would* be. Through my network of historians and spies, I have access to limitless knowledge and can conduct limitless surveillance. I have access to artifacts that expand my mind, my sight, and my hearing. I listen to all the mutterings and grumblings of the world. I feel the flutter of every butterfly wing. I am aware of every birth and every death. Every cry of misery and every gasp of joy. For all intents and purposes, I *am* a god. The only thing I lack is the spark of divinity."

Kyel sat back, folding his hands. Part of him felt anger, betrayal. Another part was just relieved to hear the truth. At least, now, he had something to work with.

"Why are you telling me this?" he asked. "Why now? Why me?"

Arvel stood up, turning his back on the old priest, who now sat staring at the surface of the table, looking decisively irrelevant. He said to Kyel, "All the rules have changed. We are now reaching the end game. And now, more than ever before, we must play to win. In the coming days, you will be tested more than any other mage in history. You must stand firm. It is the only way the Rhen will survive the coming crisis with any remnants of civilization intact. Unfortunately, you have no choice."

Kyel disagreed. "I do have a choice. Don't ever for a second think I don't." He narrowed his eyes. "And while we're at it, let's get one damn thing straight: I'm not on your side. I've never been. I'm on my own side—and I'm not convinced our goals are compatible."

Arvel folded his hands. Softly, he asked, "And what are your goals, Sentinel Archer?"

The man was trying to intimidate him. It wouldn't work. What Arvel didn't understand was that Kyel had already accepted the inevitability of his own death—a feeling that was oddly liberating. Very few things could scare him any longer. Certainly not the robed creature in front of him.

Kyel responded in an even tone, "My goal has never changed: to serve the land and its people."

"Ah," the false god smiled. "The Acolyte's Oath. Very noble. But very pedestrian. Even you must agree: the wording is rather vague."

"That doesn't change its intent." Kyel smiled bitterly. "What that oath means is I'm not your tool. I'm a servant of the land and the people of the land. And *I'll* be the judge as to which land that applies to, and which people that includes."

Arvel looked at him and drew in a long, expansive breath, his face menacing. "What exactly are you implying?"

Kyel sat forward, resting his arm on the table. "For a thousand years, your temple and its 'limitless knowledge' has known the truth about the Enemy. But instead of coming to their aid, you walled them away in the Black Lands and beat them back whenever they've emerged. What you've done is nothing short of genocide. I won't tolerate it anymore."

The man stiffened. "Then you have decided to align with Xerys against us?"

"No." Kyel shook his head firmly. "Not with Xerys. I'm taking the side of common sense and decency. I'll help you stand against Renquist and his Servants. I'll help you drive them from this world. But I will not help you destroy an entire population of people. I'll fight you to the death first."

Arvel cocked an eyebrow. "Are you aware there are three Enemy armies ravaging the North even as we speak? One less than a day's ride from here?"

"Of course, I'm aware of it," Kyel snapped. "I've done everything I can to slow them down and deplete their numbers. But we have to end this. We need to negotiate with them. Strike a treaty. Find a way we can peacefully coexist."

Arvel stared at him sidelong. "They're murdering and ravaging the very people you've sworn to protect."

"They're led by a demon," Kyel acknowledged. "But that doesn't make *them* demons."

Arvel slid back in his seat. He peered over the waxed table top with ice blue eyes that burned like coldfire. "So, what do you propose?"

Kyel shrugged, thinking the answer should be obvious. "I propose we get rid of the demon."

"And how do you intend to accomplish that?"

Kyel pushed himself out of his chair and stood up from the table. He reached down and unhooked Thar'gon from his belt. He held the talisman up and, turning it slowly, watched the spikes of the morning star glisten in the candlelight.

"With this."

Chapter Twenty-Two
Hope Besieged

Northern Chamsbrey, The Rhen

Darien bit off a strip of jerky and chewed it automatically. He was engrossed in the old leather journal in his lap. He tore off another bite and flipped a page. Master Edric's notes were scrawled on papers of different sizes and weights, as if they'd been scribed loosely and then collected and bound at a later date. The journal was full of diagrams, notes, equations, and descriptions. Edric's preoccupation with birds was evident throughout. Nearly every bird species Darien knew was documented and sketched at least once. And there were many other creatures that had been the objects of intense study. Mostly reptiles: snakes and lizards. A few insects, though it seemed Edric had abandoned that line of inquiry.

Darien's finger moved over a page as he tried to follow the logic of a particularly long and complex passage. He got lost halfway through. It seemed Edric had made up his own shorthand system. Darien had tried working forward and backward to understand how the man had arrived at his conclusions, without much success. He thought he had an idea of which general directions the Bird Man's mind had wandered, but he had no idea of the exact paths.

He tore off another strip of dried horsemeat and worried it in his mouth, flipping back to the ribbon-marked page he'd started with. He studied the diagrams of the bird intensely. It was a warbler: a palm-sized bird with a sharp beak that was common throughout Amberlie Grove. There had to be some reason why Edric had bookmarked that page in particular. It had to be a starting point…but to what?

He looked up when he heard Azár's footsteps approaching. His wife sank down next to him in the grass, crossing her legs and resting her head on his shoulder.

"Have you learned anything more?" she asked, looking down at the journal.

Darien shook his head. "I think I know what he was trying to get at, but the energy transformations would be mindboggling. I don't have the faintest idea how he could get around it."

Azár sat up and took the last strip of jerky from his hand. Popping it in her mouth, she said around the bite, "What do you think he was trying to do?"

Darien hesitated, afraid to voice his thoughts for fear of sounding like a fool. "I think he was trying to turn himself into a bird."

Azár stopped chewing and looked him over with an expression that seemed to question his sanity. "How is that possible? Birds are small. How could a whole man fit into a bird's tiny body?"

Darien said, "It's a simple matter of converting the physical to energy and then converting it back again, but you'd lose a lot along the way. A better question would be, how much of the man could you get back *out* of the bird?" Darien shrugged, his shoulders vocalizing his frustration better than words ever could.

Azár swallowed her mouthful of horse meat. "Would it not be like healing? Rearrangement of the flesh?"

"It's far from rearrangement," Darien grumbled. "It's more like reinvention. I don't know how Edric could have pursued anything like this. He was only third tier. And even if he could make it work, I can't imagine he could transform himself into anything larger than a cockroach."

Azár leaned into him, her body pressed against his. "Does it say he managed to accomplish this? Or only that he tried?"

"Not that I've found. He suggests that he did, but he never comes right out and says it."

She pulled back and looked at him. "You are not thinking of trying this thing, are you?"

"No." Darien shook his head. "I don't understand even a quarter of it yet. And there's too much risk. If something went wrong,

I could end up a quivering mass of goo."

Azár's face scrunched into a grimace. She held her hand up in a gesture against evil. "Ugh. No. I would not like you like that. You should put that book away."

Darien grinned, closing the journal and wrapping it back up in its cloth covering. "I thought you wanted to be rid of me."

"Not yet." Azár smiled mischievously, holding fast to the expression as she kissed him.

Glen Farquist, The Rhen

"Papa!"

Kyel laughed in joy, scooping his son off the floor. He crushed him against his chest, rocking his little body from side to side. Gil's soft curls tickled his cheek, and his sharp knees ground into Kyel's ribs.

"I've missed you!" he exclaimed into his son's golden hair.

"Missed you too, Papa!" Gil squeezed tighter, wriggling in excitement. Kyel sat down on a chair and set Gil on his lap. He had to pry Gil's arms away from his neck to keep the blood flowing to his head. Kyel held his son against his chest, never wanting to let go. When Gil had enough, he laughed and squirmed out of the embrace.

Bouncing up and down on Kyel's leg, he exclaimed, "Papa! Did you fight a war?"

Kyel shook his head. "Not really." Then he thought about it. "I don't know. Maybe I did."

His son's eyes widened like saucers, his mouth forming an enormous O. *"You fought a war?"*

Kyel ruffled Gil's hair playfully. "Something like that."

"What is that?" Gil asked, pointing at the morning star Kyel had set down by the door. It wasn't a very good place for a spiked weapon, he realized.

"It's a magic stick," he said, grinning.

Gil made a sharp, excited gasp. "Can I have it? Please?"

Kyel shook his head. "No. It's not a toy. In fact, Papa needs to find somewhere else to put it." He lifted Gil and set him on the floor, then rose to find a better home for the talisman.

"Wanna wrestle?" Gil asked, bouncing up and down.

Kyel picked up Thar'gon and glanced around for a place to put it. His eyes leaped to a book case set against the wall. He placed the weapon on top, out of reach of curious hands.

"Papa's a bit tired," he admitted.

Undeterred, Gil clung to his leg and tugged as if trying to pry Kyel's foot off the floor. Kyel pinwheeled his arms then pretend-fell and rolled onto his stomach, letting Gil clamber on top of him.

"I win!"

"Yes, you beat me!" Kyel gasped, trying to catch his breath as his son bounced up and down on his back.

Gil slid off, got down on his belly, and stared Kyel in the face. "Are you a king?"

"No, not a king," Kyel laughed, pushing himself up and leaning back against the wall. Gil wormed his way over to him, sliding into his lap. He wrapped himself in the drape of Kyel's arm.

"Uncle Arvel said you're a king."

"Oh, he did, now?" Kyel frowned, not certain how he felt about 'Uncle' Arvel. And this king business.

"Are you a prince?"

"No. Just a mage."

"Oh. Love you anyway, Papa." Gil squeezed Kyel's arm tight.

Kyel embraced his son back. "I love you too, Gil."

A knock at the door destroyed the moment.

With a sigh, Kyel set his son on the floor and rose, crossing to the door. He opened it just a crack and peered out, prepared to tell whichever cleric was there to go away. To his surprise, he found Alexa waiting in the hallway.

He'd forgotten all about her.

Feeling chagrinned, Kyel turned to Gil. "I'll be right back," he said, then slipped sideways out the door, closing it before Gil could get a look at Alexa. Or before Alexa could get a look at his son. He wasn't sure which he was trying to prevent.

"I was just coming to check on you," he lied. Then he realized he'd lied. And he didn't care, which was the strange thing. Dismissing the train of thought, he asked her, "Are they treating you well?"

Alexa regarded him with an expression that was three parts irritation and one part disbelief, no doubt over his lack of concern. "Yes, if you call ignoring me treating me well. I told them I'm a mage, but they don't seem to believe me. I can't get anyone to fetch me so much as a cup of water."

Kyel wondered why Alexa just didn't fetch her own water. Swallowing his misgivings, he tried to mollify her. "I'll talk to them. I'm going to be meeting with—err, the High Priest—after supper."

Alexa's face lit up. "Am I invited to supper?"

Kyel doubted she was. Arvel certainly hadn't requested her company. Kyel found himself lying to her again. "I assume you are. They have to feed you, don't they?" Lying was a lot easier, he realized, than telling Alexa the truth. Her feelings were fragile, he was finding out.

"Is that your son?" She leaned forward, trying to peer past him through the crack in the door.

Kyel stepped sideways to block her view, pulling the door all the way closed behind him.

"Yes," he admitted, knowing Alexa must have caught a glimpse of Gil.

"Why is he here?"

That was indeed a long story, and one Kyel deeply regretted. Trying to make it as short as possible, he told her, "Meiran had me bring him here. She was hoping he'd inherited the Potential from me. We thought it wise for Gil to receive an education, just in case. With Aerysius gone, this temple is the best center of learning in the world."

"That makes sense," Alexa said, nodding. She glanced up at Kyel, her eyes full of candid innocence. "Doesn't he miss his mum?"

Kyel sighed, nodding. "He does. It was a hard choice." Looking into her eyes, he realized how easy it could be to forget Alexa was a mage.

She looked suddenly saddened. "Poor dear. What are you going to do with him after—"

Kyel put his hand up, stopping her. He had just been holding his son after five months of being apart from him. He didn't want to be reminded that these few moments might be the last he'd ever get with him.

Alexa's gaze slid downward. Apparently, she realized she'd overstepped. She said quietly, "Maybe there's something you can do. Some way you can stay with him."

Kyel's anger flared. The last thing he needed was hope. "No," he said firmly.

"Maybe we can find a way," she insisted, her eyes brightening.

"It's impossible."

Alexa shook her head. "Nothing's impossible." She set a hand on his arm and squeezed it reassuringly. "Don't lose hope, Kyel," she said, then turned and walked back down the corridor.

Kyel stared after her, silently seething. Alexa was wrong. Hope was just a delusion people clung to in order to make life seem bearable. What they didn't understand was how much worse they'd feel when hope inevitably failed. He wasn't going to make that mistake. He wasn't going to be deluded into thinking that he'd have more time to spend with his son and show Gil how much he loved him.

To Kyel's surprise, Arvel relented and allowed Alexa to join them for supper. Not that it mattered. It was the most uncomfortable meal Kyel had ever been forced to sit through. Not a word was spoken that wasn't necessary. All parties sat on different sides of the table. Possibly different sides of the war. If Arvel and the old man next to him were conversing, Kyel couldn't tell. Both seemed just as intent on ignoring each other as they were bent on ignoring him.

When the meal was finished, Alexa pushed back her plate. "Thank you, Your Eminence, for your graceful hospitality," she said, breaking the resounding tension.

Arvel smiled at her indulgently. "His Eminence appreciates

your gratitude. However, he does ask that you excuse us now. We wish to spend some time alone with Kyel."

Alexa shot Kyel a questioning look. He ignored her.

"Of course," she muttered, seeming flustered. "My apologies." She scooted her chair back and, with one last, stabbing glare at Kyel, exited the room. The door closed behind her more roughly than it should have.

Kyel took his time about folding his napkin. He set it down carefully on the table. Then he turned to look at the High Priest. Or whatever the silent old man actually was. More than a puppet but less than a figurehead, Kyel supposed. He wasn't surprised when the old man rose and followed Alexa out of the room.

Kyel watched his exit, feeling somewhat grateful for the man's departure. He turned to Arvel and spread his hands. "Well. Here I am."

"Yes," Arvel said with a condescending look. "Here you are. Let's start with that woman. Do you trust her?"

"No," Kyel said honestly.

"Interesting. And yet you travel with her."

He shrugged. "I don't distrust her, either."

Arvel planted an elbow on the table, cradling his face with his hand. "I'm aware of the peculiar way you found that woman— Cadmus was able to relay the information to us before he was slain. Let's just say…I am concerned. At the very least. You see, Alexa Newell's name was added to the List years ago."

Kyel had heard the clerics of Om referring to that List once before. He'd assumed it meant some type of catalogue of deaths.

Arvel continued, "It is possible this woman you know as Alexa is exactly what she seems. And if that's all she is, then she may be a tremendous asset. With her, there exists the possibility that together you might seal the Well of Tears before you pass from this world."

Kyel's mouth dropped open. He hadn't thought of that. Arvel was right—that would be a tremendous opportunity. Although Alexa was only a Master, not a Grand Master. They would have to find a way to Transfer her at least one more tier of power.

"There is also the chance she will betray you," Arvel continued darkly. "Be very wary of her. There is only one god who has ever returned a soul from beyond the Veil. And Xerys is very real."

Kyel nodded, pondering the implications. "Point taken."

"Now, as far as the talisman you inherited from Byron Connel—"

The man suddenly went rigid, his eyes narrowing to white slits, his lashes fluttering. The knuckles of his hands turned a milky white. He sat there tensed for a long, frightful moment. Then he opened his mouth and exhaled a great gasp, his body sagging as if melting into his seat. He opened his eyes.

"We're out of time," Arvel said, his gaze shooting up to lock on Kyel's. "Lauchlin's army has arrived and has cordoned off the entrance to the valley. For all intents and purposes, we are under siege."

"What are you going to do?" Kyel asked.

Arvel pushed his chair back and rose, tossing his napkin on the table. "We are prepared to field every able-bodied priest, monk, and layman of every temple. For the past few days, we've been fortifying the valley's mouth."

Kyel followed him to his feet. "We need to negotiate."

"There's nothing to negotiate." Arvel waved him off, making his way around the table.

Kyel moved to block him. "We don't even know what he wants."

The man studied Kyel intently, as if peering deep into his soul. "Darien Lauchlin is a Servant of Xerys who has brought an army to the Valley of the Gods. What do you think he wants?" He lifted his eyebrows.

"I'm going to talk to him," Kyel said, resolute.

Arvel stared at him flatly. "He'll kill you."

"No, he won't. He already had that chance. He didn't take it." In the dungeon of Greystone Keep, Darien had been a hairsbreadth away from ending his life, Kyel felt certain. He'd seen it in his eyes. He still wasn't sure why Darien had held back.

"How do you know he won't change his mind?" Arvel pressed.

"Because I know him."

The man fixed him with a hard-as-granite stare. "And he

knows you."

"No, he doesn't. Not anymore."

Chapter Twenty-Three
Parley

Glen Farquist, The Rhen

The wind howled and shrieked like a murder. The gale battered Kyel's back, pushing him forward as he walked with Arvel and Alexa up a rise of sandstone steps that snaked upward to the crest of a low hill, the only truly defensible position on the valley floor. The steps had been worn down so much, they were almost a ramp. They led to the surface of a thick stone slab of chiseled marble: the footprint of an ancient temple, now reduced to a jumble of toppled columns.

Arvel led them across the foundation toward a group of men and women clustered at the far edge. Kyel stopped behind Arvel and watched as the man inserted himself into the group of robed priests and priestesses. He exchanged greetings and small talk, while Kyel stood on the edge of the gathering, waiting and watching, wondering how long he was going to be ignored.

After a long interval, Arvel turned and beckoned him over, the bronze sleeves of his robe billowed by the scolding wind. Kyel complied with a scowl, moving only close enough to be within earshot.

Arvel had to shout to be heard over the wind. "This is His Eminence! Ansel Stroud! The High Priest of Zephia!" He indicated a man standing next to him who wore a dark beard and a darker glower. Kyel recognized him. He'd met the man before, at a gathering of temple patriarchs. He hadn't liked Stroud then, and he liked him less now.

"I'm sure you remember Kyel Archer!" Arvel shouted at the priest, who stared at Kyel and didn't respond.

Kyel nodded a curt greeting that seemed to ruffle the man.

Arvel excused himself with a wave and a smile, moving off the foundation in a crackling ripple of oversized robes. Kyel stared after him, more unsettled than angry. He turned back to the Patriarch of Zephia, wondering who, between the two of them, was supposed to be in charge.

He leaned forward and shouted at the priest, "I'm going down there! I want to see if he'll negotiate!"

"He won't negotiate," Stroud disagreed. "We have nothing to offer him!"

Kyel thought about it. "We can tell him if he surrenders, we'll let them keep the North."

The priest took a step back, staring at Kyel with a look of gaping disbelief. "You can't just give them the North!"

Kyel shot him a disdainful glare. "They've already *taken* the North!"

With that, he swung away from the man and strode toward the stairs. The wind tore at his cloak and raked at his hair as he descended the worn steps toward the valley floor. There, a group of monks from one of the militant orders fell in around him, escorting him toward the tall cliffs that surrounded the valley.

The wind lessened as they approached the bluffs, finally giving way altogether, blocked by the walls of the bottleneck canyon that formed the valley's entrance.

Kyel followed the path through the canyon as it wound like a serpent's coils through the surrounding cliffs. The walls of the passage were high, made of stratified layers of tawny sandstone. A fast stream lined with ragged boulders ran its course along the base of the cliffs, bordered by a road only wide enough to drive a cart along.

At the mouth of the canyon, Kyel halted and looked over the temples' fortifications, in the form of mud berms, trenches, and spiked palisades warded by overlooking bluffs. The entire plain had been altered to create a narrowing path that would slow and direct the movements of an advancing army.

Kyel was impressed. He wouldn't have credited Glen Farquist's priests with that kind of tactical industry. Across the canyon's entrance, they had dug a deep trench impossible to jump across or go around. If Darien wanted his men to advance into the canyon, he would have to fill that trench with corpses.

Beyond the trench, out of bowshot of the bluffs, the Enemy army had gathered in a wedge-shaped formation. Kyel stared out at it, shielding his eyes from the sun's stabbing glare. Their numbers were far fewer than he'd anticipated. Apparently, the poisoned cider had worked even better than expected, though at enormous cost. It was just unfortunate that Darien hadn't been one of the casualties.

To his guard of armored clerics, Kyel ordered, "Wait here."

He reached down and unhooked Thar'gon from his belt. Holding the spiked artifact at his side, he walked away from the security of the earthworks and crossed the flat plain toward the trench. The wind gained strength again as he moved further from the protection of the canyon walls. But the wind was only a ghost of its former strength. The air stirred as though hesitant to add to the tension already gripping the plain.

Kyel stopped when he reached the trench. To either side of his own position, the priests had stationed foot soldiers against the canyon walls. Kyel was aware he was standing in the center of a bloodbath waiting to happen, but he wasn't afraid. With Thar'gon in his hand, he didn't have any reason to be.

Ahead, a lone figure parted off from the Enemy line and advanced toward him. Kyel knew it was Darien even before he could see his face. The darkmage had a way of moving that was unmistakable, even at a distance, like the fluid grace of a predator. Kyel held his ground, waiting as Darien approached and halted before him on the far side of the trench.

Kyel considered his adversary for a long moment, wishing he could peer into the shadows of the man's soul. When it came to Darien, he didn't know what to believe. The man seemed to be walking a thin line between reason and inhumanity. Each time Kyel saw him, Darien seemed to land with both feet planted firmly on one side or the other. Kyel wondered which side of morality Darien would be walking today.

He wouldn't know without speaking with him.

Kyel closed his eyes and, lifting Thar'gon, whispered, *"Vergis."*

The world shivered. When he opened his eyes, Kyel found himself standing an arm's length from Darien's face.

Darien danced back, his sword already halfway out of its sheath. With a smoldering glare, he slid the blade fully back again. His eyes flicked to the talisman in Kyel's hand, which seemed to give him pause.

"You've learned how to use it," he said.

Kyel lowered Thar'gon and hooked the weapon to his belt. "Hello, Darien."

The man nodded slightly. He looked more sinister than Kyel remembered, his eyes cold and void of emotion. A dark power radiated from him, distorting the air around him. Kyel found himself scrutinizing Darien's face, trying to figure out what manner of man stood before him. If he was demon or madman. Or both.

After a moment, Kyel asked, "What are your intentions?"

"I'm here to take the valley." Darien gazed at him with a frigid expression.

"Why?"

"I think you know. The temples are a threat to us. They seek to drive us back into the Black Lands. I'm not going to let that happen."

So Darien wasn't a madman.

Kyel said, "It's not your people they fear. Only your god."

"Xerys is but one god in the pantheon."

Kyel spread his hands. "You need to be reasonable. You've taken the North. You've given your people hope and sunlight and a place to live. But in doing so, you've displaced thousands. Where are they supposed to go? What are they supposed to eat? They left everything behind—"

"They will live."

Kyel winced, shocked by the vehemence in Darien's voice. He stood regarding the darkmage warily. The power radiating from Darien's presence seemed to pulsate.

Somehow, he found the courage to glare his former master in

the eye. "What about the people who *didn't* live? What about the people you killed?"

Darien shrugged coldly. "They had their chance. They didn't take it. It all boils down to this: you, Meiran, the temples—you didn't leave us any options. We threw ourselves on your mercy, and you betrayed us. Any blood that's been spilt—that's on your hands. Not ours. We tried to negotiate a peaceful solution. You wouldn't have it."

Kyel cursed Meiran. And the temples. And Darien, for always sounding rational even when trying to justify atrocity. It took him a moment to sort through the logic of it all, to come to the conclusion that just because something was rational, that didn't by default make it right.

He said, "You've already taken what you need. Any more's just greed. Work with us. We're willing to forge a treaty. We'll cede you the North, if you halt your advance and cease hostilities. Right here. Today. Otherwise, you're looking at a war of attrition that will last generations. And ultimately, we will win."

Darien stared at him for long seconds with a gaze that never wavered. At last, he said, "It's a tempting offer. Two months ago, I'd have taken it." He shook his head, stepping back. "But I'm not falling for false promises again. Tell the priests I said go fuck themselves. I'm going to turn their temples into their tombs."

Kyel gritted his teeth, his frustration on the verge of boiling over. It didn't have to be this way. If Meiran and the temples had just upheld the treaty they'd negotiated—

"Darien—"

But Darien ignored him and stalked away. Kyel growled, ripping Thar'gon off his belt. He closed his eyes, envisioning the stone foundation with its worn stairs and toppled columns. The ground shifted beneath him. He opened his eyes to find Alexa and the priest of Zephia staring at him expectantly.

"No luck." He sighed.

The priest didn't look surprised. Wind whipping his hair, he raised his voice, saying, "It doesn't matter! We have superior numbers. The terrain works in our favor, giving us great advantage. And we have a Sentinel." He stared hard at Kyel with an expression that looked almost like a threat.

"And they have a Battlemage," Kyel reminded him.

Alexa turned toward him. "It's time for you to let go of your Oath."

"No." Kyel couldn't believe she would ask that of him. She was a Master of Aerysius herself, and just as Bound as he was. He shouldn't have to argue with her about all the reasons he refused to bend on the issue.

"It doesn't matter anymore!" she pressed. "Kyel! The Oath exists to protect you from moral decay over your lifetime! But you don't have a lifetime—you have days! The Oath of Harmony doesn't apply to you!"

Her words brought Darien's image to mind, a reminder that galvanized Kyel's resolve. "I'm not turning into *him*." he snapped. "I won't do it!"

Darien dropped to a crouch beside Azár and Sayeed. He picked up a stick and drew a broad V in the dirt, then gathered a handful of rocks and took some time positioning them along the sides. He embellished his crude map with leaves and sticks, arranging them carefully.

"It's not good," he reported. He scooted a rock over, nudging it into position with his finger. "They've had time to prepare for us. They've made the entire canyon into a death trap. And they've got a Sentinel."

"Your apprentice?" Azár looked at him with confusion in her eyes. "The man who saved you from the dungeon? Will he fight against you?"

Darien scowled. "Kyel marches to the beat of his morals. He sees the value in our cause, but he disagrees with how we're going about it. He doesn't understand that sometimes you have to spill blood to save blood."

He pointed the stick at the V on the ground. "They've positioned infantry and archers along the sides of the canyon here…and here. They've left their center vulnerable. I think that's intentional. They're going to try to draw us in, then flank us. We'll have to counter that by attacking their wings." He drew an arrow in the dirt then looked up at Sayeed, "You take the Zakai and try to roll them up on the left. I'll take the center and keep the arrows off you."

"What about your apprentice?" Azár asked with a worried frown.

Darien tapped the stick against his leg. It took him a second longer than it should have to reach a final decision. "I'll deal with Kyel."

"This Sentinel," Sayeed said slowly. "How well does he know you?"

Darien ignored him.

Sayeed reached out and caught the stick, forcing Darien to look at him.

"Take mind," Sayeed said with a sharp glare of warning. "This man is more dangerous than you think. Do not underestimate him."

"I won't," Darien said, relinquishing the stick.

Chapter Twenty-Four
The Battle of Glen Farquist

Glen Farquist, The Rhen

"Look," Sayeed said, nodding in the direction of the cliffs. Darien removed his helm and, tucking it into the crook of his arm, peered out across the bunchgrass-cobbled plain. The militia of priests remained behind the protection of their trench: long lines of foot soldiers four to eight men deep. The wings of their army extended out along the base of the surrounding bluffs. Darien gazed ahead, uncertain what Sayeed was trying to indicate.

"What do you see?"

"The banners," Sayeed said. "They do not stir in the wind."

Darien stared harder across the plain. The wind surged in random gusts, and yet the banners of the temples remained becalmed. "He's learned control of the wind," he grumbled. "That means he can shield."

Azár asked, "How will that affect us?"

He shrugged. Kyel wielded Thar'gon, but Darien doubted he'd learned much control over it. And Kyel's hands were tied by the chains on his wrists. So was his effectiveness.

Sayeed pursed his lips in troubled thought. "It is an ill-omened day for battle. Perhaps it is best to wait."

"Ill-omened?" Darien echoed. "How so?"

"The moon is overhead in the daylight, looking down." The officer glanced upward toward the faded disk of the moon. "Many believe it is a sign of the gods' disapproval, for we make war against their home."

Darien cursed the Malikari love of superstition. "The gods

don't live in Glen Farquist. As far as the moon's concerned, it's a natural cycle. We can't stand here waiting for the moon to wax."

Sayeed nodded, though he looked far from reassured. If anything, he looked resigned to a dismal end. Darien decided to let the man stew, his thoughts returning to Kyel, the one variable he couldn't predict.

He said to Azár, "I want you to stay back here, out of the battle."

His wife stabbed him with an outraged glare. "I will not stay back while my husband wages war! You promised you would never ask this—"

"I *need* you behind us," Darien snapped, more harshly than he'd intended. "If something goes wrong—if they do manage to flank us—then I'll need you in reserve at our rear. And if Kyel does give me problems, then I'll need you even more. I doubt he can manage the both of us at once, coming at him from two directions."

Her expression softened somewhat. At last, she nodded. "I will be where you need me most," she conceded. "My husband is a wise commander." Without another word, she turned and walked away from the line.

Darien heaved a sigh. The battle hadn't yet begun, and already the gods seemed against him. "All right." He tugged his helm down over his head. "Let's have at it."

Sayeed shook his head in silence, looking grim. Darien ignored him and drew his sword, the blade carried by Khoresh Kateem into the Battle of Harmudi. He hoped the sword would bring him equal success. He raised the blade high over his head. Then he brought it down, leveling the point at his enemy.

"*At them.*"

The lines of infantry behind him started forward, Darien striding ahead of them with Sayeed at his side, surrounded by a protective ring of elite Zakai. He drew deeply on the magic field and fed its energy. Magelight erupted beneath their feet, a blue mist that spread quickly across the ground. He increased the energy, until the magelight condensed into cobalt tongues of whipping mist that advanced beneath the feet of his army. The magelight produced the desired effect. The first ranks of defenders edged back despite their officers' commands to hold their line.

The first volley of arrows arced toward them, darkening the air. Darien waited until they reached the apex of their flight, then lashed out at them with force. The arrows shattered overhead, showering them with broken shafts. Another dark cloud met a similar fate. And another. Darien lashed out at volley after volley, knocking the arrows from the sky with furious waves of solid air.

Another arrow cloud lofted toward them, this one far larger than the rest. Darien reached out from within, summoning enough power to shatter every arrow in the sky.

The slap of air never connected.

It reversed direction and hurled back on him.

The wall of air impacted before he could react, lifting him up and slamming him to the ground. The wind knocked from his lungs, Darien lay gasping on his back, his mind struggling to make sense of what had just happened. It took him a moment to realize every man in his guard had been affected, most lying sprawled next to him in the dirt.

Darien pushed himself up, coughing and shaken. All around him, soldiers were struggling to stand, staggering back into position to reform their rank. Some of the men remained on the ground, unmoving. Darien stood blinking in a daze, his ears ringing. His mind fumbled to understand the implications of what had just occurred.

Kyel was Bound. Had he relinquished his Oath of Harmony?

Then it hit him: Kyel hadn't directly harmed a single person. He had simply deflected an oncoming assault. It was Darien's own magic that had inflicted the damage. He cursed his own arrogance. Kyel had made himself into a formidable Sentinel in only two years without tutelage. Darien hadn't thought it possible.

Another volley of arrows launched toward them. He reacted—not fast enough. The arrows peppered the ground, pelting his armor. With a growl, Darien surged forward. His men followed, covering the remaining distance under a constant barrage of arrows, the archers across the trench loosing their shafts at will.

As they closed the distance, the arrows started coming harder, no longer arcing through the air, but hurling toward them parallel to the ground. The bodkin points clanged off his armor, almost hard enough to pierce. Men to both sides started to drop. Darien threw up a shield thick enough to slow the arrows' flight—but weak enough that Kyel couldn't repurpose it into a weapon.

When they gained the trench, Darien dropped the shield and wove a web of shadow to span the gap. The web was thin as gossamer but strong enough to bear significant weight. He stood back, channeling every drop of power he could handle into maintaining it. Sayeed and the Zakai remained by his side, keeping a vigilant watch, while the rest of the Tanisars rushed forward.

When the last foot soldier cleared the bridge, Darien sprinted across the trench then dropped the shadow-bridge. He threw the shield back up. Just in time—one last volley of arrows clattered against it.

With a cry, his warriors impacted with the priests' front lines, fighting to batter their way through. Darien drew up just short of the melee, Zakai swarming into a defensive position around him. There was little he could do against the enemy as a whole. So he started attacking the priests individually.

One by one, he dropped them to the ground. Darien stood looking from face to face. Everywhere he looked, scowls of fury turned to grimaces of agony. He moved forward, wielding death to clear a path ahead of him.

He took his time, picking his way over the corpses collecting under his feet. Men and women scrambled out of his way with looks of horror.

They didn't get far. Darien pushed further into the thick of the fighting, until the bodies of the fallen became too dense an obstacle to wade through any longer.

A thundering battle cry rang across the canyon, making Darien turn. Behind, some of their men had broken away from the main force to attack the priests' left wing, charging toward the foot soldiers that lined the cliffs. And drew up short, halfway there.

Men cried out in dismay and dropped their weapons, tottering over their feet. Others fell to the ground, then tried to worm their way forward on their stomachs. Arrows rained down from the tops of the cliffs, finding easy marks.

At first, Darien couldn't understand what was happening.

It took him a moment to realize the ground beneath the troops had dissolved into a quagmire.

Kyel.

Again, the Sentinel had found a way to reap a harvest of lives without breaking his Oath.

Men screamed, lurching for firm ground and not finding it.

Priests armed with crossbows sprang forward, slaughtering the helpless soldiers mired in the mud. Soon, the ground beneath them ran red with spilt blood.

Darien broke away from the melee and started back across the canyon.

His Zakai escort swept ahead of him, slaying anyone who stood in their path. A rank of pikemen spilled forward, charging their position. Without breaking stride, Darien threw up a hand and stopped their hearts.

Kyel clenched Thar'gon so hard that his arm was shaking. The talisman glowed with a brilliant light, radiating enough power to heat the air around it. At his side, Alexa clung to his arm, her mouth open, eyes wide in an expression of awed exhilaration. Ravaged by the wind, her hair whipped against her face, giving her a wild appearance.

Kyel watched in satisfaction as the Enemy soldiers trapped in the mud were set upon by a group of warrior-priests. The sight of their slaughter chilled him, making him writhe inside his own skin. He had to keep reminding himself that he hadn't killed even one man. Not one. Yet hundreds were dying as a result of his actions. The realization made him want to vomit. With Thar'gon in his hand, he had already decimated a third of Darien's attack force. It was as though the talisman were wielding him, instead of the other way around. He was merely the weapon's conduit, nothing more.

Worse, the raw feeling of power was exhilarating, intoxicating. It was like being a god without being godly. All trace of fear inside him had been brushed aside. With the talisman in his hand, Kyel felt indomitable.

Because he was.

He saw Darien's small band of men break away from the main force, sprinting toward those being butchered in the quagmire.

"You have to stop him!" Alexa cried.

Kyel closed his eyes and tried. "I can't! He's too far away!"

Alexa tugged at his arm. "The true strength of that artifact is mobility!" she cried. "Don't stay in one place! Go where you need to be! Use it to control the field of battle!"

She was right. He wasn't using the talisman to its full potential. But if he were...

Kyel closed his eyes, visualizing the ground behind the trench. *"Vergis."*

Darien staggered to a stop, realizing the only thing left ahead of him was dead warriors and blood-wet earth. Furious, he lashed out at the retreating defenders, burning the priests to char. Then burning the char to ash. The screams were satisfying. His gaze snapped back to the corpses of his men lying in a trough of oozing mud. His mouth went dry. His mind yet grappled with the concept that Kyel could pose any threat at all. Certainly nothing this devastating.

Reeling, Darien backed away from the slaughter.

He turned to find that the priests had regrouped. They had taken advantage of his absence to flank what was left of his assault force. Already, his men were nearly enveloped.

Sprinting forward, Darien pulled at the magic field, filling himself until he burned with charged power. Holding it steady, he drew next on the Onslaught, then wrapped the contradictory energies together in a knot. He launched that volatile missile at the charging priests. The hurling magic flew like a comet across the battlefield—

—and exploded in the air as if hitting a wall.

The recoil hit Darien in the face, smashing him to the ground. The world went red and then black. He blinked rapidly to clear his vision, gasping for breath.

Sayeed knelt at his side, blood running freely down the left side of his face. "Brother!"

His voice sounded strangely muffled. Darien saw that many of his Zakai lay sprawled across the ground, either dead or unconscious. The man nearest him had been dismembered. The head, still helmed, lay a good distance away.

Sayeed stood above him, repulsing the attacks of three monks who had seen Darien on the ground and were trying to exploit the opportunity. His blade wove through the air in great, slashing arcs. Kicking one man back, he drew a cut across another man's belly in time to parry an attack by the third. Sayeed brought his sword around in a diagonal slash that ended the fight.

He dropped to the ground next to Darien and hauled him upright by the arms.

"Can you walk?" he gasped.

Darien nodded. Gritting his teeth, he struggled back to his feet. He spat a mouthful of blood that stringed from his lips. Eyes searching for Kyel, he reached up and tightened his helmet's cinch, then started forward again. Ahead, his men were on the verge of being overwhelmed.

"Can you counter him?" Sayeed demanded.

Darien ignored the question. A group of priests had marked his position and were charging his way. His few remaining Zakai sprang in front of him, ready to shield him with their lives.

"Get down!" Darien shouted, forcing his way through the ring of Zakai. He dropped the magic field entirely and summoned the Onslaught, wielding the power of hell in both hands before flinging it headlong at the charging priests.

The men rushing them stumbled and fell screaming to the ground. They writhed in the dirt, wailing horrifically as their flesh began to dissolve. Their agony didn't last long.

"Narghul," Darien whispered.

A host of necrators bled up from the ground like shadowy

wraiths: a hellish ring of protection. Darien's blood turned to ice. It was as though the creatures sucked the heat right out of his body to feed their own existence.

He willed them forward. The necrators obeyed, ranging out across the battlefield in search of souls to consume. They were a last resort; necrators were indiscriminate in their killing.

He turned to Sayeed.

And saw Kyel standing behind him.

Darien shouted a warning, shoving Sayeed out of the way. He lashed out viciously with the Hellpower.

Kyel merely waved his hand, deflecting the assault. Darien gaped at him in shock, taking a step backward. Then another, his mind reeling toward panic.

"*Run,*" Darien gasped.

Sayeed and the Zakai obeyed, but Darien didn't follow. Instead, he turned back to face his adversary.

"*How?*" he gasped.

Kyel raised his weapon. It shimmered with power, brilliant and blinding. Darien took one, good look into Kyel's eyes. Then he turned and started running.

Kyel sensed he had one chance—one chance—to take Darien to the ground, to rid the world of him forever. He could hear Alexa's persistent voice in the back of his mind, begging him to abandon his Oath.

All it would take was one strike with the talisman. One act.

And Thar'gon was eager. He could feel its need, the weapon's desire to dominate. He swept the morning star back, preparing a strike that would send Darien's twisted soul back to his master.

Kyel growled and lowered the weapon, unable to complete the act.

His eyes tracked Darien as he sprinted away. He was losing his opportunity. His mind sifted through options.

Then it came to him. The answer was obvious.

Concentrating, Kyel willed the air to thicken around Darien. He watched the darkmage slow to a stop, stumbling, fighting to stay on his feet. Kyel tightened his grip on his weapon, concentrating harder. When Darien struck out at his invisible cage, Kyel was ready. He reflected the attack back on him. Darien staggered and fell, blood streaming down his face. He tried to get up, but Kyel thickened the air more and held him there.

He thinned the shield, allowing Darien enough air to breathe. Enemy soldiers rallied to his aid but could do nothing against the bubble of solid air that contained him. As his men watched, Darien lashed out at his prison with the magic field, with the Onslaught, with anything and everything he could throw at it.

Nothing worked.

All of Darien's demonic power was useless against Thar'gon's great might.

Kyel smiled triumphantly. He raised his hand in the air, signaling the priests to move in.

For the first time in his life, he saw real fear in Darien Lauchlin's eyes. The darkmage railed against his prison as the priests closed the distance, swords and crossbows raised. The harder Darien struggled, the stronger the shield became, absorbing his power to reinforce its structure.

Eventually, Darien gave up. He knelt on the ground, head bowed as though defeated.

Then, slowly, he looked up and locked his stare on Kyel, his eyes black pools of shadow that burned like hellish coals. He raised his hand. His lips moved silently.

A terrible chill pierced Kyel's heart. And a more terrible feeling of dread.

He whirled to find three necrators hovering behind him.

Fear clenched Kyel's throat, choking him, terrorizing him. He couldn't move, couldn't breathe. The arm that held Thar'gon sagged uselessly to his side. Like a fickle lover, the magic field abandoned him.

Wide-eyed, Kyel stared into the face of the nearest necrator and saw his own death gazing back at him. He wanted to run, but that was impossible. The fear was too raw, too paralyzing. It slithered out of his gut, tightening its grip on his chest, numbing his mind.

Kyel's hand opened reflexively, dropping the talisman.

A shadowy hand reached toward him, fingers groping to touch his face.

"Kyel!"

Something shoved him backward, hurling him away from the wraith's outstretched hand. He staggered as his mind was suddenly released from the paralyzing grip of terror. He glanced back to see Alexa standing between the necrator and himself, hands raised in the air, fingers splayed. Somehow, she was holding the demon at bay.

He couldn't leave her there. She had no chance against such a creature.

But neither did he. Kyel scooped Thar'gon off the ground and did the only thing he could do.

"Vergis!" he whispered.

The cage of air disappeared. Darien bellowed in rage as Kyel disappeared with it. His eyes darted toward the woman—

—but she was already gone. So were his minions. He felt their loss, as though a piece of his soul had been torn out of him. He stood rooted to the ground, crippled by shock and disbelief. He started forward toward the place where the woman had just been standing.

"No!" Sayeed bellowed. He caught Darien by the shoulder and spun him around. "Brother, we must flee!"

"That woman—" Darien began.

An explosion erupted on the far side of the battlefield. And then another. A shockwave hit, deafening. Darien could feel the thunder of it. Screams of death and terror erupted all around, ringing off the cliffs. More fires sprang out of the ground, one after another, traveling across the canyon floor in quick succession.

Everywhere Darien looked, priests were running aflame. The melee disintegrated into bedlam as screaming men and women fought and clawed and battered their way clear of the flames.

Darien stood stunned, watching it all unfold before him as if staring inward at a dream. Black smoke billowed over the battle-field, obscuring his sight. The entire scene seemed disjointed and surreal.

Before him, a lone figure emerged from the thick haze of smoke, moving toward him with a confident stride. At first, he thought it was Kyel, returned to slay him.

But it was not.

"Azár," Darien whispered in awe.

Chapter Twenty-Five
Branching and Unbranching

Isle of Titherry, The Rhen

"Are you sure you can do this by yourself?" Quin asked. "You're not a Harbinger."

Naia paused, one hand lingering on the balustrade, and looked back at him. Quin stood on the balcony overlooking the Crescent with his hat in hand, hair tousled by the wind. He was trying to look unruffled but failing miserably. He hadn't seemed right in days. Not since the morning they'd buried Tsula.

"I am the closest thing to a Harbinger there is left in the world," Naia corrected him. "I no longer need Tsula's guidance. At least, not to read the Crescent."

His brow furrowed. "In my time, it took twenty years to train a Harbinger." He bounced his hat against his leg. "Don't you think you might be getting ahead of yourself?"

Naia shot him a reproving look. "Most of the training Harbingers received went toward teaching them how to cope with their visions. Simply reading the Crescent is effortless."

Quin planted his hat squarely on his head. "Is that why Tsula had the personality of a rock?"

"Harbingers were trained to let go of all attachments and emotions. I think it was the only way they could protect themselves from going insane."

"I don't want you going up there," he said firmly, his face stern.

"I'm going up there," she insisted, and set a hand on his arm. "That's the reason why we're here. With Tsula gone, I might see new versions that were not available before. I have to try. I'm going to die, anyway, in just a few days—"

"No, you're not."

Looking suddenly more dangerous than she'd ever seen him, Quin stared at her piercingly. He held her gaze steady for a long moment, then leaned in to press a slow, lingering kiss on her lips.

"Come back to me," he ordered, his eyes still fixed on hers.

Naia swallowed, taken aback. And stunned by the bold feelings his kiss inspired. She licked her lips and turned away, feeling off-balance. This wasn't the Quin she had known, she realized. Tsula's death had changed him.

A bolt of understanding rocked her hard. This was Quin the way he used to be, she realized. This was the man he had been, before Amani's death had extinguished the spark within him. Naia turned slowly back around, searching his face for confirmation. Quin regarded her with a steady confidence she'd never seen before.

"I'll come back," she assured him.

Naia turned away and walked through the stone balustrade onto the arching path of transparent stepping stones. The breeze caressed her face and fanned her hair. It felt cool, even as the sun felt warm on her skin. She followed the invisible path out over the mercurial surface of the Crescent toward the Nexus.

Steadying herself, Naia passed through the thin membrane. Entering the room always reminded her of the way a stick can pass through the surface of a bubble without bursting it. Inside, she found herself once again within the dark, spherical chamber. The silver tendrils writhed across the walls like vines, twining and untwining, branching and unbranching. Naia moved forward until she was standing in the exact center of the sphere.

There, she closed her eyes and emptied her mind of all thought, until the only thing in the world that mattered was the sound of her own heartbeat. She stood there a moment, settling into the serene bliss of emptiness, letting her mind drift on the ebb and flow of her breath.

Then, from out of the darkness, a silvery filament emerged and uncoiled. It grew, branching and twirling, coiling and vining. It fed her with a soft luminescence that grew slowly, throbbing like a pulse. The darkness abandoned her, her mind washing after it.

The epitome of all storms—the storm that every other storm aspired to be—raged and ripped through the atmosphere. All was fading, all was dying. And she was dying with it.

"I can't stand it!" Naia shrieked to the absent gods.

She could feel the magic field stretched around her to its thin limit. And then it ripped. Naia screamed her life away, feeling her mind heated to boiling inside her skull.

With a shriek, Naia opened her eyes. All around her, the walls throbbed to the time of her heartbeat. Cold sweat dribbled down her face, and she gasped for breath. She stood there a moment, steadying herself until her pulse finally slowed. The vision had been too real.

And it was not the first time she had experienced it. That version was the most likely ending to her Story. Every time she came here, it was always the first version she was subjected to. She should be used to it by now. Desensitized. But she wasn't. It was impossible to grow accustomed to the act of dying.

She took a deep breath and closed her eyes again, letting her mind seep back into that dark and empty place.

The wind howled a monstrous wail as it rampaged through the mountains, terrorizing the clouds, which fled wildly before it. In front of her, Darien lay in an expanding pool of blood, more blood than any human body could possibly contain. It spread rapidly, as if seeking to saturate the entire Circle of Convergence. Or the entire world. Or the universe.

Standing behind her, Zavier Renquist lifted Quin's sword and swept it back over his shoulder. "Let the reign of Xerys begin!" he snarled, and cleaved Naia's head off.

Gasping a sharp hiss of breath between her teeth, Naia opened her eyes. Out of all the possible versions she'd been subjected to, she found that one the most chilling. Not only was it the most visceral, but it was also the most desperate, the most dire. She was left with the ominous feeling that the price of failure was much greater than any of the other versions. She didn't know where that future led; she couldn't read anything beyond her own death. But she knew with certainty that the resulting fate would be appalling.

With a shudder, Naia cleared her mind and, glad to be rid of that terrible image, closed her eyes.

Kyel advanced across the Circle of Convergence, wielding a glowing silver talisman in his hand. In the center of the Circle—in full command of it— Zavier Renquist swept out a fist. A blinding glare of light whiter than bright and brilliantly powerful assaulted Kyel from the sky. He was hurled across the terrace, the talisman flying from his hand.

The green pillar in the sky above exploded in fury. The magic field wailed in protest, in defiance, in outrage.

Then it went forever silent.

Naia's eyes snapped open. Inside, she roiled in a cauldron of despair and grief. That version of the future was the most painful, left her aching with a tremendous sense of loss. Every time she witnessed it, she was left heartbroken.

And that was the last version. There were never any more after that, only slight variations of those three. Those were her only possible futures, and all three were horrendous.

It was time to push beyond. With Tsula gone, it was time to forge ahead, to see if there were any more possibilities she hadn't yet encountered.

Naia closed her eyes and let the silvery tendrils uncoil. She cleared her mind and let the visions seep into her.

The epitome of all storms—the storm that every other storm aspired to be— raged and ripped across the atmosphere. Thunder lashed against the cliffs, and lightning the color of blood sliced wounds in the air. The wind howled a monstrous wail as it rampaged through the mountains, terrorizing the clouds, which fled wildly before it. The world screamed in mortal anguish, and Naia screamed with it.

Kyel was below them in the chamber of the Well of Tears. Wielding his silver talisman against the portal while the Reversal was still maximized.

Sprawled in the center of the Circle of Convergence, Darien lay in an expanding pool of blood. The blood was artery-red and voluminous—far more than one human body could possibly contain. It spread rapidly, as if seeking to saturate the entire Circle. Or the entire world. Or the universe.

A thunderous clap of air sent Renquist hurling to the ground. Naia looked up in terror, in hope, in desperation. She gasped in disbelief.

Blood streaming down his face, Quin stalked toward her across the glowing Circle of Convergence, Kyel's silver talisman glowing like a beacon in his hand.

"Run, Naia!" he shouted. Hefting the weapon, Quin advanced toward Renquist.

Naia froze. It was wrong. It was all terribly, terribly wrong.

"No, Quin!" she shrieked. "Leave him! Help Darien!"

Zavier Renquist rose to his feet, eyes menacing pools of shadow. He raised his hand and struck out at her with the Onslaught.

Naia screamed as the world around her broke apart, shattering like glass into a thousand tiny fragments, each with its own awful reality. She caught brief glimpses of each, each more terrible than the last.

She lived a thousand lifetimes in a heartbeat.

And a thousand deaths.

Naia collapsed to her knees, bent over in horror. Bringing her hands up to her face, she choked on tears. Quin was right: Tsula had been blocking her.

Now, her block was lifted. She realized why Tsula had placed it there in the first place: to protect her, to save her from insanity.

But she wasn't insane. Somehow, her mind had survived branching into a thousand different directions, then unbranching to become whole again. And within those myriad branches, she had caught just a glimpse of the one future they desperately needed. But that was all. Just a glimpse.

And that was all she was ever going to get. Naia felt certain she would never survive being shattered like that again.

She sucked in a deep breath through her nostrils and let it out again slowly. She waited there, kneeling, until she got her emotions back under control. Then, wiping the tears from her eyes, Naia stood up and made her way toward the tendril-encrusted wall. She took one last, stabbing glance back, then stepped out of the dark sphere, vowing to never, ever enter it again.

She could never be a Harbinger. She could never approach Tsula's courage.

Naia fled the Nexus, hardly noticing the placement of her feet as she took the glass stepping stones two at a time. She stumbled back onto the balcony of the castle, then stopped, blinking, looking around for Quin in the harsh glare of the sun.

She found him around the corner, sitting on a bench in the shade of a tree in purple bloom. He looked up, hearing her footsteps. Seeing the expression on her face, he shot out of his seat, coming toward her with his brow furrowed in concern. Naia dove into his arms, the tears already springing back into her eyes.

"I know what we have to do," she gasped, sobbing quietly against the fabric of his coat. His arms tightened around her, crushing her against his chest. His hand ran soothingly through her hair.

"What is it? What did you see?"

She pulled back and looked up at him. "We can destroy the Well of Tears without destroying the magic field."

Quin stepped back with a look of confused disbelief. "How's that possible?"

Naia shook her head as fresh tears spilled down her face. "It's possible. We can do it. But the price is so high…"

"You've seen it?" he asked. His face bled through several shades of pale before settling on gray.

She nodded. "I only saw a fragment of it. Just a glimpse. And that's all I'm going to get because the chance of it happening is so miniscule. And…" Her voice trailed off.

"And what?" he glared at her suspiciously.

"I think you're going to die, Quin," she whispered. "So will Darien. So will Kyel. Your soul will be consigned to hell. And with the Well destroyed...there'll be no coming back for you. Ever." She grimaced, bowing her head in grief.

Quin reached out and, with a finger, lifted her chin until she was gazing into his eyes.

"Do you live?" he asked.

"I think so..." she whispered.

He nodded once.

"Then it's worth it."

Chapter Twenty-Six
Gods Be Damned

The Kingdom of Emmery, The Rhen

D arien slid the oiled cloth down his sword's blade, applying all of his concentration to the effort. Not that oiling common steel was a demanding task, but it was something to divert his mind from the battle and its aftermath. All around him, tents were being broken down, fires extinguished, his soldiers going about their business with a kind of disciplined efficiency that Darien had never seen before entering the Black Lands. Even after such a harrowing defeat, his men still went about their duties with machine-like efficiency.

Darien wished he could share their focus. As it was, it was all he could do to rub his blade with the oiled rag and try not to think too much. Thinking inevitably led to remembering, and remembering was something he wanted to avoid. But there was only so much oil that could be applied to a blade without gumming it up. Darien slid *Valdivora* back into its sheath and put the cleaning kit away in his pack.

He looked up, his eyes drawn to the eastern sky, which glowed with the warmth of dawn. A breeze stirred, its breath heavy with the odor of woodsmoke and damp earth. It was a chill morning. He stood and strapped his war belt around his waist, adjusting the scabbard at his side. He scrubbed his hands together to rub the sword oil into his skin and started back to his tent.

Darien's thoughts turned to Kyel, despite his best efforts at distraction. He was tired of replaying the battle in his head, scouring his memory for things he should have done differently. After days of analyzing his strategy and actions, he kept returning to the same conclusion: that there was nothing he could have done to change the outcome.

He hadn't lost the battle because of his own lack of competence. The battle had been lost because of Kyel's superior abilities.

And that's what scared Darien most. He had control over his own actions, his own men. His own power. But there was nothing he could do to change the fact that Kyel had become far more powerful than himself. And had command of an artifact he had no hope of defending against.

Darien paused, sweeping his eyes over the encampment. He wasn't surprised when he saw Sayeed walking toward him down an aisle between tents. The man wore the same scowl he'd been wearing for the past four days.

The officer drew to a halt, looking at him critically. Appearing dissatisfied with what he saw, Sayeed made a motion with his hand, indicating a fallen tree that lay sprawled across the ground nearby. Darien took his meaning and walked over to it, lowering himself to take a seat.

Sayeed sat next to him. "Be grateful," he said. "You are alive."

Darien found the comment sadly ironic. "Am I?" he asked. His tentative existence was another source of irritation, somewhere between the world of the living and the world of the damned.

"In all ways that matter," Sayeed said. "You are a man, Brother. And, just like any man, you are fallible."

Fallible. That was not the term Darien would have used. *Ineffective* had a truer ring to it. He tossed his hands up in frustration. "I don't know how to counter him. I don't think I can."

Sayeed shrugged indifferently. "You'll find a way. He has limitations. This Oath of Harmony—that is a crippling oath. I do not understand why any mage would swear it. Especially one who is supposed to be a defender of his homeland." He reached down and scratched his leg, a quizzical expression on his face.

Darien glanced past him toward the encampment, where the last of the tents were being broken down and folded for the march. "It's supposed to prevent moral degradation. To keep someone like Kyel from becoming someone like me. It does seem limiting—yet in many ways, it's not. You saw how easily he handled me. There wasn't a thing I could do about it. Every time I attacked, he just turned my own magic against me."

"Then next time, don't attack," Sayeed suggested.

"What would you have me do?"

"The same thing he does. Think, Brother." He leaned forward, his elbows on his splayed knees. "What makes him so effective?"

Darien didn't have to think about it long. He remembered the hopeless frustration he'd felt when he realized there was nothing he could do. "He neutralizes me."

Sayeed's eyes locked on his. "Then neutralize him."

"I thought I had. With the necrators. But then…"

The Zakai officer nodded, his brow furrowing. "That woman. Was she a mage?"

"Aye." Darien stared down, absently picking at the rough bark under him. "Her name's Alexa Newell. She was a Naturalist. I didn't really know her. I just knew *of* her. She went missing a few years back. It was quite a big thing at the time. There was an enormous search. It took months. They never found a trace of her—everyone just assumed she'd died."

Sayeed grunted. "Apparently they were wrong."

"No. Not wrong."

"What do you mean?" Sayeed's brow furrowed in incomprehension.

Darien looked past him, toward the tents. He'd spent the last few days in thought, pondering Kyel's one-sided victory. Alexa's appearance at the end of the battle disturbed him most. More than anything, he feared what her presence might signify.

He said, "A mortal mage could have never confronted my necrators. Even if her soul was just as black as mine. They're *my* minions. She shouldn't have been able to command them. And she didn't just command them—she *unmade* them." It was a harrowing thought, one that smacked of forces much stronger than himself. The types of forces not Bound by the Oath of Harmony.

"Then make more necrators," Sayeed shrugged.

"I've others I can summon," Darien said absently, "but that's not the point. I need to find out what she's about and what she's doing with Kyel. I sense another hand at work here. And I don't like the implications."

Sayeed stared gravely at him, his dark eyes filled with understanding. "Whatever comes, my sword will always guard your back."

Darien appreciated that. More than Sayeed would ever know. He said with a smile he didn't feel, "Then I will never have reason to fear."

The Zakai officer ducked his head and, patting Darien on the shoulder, stood and strode back to camp. Darien remained behind on the log, watching him go. His fingers picked at the bark, peeling up thin fragments that looked like puzzle pieces. He tried fitting two together, but soon gave up and flicked the pieces away.

Darien rose and made his way toward his tent. They faced another long march that would bring them another day closer to Rothscard. At the pace he'd calculated, it would take them only three more days to reach the city and meet up with the other armies he had sent southward through the Cerulean Plains.

Reaching the tent, Darien stopped and glanced around, looking for Azár. He caught sight of her at last, a short distance away in the direction of the forest. She was kneeling on the ground, bent over her knees.

Concerned, Darien started toward her. She rose to her feet, wiping her mouth. She looked up, noticing him. A change came over her face. Her eyes widened, her jaw going slack. As he neared, she took a step back away.

"Are you ill?" Darien asked, suddenly worried. When she retreated another step, he stopped and raised his hands. He felt like he was stalking some wild creature, one prepared to bolt.

"I am fine," she said, though her voice didn't sound fine.

Hearing her tone, Darien felt genuine fear. "Come here. Let me have a look."

But his wife shook her head. She turned and walked away in haste.

"Come here!" Darien shouted at her back, starting after her.

Azár stopped. And turned around, her eyes full of misery. She bowed her head and stared at the ground instead of him. More than anything else she could have done, that one action alarmed him the most. Azár was not a submissive woman.

Darien strode toward her, fear sharpening his movements. He caught her by the shoulders and stared into her face, groping there for explanation. Azár's eyes were red and watery. As if she'd been crying. Or sick.

Darien cast his will into her, probing his wife gently with his mind. After moments, he opened his eyes, confused. His probe had returned only a strong sense of health. There was nothing wrong with her. He sagged in relief. Just to make sure, he felt her again. This time, he sensed something else, something he'd overlooked the first time.

There was another presence, deep down inside.

Darien choked, letting go of Azár and stepping back. His mind went numb. His heart stopped. The world crumbled.

"Husband—"

He backed away from her. Azár started after him, panic on her face. Darien raised his hands, fending her off. Then he whirled and strode away, moving across the camp as quickly as he could without breaking into a run. His vision swam, his thoughts paralyzed. He wasn't aware of where he was going. It didn't matter; he just needed to escape.

Darien fled the camp and followed a deer trail into the forest, moving like a man walking in his sleep. Or in a nightmare. At last, he staggered to a stop in a small clearing.

There, he fell to his knees. He brought his hands up to his face and allowed the pain to come. He wanted to throw his head back and rail at the vengeful gods.

He'd already lost one child without having the chance to know it. Now he would lose another. And the mother who bore it.

The gods were worse than cruel. They were ruthless.

It was some time before he found the courage and composure to return to camp. Darien walked automatically, striding with his head lowered, eyes locked on the ground in front of him. He couldn't look up, couldn't let the men see the defeat on his face.

He found his tent still intact. Darien batted the flap out of his way. Azár was within, sitting cross-legged in their bedding. She looked up as he entered, her face just as raw and devastated as his own.

Darien sank down beside her on the blankets and wrapped his arms around her, feeling her body shudder as she cried softly against him. He closed his eyes, reaching through her to feel the small life within. It was there: a miniscule heartbeat, faint and rapid, like the flutter of hummingbird wings. The feel of it brought a knife-sharp stab of pain. He squeezed her tighter.

"I did not know how to tell you," Azár moaned against his chest. "I did not know how to tell you that you will have another child who will not—"

"*Stop,*" Darien growled, choking on the word. He let her go, pulling back. *"This child will live!* You will *both* live! I don't care how many eternities I spend in hell—I am *not* leaving this world until both of you are safe. Gods be damned, I'll find a way!"

Azár was sobbing. He clutched her against his chest, burying his face in her hair. He wanted to murder the gods, to take everything from them, the way they'd taken everything from him. He wanted vengeance. But the gods were out of reach, beyond his capacity to cause them pain. So he turned his attention to his wife, instead.

All he could do was hold her. And cry with her. So that's what he did.

Chapter Twenty-Seven
Sense of Purpose

Glen Farquist, The Rhen

"Papa, what's a Sentinel?"

Kyel scooped little Gil off the floor and planted him down in his lap. Smiling sadly, he said, "It's someone who stands watch. Someone who protects."

It was hard, putting the essence of who he was into words such a young child could understand. Especially a child who was losing his father. Kyel figured he had to be exceptionally careful about what was spoken and what was left unsaid. Years later, when his son thought back on him, the words said today would likely be remembered best.

"Do Sentinels have magic?"

Kyel nodded, fighting back tears. Gil was asking all the wrong questions, the kind he didn't want to answer. Or maybe they were the right questions. Regardless, they hurt.

"Yes, Gil. Sentinels have magic."

The boy's face lit up. "Do magic, Papa! Do magic!" He bounced up and down in Kyel's lap, his eagerness too great to be contained in his little body.

But it was not the time for magic.

Kyel ran his hand through his son's hair. "No, Gil. Not today. Papa's tired."

"Pleeeeease?"

"No." Kyel shook his head. He gazed into his son's face. At his warm blue eyes. At his soft skin. His full lips. Soft ringlets of hair. Gil was perfect in every way. Kyel took in each feature, one by one, trying to imprint them on his mind. Each was equally important, the most important thing in the world.

"What do you protect, Papa?"

Kyel's hand was trembling, so he clenched it into a fist. It took him a moment to answer. He knew he had to tell Gil just enough of the truth without being too candid.

"I protect you," he said finally. "And your mum. And anyone else who needs protecting."

Gil's lips twisted, his little eyes scrunching in thought. He sat there for a moment looking very skeptical. Or very concerned.

"Who protects you, Papa?"

Kyel opened his mouth. Then closed it again, not having the faintest notion how to respond. He thought hard about it. He couldn't tell Gil the truth: that no one protected him. That he was going to die in a matter of days. That Gil would never see his father again. That these scant moments would be the very last they had. Kyel swallowed back the tears that tried to come and fought the sorrow off his face. He couldn't break down. His strength was the last and best gift he could ever give his son.

"Who protects you, papa?" Gil asked again.

From some deep place of courage he didn't know he had, Kyel managed to dredge up a wavering smile. "That's what magic's for."

"Will there always be magic?"

Another unfortunate question.

"I hope so."

"I hope so, too."

With a smile, Gil threw his arms around Kyel's neck, wrapping him in a squirming bear hug. Kyel grimaced against the grief that clawed at his chest. He gathered his son in his arms and hugged him tight, cherishing the feel of him.

Into Gil's soft curls, Kyel said softly, "You need to know how much I love you. And how proud I am of you."

The little body wriggled in his arms. In a voice muffled by Kyel's thick shirt, Gil said, "I love you too, Papa. You're the best Sentinel in the world."

Kyel pulled the door softly shut, cutting off the steady sounds of Gil's snoring. He squeezed his eyes closed against a stab of sorrow. It wasn't fair. A little boy shouldn't have to grow up without a father. He reached up, rubbing his eyes. He took a deep breath. Then he strode away.

He made his way through the warren of passages that formed the living quarters of Om's Temple. He rounded the last corner that led to the main entrance and there drew up. He hadn't expected Arvel to be waiting for him. But he wasn't surprised to see him, either. Avoiding eye contact, Kyel asked, "You're going to get him to his mum, right?"

The god-priest flashed Kyel a dour smile. "Of course. It is the least we can do. Don't let your thoughts be preoccupied with your son's welfare. Gil will be taken care of."

Kyel nodded, his shoulders sagging.

"Are you ready?" The smile on Arvel's face was fixed as if etched there. "The Temple of Death is expecting you."

Kyel paused. "I would like to ask a question."

Arvel's waxen smile slipped just a fraction. "You wish to know if the gods are real."

Kyel was surprised the man had anticipated his question. Nevertheless he nodded, figuring he was owed the truth. Arvel raised his hand, beckoning Kyel to follow. He led him through a doorway into a spacious chamber dominated by a table surrounded by many chairs. Kyel took a seat, while the cleric settled across from him.

Clasping his hands together, Arvel informed him, "There is only one goddess."

"Which goddess is that?" Kyel sat back in his chair, bringing a leg up.

Arvel smiled blandly. "She has gone by many names since the beginning of the world."

"So why the secrecy?" Kyel pressed.

"Because." Arvel shifted in his seat, his face becoming very serious. "The temples are not religious entities, as you've been raised to think. They are entirely political. The temples are institutions created to defend humanity against our most ancient of all adversaries."

"Mages," Kyel guessed.

Arvel nodded. "If not for the temples, mages would dominate the earth, oppressing the vulnerable masses. They've done so in the past, and they would do so again. For millennia, the temples have resorted to the one force on earth capable of challenging the power of magic: the power of faith."

Kyel frowned. "Then how do you perform your miracles?"

"Each temple was entrusted with magical artifacts. And from these artifacts, we have achieved the "miracles" that buy us the faith we need. There is only one temple that does not need to rely on artifacts of magic."

"And which temple is that?"

"The temple of the One True Goddess. The Temple of Isap." The smile on Arvel's face stagnated.

"What of the Catacombs?" Kyel pressed. "The Atrament… none of that is magically conceived?"

"All of that is Isap's domain."

It all made perfect sense, Kyel realized. Arvel's story explained so many inconsistencies he'd always wondered about. But the story did have one gaping hole. Leaning forward in his seat, Kyel pressed, "Then what of Xerys?"

Arvel slouched, his body seeming to deflate and collapse in on itself. "Xerys does, in fact, exist. But he is not a god."

Kyel frowned. "Then what is he?"

Arvel's glasses had slipped down his nose. Pushing them back up, he explained, "Xerys was the first mage, the most beloved of all of Isap's creations. He was born of magic and tasked with protecting all things magical. But Xerys became too enamored by what he guarded. He came to believe that creations born of magic were elevated above those who were born mundane. He decided it was the place of humanity to serve magic, and not the other way around. This belief was contrary to Isap's vision of her creation.

"So Xerys earned Isap's displeasure. He was banished from this world and imprisoned in another plane: what you call hell. Contrary to what you've been taught, Xerys is not the source of evil in this world. Evil is a construct, nothing more. But Xerys has no compunctions against using what we call 'evil' to his advantage, if doing so advances his own interests."

Kyel stared at Arvel, feeling physically shaken. Every tenant of faith he had ever nurtured had just been broken on the wheel of truth.

The implications were vast. They redefined his very purpose.

"So…Xerys' Servants are not demons?"

Arvel's wan smile returned. "Oh, they are most certainly demons. They are creatures of spirit who, like Xerys himself, are forbidden from ever entering Isap's domain. They have chosen to side with Xerys, so have been banished to spend eternity in the company of the master they serve."

Kyel nodded. "And what of the Hellpower?"

Arvel smiled morosely. "The Hellpower is the type of magic that exists in Xerys' realm. It is the antithesis of the magic field."

So many answers…and yet each answer spawned a host of new questions. Kyel wondered how many years it would take to get to the bottom of it all. If there was, indeed, a bottom.

He sighed wearily. "I don't understand. What are the Servants trying to accomplish? What are they looking to gain?"

Arvel shrugged, as if the answer should be obvious. "Xerys wishes to be freed from his confinement. That is the goal his Servants work toward. And that is the reason why we must oppose him. For, if Xerys is ever freed, humanity would be once again pressed into servitude by those with magic, and mages alone would rule the world."

Arvel looked down at the tabletop. "Zavier Renquist plans to halt the Reversal of the magic field using the Hellpower, just as he tried to do a thousand years ago. Only, to release enough of it, he would have to open the Gateway wide enough that it would free Xerys from the Netherworld."

Kyel stiffened as the priest's revelation sank into his chest like icy fingers groping for his heart. His first thought was of Gil. He'd told his son he was a protector. And he could think of nothing in the world more important to protect.

"What must I do?" he asked.

For the first time, Arvel's smile grew beyond bland, into something eager. Something sinister. "Stop Renquist. Stop his Servants. Before they gather enough power to release Xerys into this world."

Chapter Twenty-Eight
Transformations

Isle of Titherry, The Rhen

A bleakness encased Naia's thoughts as she stared down at the ever-changing surface of Athera's Crescent. Her gaze followed the flowing patterns that moved across it, patterns that reminded her of ripples propagating across the surface of a lake.

The day was bright, and a gentle breeze cooled her skin, but nothing could take her mind from the myriad possible destinies she had witnessed in the Nexus. Nothing could alleviate the sorrow that filled her heart. It didn't matter which future destiny held in store for her. All seemed equally bleak.

Naia sighed, pushing her hair back out of the way of her vision. Turning away from the Crescent, she made her way back into the castle. She found Quin in his room, stuffing the last of his possessions into his pack.

"Are you ready?" she asked.

He nodded, flashing her a smile that didn't quite reach his eyes.

Naia clasped her hands together as she moved across the room toward him. The new shadow staff he'd carved was leaning against the wall beside the bed. She had forgotten to ask if he'd ever finished it. Reaching out, she laid her hand upon the staff, stroking its wax-polished surface. Instantly, an ominous feeling jolted up her arm, making her flinch. Naia retracted her hand quickly. It was the same feeling she'd gotten the first time she'd touched the staff. The thing felt evil, although Quin kept insisting it wasn't.

Moving away from the staff, she asked, "Why are we going to

Rothscard?"

Quin tied his pack closed, giving the cord one good, last tug. "Because you said we need to find Kyel," he said as he swung the pack over his shoulder.

Naia's brow furrowed. "And why do you think Kyel will be in Rothscard?"

Quin shrugged. "Because it's the logical place for him to be." His eyes roved quickly over the room, scanning to make certain there was nothing left behind. He took the staff into his hand. "Being a Sentinel, Kyel would want to be near the Front. But the problem is, we've been here too long. So the Front's not likely where we left it. With the Reversal so close, Darien's had no choice but to push southward. And any invading army would make Rothscard their target."

"Then the war's already begun. What are we going to do?" Naia whispered, feeling that they'd already failed before even setting off.

Quin appeared to think about it a moment. "Well, we'll just have to improvise," he said, holding the door open for her.

The Kingdom of Emmery, The Rhen

The demon-dog yawned enormously. The beast gazed across the fire at Darien with a questioning look. Its ears perked, its head whipping toward the darkness. The hound rose to its feet, emitting a low growl, intent on something outside the circle of light. Then it relaxed, apparently satisfied. The thing turned in a slow circle, then finally settled back down, closing its baneful eyes.

Darien ignored the thanacryst, his attention riveted on the journal in his lap. He held his head in his hand, fingers clasped around a fistful of hair. His eyes scoured the page as if his life depended on the information contained there. Or another life, far more precious. All he knew was that the secrets unlocked by that journal were so important that Edric Torrence had lain down his life to pass them on.

He didn't look up at the crunch of approaching footsteps.

"Report," Darien ordered, flipping a page.

"Warden, we have only four crates of salted fish remaining and one cask of wine," his quartermaster informed him.

Darien glanced back over the last solution on the page. Absently, he said, "The fish should get us there. Ration the wine."

"Yes, Warden."

As the officer moved away, Darien tried repeating Edric's calculations in his head. He quickly found them too much to keep track of. With a grunt of frustration, he reached into the cloth sack at his side and pulled out a pot of ink and a writing stick. The *elam* wasn't sharpened, but that took only a moment's thought to fix. Unrolling a strip of parchment, he started scribbling, altering magnitudes to account for his own abilities.

The resulting number was extraordinary.

"It'll work," he muttered.

"What will work?"

Twisting, Darien looked up into Azár's face. She'd come up quietly behind him, and even the thanacryst hadn't alerted him to her presence. The beast appeared to be sleeping, its hind foot twitching just a bit. He set the parchment down and stoppered the ink pot.

"I think I know how Edric did it," Darien said, closing the journal and slipping it back into its embroidered cover.

Azár sat down beside him, her face lit by interest. "How is that?"

Darien reached up and scratched the whiskers on his jaw, wondering if he had enough understanding of Edric's methods to replicate the experiment. He decided the risk would be minimal. "It's complicated. I'm still trying to figure out why he felt flight was so important. I'm not sure what the value is, other than mobility. Still, I'd like to try it."

Azár turned away from him and gazed into the fire. The light of the flames danced across her face, tracing her features in acute contours.

"I do not like this idea," she said at last. "What if you turn yourself into a bird and cannot change back?"

That had been his first concern. Which was why he'd worked out both the forward and reverse solutions several times, just to make certain. "That wouldn't happen," Darien assured her. "The energy works out the same in both directions."

He stood up and wandered around the campfire to the demon-hound. The beast sat up on its haunches, its tail thrumming against the ground. Darien ran a hand through its matted fur, giving the thing a good scratch behind the ears.

"I could try it. See what happens," he suggested. "Master Edric obviously thought it was import—"

Azár cut him off. "This is not a good idea. It sounds dangerous."

She had made up her mind, he saw. And when Azár was adamant about something, she wasn't likely to relent. Which meant he would have to test his theory without her consent.

Darien gave the demon-hound one last, good scratch. Then he closed his eyes and wrenched as hard as he could on the magic field, forcing it in, filling himself as quickly as he could to the point of saturation.

"NO!" Azár screamed, realizing too late what was happening. All at once, a writhing mass of blue flames enveloped Darien, erupting into an inferno of blinding brilliance. She leapt to her feet, lunging for him—

A flurry of wings beat against her face, knocking her backward with a startled cry. Panicked, she screamed her husband's name.

But he was gone. Only a shimmering afterglow of his image remained in his place.

A shrill screech pierced the air. Azár's stomach lurched in fear. She scanned the line of trees, desperately seeking the source of the cry. Then she saw it. There, silhouetted against the stars, the dark form of a bird rose swiftly into the sky.

"Sayeed Zakai!" she screamed, terror in her heart.

She staggered backward over uneven ground, eyes pinned on the falcon as it darted across the thin crescent of the moon. Another shriek pierced the night.

She heard footsteps sprinting toward her. Then Sayeed was at her side, eyes wide and alarmed.

"Are you harmed? What happened?" he demanded.

"There!" Azár cried, pointing upward, her finger tracking the bird's motion. It gained height in slow circles, finally leveling out to skim gracefully overhead.

"How…?" Sayeed gasped.

The demon-hound gazed upward, cocking its head.

The falcon let out another piercing screech. It dipped its wing and veered away, soaring toward the mountains in the far distance.

"He is not coming back!" Azár cried, watching the bird flapping away.

Face aghast, Sayeed gripped her arm, his fingers biting into her skin. The cries of the falcon grew fainter. Soon its form was lost, slipping away into the shadows of the night.

Tears streaked Azár's face. A feeling of futility washed over her, weakening her knees. Sayeed caught her up, supporting her weight against him.

"He will come back," he reassured her. But she could tell by the sound of his voice that he was just as concerned as she.

"What if he doesn't remember he is a man?" she whispered.

They stood by the fire as the night dragged on, measured by the moon's slow progress.

They stood there until the coals grew cold and dawn broke across the horizon.

When Sayeed finally picked her up and carried her back to her tent, Azár didn't resist. She was barely aware of the officer settling her into bed, arranging her covers over her with the care and compassion of a brother. Feeling more alone than she could ever remember, she fell into a deep and troubled sleep.

Azár awoke to the feeling of a hand stroking her face, running tenderly through her hair. She opened her eyes and stared up through the shadows of the tent into the solemn face of her husband.

Her anger exploded. She shot bolt upright. Enraged, she swept out a hand, striking Darien in the face.

He closed his eyes, accepting the blow.

His lack of response angered her more. Azár hauled her arm back to strike him harder. This time, he caught her wrist.

"I'm sorry," he said.

Her anger melted. Sadness took its place. Exhausted, she collapsed against him.

Glen Farquist, The Rhen

Kyel followed the white-robed priest down the long hall toward the main sanctuary of the Temple of Death. Through the glass, he could see the temple's garden courtyard, with its long reflecting pool bordered by manicured shrubs. White and black swans plied the pool's waters and roosted along the shore. Beyond the garden rose the verdigris dome of the sanctuary, replete with its hundreds of stained-glass windows.

The sound of their footsteps rang off the walls as the gangly priest he followed turned a corner and led him down a narrow hallway that ended at a door. Kyel waited as the young man knocked twice, then opened the door and stepped back. Kyel nodded his gratitude and moved past, turning to confront the old man who sat waiting for him behind a wooden desk.

At the sight of him, Luther Penthos rose to his feet. Kyel walked forward, taking the priest's hand. Strangely, he felt none of the hesitance he'd always experienced before in the presence of this formidable man. Luther Penthos was Naia's father, as well as the High Priest of Death. Kyel's history with him had been turbulent. He had no reason to think that had changed.

"Your Eminence," he said in acknowledgement.

"Grand Master Archer." There was no trace of a smile on the priest's face. "I wish I could say it is good to see you again, but I'd be lying. Have you had word of my daughter?"

"No. Nothing." Kyel shook his head, feeling a pang of regret.

The old man nodded, slouching just a bit. "If you happen to see her before…well…" His voice trailed off. "Please tell her that I love her."

Kyel nodded. "I will, Your Eminence."

Setting his pack on the floor, he took a seat. He let his gaze travel around the room, looking over the assortment of books, tapers, lamps, and scrolls the man had amassed. The High Priest's study looked much more cluttered than the last time he'd seen it only months before. As though the man's enthusiasm for life had fled with his daughter.

"So." The old priest folded his age-spotted hands on the desk. "I hear you desire an escort through our Catacombs to Rothscard. I suppose I should warn you that Rothscard is not a safe destination at the moment. The city is under siege. We can get you in but, considering the size of the Enemy host, your sojourn may prove dangerous."

Kyel took the man's meaning. He said softly, "I'm not entirely defenseless."

Penthos raised an eyebrow. "So I've heard. I would like to thank you for a laudable defense of this valley. I fear, however, that such an outcome may not be easily replicated in Rothscard. The Enemy host is well over a hundred thousand strong, with more arriving each day. Rothscard is almost certain to fall."

Kyel glanced up at a painting that depicted one of the aspects of the goddess Isap. Remembering what Arvel had said about the goddess, Kyel stared harder at the image. In it, Isap appeared as a human woman with an elaborate headdress, holding a tall, stringed instrument. Her face, covered by an opaque veil, was unknowable. She could have been any woman, or every woman.

Looking back at Penthos, Kyel said, "I'd be grateful for help getting to Rothscard. But I'm not going there to defend the city. My goal is to destroy Xerys' Servants."

The old priest's eyes hardened to steel. "Then you will have all the aid I can give you. We no longer fight a war against the Enemy. That war is already lost. What we fight for now is the future of humanity. And that is a battle we can't afford to lose."

Kyel inclined his head. "I understand, Your Eminence."

Chapter Twenty-Nine
Every Advantage

Rothscard, The Rhen

The sound of his boots crunching on pebbles had occupied Darien's attention the entire morning. The noise grated on his nerves. He was growing fed up with it.

And with his wife's relentless silence.

Azár hadn't spoken to him all day, had made a point of showing him her back and throwing glares at him when she thought he wasn't looking. She had managed to walk at his side while successfully ignoring him for hours, her face set in a perpetual scowl. He'd had enough of it.

Darien let out a long, frustrated breath, groping for patience. "I'm sorry," he said in as gentle a tone as he could manage. "I gave you a fright. I ought to have warned you."

Azár's eyes glinted with ire. She was silent for a long minute. Then she responded, "Why did you do it?"

Darien breathed another irritated sigh. "Because I need to find an edge. Kyel handled me too well back there. With that talisman, he's stronger than I am."

Azár cast him a look of troubled doubt. "How can turning into a bird help you defeat your apprentice?"

Darien shrugged. "Mobility. Recognizance. I can go places no one could expect. Other than that…I don't know. I'm sure there are other advantages."

She tossed another glare his way. "Why didn't you return?"

"I *did* return."

"You were gone all night!"

He wanted to growl. "I told you. I'm sorry. Now, can we be

done with it?"

"No," she snapped. "Tell me why you were gone so long."

He scrubbed his hands through his hair, trying to find the right words to explain his actions. It was far more difficult than it seemed. Perhaps because, at the time, he hadn't been thinking in words.

His brow furrowed. "At first, I was just taken with the feel of flying. The freedom of it. I've never known anything like that. And my thoughts were different." He struggled, searching for a way to explain it. "They were bird thoughts. Not human thoughts. All I could think about was getting away, of escaping. So that's what I did."

Azár looked appalled. She whispered, "You forgot you were a man."

Darien shook his head. He still had a hard time understanding all of it. "I didn't forget. It's just that…being a man didn't seem all that important at the time. I had other needs that were much more powerful, and I didn't know how to override them."

The look in Azár's eyes could have melted glass. "Don't *ever* do that again! What if next time, you cannot control it?"

She was being unreasonable. He had just discovered a wonderful new advantage. Darien had no idea what purpose it could be put to, but he couldn't discard it just because his wife was worried for his safety.

"Next time, I'll be stronger. I'll have more control."

"There will not *be* a next time." Her tone left no room for argument.

Darien clenched his fists. "There will. I need to find and use every advantage I can. *Every* advantage. Don't you understand?"

He glanced significantly down at her middle. When she realized what he was staring at, her hand went immediately to her belly, as if seeking to shield the small life within.

She scowled. "How will changing into a bird save our child's life?"

"I don't know. But it might."

"You are stupid, Darien Lauchlin. I will not—"

He'd had enough. There was nothing more to be said about

the issue.

Darien opened his mind to the magic field and tugged at it violently. He stumbled midstride. There was a brilliant flash. Then he was falling—

Reflexively, he shot his arms out to catch himself. But he kept falling, falling upward. Falling away from the ground, flying—

The pull of the sky...

He beat his wings, climbing higher. Below, a tangled line of people wound through the trees. He circled above them, searching for an updraft. Finding one. He relaxed and let the warm air currents lift him higher.

The feel of the wind...

Everything below was impossibly sharp, impossibly vivid. He could see every detail of every face. New colors he had never before seen. A glowing fluorescence that dappled the ground. Far away beneath a tree, something moved—

Prey...

He tucked his wings and dove toward it. Then:

War. Child...

He pulled up, reminded of his purpose. He banked sharply and set his course parallel to the river. Ahead, he could see a great black plume of smoke that resembled a bank of clouds.

The city...

Below, the forest ended, and a vast grassland began. A great mass of people spread like a dark ocean across the plain. There were horses, fires—

Danger...

He wheeled away, but not before marking the colors of the banners. He angled back toward the river, pumping his wings, soaring over the forest, to the drawn-out column of men and women—

Azár...

He skimmed lower, finding a path between the trees, lower still, meeting the ground—

He staggered and fell to his knees, roughing the heels of his palms on the pebbled surface. He glanced up—

—into Azár's startled face. Sayeed was already running toward him. People were backing away, eyes wide with fear, holding up their hands in a ward against evil.

He lurched to his feet. Sweat streamed from his brow, drained into his eyes. He swiped a sleeve across his face. He was panting. Weak. He staggered.

"I did not believe it," Sayeed gasped, putting an arm out to steady him. His face was full of wonder. Or fear. Darien couldn't tell which.

He turned to Azár. Before she could say anything, he held a hand up. "I know. I'm stupid."

To his disbelief, his wife grinned.

Isle of Titherry, The Rhen

The shrine of Death didn't look familiar, although it should have. The last time Quin had seen it had been under the spell of everlasting winter. But that spell was broken. Now the Isle of Titherry lay basking under the warm spring sun, enjoying a thaw that had been delayed for years—ever since the collapse of the Hall of the Watchers.

When Aerysius had fallen, its Circle of Convergence had died with it, its conduit severed from Athera's Crescent. Without that input, the Crescent had resorted to pulling the energy it needed directly from the air around it, encasing the isle in a winter that didn't end. Now that Quin had repaired the conduits, Athera's Crescent was functioning just as it was designed to do.

Quin turned to Naia, his eyes running over her. She was occupied with the business of lighting the shrine's assortment of tapers. It was almost like a graceful dance that swept her from one end of the room to the other. Quin watched her as she worked, lighting one taper from another by means of a wooden splint, moving in what seemed a random order back and forth across the shrine. He had a feeling there was nothing random at all about her movements. He stood back and watched, enjoying the fluid grace of her body.

"I've been thinking," he said, staring at her back. "These visions—or versions—that you have. Is Zavier Renquist in each of them?"

"Yes," Naia responded without pausing in her candle-lighting.

Quin's eyes wandered across the walls of the shrine, taking in a series of numbered frescoes painted there. "What if Renquist was taken out of the picture? I mean, could he be blocking your ability to see past him? Like Tsula?"

Naia didn't pause. "I don't know," she said with her back to him.

"But it's possible, right?"

She turned slowly around to stare at him with a skeptical look. "I suppose. Why? What are you thinking?"

"It strikes me as odd that Renquist was Tsula's husband. It's highly irregular for Harbingers to marry anyone, much less a Prime Warden. Maybe Tsula wasn't helping him intentionally... but that doesn't mean she wasn't helping him unintentionally."

Naia frowned with a look of intense concern. "Do you think he knows what we're about?"

"I don't know," Quin muttered. It took him only a moment to arrive at a decision. "You go on ahead to Rothscard. Show me the way to Bryn Calazar. I'll meet up with you when I'm done."

"Done with what?" Naia asked, moving toward him. She extinguished the wooden splint with her fingers and set it down. She stared at him intensely.

Quin took her hand and kissed it. "There's something I need to do that I should have done a long time ago."

"And what is that?" Naia whispered with a look of dread.

Quin smiled dangerously. "I'm going to kill Zavier Renquist."

Rothscard, The Rhen

Kyel's gray stallion shied away from a street dancer's brightly colored ribbons. He reined in and brought the animal under control. He couldn't believe anyone could be dancing and flipping around ribbons in the midst of a siege. But people had to put food in their mouths, he supposed, even under the direst of circumstances. Reaching into his pocket, he pulled out a coin and tossed it to the woman, figuring she needed it more desperately than he did.

His escort of blue-cloaked guardsmen were having a difficult time holding back the crowd as they waded through Rothscard's unruly streets. The city was bursting with masses of people swarming the shops and market stalls, scrambling to find food and supplies. The city guard was hard-pressed to keep order, often resorting to bludgeons and swords to maintain some degree of civility.

Most of the markets were already emptied, the street vendors sold out of wares. The storefronts had been boarded up, the shopkeepers fled. The only commodity Rothscard seemed to have in good supply was an abundance of prostitutes and opportunists, the former touting their wares in exchange for food, the latter pushing medicinals at criminal prices. The stench of smoke and fear-sweat combined to yield a heady miasma in the air.

The gates of Emmery Palace were heavily guarded. Kyel was ushered through quickly, garnering more than his share of shocked looks and stares. The people of Rothscard were no longer used to the sight of a black cloak. Most of the population took heart in the sight of it. Others looked on in fear.

His escort led him through another gate into the Inner Ward of the palace, past fountains hedged by immaculate gardens. At the palace steps, he was relieved of his horse and greeted by a flustered-looking minister who bowed and blotted his brow with a folded kerchief.

"This way, Great Master. The Queen and Prince await you in the council chamber."

The council chamber was an upgrade, Kyel decided. The last time he'd visited Emmery Palace with Meiran, Romana had relegated them to the Blue Room. Kyel took it for a good sign; perhaps he was finally being taken more seriously. He followed the minister through a series of long hallways dripping with chandeliers to a set of double doors.

The minister pulled open the doors with a flourish and announced, "Grand Master Kyel Archer of the Distinguished Order of Sentinels."

Kyel stepped into the room, feeling irritated and rather embarrassed by the pomp and formality. He wasn't there to exchange courtesies, and he didn't care a whit about decorum. His business was far more serious in nature.

The council chamber was dominated by a long table carved from a single piece of burl wood. Queen Romana and her husband rose from their chairs, the only two people in the room. Kyel walked forward, not bothering to kneel; he was a mage, and therefore the equal of any queen. He sat next to them at the table, waving away a servant who scurried forward to offer refreshments.

Kyel's gaze travelled over the royal grandeur of the chamber, at the gilt wall panels and elaborate sconces. All eclipsed by the majesty of the Queen herself. Romana's presence saturated the room. She was no longer the young girl he remembered meeting two years before.

The Queen was staring at him expectantly, no doubt waiting for him to speak. It took Kyel a moment to form words. This was the same woman who, upon their first meeting, had ordered him arrested and had him placed in chains. He'd been completely at her mercy, and at the mercy of her husband, Nigel Swain. Kyel sat looking back and forth between the two of them. He folded his hands on the table, taking a moment to collect himself.

"Thank you for receiving me," he said at last. He was surprised by the confidence in his voice. He couldn't have managed that tone even a few months before.

"Thank you for coming, Grand Master Archer," Romana said, inclining her head.

Her husband stared at Kyel with a narrow, unblinking gaze. Swain had been Romana's captain of the guard before he had become the Prince Consort. He was also the Guild blademaster who had trained Darien in the sword. He was perhaps the most uncompromising man Kyel had ever met, and the most single-minded.

Swain said coolly, "I'm not sure how you arrived, considering our city is under siege. But we would appreciate any help you can lend us."

After two years of knowing him, Kyel still wasn't sure whether or not he liked Swain. Looking at Romana, Kyel said, "I'm sorry, Your Grace, but I'm not here to defend Rothscard. I'm here to destroy Darien Lauchlin."

Swain nodded slightly, while Romana canted her head at Kyel's words.

"A worthy goal," she pronounced with an undertone of skepticism. "However, I fear it is unachievable. And unnecessary. By all reports, the Reversal of the magic field is imminent. I am told the event will send Xerys' Servants back to whatever hell they came from."

Kyel shook his head. "There's more to it. The temples believe the Servants plan to stabilize the magic field using the Hellpower. Not only would that halt the Reversal, but it would release Xerys fully into this world. We don't know how they indent to accomplish it. But we do know it's possible."

Romana and Swain exchanged a horrified look weighed by experience and understanding. The Queen turned back to Kyel. "What do you need from us?"

Kyel said, "I need your army, Your Grace."

Romana's eyebrows shot up, her face frozen halfway between disbelief and amusement. *"Again?"*

Kyel realized he had just spoken the same words he had uttered upon their first meeting. Only, then, he had been Darien's emissary to the throne of Emmery.

"I need men behind me," he explained. "I can't bring Darien down by myself. I'm Bound by my Oath of Harmony. But I can weaken him. And I can contain him long enough for others to move in and finish him."

Romana nodded slowly, looking thoughtful. She brushed a wisp of hair out of her face, for a moment looking like the young woman Kyel remembered meeting for the first time. But the moment was fleeting, and the imposing monarch was quick to return.

Formally, she announced, "Sentinel Archer, you may have whatever resources we can spare to hunt this demon down."

"Thank you, Your Grace." Kyel said with a nod. "I will make

do with whatever you can give me."

"I'll assist you personally," said Swain. "I need to finish what I started back at Orien's Finger. I should have never let Darien walk away from there alive."

Kyel remembered when Swain had stood with his sword raised over Darien, preparing to strike a blow that would have ended his misery. For some reason, the Prince had stayed his hand. Kyel wondered how events would have transpired differently if he had let the blade fall.

"There's another matter we need to speak of." Swain's face was etched in troubled lines of concern. "Another mage arrived in the city this morning. A woman calling herself Master Alexa Newell. Do you know her?"

Kyel stared at him in shock.

"Yes, I do," he gasped. "She's here?"

When Alexa hadn't returned, he'd just assumed she'd been slain by Darien's necrators. And while he was grateful that she had saved his life, Kyel hadn't mourned her. Her appearance in Rothscard was all too coincidental and disturbing. Why hadn't she returned to him in Glen Farquist? And how had she arrived in the city ahead of him? Far too many questions still surrounded Alexa for Kyel's liking.

"She's here," Swain confirmed. "I had her arrested and taken to the Citadel. I don't like what I can't explain, and I like it even less when my city is under siege."

"I understand." Kyel said. "I would like to speak with her."

"I'll take you to her."

Kyel rose from his seat. Queen Romana stood and took him by the hand. She said with a smile, "You have grown so much since the first time we met. More than I would have ever imagined possible. You have become every inch a Sentinel, Kyel Archer."

Kyel felt certain it was by far the greatest compliment he'd ever received, and he knew he should feel proud. Two months ago, he would have. But too many events had transpired since. Instead of feeling bolstered by Romana's words, they only served to make him feel saddened.

Because the Queen was wrong. What she sensed in him was not confidence. It was simply resignation.

Chapter Thirty
Legacies

Rothscard, The Rhen

The encampment of the Malikari legions sprawled across the plains, beginning at the banks of the River Nerium and extending in every direction to the distant horizons. Thousands upon thousands of tents pitched in orderly rows radiated outward like the spokes of a wheel from the center of camp. In the far distance, the walls of Rothscard gleamed a bloody red, reflecting the saturated colors of the sunset. Black smoke billowed from the city, roiling overhead like heavy storm clouds.

Darien ordered his Tanisars to pitch their tents on the western margin of the encampment, then continued on to the command tent with Azár and a small retinue of Zakai. At the sight of their small group, men and women ran forward to line their passage, shouting and cheering and shaking weapons in the air. What surprised Darien most were the long rows of tethered horses that had been assimilated into the encampment. Apparently, the horse lords of the plains had honored their commitment.

They found the command tent abuzz with uniformed officers trickling in and out of the pavilion's entrance. A spectacularly garbed man with a tall plume on his hat intercepted them, then ducked aside to confer quietly with Sayeed in the language of the clans. After a short moment, Sayeed nodded and returned to Darien, his expression concerned.

"Your presence is requested within. You are to enter alone."

Darien frowned, wondering which warlord would be arrogant enough to greet his arrival with demands. Nevertheless, he raised his hand, cautioning Sayeed and Azár to remain outside. Whoever it was that awaited within, he wanted to confront them alone. His pregnant wife need not look on.

Darien followed the officer into the pavilion. Lining the walls were men and women who immediately clamored to their feet and, bowing, streamed out of the tent. A group of officers leaning over the map table turned and, upon marking his arrival, shifted their gazes to the floor. They filed past him, avoiding his eyes on their way out. Even Darien's plumed escort didn't remain long. The man bowed deeply then took his leave, untying the tent flaps from the support posts and letting the fabric fall. Soon, the entire pavilion stood dim and empty.

Only, it was not.

There was a rustle on the other side of the tent's partition. Darien turned, stiffening with suppressed tension. His hand moved to the hilt of his sword.

The partition was drawn back to admit two men—the only two men in the world whose very presence made Darien's nerves prickle. Without hesitation, he went to his knees and bowed forward, pressing his forehead against the rugs, his palms beside his face. He remained there, unmoving, until the rustle of robes told him both men had taken a seat. Time dribbled forward, marked only by the ebb and flow of his breath.

At last, a deep and familiar voice announced, "You may rise."

Darien pushed himself upright, feeling the blood drain from his face. He shifted into a cross-legged position, hands clasped in front of him. He raised his gaze slowly, hesitant to look Zavier Renquist in the eyes.

The Prime Warden regarded him for a long moment without moving. He was seated on a rug, wearing the formal blue robes and white cloak of his office. Beside him sat Cyrus Krane, ancient Prime Warden of Aerysius, and Renquist's second-in-command. Krane's dark eyes surveyed Darien suspiciously. The man had never liked him. He'd never thought to question why.

Renquist favored him with a fatherly smile. "Welcome, Darien. How is your health?"

Darien's eyes ranged from one man to the other. He answered

guardedly, "My health is good, Prime Warden." His back remained stiff, his fingers locked together with rigid tension. He sensed danger in the air, and his muscles were responding.

Renquist nodded. "By all reports, you've done exceptionally well. You have managed to secure the whole of the North. Even the great city of Rothscard shall soon fall before us. As I predicted, you have truly become the greatest Battlemage in all of history."

Darien bowed his head, feeling a flush of humility tempered by apprehension. "Thank you, Prime Warden."

Again, Renquist supplied that same, fatherly smile. Darien didn't trust it.

"Now, let us speak of recent developments." The Prime Warden sat back and adjusted his posture. His many-stranded silver necklace shimmered in the lantern light. "I received word that Byron Connel was slain in battle. And that his talisman fell into the hands of a Sentinel. Two events which are…most unfortunate."

Darien licked his lips, a faint shiver tingling his spine. He thought perhaps Renquist blamed him for Connel's death. The man didn't say it outright. Still, there was something that hung in the air between them, like a cold and threatening undercurrent.

"The information you received is accurate." Darien looked from one Prime Warden to the other. "The Sentinel's name is Kyel Archer. He was my acolyte." He hesitated, unsure of how much information he should share. Too little could rouse suspicion. Too much might get him killed. "A woman who travels with Kyel taught him the use of the talisman. It is my suspicion he inherited Meiran's legacy, which would make him eleventh tier."

"Eleventh tier," Renquist echoed, his voice a low rumble. Almost, Darien thought he saw a fleeting smile on the man's face. The expression was there for only an instant, then was gone. If it had ever been there in the first place.

The Prime Warden said, "That would explain why this Sentinel was able to repulse your attack at Glen Farquist. So, Darien. What do you intend to do about him?"

Darien didn't answer immediately. Instead, he took a moment to think over his response carefully. "Kyel's not immune to my necrators. Or my thanacryst."

A glint of metal on Renquist's hand caught Darien's attention. The Prime Warden was wearing a ring he'd never noticed before. A silver ring set with a lapis stone. And upon that stone, depicted in gold overlay, was an ancient rune, one he knew well: *Dacros*. The first rune in the sequence that commanded the Well of Tears.

Darien frowned at the presence of the ring, uncertain of what it meant.

Renquist's face became very solemn. "There is one last matter to speak of. As you know, the Reversal of the magic field is nearly upon us. As things stand, we do not have much time left in this world."

Darien gazed at the floor, not wishing to be reminded. He'd promised Azár he would find a way to save her and the child she carried. But as the days crept by, the more it became apparent he had made a promise he couldn't keep.

"I believe there is a way to change that destiny," Zavier Renquist said softly.

Darien's eyes snapped up. Hope shot through him with the force of a lightning strike. *"How?"* he gasped.

Renquist spread his hands. "There is a way to halt the Reversal, though at great expense." His stare dug into Darien's eyes as if boring into his soul. "Tell me. How much of yourself are you willing to sacrifice in order to save your wife and unborn child?"

Darien's heart stopped. He gasped but couldn't draw breath. His mind stumbled to a standstill. *"Anything,"* he managed, surging to his feet. "What must I do?"

Zavier Renquist rose to stand in front of him. Clasping his hands behind his back, he said in a calm voice, "A thousand years ago, we had a plan to halt the Reversal. It involved combining the might of eight Grand Masters using the eight Circles of Convergence. Hence the covenant of the Eight Servants came to be. As you know, there are no longer eight Servants. Or eight Circles of Convergence."

He paced around the margin of the tent, circling Darien like a raptor. "But eight Grand Masters are not truly necessary. Only the vitrus of eight Grand Masters is needed."

Shaken, Darien looked at him in incomprehension. "So we need to combine thirty-two tiers of mage-power? How can that be done?"

Renquist stopped pacing and turned to face him. "Through the Onslaught, you already have access to eight tiers. If you are correct in your guess, then this Kyel Archer has inherited eleven. That leaves us lacking only thirteen tiers. Cyrus and Quinlan each have five. All we will need, then, is three more tiers."

Darien's heart froze. "No." He shook his head adamantly. "Not Azár."

Renquist waved his hand, dismissing the idea. "Of course not. I was thinking, rather, of the former priestess who inherited half your legacy. Together, we can save the lives of every living mage. Including the lives of your wife and child."

Darien could only stare at him, rendered speechless by a blaze of hope that was incapacitating.

Zavier Renquist smiled triumphantly. But the smile didn't last long. His face darkened again almost immediately. "I doubt your acolyte will be willing to lay down his life willingly. You will need to dispatch him and absorb his legacy. I'll take care of the others."

He took a step forward. "You will be my conduit, Darien. You will absorb all thirty-two tiers of combined vitrus. And, reaching through you, I will be able to halt the Reversal." His expression turned grim. He placed a comforting hand on Darien's shoulder. "Of course, as a consequence, you will not live to see your child born."

Even those words couldn't cool the flame of hope that had ignited inside Darien. It raged like a firestorm, consuming him utterly. He retreated a step, shaking his head. *"I don't care.* My life's not important."

Renquist gazed at him sadly. "Thank you, Darien. Know that your sacrifice will save many lives…and return the sunlight to Malikar." He hesitated then. Dropping his gaze to the floor, he spoke in a troubled voice, "You are like a son to me, Darien. Your loss will be deeply felt."

It sounded heartfelt. His own father had died long before Darien had reached adulthood, before he'd ever had a chance to make him proud. Zavier Renquist could never take his father's place. Nevertheless, he felt moved by the Prime Warden's expression of sentiment.

"Now go." Renquist dismissed him with a wave. "Find a way to strip your acolyte of his legacy."

"Aye, Prime Warden." Darien effected a formal bow, bending at the waist. He turned to leave but paused, turning back. "Prime Warden, might I ask a boon?"

Renquist nodded. "Of course."

"Please don't speak of this matter to my wife. I don't wish her to know."

Compassion filled Zavier Renquist's eyes, and he dipped his head. "Rest assured. Your wife will remain in ignorance."

Darien bowed again, lower this time. And then he left the tent.

Chapter Thirty-One
Promises and Lies

Death's Passage

Quin opened his eyes to the bleak grandeur of never-ending darkness.

Around him, a faint green light awoke and brightened gradually, until it was vibrant enough to see by. Turning, Quin found he could make out rough granite walls to either side: a passage that curved ahead of him as it sloped downward. It took him a moment to realize he was viewing the world through the hellish light of his own damnation. Looking down at his body, he could see the diffuse green aura that surrounded him. It didn't seem as potent as it had before.

There was a scuffing noise, and suddenly Naia was there with him. She drew up at his side, pausing as a mist of magelight crawled out of the shadows to linger at their feet. She placed a hand on his back and told him softly, "This is where we part."

Quin glanced at her in surprise. He'd figured he'd be journeying most of the way through the Catacombs in Naia's company. In truth, the thought of forging on alone was more than a bit unsettling.

Naia pointed to a fork in the corridor ahead that veered off to the right. "Follow that passage all the way to the end. It's long, but you shouldn't get lost. The exit will take you to a subbasement of the Temple of Death in Bryn Calazar."

Quin eyed the corridor warily. "Won't I be marked?"

Naia shrugged. "Possibly. If you are, I trust you'll know how to deal with the situation."

Quin stared at her sideways. "I do. I'm just shocked to hear you condoning such methods."

She smiled at him sadly. "We've gone far past the point where our actions can be limited by what I condone. The stakes are far too high."

Quin stared at her in admiration. Naia had come a long way from the woman who had once been defined by the chains on her wrists. She spoke from a place of calm practicality, in a way he found vastly alluring.

"Keep talking like that, darling, and I might never leave."

"Be very careful, Quinlan," she said. "That man is a monster."

"I'm a monster, too," he reminded her.

Naia shook her head. "No, Quin. You're not. Maybe you once were. But not anymore."

Looking down at the green aura that surrounded his body, Quin found himself in disagreement. But the thought fled quickly as Naia leaned in and pressed her soft lips against his. The kiss was long, and it left him dizzy and breathless.

"Go softly," Naia whispered when they parted. "Don't do anything that will get you killed. Again. Promise me you'll come back."

Quin shook his head. "I can't make that promise."

"Then promise me you'll try."

"I promise I'll try," he said, and leaned in to kiss her one last time. Then, settling his hat properly on his head, he turned and headed down the corridor.

Rothscard, The Rhen

Kyel followed Swain across the palace grounds to the sprawling hulk of the Citadel. There, the Prince led him down a flight of spiral steps into the dungeon beneath. It was not Kyel's first visit to the prison, and memories of his incarceration were bleak. They walked down a long corridor lined with wooden doors, stopping before the last.

Swain leafed through an iron ring of keys, at last settling on one, and poked it into the lock. With a click, the cell door popped outward just a crack. Swain glanced sharply at Kyel, then pulled the door open the rest of the way. Kyel stepped forward and peered within.

Alexa careened into his arms. Her body smacked against him, her arms squeezing him tight enough to choke him. Kyel reached up and, taking her by the wrists, disengaged her firmly and pushed her back. Alexa stared up at him with a wounded pout. She opened her mouth to say something.

He cut her off before she could get the words out. "Why are you here? How did you *get* here?"

Alexa's eyes darted to Swain then back to Kyel. She looked flustered, at a loss for words. "I don't know how I got here," she said frantically. "The last thing I remember was the battle. Then I woke up just outside the walls. I-I can't explain it! I know it doesn't make sense, but I don't know what to think. Kyel, I'm *scared.*"

Kyel didn't believe her. Every time he lowered his guard and started to trust her, Alexa invariably did something that made his doubt spike all over again. Frustrated, he grappled with his options. He didn't know whether to leave her in the cell or risk taking her with him. Of course, she could always get out on her own; she was a mage. If she really wanted to leave the cell, Alexa could in a heartbeat—but not without risking her Oath of Harmony.

He glanced at Swain. "Can I take her out of here?"

Swain's eyes narrowed. "How well do you know her?"

An excellent question. Kyel had to think about it hard before realizing that he really didn't know much about Alexa at all.

"I know her well enough," he lied.

The Prince stared at him. Doubt was plastered on Swain's face, and Kyel couldn't blame him. "All right," he growled. "I'll release her into your custody."

Kyel looked at Alexa, studying the expression on her face, searching for a reason to doubt her. Seeing none, he took her by the arm and let Swain guide them back out of the prison. No words were spoken as they crossed the Inner Ward back to the palace.

When they reached the entrance to the guest wing, Swain

glanced at Alexa and said, "If you need me, I'll be around." His eyes stabbed one last, menacing threat before he turned and left.

It was not Kyel's first stay at Emmery palace. He remembered the opulence of the guestrooms. Nevertheless, he was surprised at the size and luxury of the eight-room suite Romana had arranged for him. Kyel waited for Alexa to enter and then caught her by the arm and spun her back toward him.

"All right," he snapped, slamming the door shut. "I want answers."

"What?" She looked at him with a fearful expression.

"The necrators," Kyel reminded her. "They didn't touch you. Well, maybe they did, but they sure didn't harm you. If anything, *you* harmed *them*. So what really happened?"

Alexa shook her head furiously. "I don't know. Honestly, I don't!" She tugged at his arm, face pale and desperate. "I saw them closing in on you. I thought if I distracted them, maybe it would give you a chance to get away. I don't remember anything after that!"

Kyel could feel a hot spark of anger igniting in his gut. Too many strange events converged around Alexa like iron filings to a lodestone. He said, "Well, you're obviously here, so how did you *get* here?"

She threw her hands up. "I don't know! That's what I'm trying to tell you! I woke up here this morning. I don't remember anything before that. I really don't. I think…"

"You think what?" Kyel demanded.

Her face went blank, her eyes slipping to the side as if in thought. Very slowly, she said, "I think I was brought here. But I don't know how."

Her explanation did nothing to ease Kyel's doubt. Rather, it had the exact opposite effect. "How could have been brought here without knowing it? The attack on Glen Farquist was ten days ago! What have you been doing for the last *ten days?*"

Alexa staggered back. Her face was flushed, either in anger or in desperation. "I don't know! I don't remember!"

Kyel held his hand up. Thoughts tumbled around in his head then gradually began totaling themselves. The sum wasn't in

Alexa's favor.

He said, "Look. It all boils down to this: can I trust you? The more I think about it, the more I think the answer is no."

She opened her mouth to speak, but he raised his hand again. "You've never told me a lie, at least none that I can verify. And you've helped me a lot, with the talisman and the necrators. But you've also never told me any truth that I can verify. Not one. Everything you say, I have to take on faith. But my faith's running out. Tell me something I can validate. Right now. Or you're going back to that cell."

Alexa shook her head in desperation, her eyes wide enough to eclipse the moon. "What am I supposed to do? I can't remember!"

Kyel could only shrug. Her response confirmed his doubts. "Then I'm sorry. I'm going to get the guards now." He started to open the door.

She shot out her hand, grasping him by the shoulder. "I banished his necrators!"

Kyel turned back around. Warily, he said, "Explain."

Tears were collecting in Alexa's eyes. "I *banished* Darien's necrators!" she repeated. "I sent them away!"

"Sent them where?"

Softly, she whispered, "I sent their souls to Oblivion."

Kyel pulled away, taken aback. "Necrators don't have souls."

She clasped her hands in front of her, shaking her head emphatically. "Necrators *are* souls! Collections of souls enslaved to the master who commands them."

"So how does this prove anything?" Kyel asked. "You're telling me you can command his minions. Wouldn't that make you a demon as well?"

"No!" Alexa shook her head furiously. "I'm a Naturalist. I'm an expert at Natural Law—that's what we do! And necrators are *unnatural.* That's why I can unmake them. If I were one of Xerys' Servants, I would have commanded those necrators to destroy you."

"All right, enough." Kyel sighed, rubbing his temples. His brain ached. And, he had to admit, what she was saying made sense. He stepped back out of the doorway.

"I'm just trying to help you, Kyel," Alexa said, her eyes pleading. "I promise."

Kyel sighed and closed the door.

The nameless Zakai officer bowed low before Darien. The man probably had a name, but he hadn't bothered to learn it. Darien realized he knew very few of the names of the men sworn to serve him. It was better that way. Better to keep a distance. He didn't want to be able to put too many names with too many faces. It made it much easier to bury a man.

He leaned forward, using a stick to probe at the fire he'd built a good distance away from camp. He'd wanted to be alone. Away from the soldiers. Away from Azár. His thoughts were rampant, like a crowd of voices all shouting in his head, drowning out the rest of the world.

"Warden, the pavilion has been made ready for your use," the nameless officer reported.

Darien glanced up, glaring at the man for disrupting his solitude. "What about Renquist?"

"Both Prime Wardens have returned to Bryn Calazar."

If the soldier was put off by the look on his face, he didn't show it. No Zakai would. Darien figured he could punch the man in the groin and the soldier would probably just thank him for it.

He gave a grunt and poked at the fire again. The officer bowed and walked back toward the heart of the encampment. Darien stared after him, his eyes tracing the rows of tents while the thoughts in his head clamored for attention.

He rose and kicked dirt into the fire, smothering it. He could have used magic—it would have been easier. But sometimes it felt better to perform a task unaided. He girded his sword belt around his hips and drew his pack on over his shoulders. Then, fingers hooked in the straps, he made his way over the trampled grass back toward the heart of the encampment.

As he moved between rows of tents, the familiar sounds and

smells settled his nerves. The camp had a life and rhythm of its own. Right now it was winding down, getting ready for the smooth transition into night. The sun had already set, its light just a gray smear on the western horizon. Voices carried on the air from every direction. Laughter rose somewhere in the distance then faded again like a tide. The smell of searing meat invaded his path, making his mouth water. In the back of his mind, his thoughts still churned, still vied for dominance. It was all he could do to ignore them.

It took him awhile to reach the command tent. Darien pushed back the flaps and entered with an intense feeling of unease, half-expecting Renquist to appear out of the shadows. But the nameless officer had been right: both Prime Wardens were truly gone. Wearily, Darien pulled off his boots and pushed back the cloth partition. He stood there a moment, just looking. The four-poster bed looked the same as he'd left it. Connel's book of poetry rested open on its pedestal. The colorful woven rugs were arrayed across the floor in the same overlapping pattern he remembered. As if the tent hadn't been packed up and moved dozens of times over hundreds of miles in his absence.

Darien's gaze travelled across the floor, coming to rest on Azár's back. He was surprised to find her kneeling on the rugs on the other side of the bed, taking items from a chest. She glanced over her shoulder at him, then rose gracefully with a smile. He slid his pack off and stood for a moment, just staring at her. Then he crossed the space and wrapped his arms around her from behind. His hands came to rest on her middle, on the slight bulge that had started to form there.

He asked, "How are you feeling?"

"Better."

He drew a deep breath, taking in the scent of her. "Your hair smells good."

"Yes, well, you stink." He could hear the smirk in her voice. It made him smile. He held her tighter.

"Do I, now?"

"You smell like that hound when it gets wet."

Darien couldn't help but grin. He released her and opened

himself to the magic field, filling his mind with its sweet song. A soft blue light sprang into being around him, rippling over his body in azure waves. After a moment, he let it fade. Then he glanced down, verifying that his clothes were now just as clean as they smelled. He slipped his arms back around her.

"Better?"

"Yes." He heard the smile in her voice. "That is better."

Softly, he kissed her hair. As he did, he felt inside her, probing, exploring, until he felt her heartbeat. And beneath that sound there was another—softer and intensely faster. Darien concentrated on that sensation, bent all of his will into exploring it. At last he felt it: the faintest, tentative echo of identity.

"You carry a baby girl," he whispered, his voice full of awe.

"I know."

The smile was gone from his wife's voice. Only sadness remained. Sadness and despair. She twisted away from him. "I am going out."

He let her go, staring after her as she shrugged on a robe and fled through the partition. Darien closed his eyes and drew in a long, shuddering breath. He let it out again slowly. Collecting himself, he moved back out into the empty gathering space. Instead of following his wife, he moved to the table. He gazed down at the maps that were strewn across its surface, shoving his feelings aside. They were an unnecessary distraction.

No harm would ever come to his wife or his daughter, he decided.

He wouldn't let it.

Darien pinned his focus on the maps, studying them with an acute sense of purpose.

Chapter Thirty-Two
Servants of Xerys

Bryn Calazar, The Black Lands

Quin emerged from the Catacombs into the death-dim shadows of a temple basement. The space seemed abandoned, the dark stones floured with old dust. The smell of mildew dampened the air, and the constant sound of dribbling water echoed softly through the darkness. Quin started forward, the sound of his footfalls jolting the quiet.

He walked up an aisle lined with thick, dark pillars that supported a vaulted ceiling. Overhead, the roof seemed to sag in exhaustion, burdened by weight and old age. He reached a set of stairs and paused, looking up at walls encased by shadows that convulsed with sporadic torchlight. Quin closed his eyes, taking a moment to ease himself into the old mindset of hyper-vigilance. It took longer than expected. Centuries of indifference had dulled the sharp edges of his mind.

In his former life, Quin had lived every moment in such a state. Because of his temperament, he had been identified young and trained in secret to three different orders at once, in an experiment that went far outside of ethical boundaries. He had become a perfect alloy of magical expertise: Arcanist, Empiricist, and Battlemage—an unexpectedly dark and potent combination. Quin's unique skillset made him the most dangerous kind of assassin: a mage-killer. An ambush predator capable of disappearing into the shadows or striking from a distance. And under the rule of Zavier Renquist, the need for his talents had experienced a renaissance.

No one in Aerysius had ever suspected him. Quin's victims

died of natural causes: heart attacks, aneurisms, falls… The tools he'd created left no magical traces, no indications of foul play. And if a particular death seemed too coincidental, Quin had made certain he was the last person in the world anyone would suspect. He'd lived a quiet life: just an introverted, cynical artisan who never left his workshop. A talented Arcanist known throughout the world for his capacity to create. Only three men in all of history had been aware of his capacity to destroy.

One of those men was Zavier Renquist, who had commissioned his training all those years ago. Renquist called what Quin did "shadow diplomacy." Quin had found that ironic at the time, because his brother had always been the diplomat in the family. And yet it was often Quin's negotiations, more than Braden's, that had the most impact.

Beneath Quin's feet, the temple rumbled.

He paused, listening. The noise of dripping water seemed amplified in the stairwell. Above, one of the torches flared, the shadows flinching in response. Cautiously, Quin moved forward, stepping into a broad streak of torchlight.

From the corner of his eye, he caught a faint motion. His gaze ticked toward the young priest of Death who had been unfortunate enough to notice him. Quin willed the man dead then stepped over the corpse. Clutching his shadow staff close against his body, he crossed the shrine toward the door.

He peered outside, shooting a glance up and down the dark street. The ash-paved road was empty, save for one lone man who limped toward him, head wrapped in the gray scarf of Bryn Calazar's underclass. Quin stepped into the street, tipping his hat at the fellow. He caught the glint of suspicion in the man's eyes as he walked away.

Quin turned a corner and stepped into a narrow alley between the crumbling walls of two deteriorated buildings. There, he set his pack down and rifled through it. He withdrew a black vest made of a glimmering fabric that was dizzying to look at. Righting himself, Quin pulled on the vest. Immediately, the clothing he wore shimmered and blurred, distorted by a wave of magic. When he stepped out of the alley, he wore the thread-bare and soot-stained rags of a Calazari coal-digger. A mangled gray scarf hung from his shoulders, and his feet were bare and blackened. Quin wound the scarf around his head as he walked, tucking it into place.

He followed the street to its inevitable end, then turned onto a more populated thoroughfare. Adopting the bow-legged stride of a tunnel-dweller, he walked with his shoulders slumped in the general direction of the harbor. The streets became crowded—too crowded, under the circumstances. Looking around at the intersections teeming with foot traffic, Quin began to wonder if Bryn Calazar had ever been evacuated.

As he walked, he was constantly jostled by citizens in too much of a hurry to dodge him properly. Cadak was the busiest quarter of the city, and the most impoverished. Most people scurried about wrapped in throws and blankets, their skin unwashed, open wounds festering on their legs. Gas lanterns bordered the street, hazy orbs of light that faded in and out, at the mercy of roving clouds of coal-smoke. Quin followed the street as it curved, rising, to the top of a low hill.

At the summit, he paused and caught his breath. Below, at the bottom of the cliff, a broad expanse of ocean unfurled before him. He could hear the crash of the waves as they broke against an offshore reef, could feel the thick humidity in the air. But there was no scent to the ocean. The miasma of coal-smoke overwhelmed even the taste of salt in the air. Quin stood there for a long time, listening to the gentle rhythm of the waves, remembering the myriad gulls and sails that had once bobbed on the surface of the crystalline water.

Gazing out across the harbor, Quin realized how much he missed Bryn Calazar. Not this decapitated and resurrected monster of a city—he missed Bryn Calazar as it had been a thousand years ago, as it would never be again.

Across the harbor, overlooking the ocean, limestone cliffs capped by a modest-sized temple drew his attention. In that spot, the Lyceum had once stood, its arching domes and graceful minarets a wonder of the ancient world. The Lyceum had survived wars, dynasties, millennia...

…until his own choices had destroyed it.

A low rumble overhead echoed Quin's mood. He glanced up at the sky. The black clouds above looked even more volatile than usual, racing toward the horizon. The lights within their murky depths strobed as if incensed. Every once in a while, the lights would flare in unison, sending branches of lightning spiderwebbing across the sky. The sight was chilling. He knew what he was witnessing, for he had seen it before: the first throes of the magic field, as it cringed in anticipation of the Reversal.

Quin thrust his hands deep into his pockets and turned away from his memories. Keeping the harbor on his right, he set his course for the ziggurat.

Rothscard, The Rhen

Darien folded his arms, looking around at the tight circle of war chiefs gathered in the command tent. Of them all, the general of Bryn Calazar's army stared back at him the hardest. Masil ul-Calazi resented him and made no effort to hide it. Darien didn't care. The man was capable and efficient. He'd secured the whole of the western plains while Darien's Tanisars had been raiding down the far side of the Craghorns. Ul-Calazi commanded the largest professional fighting force in the world. It would be foolish not to take him seriously.

Speaking with his hands as much as his mouth, the general explained, "When we first arrived, the defenders would ride out from their gates in groups of roughly two hundred and attack our flanks. They would hit us quickly and then flee back behind their walls. Since then, they have engaged in no offensive maneuvers."

Darien nodded, taking in the information and saying nothing. His gaze was focused on the general's eyes, which stared back at him flatly. He was beginning to get the impression that, to ul-Calazi, war was only about numbers, timing, and probability. Darien found himself in agreement.

"Have you met any magical defenses?" he asked.

The general scratched the side of his nose, his mouth pursing.

"There has been no magic used against us."

Which was well. Darien had been hoping Kyel wouldn't follow them to Rothscard. Or worse—arrive ahead of them. Resting his hands on his thighs, he nodded thoughtfully. He swept his gaze around the circle of officers, then directed his response to ul-Calazi.

"Prepare your men for an assault. We'll attack the Lion's Gate at dawn. While you've got their attention, I'll create a breach in the eastern wall…here." He planted a finger on one of the maps spread out on the floor between them. "As soon as I do, abandon the gate and make for the breach."

Ul-Calazi glanced down at the map, dropping his hand. "What opposition should we expect within the walls?"

Darien tapped on the map, indicating a dense section of the city snug up against the eastern wall. "This quarter's called the Regret. It's mostly peasant shacks and fishmonger huts. It's also about as far away from the Citadel as you can get. They won't be guarding it. Just get there quickly, before they have time to plug the hole. We'll be fighting in the streets, house-to-house. It's going to get bloody."

The general waved his hand, as though dismissing Darien's concerns as trivial. He inclined his head stiffly. "Is that all, Warden?"

"That's all."

As the men and women rose from the floor, Darien commanded, "Sayeed. Remain."

His First turned back toward him, lingering on his feet as the other war chiefs cleared the tent. When they were alone, Darien gestured for him to sit, then rose and replaced the various maps he'd been using back on the table. He fetched a jug and two tin cups from an assortment of supplies stashed along the wall, then took a seat on the spread of rugs. Guessing his intent, Sayeed's eyebrows rose in question, even as his expression tightened with worry.

Very deliberately, Darien set the cups down between them and unstoppered the jar. He poured enough rika into each cup to fill it halfway. He then lifted his cup and emptied the contents into

Sayeed's. As he did, the man's eyes snapped up to lock on him. Keeping to the ritual, Sayeed gave Darien back his share and, watching him drink it down, followed suit.

Darien refilled both cups then sat back, resting his hands on his knees. He said, "I've a favor to ask of you."

Sayeed's gaze never left his own. "You may ask me anything, Brother."

Darien warned him, "It's an awfully big favor."

He drew in a deep, troubled breath, feeling his emotions squirm inside him. He didn't like letting them out; admitting his fears made him feel wretchedly uncomfortable. He knew the rika was meant to help with that but, of course, it didn't. Nothing could.

He poured Sayeed another cup, then filled his own to the brim, knocking the liquor back in one swallow. "The magic field will reverse its polarity in two days. Then I'll be returning to the Netherworld."

Sayeed stared at him in silence a long minute before pouring them both another round. He said softly, "And your wife carries your child in her womb."

Darien froze, pausing in the motion of lifting his drink. For a moment, he sat still and silent, gazing down at the scrollwork pattern of the rug. "How did you know?"

Sayeed's whole body appeared to deflate. "She is sick every morning. Brother…I have no words…"

Darien set his cup down hard. "Forget words. I've a problem to solve. And I need you to help me solve it." He didn't want the man's pity. That was the last thing in the world he needed.

Sayeed nodded, his face hardening. "Of course. Forgive me."

"There's a way to stop this," Darien said. "To stop the Reversal."

"*Ishilzeri!* How? What must we do?"

Darien raised his hand. "Stop. You can do nothing—it's all on me. And I won't survive, so I need you to—"

Sayeed shook his head vehemently. "You have no way of knowing that—"

"I do," Darien insisted. "Remember when you swore to be my

brother? You told me that, if I should ever fall, you'd provide for my family. Tell me those weren't just words. Tell me you meant it." He pinned his stare on Sayeed's face as he waited for a response. It took long seconds to come.

"Of course I meant it." Sayeed's voice sounded hoarse. He stared past Darien at the wall of the tent, looking deeply troubled. Darien hoped it wasn't because the man had changed his mind.

"Then would you do that for me, Brother? Will you care for my wife and daughter after I'm gone?"

Sayeed placed his cup upside down on the rug, then firmly clasped Darien's arm with both hands. He said gravely, "I swear I will guard your family with my life and provide for their needs. And I will make certain your daughter grows to womanhood knowing of the man her father was. It is far more than my obligation. It is my honor."

Darien nodded, feeling suddenly incapable of trusting his voice. To cover, he lifted the jug and poured each of them a fresh cup. He drank his down, listening to the great, brooding silence that had settled between them. He felt comforted by Sayeed's pledge. But at the same time, he felt disturbed by his own reaction to it. He had expected to feel the sadness, the frustration, the grief.

He just hadn't expected to feel the envy.

Naia stared out through the curtained window of the carriage that carried her, rattling along, toward Emmery Palace. The city teemed with panicked residents who filled the streets, shouting and shoving their way through the bedlam.

By the time her carriage drew up in the manicured courtyard of the palace, Naia was already on edge. Athera's Crescent had shown her visions of Rothscard under siege, and those visions had always led to dark and uncertain futures.

A group of blue-cloaked guardsmen rushed forward to attend her. One man with captain's bars peered in through the carriage window. His face had been scarred by the pox, his hair white and peppered with gray.

"Come on out," he ordered. "What business have you?"

Naia threw open the carriage door and hopped to the ground without waiting for a footman. She informed the captain, "I am Master Naia Seleni of the Order of Harbingers. I am here to request an audience with the Queen."

"You claim to be a mage?" The captain sounded skeptical, looking her up and down intently. "Let's see the chains on your wrists."

Naia froze. She hadn't anticipated such a question. She had lost the markings of her Oath before her journey to Titherry. Her mind searched frantically for excuses—anything to distract from the glaring absence of the chains.

The captain's eyes narrowed. In a rigid voice tempered by ice, he said, "Bare your arms. If you like, you can do it away from my men. But unless you've got the marks of the Oath on your wrists, you won't be going anywhere near the Queen."

Naia stared at the captain in dismay, having no idea how to react. If Romana found out she'd given up her Oath, the Queen might go so far as to order her execution. Staring at the captain fixedly, she said, "You wish me to prove that I'm a mage? There are other ways."

A blue mist of magelight appeared at her feet. Startled, the captain stepped back with a look of alarm.

"I am a Master of Aerysius," Naia proclaimed. "Do you still doubt?"

The captain stared at her hard, unblinking. A small drop of sweat dribbled down his brow. His hand tensed and then untensed on the hilt of his sword. His lips compressed to a fine line, his jaw tightening. He took another step back.

"Run, Jeffers!" he growled.

The captain drew his sword, his men fanning out behind him. One of the guards turned and lit out across the courtyard.

Something struck Naia from behind.

Her knees buckled, her vision erupting in a shower of sparks.

Chapter Thirty-Three
The Pain of Truth

Rothscard, The Rhen

Kyel Archer stood on a turret overlooking the Lion's Gate, the banners of Emmery Palace fluttering behind him. A breeze stirred the air, moving in from the river delta. Kyel stared off in that direction, hoping for a glimpse of the ocean. But Rothscard was still a good distance from the shore, and the tower wasn't tall enough to offer a view of it.

A different kind of ocean spread out from the base of Rothscard's walls. The Enemy encampment extended to the horizon, arranged in perfect geometric patterns. There were so many more tents than he had expected. Kyel tried not to let the numbers intimidate him, but it was hard not to. His hand tightened around Thar'gon's haft, seeking and finding comfort in the weapon's extraordinary might.

He turned away from the parapets. As he did, a jolting shock seared down his nerves, making him reel. He shot his hand out and caught himself on the coarse stone of a merlon. All around him, the lines of the magic field stretched and then recoiled as if bludgeoned. The aftershocks continued for a while, the field lines convulsing spastically before evening out again.

Kyel stood panting, taking a moment to collect himself. He knew exactly what had happened, and it scared the hell out of him. The Reversal was imminent, and the magic field was already cringing in anticipation.

Filled with dread, he fled the ramparts and turned his attention to navigating the escalating confusion of Rothscard's streets. Even the black cloak on his back didn't spare him from being pushed and jostled, shoved and elbowed. A climate of panic had infested the city, which was getting worse as the siege dragged on. By the time he gained the palace grounds, Kyel felt as though he'd been on the receiving side of a tavern brawl. The streets were becoming dangerous, nearly impossible to negotiate.

As he crossed the Inner Ward, a commotion across the courtyard caught his attention. Near the Citadel, a group of guards had a woman on the ground. Two men had thrown their weight on top of her, pinning her down, while another man struggled to lock a set of manacles around her wrists. To Kyel, the entire scene looked brutal and irregular. There were far more guards than it should take to arrest one woman who wasn't resisting. Concerned, he hastened toward her, wondering what she had done to deserve such treatment.

They rolled the woman over, and Kyel got a glimpse of her face.

Recognition slapped him in the stomach, tearing a gasp from his lips. He lurched forward, shoving his way through the cluster of shocked guards.

The woman on the ground peered up at him, squinting, as though staring into the sun. Her face was streaked with bloody grime, her dress torn and filthy.

"Kyel?" she muttered.

A grizzled captain with a pox-scarred face shot between them, waving him away. Seeing the color of Kyel's cloak, the guardsman's face twisted into a grimace.

"Do you know this woman?"

"I know her," Kyel growled, dodging past him. He dropped down to Naia's side and, setting a hand on her back, healed the cut on her scalp before the man could protest.

The captain caught his arm, trying to pull him away. "This woman's a darkmage! She admitted it freely!"

Kyel jerked his arm out of the man's grip. He looked down at Naia, suddenly troubled. Her wrists were bound by wide iron bands that hid the presence of any markings that might be there. Or any scars. Remembering the body of Sareen Qadir lying dead on the floor of the shrine, Kyel had to admit that the guards might be right.

His eyes went back to Naia's face, searching there for answers. But her eyes were closed; she'd fallen into the healing sleep. He wasn't going to get any information from her. So he went with his gut.

Kyel stared flatly at the officer. "I'm not asking. I'm telling. Get the damn restraints off her."

The guard captain didn't move. The man stood frozen as his men looked nervously on. Frustrated, Kyel reached out from within and tore Naia's shackles off himself. They opened of their own accord, slipping to the ground with a metallic clink. The guards surged back, hands darting for their weapons.

Kyel's stare remained fixed on Naia, at the set of awful scars that encircled both her wrists. A feeling of profound sadness crept over him. Anger followed quickly. With a disgusted growl, he heaved Naia into his arms and lifted her from the ground.

The captain bellowed after him, "She's a godsdamned dark-mage! And you're one, too, for helping her!"

Ignoring him, Kyel carried Naia toward the palace, mired in his own turbulent outrage.

Bryn Calazar, The Black Lands

The dark avenue Quin followed split into two smaller avenues, forking around a short temple that squatted like an abandoned god in the midst of the intersection. The temple's walls leaned drunkenly to one side, its parallel columns bent at a painful angle. The entire structure looked ready to fall over. It was a miracle it already hadn't.

The city streets still buzzed with people who, for whatever reason, had chosen to ignore the order to evacuate. Tall-wheeled rickshaws sped by, pulled by bone-thin youths, while merchants dragged carts behind them laden with trade goods. Quin walked down the center of the street, careful to maintain the shambling stride of the city's malnourished underclass. A peddler, mummified in cloth, noticed him and sprang forward, thrusting a skewer of roasted vegetables under his nose.

"Five darham!" the peddler shouted in the Calazi dialect, waving the skewer. "Five darham! Delicious!"

"No thank you," Quin said, pushing the skewer out of his way.

The man was undeterred. He jogged after Quin, waving his skewer. "Four darham! Very fresh! You should taste!"

Quin waved him away, quickening his pace. A woman ahead of him carried a howling baby strapped to her back, its thin legs kicking in exclamation. Quin veered around her, almost tripping over a broken cobble in the street. Up ahead, he could see the tall, step-sided ziggurat thrusting its weight above the skyline. He set his course toward it, boring his way against the flow of foot traffic. Vexed pedestrians dodged and jostled him, raining him with curses and threats. Quin ignored them all and shambled onward.

The avenue narrowed abruptly, tall walls erupting on both sides of the street. Quin turned onto a winding alley lined with merchant stalls, each stuffed with odd assortments of pottery, textiles, and iron-forged wares. Eventually, the cobbles ran out. The street continued on, paved with tarry mud that reeked of stale urine.

Quin halted at the base of the ziggurat. His eyes traced the long, ramp-like steps that slanted upward at an intimidating angle. There were no guards stationed around the temple's base, at least none visible. He paused long enough to make certain the fabric of his head scarf was tucked in tight, then started up the stairs.

The steps were grueling and precarious, much taller than they were narrow. His legs burned by the time he reached the temple entrance only midway up. There, recessed in a split in the rise of steps, two black-mailed sentries warded the entrance to the Grand Temple of Xerys. Though they remained thoroughly motionless, Quin knew the sentries had marked his approach.

Which was why they slumped dead, like toppled suits of armor.

Unwinding the scarf, Quin stepped around the bodies and slipped into the dim corridor beyond. A narrow passage led straight back into the temple's dark interior, lit at long intervals by lanterns ensconced along the walls. Quin moved forward cautiously, using just a dribble of magic to soften the sounds of his footfalls. A little ways in, he found an opening in the wall that led to a side passage. He turned onto it, finding himself in a short corridor that led to a series of rooms partitioned by brightly-colored fabric. Quin stopped at the first drape of gauzy cloth and, pulling the fabric aside, slipped through the doorway.

Warm light greeted him within, along with the heady odor of perfume. Sounds of conversation and laughter drifted from an adjoining chamber. Backing against a wall, Quin wove a web of shadow and tightened it around his body. Within the shadow-web, he could go unremarked by the casual observer, nothing more than a fuzzy distortion in the air. He moved toward the light and the laughter, stopping before a thin drape of turquoise gauze.

He pushed the curtain aside just a fraction and peered within. The chamber on the other side was ornately tiled and contained a luxurious octagonal bath ringed by pillowed sofas. Men and women lounged in and around the water, in various stages of undress. Judging by their well-nourished bodies, the men were most likely priests of Xerys. Which would make the women attending them either acolytes or slaves, if there truly was a distinction.

He let the fabric sway closed then retraced his steps, taking a moment to tighten his shadow-web.

Back out in the hallway, Quin moved to the next fabric-draped doorway. He parted the curtain and slipped into a long, dim chamber lit only by the glow of a single lantern. He stood quietly for a moment, just listening to the sound of the room's emptiness, assessing his surroundings. Dark silhouettes of furniture lined the walls. The oil lantern sat on the floor in the corner behind him, casting a timid glow. He crept further in, drawn toward an unlit doorway at the far end of the room.

"Your hatred is so loud, I could hear it echoing from Titherry."

Quin squeezed his eyes shut as a feeling of defeat seeped through the pores in his skin. He released the shadow-web, since it no longer served a purpose.

If it ever had.

He turned slowly around to confront the dark figure that moved forward to eclipse the lantern light.

"You knew I'd come," Quin surmised.

The shadow nodded. "Of course I did. In truth, I was counting on it."

Quin groaned. Renquist must be a sensitive—and a damn powerful one, to feel his emotions across such a broad expanse of ocean. He hadn't suspected that. But there was so much that revelation explained. Suddenly, a thousand different things made a thousand different kinds of sense.

Quin asked, "What do you want from me?"

He leaned his staff against the wall and curled his fingers around the hilt of his sword, the one artifact in the world capable of dampening a mage's gift. He could feel Renquist's strength from across the room, a dark and potent energy that exuded from his presence to oppress the air. Renquist's power had grown tremendously since the last time Quin had seen him, making him wonder if the Prime Warden had been sitting in Bryn Calazar drinking in mage power. And mage lives.

Renquist took a step deeper into the pool of light. The wavering glow of the lantern defined his face in jagged angles and sharp planes. His eyes burned through the shadows like glowing embers.

He said, "You have something I deeply desire."

Quin drew his sword with a metallic hiss, holding the tip leveled at the demon's heart. Or where his heart should have been. Quin doubted Renquist had ever had one.

"I didn't think you had such confidence in my abilities."

He was awarded with a condescending smile. "It's not your abilities I have confidence in, Quinlan. It's your stupidity. You have defied me twice. Once with Braden. And now with Darien. You have a knack for leading my most talented pupils astray."

Quin scoffed. "Darien isn't like Braden."

"No," Renquist agreed. "He's not. Darien is much more competent and powerful than your brother ever was. Which is why I need your assistance."

Quin felt his heart pounding against his ribs. With every word, Renquist's voice clawed deeper into his chest. "What makes you think I'll help you?"

The demon smiled. "You'll help me because Darien is determined to do exactly what you and your brother gave your lives to prevent all those years ago. You see, Darien knows a way to halt the Reversal. And he is willing to open the floodgates of hell to accomplish it."

"No." Quin shook his head. "Darien wouldn't do that."

Renquist took a step toward him, smiling kindly. "Wouldn't he? Perhaps you don't know him as well as you think."

"I know him well enough." Quin drew the sword back over his shoulder, winding his arms as he backed away. He didn't get far.

A noise behind him made him turn. Cyrus Krane stood in the doorway, flanked by three of his sinister pets. The necrators glided silently forward like obsidian death. Quin backed away until he found himself pinned against the wall. He didn't know if Krane's necrators could harm him, but he didn't want to find out.

Renquist continued, "If you know Darien, then you know he already lost one child. How must he feel, knowing he is about to lose another?"

Quin lowered his sword, his arms sagging to his sides. He opened his mouth to deny the man's words but then stopped himself. Zavier Renquist never lied. He never had to. The truth was always much more painful.

Quin swallowed heavily. "Who's the mother?"

"Darien's wife. The Lightweaver, Azár."

Quin glared his hatred at Renquist, shaking his head in disgust. "You really are a demon, aren't you? It's not good enough for you to destroy a man. You have to destroy all that he is and all that he loves. And even then, you're still not satisfied." He regarded Renquist a long, searching moment. "You still haven't explained why you need me."

"I don't need you at all," the Prime Warden responded in an ice-calm voice. "The strength of the gift inside you will be enough to suffice."

Quin's stomach froze like a block of ice. He pressed himself against the wall as close as he could.

The light of the lantern winked out. An encompassing blackness settled thickly around him, cold and terrifying. Quin couldn't see the necrators, but he could feel them there, just on the edge of his senses. Gliding toward him through the darkness.

Rothscard, The Rhen

Kyel's hand trembled as he offered Naia a glass of water. She sat on a sofa, rubbing her temples, looking up at him with dark eyes that bore no degree of malice. Still, Kyel couldn't drag his gaze away from the scars on her wrists, repulsed by the sight of them.

"Explain yourself," he said, crossing his arms.

Naia took a sip of water then smiled patiently. "I'm not a dark-mage, Kyel. I'm just a mage." Her eyes were kind, compassionate. Just the way he remembered. "Bound or Unbound, it makes no difference. I'm still the same person you've always known. I haven't changed."

"You broke Oath!" he growled, filled with both anger and fear. When—not if—Romana found out about her, the Queen would order Naia put to death. Kyel knew he couldn't argue with that decision. The thought made him want to retch.

Naia raised her eyebrows, fixing him with a disappointed look. "I did it to save you. Sareen was killing you—"

Kyel raised his hand, cutting her off. She had condemned herself by her own words. The realization made him feel intensely sad. He blew out a protracted sigh, resenting the hell out of her. He would have to tell Swain. Sooner, rather than later.

Naia was a mage, so the Citadel couldn't contain her if she decided to walk out.

Swain and Romana wouldn't want to take that risk.

Chapter Thirty-Four
The Regret

Rothscard, The Rhen

Darien sat his horse, Sayeed and his Zakai at his side, watching the gray light of dawn bleed slowly across the horizon. The morning was cold; he could feel the chill of his armor even through his padded gambeson. Dark clouds had moved in sometime during the night. Deep within their depths, Darien could see swarms of flickering lights. The lights seemed to wince in time to the pulsations of the magic field. The disturbances were entirely unnatural. The feel of them grated like sandpaper down his nerves.

He stared out across the wide swath of denuded ground that stood between their ranks and Rothscard's high walls. To the left of his Tanisars, the army of Bryn Calazar was amassed before Rothscard's north gate, spread out across the grassland like a tumultuous black sea. At their rear, the horse warriors of the Jenn had collected in a vast, milling horde.

Thin columns of smoke rose at intervals from Rothscard's crenelated ramparts, from fires lit to heat oil and pitch and add an element of horror to the missiles of the trebuchets. Rothscard's commanders had positioned the bulk of their defenses along the north wall in anticipation of an attack on the Lion's Gate. The rest of the city's battlements remained relatively undermanned. So far, his feint was working.

A sonorous horn cry rose over the plain, followed by a disciplined stillness no army of the Rhen could ever rival. Amongst the Malikari legions, not a soul moved. There was no clatter of weapons, no rustle of armor.

Just an unnerving silence that clung like a pall over an army of one hundred thousand men, a silence that thundered louder than any war drum ever could.

The general of Bryn Calazar's legions raised his sword. Upon his signal, every throat in the ranks behind him bellowed a whip-crack war cry.

There was a pause.

Then, faintly at first, deep-throated drums began tapping out a measured cadence. The drums gradually increased in tempo and intensity, the resonant booms rising in crescendo over the plain. The pulse of the drums continued, relentless and precise, rattling the air until Darien could feel their rumble in his chest. Another staccato shout bellowed from thousands of throats, then another, just off-beat. The resounding noise swelled to a climax, sustained there for minutes, then ceased with a final, thundering *BOOM*.

Stillness followed.

A lone war horn brayed languorously.

Then, with a tremendous cry, the whole of the Malikari army broke forward at a run.

The thunder of their charge was deafening. As the front ranks came within bowshot of the walls, dark arrow clouds began arcing downward, dropping soldiers at random. Trebuchets mounted to the ramparts joined in, hurling projectiles coated with Hell's Fire that blazed like long-tailed comets across the sky, tearing great swaths through the advancing army. Men and women were set ablaze with sticky flames that spread quickly to devour anyone nearby.

Ul-Calazi's men raised ladders against the walls that were immediately flung back, only to be raised again. All the while the trebuchets worked tirelessly, hurling their blazing payloads at the attacking army. One of the siege engines erupted in flames, the men tending it hurled from the battlements. Another trebuchet exploded seconds later, taking its attending crew with it.

A great cry rose from the battlefield, and then the dark host parted to admit an armored battering ram, covered and shielded. It was drawn by many teams of horses that were then unhitched before they were brought within bowshot. From there, men ran forward to push the ram up against the gate. Hot oil and flaming arrows flooded down from above like scalding rain. For every man that dropped, another took his place, the ram moving inexorably forward.

Darien swept his gaze over the fortifications, noting the lack of soldiers on the eastern side of the city. As predicted, Swain had pulled the bulk of his forces from that section of wall, leaving its defenders spread few and thin.

A resounding shout brought his attention back to the Lion's Gate. A brilliant gold shield had insinuated itself between the ram and the gate, repulsing their efforts. The ram battered futilely against the shield, while Malikari infantry screamed their frustration at the unyielding walls. Flights of arrows splattered the ground, felling men like trees.

Seeing that golden shield, Darien swore a curse. He'd hoped they'd left Kyel behind in Glen Farquist.

His eyes scoured the battlements, searching. But the city was too far away to make out the faces of the men defending it. His frustration mounded by the second. It felt like the battle had reached a critical climax and was ready to implode. He looked at Sayeed.

"Are you ready, Brother?" he asked.

His First nodded. "We are ready."

"Then let's have at it."

He kicked his boots into his horse's sides, clutching the stallion's mane in his fist. The animal surged forward, moving quickly up to speed, its hooves tearing up the grassland as it raced toward the city's eastern wall. Sayeed's horse labored alongside his own, his men fanned out behind them.

Ahead, the few soldiers guarding the east gate noticed their approach and started scrambling. A few panicked and loosed their shafts early, which fell well short of hitting their marks. Darien drew his mount up and motioned his men to move into position at his sides. He glanced up and down the face of the wall, getting a better idea of the defenses. Urging his stallion into motion, he veered the horse toward the gate.

As they came within range, groupings of arrows began arcing down from the walls. Darien deflected the shafts before they could find purchase. When they neared the gate, he slid off his horse, then sent the beast on its way with a slap on the hindquarters.

He opened his mind to the magic field, gathering it in and holding it at ready. The field thrashed wildly, already tormented by the coming Reversal. He tightened his grip on it, despite its protest. The feel of it rubbed his nerves wrong, made his skin crawl.

Darien concentrated on the masonry that lined the gate, feeling inside the stones and applying pressure to the weakest joints. Fine cracks erupted all along the wall, racing outward like spiders' veins. Flakes of granite showered down. Above on the battlements, the soldiers realized their danger and retreated to the towers. Darien concentrated harder, bending all the brute force of his will into the effort. Chunks of stone sprayed from deep fissures, and a terrible groaning noise rumbled from deep within.

Still, the wall stood.

Darien reached for the Onslaught and used the Hellpower to augment his strength. Within seconds, he felt the blocks surrounding the gate start to *shift*. Huge chunks shivered and disappeared, leaving gaps in the stone arch. More stones shivered and then gave way, raining shards of crumbled rock onto the ground. Then, with a deafening roar, the entirety of the wall collapsed into a mounded berm of jagged stone.

Darien's men scrambled forward, leaping onto the rubble as arrows pelted down from the towers still standing. Darien deflected the arrows and scrambled after Sayeed into the breach. The debris shifted beneath him, the stones turning underfoot. It was harrowing minutes before he followed the Zakai off the scree. Skidding down the last few crumbling steps, Darien stumbled to a stop, then glanced around to get his bearings.

They had breached the wall in a remote section of the city called the Regret. The quarter was populated mostly by criminals and unfortunates, its slums and back-waters burgeoning with black-market trade. Ahead, his Zakai patrolled the street, moving in zig-zag patterns from one side to the other, crossbows cocked, swords held ready. Darien walked behind them, his eyes scanning the long, dilapidated layers of shanties stacked one atop the other. Drying laundry flapped like colorful banners above the street, hanging from clothes lines that crisscrossed above. The smell of the place was a cloying combination of mold, wood smoke, and rot.

Ahead, a disjointed collection of slum dwellers had amassed at the end of the street, armed with a variety of impromptu weapons. Seeing the advancing Zakai, the mob broke toward them.

"No mercy," Darien ordered. The Zakai sprinted forward. He ran after them, sword in hand, bringing the Onslaught to bear against Rothscard's luckless defenders.

Kyel tightened his grip on Thar'gon, nervous sweat trickling from his brow. Alexa stood at his side, clinging to his arm. He wasn't sure whether she sought to steady him or steady herself. He was starting to have a hard time keeping focus. The power Thar'gon channeled was wild and difficult to control in the amounts Kyel found himself wielding. With the talisman's aide, he'd been able to force the massive battering ram back from the gate, but only at great risk to his Oath. He hadn't killed any of the attackers directly, but it had been too close for Kyel's liking. He'd narrowly avoided immolating a siege engine, along with all of the men tending it.

At his side, Nigel Swain stood shouting orders at the top of his lungs. There was frenzied fighting all along the battlements. Ladders were being raised from below, more and more each minute—too many to deal with all at once. Little by little, the Enemy was making their way onto the walls and expanding the footholds they gained. Up and down the ramparts, Enemy warriors were capturing the wall-mounted trebuchets and turning them against the city's own defenses. Soon, Kyel found his attention pulled away from the gate, forced to defend Rothscard against flaming projectiles hurled from its own walls.

A concussive blast exploded against the tower behind him.

Kyel threw a ward up—probably the only thing that saved his life—but couldn't expand it in time to save the soldiers on the tower who fell, engulfed in roiling flames. Kyel extinguished the flames but not the pain. The men continued to writhe and scream, while Kyel looked helplessly on. He couldn't heal them without physical contact, and he was too occupied trying to prevent another such catastrophe.

Alexa tugged harder on his arm. "It's not enough!" she cried. "We are losing this battle! You must make a choice—between preserving your Oath or preserving the Rhen!"

Angered, Kyel waved her off. She could be doing a lot more than she was, he thought, watching another tower erupt in flames, men thrown from its walls. Kyel cursed in frustration. He'd let that one get by him.

At his side, Swain stiffened. "Something's wrong," he said, his voice barely audible over the rage of the battle

Kyel shouted, "What?"

Reaching up, the Prince ripped his helm off and moved to a crenel overlooking the plain. His face was covered in soot, except for branching streaks where sweat had eroded the grime. He finished his study of the battlefield, then turned back to Kyel with a look of alarm. "They're not using Darien."

Kyel froze. He hadn't noticed Darien's glaring absence from the battle. The thought made his stomach wrench. "Then where is he?"

"Gods be damned!"

A merlon exploded beside him, flinging them backward. Swain recovered quickly, blood leaking from a gash over his eye.

Another, larger, explosion rocked the city.

Kyel stared out across the skyline, to where a wide plume of smoke rose and was spreading swiftly.

Swain started swearing fluently. He shouted at his officers, "Pull everyone you can off the gate and get them down to the Regret! Gods' whoring mother, they've already breached the fucking wall!"

Darien backed away from the fires consuming the Regret's layered shanties and turned to follow Sayeed into a narrow alley. The fires were spreading hungrily, leaping from rooftop to rooftop, much faster than he'd expected. Panicked residents fled before the roiling heat of the flames, taking to the streets—sometimes through doors, more often through windows. The morning had gone dark, the sky blackened by billowing smoke swarming with embers. The air was filled with horrendous shrieks, the kind that only came from the throats of the dying.

A window broke overhead, raining shards of glass down right in front of him. A woman followed, streaming fire behind her and screaming all the way to the ground. Darien lurched backward, filled with revulsion, then turned to jog after Sayeed toward the street.

At the intersection, Sayeed caught him by the arm and nodded toward another group of men collecting a ways up the street, a combination of city regulars and armed citizens. Darien wrapped a glowing shield around himself and motioned for Sayeed and his men to remain behind. Drinking in the Onslaught, he strode alone up the center of the street toward the gathered resistance. Seeing him haloed by an aura of green energy, the mob became chaotic. Most of the men started backing away. Others turned and bolted. Darien summoned a mist of magelight and sent it slithering ahead of him. More men fled. The rest broke toward him.

Something *cracked* against his shield. Darien whirled to see a soldier reloading an arbalest, in the process of fighting with the crank. He threw the Hellpower mindlessly at the man. The soldier melted, dissolving with a sizzling hiss.

Darien turned back to face the charging militia.

Sayeed sprang in front of him and struck out at the first man, slicing his head off, then kicked another man back against the side of a building. He ducked an oncoming strike, then whirled to thrust his sword into his opponent's chest.

The rest of the attackers exploded in a rain of gore.

Sayeed whirled to look at Darien with startled eyes.

"Where is ul-Calazi?" Darien growled.

He kicked the severed head out of his path, then glanced back in the direction of the breach. The Calazari reinforcements should have arrived minutes ago. Ahead, more blue-cloaked soldiers poured into the end of the street. Defenders worked feverishly to seal them off, erecting a barricade that consisted of any lose items they could scavenge from the surrounding buildings. Already, in the span of minutes, hundreds of soldiers had collected behind that barricade. Very soon, there would be thousands. For the first time, Darien started to doubt. He had brought only his warband to capture the Regret, but it would take more than that to keep control of it.

He wondered if Ul-Calazi had abandoned him intentionally.

Growing nervous, Darien scanned his surroundings, searching for a good defensive position they could retreat to. As an extra precaution, he summoned his array of necrators and sent them ranging ahead. He wasn't sure they would be enough. But they were all he had.

Kyel pulled his horse to a halt and swung down from its back, striding across the street toward the lowered portcullis that sealed off the Regret Quarter. Swain tossed his horse's reins to a soldier and then ran over to take reports from a cluster of officers. Kyel slowed to a stop, daunted by the mayhem that reigned on the other side of the gate.

Through the portcullis' rusted bars, he could see that a large section of the Regret was already enveloped in flames, the smoke so thick it was impossible to estimate the extent of the destruction. A terrified mob had gathered on the other side of the portcullis. People were struggling to reach a small sally port beside the gate. The crowd surged violently. Panicked residents shoved and fought their way forward. People were starting to get trampled, while others were desperate enough to try climbing the portcullis despite iron spikes meant to discourage such activity.

Outraged, Kyel crossed back toward Alexa and said to her, "We have to stop this here. Can you banish his necrators?"

Alexa nodded. "If I get close enough."

Kyel bit his lip, trying to think of the best way to proceed. "Stay by me," he ordered. He crossed the street toward Swain.

"This is a godsdamn disaster," the Prince growled.

Glaring in rage at the gate, Kyel said, "I'll control him. Have your men finish him off."

Swain flashed him a devil grin and freed his longsword from its wooden sheath. He waved Kyel and Alexa back against the wall, then shouted the order to raise the portcullis. There was a groaning shriek of fatigued gears and clattering chain. The portcullis shuddered upward to admit a frantic hoard of rampaging people who streamed past them out of the Regret. It was minutes before the flood drained to a trickle. When it did, Swain ordered his men forward. They moved through the gate at a dogtrot, faces pale and rigid. Kyel couldn't blame them. They knew exactly what they advanced toward.

Side-by-side with Alexa and Swain, Kyel followed the soldiers into the Regret.

Chapter Thirty-Five
Duel with a Devil

Rothscard, The Rhen

Darien led his men across a war-torn square that had, only minutes before, been part of the Rhen's largest covered market. The slatted roof had burned away, leaving only the scorched bricks of merchant stalls intact. Darien swiped his hand out, throwing a concussive blast that sent a group of city regulars hurling to the ground. Only a few managed to get back up again. By the time the Zakai arrived, most of the survivors had fled. His warriors dispatched the rest.

Looking back, Darien saw that an entire company of Blue-cloaks had flanked them and were closing on their rear. He recalled his necrators to his aid. They rose around him, shadowed wraiths that served with mindless hunger. With a whispered word, he sent them gliding toward the encroaching soldiers.

A shout from Sayeed made him whirl back around. Dozens more guardsmen were pouring into the other side of the market. His necrators weren't done eliminating the threat behind. Darien drew in the exhilarating taint of the Onslaught, wielding it against the men-at-arms ahead.

Immediately as he struck, a group of his own warriors were lifted off their feet and thrown brutally backward. They collided with the sides of the tall brick buildings, their skulls and spines shattering on impact. Darien froze in place, numbed by shock. Sayeed started forward, but Darien threw a hand up, stopping him.

"It's Kyel." He swore a curse.

Sayeed hissed in frustration, raising his sword. "Can you counter him?"

"We're about to find out."

Darien intensified the glowing shield that warded them, reinforcing it with the Onslaught. He scanned the way ahead, searching rooftop to rooftop, window by window. Confounded, he moved warily forward, Sayeed at his side, a half-dozen injured Zakai behind them. They were all that was left of his warband. The remainder of his men lay dead and broken in the street behind them.

The market square was eerily quiet, save for the crackle of flames still gnawing at the bones of the surrounding district. Ash drifted through the air like snowflakes, borne on a wicked-hot breeze.

Darien tried to swallow, but his throat was too dry to perform the action. He turned slowly around, scanning the alleys, seeing nothing. The day had become eclipsed, a totality of smoke that darkened the sun.

A distant clattering echoed toward them, sharp noises ringing off the surrounding walls: the sound of hoofbeats. Darien whirled toward the end of the street, bringing his sword back. Sayeed moved into position at his side, his blade held ready, glancing up and down the street.

All at once, a lone horse erupted from a side street, careening toward them at full gallop, empty stirrups bouncing at its sides. Startled, Darien lowered his sword and backed away. The horse didn't slow its charge, but angled toward them as if aiming to run them down. Darien leaped out of the way, Sayeed throwing himself in the other direction. Before Darien could recover, scores of soldiers spilled into the market, converging on them from all sides.

The Zakai leaped forward to ring them defensively. Sayeed raised his sword, his fingers flexing and unflexing their grip on the hilt. Blood and grimy sweat ran down his cheeks, dripped from his chin. His lips drew back in the rictus of a snarl. He stepped behind Darien, turning to ward his back.

The Bluecloaks closed the distance and engaged with fury.

Darien seized the magic field, lashing out with it violently. A roiling conflagration of flames consumed the center of the square, devouring everything in its path. Soldiers screamed and fell, thrashing on the ground before quickly succumbing. Those who tried to outrun the flames didn't get far. The entire market was ablaze with whipping whirlwinds of fire that twisted high in the air.

When there was nothing left to consume, the flames died down. It took Darien a moment to realize that only Sayeed and himself remained alive in the square, crouching in a perfect ring of uncharred cobbles.

Trembling, Darien pushed himself to his feet. His anger burned raw, hotter than the flames.

"Visea," he whispered, recalling his necrators.

Swain cursed and ordered his reinforcements into the market. Kyel stood glaring at the black smoke that roiled from the center of the square ahead, wondering how many soldiers had been devoured by Darien's assault.

Suddenly, a terrible feeling overcame him, making the hairs on the back of his neck stand on end. A ghastly chill seeped through his skin, freezing his heart in a thick layer of ice. The cold was insidious and complete, terrifying. He'd felt that feeling before and knew exactly what it meant.

He wasn't surprised when the song of the magic field died inside him.

From out of the ground, shadowy forms rose to encircle them. The necrators made no move to advance, but lingered, wavering, as if uncertain of their purpose. Kyel turned slowly, raising the talisman. He was cut off from the field, but he could still feel magic in the weapon. Considering the number of shades surrounding him, Kyel figured it wouldn't be enough. But perhaps he could take a few of the demons out with him.

"You can't fight them, Kyel," Alexa said with calm resolve. "But I can."

Walking forward, she moved toward the nearest living shadow.

The necrator's ebony form rotated slowly, centering on her. Alexa muttered a phrase in a language Kyel didn't recognize. The necrator immediately vanished.

As Kyel looked on, Alexa moved toward the next demonic shadow, dismissing it casually. Then she went on to the next, making a slow circuit of their position. One by one, Darien's necrators popped out of existence, until only one remained. Alexa halted in front of it. With a smile, she waved her hand.

The necrator steamed and hissed as it dissolved.

Darien staggered, the pain of loss slamming into him like a sword thrust, tearing the breath out of him.

"Brother!" Sayeed cried. "Are you wounded?"

It was all Darien could do to shake his head. His screaming nerves were like phantom pains from a lost limb. His minions were gone. All of them. Unmade.

He wavered, feeling unstable, then took a step forward.

An invisible wall of air slammed over him, imprisoning him. He brought his hands up, testing the limits of a cage he couldn't see. He couldn't penetrate it, not with his hands, not with magic. He groped at it frantically, nervous sweat streaming down his face.

The square around them erupted in fire. Shattered cobblestones rained down on their heads like falling hail. Darien dropped to the ground beside Sayeed as another fiery explosion scorched the air around them. The intensity of the heat nearly overwhelmed his shield. At first, Darien thought it was Kyel attacking them. Then he realized it wasn't.

"They've turned the trebuchets on us," he rasped. The first two projectiles coated with Hell's Fire had missed them, but the soldiers tending the siege weapons would be recalculating their aim.

Another flaming missile arced toward them from the ramparts, trailing a tail of smoke behind it. Darien closed his eyes and put everything he had into an absorption shield strong enough to cover both himself and Sayeed. The missile hit, its flames gushing in a whooshing fireball that overwhelmed his shield. The searing heat scorched Darien's skin even as he fought to heal himself. At his side, Sayeed screamed in agony. Darien dropped to the ground, holding the man who called him brother, healing Sayeed as he burned.

Another flaring missile hit, disgorging its payload of flames. This time, Darien diverted the heat from the air and channeled it into the ground, a reservoir big enough to absorb the energy. Another projectile exploded around them, followed by another. Each time, he diverted the heat of the flames into the ground.

But the street was starting to heat up. His tactic wouldn't save them much longer. Trembling, he held Sayeed clutched against him and fought with all his might to keep ahead of the flames.

He was starting to panic. The nightmares that plagued him endlessly, of being roasted alive, were no longer just torturous memories—they were quickly becoming reality. With every shuddering attack, his defenses slipped another crack. He could no longer keep the agony of the flames at bay. Waves of heat roiling off the ground distorted his vision. And still the trebuchets thundered, wearing him down a little more with each strike.

He knew he was at his end when he could no longer feel the pain. He clenched his teeth and held Sayeed tighter.

All at once, the bombardment stopped.

Darien remained hunkered down, waiting for the barrage of flames to resume. When they didn't, he chanced a glance up at the battlements and saw that every last trebuchet was on fire. Ul-Calazi's men had finally overrun the walls.

In his arms, Sayeed lay limp, but alive.

The world reeled around Kyel. He gasped, filled with a euphoric excitement he couldn't explain. Before him, crouched on the ground, Darien knelt in a blackened ring of smoldering bricks that glowed red at the edges. Even though the city was falling around him, Kyel felt triumphant.

He felt a tug on his sleeve. Alexa stared up at him, her eyes wide and feverish. "You have him down!" she exclaimed. "Now end this!"

Kyel shook his head, wishing he could.

Her face flushed brightly. "You are dead in two days! What does your Oath matter?"

"It matters!" Kyel jerked his arm out of her grasp. He didn't have the energy or the desire to argue with her. He was still maintaining the cage of air around Darien, and the effort was taxing.

At his side, Swain growled. "I've had enough of this."

He reached behind his back and tugged at the cinch straps of the harness that anchored his armor. His breastplate slid off, falling to the ground. Swain trudged forward, armored only by his chain hauberk and gambeson.

"Release him," he shouted over his shoulder.

To Kyel's dismay, Swain drew his sword and stalked down the street in the direction of the market. Kyel stared after him, incredulous. He thought he could guess the man's intent, and it scared the hell out of him. Even so, he released the prison of air around Darien.

Kyel strode forward, Alexa at his side, trailing Swain down the street. He stopped at the edge of the square, silently absorbing the devastation.

Darien still crouched in a smoldering ring of blackened stone, while all around him the remains of collapsed buildings yet smoldered. Corpses lay sprawled across the ground, most reduced to charred skeletons. The smell was ghastly, a combination of sulphur and roasted flesh. Kyel brought his hand up to his mouth, fighting back bile.

Ahead, Swain approached Darien cautiously, blade drawn and carried downward at his side. Darien stared reproachfully up at him from the ground, his face a mixture of rage and pain and some other emotion Kyel couldn't identify.

Darien lay the man in his lap down on the cobbles, then rose unsteadily to his feet. Dark power seethed from his body, bleeding into the air in distorted waves. He was drawing hard on the Onslaught, Kyel realized. Preparing for a strike. Wary, Kyel tightened the protective shield around Swain.

The Prince halted. He stood hefting the hilt of his sword in his hand, as if testing the weight of it. He acknowledged Darien with a nod, and said in a calm voice, "Just you and me, like the old days. But this time, only one of us walks away."

Kyel felt his stomach clench. Darien was the best swordsman he'd ever known, but Swain was a blademaster, the man who had trained him.

Darien stood motionless in the street, eyes fixed on the slow motion of the Prince's blade. His gaze slid slowly upward to lock on Swain's eyes. He nodded slightly.

Reaching up, Darien unbuckled his chinstrap. He tugged his helmet off and tossed it on the ground, shaking out a mane of sweat-matted hair. His face was darkened by sooty grime that left a perfect delineation where the protection of his helm had ended. The look in his eyes was cold as death.

Swain took a step forward, his eyebrows raised in question. Darien glowered at him for a moment then reached up and unfastened the buckles of his harness, dropping his armor to the ground. His hand traveled to the hilt of his sword and drew the weapon from its sheath. It wasn't the same sword Kyel remembered; it was a scimitar. Kyel didn't know much about the mechanics of swordplay, but he couldn't help wondering if Darien's training with the longsword would translate well to this curved, sleeker blade.

Swain approach slowly, his weapon extended in front of him. Darien brought his sword up, lightly tapping Swain's blade.

The Prince exploded into motion.

He swept forward with a lightning series of attacks that sent Darien retreating.

Swain's sword moved so quickly, so precisely, that Kyel's eyes couldn't keep up with it. The violent hammering of steel against steel rang sharply off the walls, echoing through the square.

Behind Darien, the Enemy soldier he'd been protecting stirred, leveraging his torso off the ground. Seeing Darien circling Swain, the man's eyes went wide, first in surprise. Then in fear.

Kyel understood why. Darien was at a clear disadvantage. The sword in his hand was shorter than Swain's. The Prince had a much longer reach, and Darien was forced to keep dodging and retreating. While Swain's motions were crisp and precise, Darien moved his scimitar in great, sweeping arcs.

He swept out with a feint. Swain dodged, rotating his blade and deflecting the blow. He brought his sword up and held it out in front of him, keeping Darien at a distance. Then he brought the blade back over his shoulder and swept it down. Darien ducked under the attack and used his momentum to shove Swain forcefully aside.

The Prince whirled around, scoring a cut across Darien's back. Then he launched a crisp sequence of attacks that battered him to the ground. Overwhelmed, Darien raised his sword over his head to fend off Swain's hacking cuts.

He struck out with a foot, taking the Prince behind the knees and sweeping his legs out from under him. Swain hit the ground and rolled, somehow ending up on his feet. He sprang back, then whirled, delivering a slice that cut through Darien's gambeson, drawing a line of blood across his ribs as he rose from the ground.

Kyel gasped, appalled by the sheer brutality of it all. The harsh clangs of steel impacting with steel drove home the viciousness of the fight. It was starting to sink in that one of the two men before him was going to die a brutal death. Kyel dreaded that moment.

Swain struck again, batting Darien's sword aside. Darien danced back, drawing his long dagger from his belt. Crossing both dagger and sword, he interrupted Swain's next strike with a scissoring motion. The two men circled slowly, each waiting for an opening.

All at once, Darien lunged. Moving both dagger and sword together, he parried Swain's attack with the dagger while throwing a high cut with the sword. The curved blade took the Prince in the neck, continuing its slice down through tissue and bone. Darien tore the sword out, fanning the cobblestones with blood. He stepped back, weapons held ready, even as Swain fell.

Chest heaving, Darien stood over the Prince and watched him bleed out. Callously, he wiped his blade clean on the fabric of

Swain's leggings. Then he returned both weapons to their sheathes and turned to fix his stare on Kyel.

"Your turn," he said.

Kyel understood. There was nothing more he could do. The city had fallen and would soon be overrun. He couldn't stop Darien, not by himself.

Darien glared at him hard, his expression going from dark to demonic. A terrible green light suffused him, pulsating, sucking the light from the day. The shadows of the square deepened, the air growing fiercely chill. It was terrifying to behold, especially since Kyel knew what was happening: Darien was filling himself to saturation with the combined might of both the Onslaught and the magic field. Preparing a strike that Kyel couldn't deflect, not even with Thar'gon's great aide.

"Darien, no!"

Naia hurled past Kyel, inserting her own body between the darkmage and himself. Darien's expression changed, fading through various degrees of rage into something that looked like regret. The green aura around him slowly waned but didn't fade completely.

Naia took a step toward him. "Please, Darien. You need Kyel to destroy the Well of Tears."

Darien recoiled as if struck.

The glow around him winked out. He looked back and forth between Naia and Kyel with the haunted face of a condemned man. He shook his head. "That's not possible."

"It *is* possible!" Naia insisted, closing the gap between them. "Come away and listen. You sent Quin to Titherry for a reason. We have your answer, Darien! The answer you wanted us to find!"

Darien looked dazed, as if the sight of her was like venom, paralyzing his ability to react or comprehend. His mouth moved, fumbling silently, at last forming words. "Quin? You came with Quin?"

She halted before him, commanding, "Afford him clemency!"

To Kyel's disbelief, Darien obeyed. Nodding, the darkmage

turned to address him. "A truce, then. Your life is under my protection." He turned back to Naia, his face telling a dismal story of boundless guilt. He said softly, "Naia. I don't know what to say…I don't have the words…"

Naia stared at him a long, hard moment. "Then don't speak."

Chapter Thirty-Six
Freedom of Will

Rothscard, The Rhen

Darien closed his eyes as Azár fell into his arms. He sagged against her while she hugged him tight, maybe tighter than ever before. She sighed happily against his ear. "Thank the gods you are safe. Did you take the city?"

"Aye, we did," he said, letting go.

"*Ishilzeri!* My husband is a great commander!"

"Your husband is exhausted."

Darien turned and started pulling off his armor, tossing it piece by piece on a rug laid out on the ground. When he was down to just his leggings, he strode over to a cask of water standing upright against the side of the command tent. He plunged his head in, then righted himself with a great gasp, whipping his hair back and spraying water everywhere. Azár brought her hands up, shielding her face. There was laughter in her eyes. Darien bent to pick his shirt back up, using it to wipe the wet grime from his face. Shoulders sagging, he walked toward the tent's entrance.

"You should lie down," Azár said, plucking the dirty cloth out of his hands.

He'd forgotten he was holding it; his mind felt dazed. He was battle-weary. No, it was more than that. He was grieving, Darien realized. He'd killed his mentor. No matter what else Nigel Swain had become to him, he would always be that.

He paused and turned back to the soldiers lingering behind him. "A moment, Sayeed."

His First hurried over, concern on his face. He had been acting odd, ever since the battle. Darien didn't understand why. Sayeed had begun treating him as though he'd taken a mortal wound. His apprehension was almost palpable.

And irritating.

"We'll need some fresh horses for the morrow," Darien said. "And round up what's left of the Zakai. It'd be wise to enter the city by procession, to demonstrate our strength. I want the Zakai to ride at my side. I'll need a guard of honor."

Sayeed stared at him blankly, as though he hadn't understood a word.

Darien raised a weary eyebrow. "Horses. Zakai."

The man ducked his head more deferentially than he ever should have. "Of course."

Darien clapped him on the back and sent him off. Then he ducked into the dim interior of the tent and trudged wearily through the cloth partition. He stripped and sank into bed, falling instantly to sleep.

When Darien open his eyes, he found Azár lying soft and naked at his side, her body only half-covered in blankets. It was night, but the ambient light was enough to reveal her features. Darien traced the gentle curve of her body with his gaze. She was beautiful. Perhaps the most beautiful thing he'd ever seen. She stirred, her eyes blinking open enough to look at him.

"You're awake," she said groggily, stretching. "You slept through dinner."

Which explained his vast hunger. Darien sat up, letting the covers fall off him, and rubbed his eyes. He wondered what time it was. He still felt bone-weary.

"How does one become a Servant?" Azár asked, setting a hand on him. "Is there some vow or ritual?"

The question came out of nowhere and caught Darien by surprise. Rubbing his eyes, he answered guardedly, "There's a vow."

"And did you speak this vow?"

He frowned, not liking this peculiar line of questioning. At best, it brought on feelings of shame. "I did," he admitted.

"Will you teach it to me, so that I might speak it also?"

Darien winced, shocked by the question. Azár was beautiful and good. Unblemished. The thought of her becoming a creature such as himself was horrifying. Shaking his head in dismay, he asked, "Why would you wish that?"

She sat up and set her hand on his own, gazing into his eyes. "Because our time in this world grows short. And I am scared. I have only just found my husband. I do not wish to lose him." She leaned into him, kissing his cheek. "Where you go, I go."

"*No.*"

Appalled, Darien jerked back from her. He threw off the covers and stood up.

Confusion rampant on her face, Azár asked, "Why not?" She drew her knees against her chest.

Darien stood gaping down at her, not knowing what to say. Hoarsely, he whispered, "Because where I'm going, you can't follow."

Azár's face darkened, her eyes narrowing. "Why not?"

He hung his head, feeling suddenly sad. He wanted to stay with her. To grow old with her. To love and raise his daughter. He sank back into bed and, with a sigh, pulled her close.

"You don't belong there," he said softly.

"Neither do you."

He breathed a sigh and assured her, "You have me now. And when I move on, you'll have my memory. Keep me alive in your heart."

"You already live in my heart."

Darien took a long, steadying breath, trying to stuff his emotions back down deep where they belonged. He couldn't afford to acknowledge them. He owed her that much. He wanted to tell his wife he loved her but couldn't bring himself to speak the words.

He knew that saying them would only hurt her more.

Somehow, he'd fallen back to sleep.

Darien woke to empty blankets and a devil-dog licking his face with a sticky tongue. Groaning, he raised his hands up to fend the damn thing off. He squirmed his head from side to side, trying to escape its fetid breath.

"All right! Enough!"

The hound drew back and stared down at him with hollow eyes. He snapped his fingers and pointed to the corner. But the thing disobeyed him, instead trotting out through the cloth partition. Darien ran his arm over his face, then grabbed a handful of blankets to wipe off his arm.

The partition flapped open, and Azár stepped through. A warm smile brightened her face. "It is good you are awake. Your Zakai and horses await you outside. And you have a visitor."

Darien grunted and pushed himself out of bed. He started toward his wooden chest, but Azár's hand on his arm stopped him.

"I brought out the outfit you wore at our wedding." She motioned toward a chair.

There, laid out neatly, was the embroidered black tunic the tailors of the Jenn Asyaadi had made for him. He'd forgotten he owned it. He moved to the chair and held it up, then pulled on the pants. He had to rely on Azár to help him with the tunic. He couldn't button the sleeves on his own.

When she was done, he tied back his hair then turned toward her. He brought a hand up to trace her cheek. "You should wear your red gown."

Her eyes widened in surprise even as her hands went to her belly. "You wish me to come with you?

Darien nodded, smiling. "I'm not entering our new capital without my wife."

Azár glowed with excitement. While he collected his weapons, she produced the red gown she'd worn the day he'd proposed marriage to her. He watched her pull it on, then took a step back, admiring. Pregnancy suited her, he decided. Azár's olive skin seemed even softer than usual, her hair lustrous and sleek. Her dark eyes glowed with excitement and affection.

Offering his arm, Darien led her through the partition into the gathering area of the tent. So intent was he on his wife, that he almost didn't notice the lone figure in the corner. He glanced up and froze.

Naia stood with her hands clasped in front of her. Her gaze trailed from Darien to Azár, then back again with a questioning look.

Composing himself, Darien led Azár forward. Very rigidly, he said, "Azár, this is Master Naia Seleni. Without Naia, I couldn't have sealed the Well of Tears." He turned to Naia. "I would like to introduce to you Lightweaver Azár." He added, "My wife."

Naia blinked her shock but recovered quickly. She put on a welcoming smile and took Azár's hands into her own. "I am most honored to meet you, Lightweaver Azár. Congratulations on your nuptials. I wish you both much joy and happiness."

Darien shifted his weight from one foot to the other, and stood fidgeting with the collar of his tunic. Beneath the thick fabric, he was already breaking a sweat.

"Thank you for receiving me," Naia said. "I have come to accompany you to the palace. But first, I need you to do something for me." She lifted her hands, offering an object out to him. "I'm going to ask you to put this on."

When he saw what she was holding, Darien's breath clotted like blood.

Fear clenched his chest in an iron fist and *squeezed*. His heart terrorized his rib cage, his mind staggering toward panic. Reflexively, he reached out and groped for the Onslaught, wrenching it into him.

"Get that thing away from me!"

"Stop!" Naia held up the Soulstone before his eyes. "Quin repaired it—it can't harm you."

"How could you? You know what that damn thing did to me!"

Naia dropped her hand, the medallion dangling from her fingers. Her face set in patient lines, she moved toward him, speaking calmly, "You know me, Darien. I would never ask this of you unless I thought it truly imperative. And it *is* imperative."

She raised the Soulstone again, offering it out to him in her palm. "Take it. It can't harm you again. You're dead; there is no gift left within you. Nothing to fear."

Darien looked back and forth between Naia's face and the medallion in her hand. Little by little, reason returned to him. He let go of the Onslaught, letting most of it drain away, holding back just a little. His eyes ticked down to the glowing stone, then back up to Naia's face.

At his side, Azár snarled, "Is that the thing that killed my husband? Are you a witch, come to claim his soul? I will—"

"No." Darien shook his head, eyes transfixed on the stone. "I trust her."

"Take it," Naia urged. "Take it and put it on."

He looked at her sideways. "Why?"

Naia met his gaze unflinchingly. "Because that is what you are destined to do."

Darien nodded, at last understanding. Naia had journeyed to Athera's Crescent with Quin. She must have gained some knowledge he wasn't privy to.

He reached out and grabbed the glowing medallion. As his fingers closed around it, the feel of the cool stone shot fear into his chest. His mouth went dry, his heart thundering. He clenched his jaw, fighting against panic as he brought the thick bands of the silver collar up and wrapped them around his neck.

"Azár," he said. "Fasten it for me."

"Husband—"

"Do it."

For the second time in his life, he heard the horrifying sound of the Soulstone's clasp snapping closed.

Darien cried out as the stone's power raged into him. He sagged to his knees, folding forward. A savage torrent of energy streaked up his nerves and assaulted his mind. The violence of it was appalling. Recognizing the feeling for what it was, he didn't struggle against it. He could feel the power within the stone pour into him, filling his mind with a warm, wonderous feeling he'd entirely forgotten.

The Transference ended as abruptly as it had begun. Darien knelt trembling and gasping on the rugs, staring up at Naia's face in outright amazement. He reached up and uncinched the clasp, letting the collar slip off his neck. His mind raced frantically to understand the implications of what had just happened.

Through shivering breaths, he demanded, "Why?"

Naia bent over, a warm smile on her face. "Don't you understand? *You're alive.*"

Darien stared at her numbly.

It took him a moment to realize she was right.

Then another moment to see the irony.

That was the one thing he'd been lacking, the only thing separating him from life. It was the spark of the gift that had been ripped out of him upon his death, now given back to him by the very object that had stolen it in the first place.

"I don't understand," he whispered.

Azár dropped to his side and hugged him protectively.

Naia smiled to reassure her, then said to Darien, "You lost the legacy of power within you when you died. Since then, your link with Xerys has been the only thing keeping you in the flesh. Your gift has now been restored. You no longer need to fear your Master—Xerys has no power over you anymore. Your destiny is your own, to do with as you wish."

Darien struggled to his feet, panting to catch his breath and leaning heavily on Azár. He was filled with a numbing euphoria.

He took Naia's hand and gasped, "I don't know how to thank you."

But Naia shook her head, retracting her hand. "Don't thank me, Darien. This is no gift."

"What do you mean?" He stared at her in incomprehension.

"Trust me. You will understand."

Frowning, Darien nodded. He closed his eyes, fighting to calm his breath and steady his mind. Azár drew him aside, shooting a sharp glare at Naia. Rubbing his back, she whispered something in his ear that fled right by him. He wasn't paying attention. His head still reeled from the Transference, and he was still struggling to make sense of this new position he found himself in. He was still a Servant of Xerys. But he no longer had to be his Master's slave.

"Are you able to continue?" Azár asked gently. "Or should I tell the Zakai to stand down?"

Struggling out of his thoughts, Darien shook his head. "No. This should be done now, not later."

He swiped his sleeve across his brow, wiping off at least some of the sweat. He paused for a moment to collect himself. Then, taking Azár by the hand, he walked on unsteady legs out of the command tent and into the cool morning air. He had to squint against the sun; it seemed enormous and far brighter than ever before. Darien looked around in amazement, at a world saturated with color. He'd forgotten what it was like, to have his senses augmented by a mage's gift burning inside him. An entire division of cavalry stood arrayed before him, brilliant banners flapping in the breeze. Darien paused, allowing himself just a moment to marvel at the sight.

The silhouette of a man, backlit by the rising sun, approached leading a horse. As he neared, Darien recognized Ranoch, the clan chief of the grasslands Jenn. The stallion behind him was tall and fine, its black coat sleek and gleaming in the sun, its bridle quaking with jewels and tassels. A richly embroidered blanket had been draped over its back, sewn with tassels that reached almost to the ground.

Ranoch halted before him. He offered the horse's reins to Darien. "This is Turtak, the finest stallion of my herd. He is a gift."

Darien looked upon his new mount in admiration. He raised his hand and stroked the silken fur of the stallion's neck. He said in wonder, "He is a tremendous gift. You have my gratitude."

He moved to mount the horse, but a low growl from behind him made him turn. Behind him, the demon-hound stood, feet spread widely apart, its hindquarters raised as if ready to spring. The beast's gleaming eyes were trained on him, its lips drawn back to reveal a mouth full of heinous teeth. The thanacryst's growl deepened, became threatening.

"Theanoch," Darien ordered it, feeling suddenly unsure.

The hound sprang.

The beast slammed into him, hurling him backward to the ground and knocking the air from his lungs. Stunned, Darien groped for the magic field but couldn't catch hold of it.

The hound clamped its jaws around his thigh and began to maul him. Darien howled in pain, kicking and beating his fists against the creature, trying frantically to dislodge it. He rolled away, feeling the teeth rip the flesh of his leg.

Desperate, he reached for the Onslaught. But the power of hell was useless against hell's minions.

The demon-dog sprang on top of him, pressing him against the ground. Its maw closed around his shoulder, its teeth sinking deep into the tissues. The hound shook him violently, thrashing him back and forth across the ground, as his blood sprayed the grass.

A terrible agony took hold of him as the hungering beast began to feed off his newfound power. The jaws released his shoulder and closed on his neck.

Darien caught hold of the magic field and speared it into the creature with all the vast strength of his mind. The hound flinched but didn't let go. If anything, it clamped down harder.

Hot blood drained from his neck, saturating his tunic. Darien was vaguely aware of Sayeed standing over him, thrusting his sword into the demon-hound over and over, to no effect. Darien's vision went dim. His breathing became gurgling.

As a last resort, Darien used the last scrap of his failing power on himself.

The jaws released him. He sprang up from the ground and twisted, snarling in outrage. His adversary's gleaming eyes narrowed. The beast drew back, preparing to spring. Darien didn't give it the chance.

He launched himself at the creature, tearing a long gash in its neck. The demon-hound yelped in pain, twisting away. Darien stalked the creature in a slow circle, growling menacingly. For the first time, there was fear in the thanacryst's eyes. Darien wondered why. Then, looking back at himself, he realized with shock:

He was no longer human.

He was a hell-hound.

Darien lunged, his jaws snapping closed around the beast's head. He twisted, his teeth sinking deep into the animal's flesh as he fought to wrestle it to the ground. The hound resisted, thrashing about and whining in pain. He locked his jaws, digging deep into the dirt for leverage. The delicious taste of demon-blood filled his mouth. He clamped down harder as the beast's struggles became desperate, then gradually weakened.

The thanacryst's legs beat against him, over and over. The struggling slowed. Then, with one last, forlorn whimper, the demon-hound went limp. Darien waited, his teeth sunk deeply into its flesh, until he was certain the thing was dead. He unlocked his jaws and released it.

And released the magic that sustained him.

He sank to his knees, his strength draining from him. Blood saturated his tunic, gushed from the wound in his neck. He healed the injury, but then exhaustion hit him like a hammer blow. Sayeed caught him before he could fall and eased him the rest of the way to the ground.

Darien lay in the blood-wet grass, gaping up at the sky as the rest of the world blurred around him.

"Rest," his brother commanded. Darien obeyed, closing his eyes.

Chapter Thirty-Seven
The Price of Betrayal

Rothscard, The Rhen

The western sky was the faded yellow of an old bruise. Darien stared out at the sunset and cursed himself, regretting how long he'd slept while letting the daylight go to waste. Zakai moved immediately to cluster about him, much more protective than they had ever been before. The carcass of the thanacryst had been dragged away, but there was still a dark stain in the grass where the beast had fallen. Demon blood. Too dark to be human. He stopped and stood there still, gazing down at the place where the hound had fallen, a deep sadness working it's way into his bones. He hadn't realized how much the beast had wormed its way into his heart. It felt like a little piece of him was gone, bled away into the grass.

Darien lifted Azár onto her horse, a golden palomino with a silvery mane. Moving to his own mount, he climbed onto Turtak's back. He took the braided reins in his hand and directed the horse forward with the pressure of his legs. The stallion snorted and moved into a trot, head and tail carried proudly high. Darien guided the animal into a gap in the long column of soldiers, behind a small vanguard of Zakai. There, he pulled the horse to a halt and waited for his wife to draw up at his side.

On his signal, the soldiers started forward. Their column marched to a cadence tapped out by a single drum, an irregular pattern that had a rustic wildness about it. To Darien, it seemed an odd rhythm to march to. Nevertheless, the horses and men seemed born to it.

The procession moved forward as a unit, moving off the grass and onto a wide and rutted road. Darien stared in front of him at the mangled city ahead. The victory they had won felt more bitter than sweet. Rothscard as he had grown up knowing it was no more. The city once heralded as unconquerable had fallen under his sword.

The procession reached the remains of the Lion's Gate. The arch above the gate had fallen, the rubble already cleared away. On the other side of the walls, he could hear the sounds of the city, a restless and growing panic. The air moving toward them carried with it a malodorous blend of smoke, death, and spilled sewage. Their assault had crippled parts of the city's infrastructure. It would have to be rebuilt.

Above them rose a pair of limestone turrets that looked gnawed by the teeth of a monster. Remains of the portcullis had been pushed aside, its lattice grate bent into a distorted, cross-hatch pattern. The gate itself had been shattered, its wood carried away to be used to fuel Malikari fires. Beyond the wall, the sounds of a terrified populace grew boisterous and frantic.

At the sight of their vanguard, the crowds erupted into a collective outcry of terror and fury. Darien's stallion tossed its head, spooked by the thunderous clamor. They processed down a broad avenue lined with mailed sentries who were hard-pressed to restrain the surging masses. The entire crowd behind them churned like a boiling pot as individuals vied for a better view.

Until they caught sight of him.

It was like a strange ripple that passed through the crowd, flowing behind Darien as he passed. People stilled and fell quiet, their eyes filling with awe and horror.

Silence trembled in his wake.

Darien's ears rang with the hollow sound of his horse's hooves striking the blood-stained cobbles. The animal lifted its legs smartly, as if purposefully strutting to impress the crowd. To his left, Sayeed fought to keep his spirited mount in check. And on his right, Azár rode straight-backed and elegant, her red gown flowing over the sides of her golden mare.

They rode along the wide boulevard that paralleled the Grand Canal. The avenue they followed led through the center of the city, under the shadows of tall, sloped-roof buildings joined together in long rows. All along their path, the crowds remained dense and frantic. Only the threat of the soldiers' weapons prevented the populace from spilling into the street. The avenue ended at a large, tree-covered hill that contained the palace grounds.

They were met at the gate by a company of Tanisars, while the rest of the procession continued on through the city. Riding within a tight guard of Zakai, Darien entered the grounds of Emmery Palace. He directed his horse around the girth of the Citadel, through acres of torn-up gardens and trampled lawns. Ahead, above the substantial wall that curtained the Inner Ward, the towers of the castle came into view, high turrets of white limestone capped by crenelated ramparts. Smoke yet billowed from the eastern wing, and one of the turrets was partially collapsed. Emmery Palace had not fallen easily.

Their party gained the courtyard, where they were met by a small group of elite Zakai who took the reins of their mounts. Darien dismounted and helped his wife climb down from her horse's back. Together they strode, arm in arm, up a wide span of steps to where a group of the city's former ministers awaited them under the castle's broad portico.

Darien stopped at the top of the steps, hand resting on the hilt of his sword, his gaze sliding from one horrified face to the next. The ministers stood sweating and fidgeting, as if too fearful to act. At last, a balding man in a rumpled suit walked pale-faced toward him. Halting a good distance from Darien, he went to his knees then bowed forward to the ground.

There was a rustle of nervous motion. Then the other ministers followed suit, abasing themselves on the ground, granting him the obeisance usually reserved for a Prime Warden.

Darien stared down at them, coolly considering the gesture, giving them ample time for the humility of the act to sink in. His mother had sometimes waited minutes before acknowledging a petitioner. Darien had learned many things from Emelda Lauchlin, not the least of which was how to intimidate.

He'd learned that lesson well.

After long minutes, he uttered, "You may rise."

The group of ministers regained their feet, more than a few tottering dizzily. The balding man came forward, wringing his hands nervously.

"Welcome to Emmery Palace, my Lord."

"I'm not a lord," Darien snapped. "Where's Romana?"

"My Lo…" The minister's voice trailed off as he visibly struggled to find a more suitable honorific. He finally settled on "Great Master," a generic title that could be applied to any mage. When Darien didn't correct him, he stumbled on, "The Queen awaits you in her throne room."

"*Former* Queen."

The man paled even whiter. Swallowing heavily, he bobbed his head. "The former Queen awaits you."

The minister turned and beckoned their party forward. Offering his arm to Azár, Darien strode beside the man into the guts of the palace. The tiled floor of the foyer was sticky with blood. The room reeked a strong metallic odor, which combined with the choking smell of smoke. As they crossed the wide room, Darien had to watch his step, picking his way over the wreckage of a chandelier that had fallen from the ceiling, its crystalline remains scattered across the floor. A wide smear of blood streaked the tiles where a corpse had been dragged away.

The minister turned and led them down a wood-paneled hallway that ended at a set of double doors. The man paused for a moment, then pulled both doors open with a flourish. Darien guided his wife through without sparing the minister a glance, his eyes fixed on the pair of chairs sitting on a dais at the far end of the hall. Emmery's throne was a tall, elaborately carved piece of rosewood, set with velvet cushions. To its right sat a similar throne, smaller and less ornate.

Darien's eyes were drawn to the group of people clustered together on the far end of the dais. Romana Norengail stood with one hand draped over a wood banister. The look on her face could have curdled milk. Beside her stood Kyel and the woman who had banished his necrators. Her presence in the throne room troubled Darien more than anything else.

A terrified servant lingered off to the side, holding a trembling platter laden with filled wine glasses. None of the Queen's company seemed to be partaking.

Letting go of his wife's arm, Darien climbed the steps of the dais and approached the Queen. But instead of halting before Romana, he angled toward the servant and scooped a wine glass off the tray. He slung himself down on the Queen's throne, slouching back with deliberate arrogance. He drained the wine in one swallow.

To Romana, he said, "My condolences on the death of your husband." He opened his hand and let the spent glass fall from his fingers. It shattered on the tiles.

The Queen shot him a hateful glare. "My condolences on the death of your soul."

Ignoring her, Darien beckoned his wife forward, motioning her toward the smaller throne. With a calm and regal grace she'd never shown before, Azár flowed across the dais and assumed her place at his side. Darien smiled at Romana.

He nodded toward the doors. "If you leave now, you leave with your head." Thinking on it, he corrected himself. "Well, you'll be leaving either way. I'd just prefer you not bloody up my throne room."

Romana shot him one last, vicious glare, then turned and moved with an unhurried stride out of the hall, her life and dignity intact.

When the doors closed behind her, Darien allowed himself a smirk. He beckoned the servant with the wine forward, claiming a glass for his wife and another for himself. He looked up to find Naia gaping at him, her face aghast. He didn't care. With a toss of his head, he commanded her:

"Talk. Start with the Soulstone."

Naia shared a nervous glance with Kyel, then stepped forward. For once, she seemed at a loss for words. After a moment, she said, "The Soulstone was created by Quinlan Reis."

Darien blinked. The revelation was both surprising and disturbing.

Naia went on, "Quin did what he could to fix the medallion's

297

gemstone. The stone now functions better than he ever intended. So well, in fact, it can create new legacies by drawing vitrus directly from the magic field itself. With it, we have the ability to recover our lost numbers—conceivably, anyone with the slightest scrap of the Potential can be imbued with the gift."

Darien sat quietly, letting the information sink in. When it had, he needed another glass of wine. He motioned the servant with the tray back and helped himself.

"Why was it necessary I put it on?"

Spreading her hands, Naia explained, "I needed to be able to speak freely about what Quin and I discovered. And you need to be able to act on that knowledge, even if it contradicts Xerys' interests."

Darien set the empty glass down on the floor. "Then speak."

Naia nodded. "On Titherry, we found one last Harbinger who taught me how to read Athera's Crescent. With the Crescent, I saw there are only three possible futures still available to us. There are an infinite number of variations of those futures, but it boils down to this: we must destroy the Well of Tears."

"How is that possible?" he whispered.

Naia turned to look at Kyel over her shoulder. "We need Kyel's talisman. He can use it to shatter the Well of Tears, but it needs to be done at just the right time. The magic field will fail completely before it flips. Most of the Well's defenses rely on magic—when the magic field falters, the Well will be vulnerable."

Kyel stared at her sideways, looking intensely skeptical. "I can't shatter anything without magic."

Naia insisted, "Somehow it works. In my visions of this future, you always wield the talisman successfully, even in the absence of the magic field."

Darien realized he already knew the answer to that problem. "Thar'gon is a magical reservoir," he said. "It'll work."

Naia turned back to Darien. "If we destroy the Well, then the portal between worlds will collapse. And the recoil will knock the magic field back into its proper alignment."

Darien gnawed on that for a moment. It was an enticing alternative to Renquist's dire strategy…too enticing. There had to be a reason why Renquist had chosen to ignore that option. He took another glass of wine, drank it down in one swallow, then replaced the spent glass on the servant's tray.

"What are the risks?"

"If we fail, then Renquist will bring Xerys fully into this world."

Darien nodded slowly. Naia had seen Renquist's plan in the mirror of Athera's Crescent. He couldn't help wondering if she had seen his own part in it. He studied her eyes, looking for sign of doubt. But in Naia's dark eyes, he saw only hope.

False hope, he felt certain.

"And why would releasing Xerys be so terrible?" he asked.

Naia's mouth dropped open. The hope in her eyes chilled to icy dismay. "Did you truly just ask that question?"

Darien sat forward. "I did. Xerys is not evil. He has been tasked with the preservation of the magic field. He is simply carrying out his duty. But, then, aren't we all?"

Naia shook her head slowly, as if dazed. After a long moment, she breathed, "No, Darien. Not at that price."

He shrugged. She still embraced the false narrative that Xerys was an evil god. That Chaos was malevolent by nature. She didn't understand that the magic field was born of Chaos, that Chaos itself birthed every destiny.

But he understood part of Naia's hesitance. Xerys was, at best, a callous and indifferent master without compassion for the masses. If Xerys was allowed to cross into the world, it would precipitate a purging of the temples and risked a genocidal war that could last generations. Thousands would die. Perhaps hundreds of thousands. And, yet, it was conceivably worth the price. How much was the existence of magic worth? Could anyone put a value to it?

"What are our chances of success?"

"Not good," Naia admitted in a dismal tone. "Quin went to Bryn Calazar to try to assassinate Renquist and Krane. He hasn't come back."

Which meant Quin was dead. He would have no chance against Renquist. Darien couldn't imagine what the man had been thinking. He sagged, collapsing back into the throne. He shook his head, feeling an aching grief as familiar as breathing. He'd lost enough kin in his life that he should be used to the ache of it by now.

But he wasn't.

Forcing his emotions aside, he looked back up at Naia and started weighing his options. Renquist's plan had a much higher chance of success. But a success that came at tremendous cost. Naia's proposal had a great risk of failure, and that failure would mean the death of all mages.

Including Azár. And their child.

But perhaps he could hedge his bets. Darien's gaze slipped to Kyel and the woman from Aerysius he had taken up company with. It was Renquist's will that he absorb Kyel's power along with Naia's. Darien didn't know how that made him feel. Kyel's opposition had hurt—hurt with the bitter ache of betrayal. But Darien respected it. Through all that had transpired, Kyel's chains and integrity had remained intact. Not like his own. In the end, Darien decided that Kyel's life was worth something, worth enough to give him a chance. Naia's life, as well. And if her plan failed, then there would still be time to carry out Renquist's command.

Darien gave a slight nod. "You have my support."

As soon as the words were out, a terrible feeling of loss welled within him. It was a harrowing feeling. A life-twisting feeling. Suddenly ill, Darien broke into a clammy sweat, clenching the armrests of the throne. Rocked to his core, he sat upright with a gasp of understanding.

He had betrayed his Master, so his Master had betrayed him.

He had lost the Onslaught again, just as he had in Tokashi's dungeons. Only, this time, he'd lost it permanently.

He leaned forward, hands on his knees, and sat there panting, sweat streaming down his face. Azár leaned into him, setting a hand on his back, her face full of concern. Kyel started forward, his companion moving alongside him. Darien looked up, feeling a lightning-like stab of fear.

"Don't bring that woman near me," he snarled.

Kyel halted and threw his hand up, blocking the woman from moving forward. He stared a question at Darien.

Darien rose to his feet, feeling besieged. "Her name is Alexa Newell. She was a Master who disappeared from Aerysius four years ago. She's not on your side."

"I have no reason to doubt her," Kyel said.

"Then let me give you one." Darien paced forward, skirting their position. "She banished my necrators. Only a darkmage could do that. And not just any darkmage—only one with the talent to command the undead."

Kyel's stare shot to Alexa. A peculiar smile formed on her face. A knowing smile, full of confidence and audacity. She trained that smile on Darien like a weapon.

"Where is your hound, Darien?" she asked. Her smile became a gloating sneer. "Where are your necrators? Why don't you summon them?"

Darien's insides twisted as he realized his danger. He closed his eyes, his shoulders sagging under the heavy burden of defeat. She had him, and she knew it.

Azár rose from her seat and moved to stand at his side. The fear in her eyes told him she understood every nuance of his plight. She set a hand on his back. He barely felt the touch. His mind and senses stood frozen.

The woman's eyes widened, her smile triumphant. She whispered a word. And with that whisper, commanded shadow. All around the room, necrators bloomed upward from the floor, coalescing into obsidian forms.

Darien's heart chilled with terror—a primal, feral emotion unlike any other. At his sides, his hands grew cold and started trembling.

The woman spun to Kyel. "Look at him—he's defenseless! Kill him now and absorb his gift—then even Renquist himself will not have the might to oppose us! We will destroy the Well of Tears together. Act now and rid the world of this monster!"

Kyel stepped back away from her, his face gripped in a war of conflicted emotions. Darien could see the struggle in him. It was brutal.

The woman reached out and tugged on Kyel's arm. "Listen to me! Your Oath doesn't matter anymore! This is your chance! You can slay him right here!"

In defiance of the necrators, Darien mustered the last, fraying thread of his courage. He taunted Alexa, "Why don't you do it? I'm here. Take my soul."

He spread his arms, inviting her to attack. The woman narrowed her eyes, visibly seething. But she did nothing.

"You can't, can you? That's why you need him." Darien dropped his arms and said to Kyel, "She's Renquist's insurance, should I turn against him. He needs one of us dead."

He turned his glare back to Alexa. Staring at her and her only, Darien pronounced with confidence, "She's not living, Kyel. She's like a necrator herself. She's Renquist's minion."

Kyel backed slowly away. "Then why didn't she just kill me herself?"

Darien stood focused on Alexa. "She's a conduit. A soul-siphon. She needs us together, in close proximity. That's the only way she can wrench the gift out of one of us and Transfer it to the other."

The woman's smile grew slowly exultant. "So you found me out, fool. I applaud you. Only, you're wrong about one thing."

"What is that?" Darien asked.

She scoffed. Then she spread her hands. "I *can* kill you myself."

The ring of necrators swept forward. Darien threw his hands out to stop them—a futile effort. There was nothing he could do. But they didn't touch him. Instead they surrounded him, containing him.

The woman walked toward him, confident, triumphant.

She parted the ring of shadows and stepped inside the circle.

She raised her hand.

Darien doubled over as vicious agony clawed at him from the inside, tearing rapidly through every fiber of his being. He knew what it was—and the terror of that knowledge was incapacitating. The woman had captured him in a terrible link that was ripping his newfound gift out of his soul. Darien dropped to the floor, howling in mortal anguish as he thrashed in his death throes.

With a cry, Azár sprang in front of him. A wave of Alexa's arm sent her flying backward.

A jarring thump was followed by a shrieking scream.

Life and power crashed back into him. The song of the magic field surged, soaring with fury in his head. He was filled to bursting with power, but it wasn't a power he could use. It collapsed into silence as swiftly as it rose, held in check by the presence of the necrators.

Darien lay twitching as the pain slowly released its grip. At last, his body relaxed, and air returned to his lungs. He thrust out a hand and pushed himself upright.

He sat blinking, too shocked and too weakened to move. It took him long seconds to realize what had happened. The woman knelt on the floor, her fingers groping at the hilt of Sayeed's sword, sunken like a lance through the center of her chest. Alexa's face went slowly slack, her eyes rolling back. She slumped forward, driving the blade in further.

Still, the necrators remained. She hadn't commanded them to leave.

"Darien…"

It was the smallest, weakest sound. He turned and glanced behind him.

Azár lay sprawled on the floor, her lids heavy, her eyes staring upward. She wasn't moving.

"No."

Darien shook his head in denial even as he scrambled toward her. He collapsed at her side, pulling his wife into his arms. She was alive, but barely. Blood drained from her scalp, her nose, her mouth. Her eyes stared up at him, her lips moving wordlessly. He had no idea what she was trying to say. All he knew was that she was dying. And there was nothing he could do about it.

He was losing his wife. He was losing his daughter. He was losing them both.

Darien lifted Azár's head until her face was pressed against his. He closed his eyes and silently begged her not to go.

But she was going. He could feel her dying.

So he did the one thing he could. He kissed her softly and told her he loved her.

His voice was the last sound she heard. A slight smile touched Azár's lips as she died.

Immediately, Darien felt the stir of energy in his arms as the conduit of Transference between them opened. Power gushed into him from his wife's broken body, invading his own. Darien's muscles locked rigid—he couldn't let go—as Azár's body shed its two tiers of power like a parting gift.

He screamed in outrage, in defiance, in futility.

When it was done, he collapsed on top of her, weeping scalding tears of grief. He clutched her tight in his arms and pressed his face against hers.

"Brother. Come away."

Hands encircled him, tugging at him gently. He jerked away. He wasn't ready to let her go.

"I'm so sorry, Darien."

That was Naia's voice.

His tears flowed freely, wetting his wife's soft cheeks.

"Take him somewhere he can mourn," Naia whispered.

Hands encircled him again.

"Leave me alone," he rasped, and clutched Azár harder.

Naia sank down beside him and set a comforting hand on his shoulder. Her touch was a rude invasion. He tried shrugging it off.

"Let me care for her, Darien," Naia said in the compassionate and composed voice of a priestess.

For some reason, her words made him weep harder.

"Come away, Brother," Sayeed said.

Darien didn't fight him. With one last kiss, he let his wife's body slide out of his arms and settle on the floor. Then he rose from the ground, trembling and broken, a thin fragment of the man he'd been just moments before.

Leaning heavily on Sayeed, he let his brother guide him out of the ring of necrators.

Chapter Thirty-Eight
Broken

K yel took a step into the shrine.

Beneath his feet, the floorboards gave an exhausted groan. The sound startled him. He jerked to a halt, planting a hand on the cold stone wall. Standing rigid in the doorway, he gazed straight ahead into the dimly lit shrine, a small room with oppressive walls, not much more than a niche carved out of the temple's long nave. The shrine was filled with a gloomy light shed from dozens of small candles spread across the floor. Kyel lingered in the doorway, a silent and uninvited spectator, not wanting to infringe on the privacy of the scene playing out within.

"You can come in, Kyel."

He winced at the sound of Naia's voice. Swallowing, he moved hesitantly toward her, stepping with care through a meandering forest of flickering candleflame. Naia knelt at the far end of the shrine over the body of the dead woman. With the patient care of a sister, she fussed over every detail: smoothing fabric, arranging hair, painstakingly composing every feature. Kyel stood in awe of Naia's talents. In a short span of time, the former priestess had transformed a broken and bloodied corpse into an exotic beauty that seemed reposed in peaceful slumber.

"Who was she?" he asked, watching Naia stroke a silken lock of hair into place.

"His wife."

"I know that," Kyel grumbled. "But who *was* she?"

Naia didn't respond immediately. Her hand stopped moving.

She knelt quietly, gazing down at the woman with a whimsical expression on her face. "I don't know," she said at last. "Someone very special, I think."

Kyel believed that. He knelt beside Naia, pondering the woman laid out before them. She was small, even dainty. But there was something about her face that hinted at something stronger within. He thought Naia might be right. Darien had chosen an exceptional woman to love.

He sat down on the floor. "I've been thinking," he said. "About Alexa. She was killing him, and Darien couldn't do anything about it. Her necrators had him paralyzed. I wonder if that means…?"

"That he's not evil anymore?" Naia shook her head. "It's not that simple. Darien's the same man you met at Greystone Keep, the same man I fell in love with. In all this time, he's never changed. The only thing that's different are the circumstances surrounding him. Darien has pulled his support from Xerys. Nothing more. And now his master has abandoned him."

Kyel looked back down at the dead woman. He sat there in silence for a long time, contemplating Naia's words. Pondering his own emotions, which surprised him. He realized there was still a small part of him that held out hope for Darien. He wasn't sure if that made him feel better or worse about himself.

Suddenly, the floor beneath him lurched.

Kyel started, groping at the wall for stability. Naia pushed herself off the ground. She stood glancing about, her face paling.

Kyel could feel the entire magic field quaking, like a powerful aftershock. He rose to his feet, his hands clutching his head. The field lines grated against each other, raking like a dull knife down his nerves.

"It's getting bad," he gasped.

Beside him, Naia turned in a slow circle, staring up at the ceiling. "It is. We need to be getting up the mountain. I fear our time is running short."

Kyel was thinking the same thing. "I hope Darien is up for this."

She shrugged dismissively. "He doesn't have a choice." Her

gaze trailed over the dead woman. "She's ready. I'll go get him."

Darien stared at the passionless flames in the hearth, feeling trapped in a universe of nothingness. The nothingness was like a thick cotton blanket that enveloped him, encasing him completely, muffling out the world. He was dimly aware of time sliding past him. But it had nothing to do with him, so he paid it no mind. He thought perhaps he might be cold but couldn't tell for sure. He could feel the creeping fingers of madness groping over him, and welcomed them in.

"Darien."

A hand settled on his shoulder. He resented the feel of it. The touch was an invasion he couldn't bear and couldn't ignore. He moved slightly, pulling away from it.

"It's time." It was Naia's voice, knifing through the comforting layers of detachment. "We have to be going. Would you like to say goodbye first?"

Hurt stabbed through him. He wanted to retreat back into the world of nothingness and dancing flame.

"Come, Darien. Let me help you up."

Hands eased him to his feet. He followed where those hands led, lacking the will to resist. He let Naia guide him away from the hearth and back through the sitting area of the suite. Vaguely, he was aware of Sayeed standing and moving toward him, a deep scowl of concern on his face. But Naia shook her head, and the officer came no closer. Darien gazed at him dully, as if through a thick screen of lead.

The door closed behind them softly.

Naia's hand on his arm kept him moving. It was the only thing that did. Darien followed her along corridors and down flights of stairs. Out into a dark and blustery night. Wind raked his hair, clawed tears from his eyes. Or maybe it wasn't the wind. He didn't know. Smoke rode the scourging currents of air, thick and caustic. He thought perhaps the city burned. He hoped it did.

The wind whipped his senses back into focus, and he became slowly aware of his surroundings. He realized Naia had led him out of the palace grounds, that they were moving through the city streets. Frantic citizens hastened by, their children and possessions in their arms. In the distance glowed a luminous orange cloud. He could hear the sounds of screams.

Naia swept a door open and closed it behind them. Darkness settled around him, lit only by a soft, wavering light. And silence. Darien closed his eyes, savoring the quiet. Naia led him forward, moving through a gauzy haze of muted light.

Her hand released him.

"I'll wait here," she said softly.

Darien could feel her moving away. He knew what lay before him. He didn't want to look. But he did anyway.

Azár lay on the floor, surrounded by a sea of candles glowing with a timid light. At once, his shield of detachment fell away, and he was instantly engulfed in a holocaust of grief. Darien sank to his knees, taking his wife's limp hand into his own. He sent his will plummeting into her, probing, seeking, to find only emptiness. An emptiness more eternal than the world that imprisoned him.

He closed his eyes and let the despair come. But it was fleeting, replaced quickly by rage. A savage anger consumed him, burning away reason.

Growling, Darien clenched Azár's hand and sent a violent deluge of healing energies flooding into her body. He forced his will into her, prying and tunneling into every sinew and tissue, assaulting her violently. He pulled with all his great might at the magic field, filling himself to the point of pain, channeling every last drop of power he could wrest into her. Until she glowed with brilliant energies that streamed off her in sad, radiant waves.

"*Stop, Darien!*"

He ignored the command, intensifying his efforts, until the pain became excruciating. With a cry, he released the magic field and slumped forward.

"You have to let her go." Naia's voice was filled with compassion and good sense.

He knew she was right. The knowledge defeated him, forcing him to give in to the futility of it all. Darien released Azár, laying her down to rest. Then he turned and glared up at Naia with wrath in his eyes.

"I'm so tired of this world," he grated. "I want nothing more to do with it. People say hell is a place of torment. Well, I've been there. And believe me, hell's a much kinder place."

He surged to his feet and made for the door of the shrine. But he halted as something caught his attention: a frieze of the Goddess of Death, carved into the wall beside the doorway. The sight of it tore him wide open.

"Damn you, bitch," he snarled as he fled.

It took Naia long minutes and many steps to catch up with him. She wove through Rothscard's frantic streets, dodging panicked mobs of citizens. Ahead of her, Darien carved his way through the densely packed avenues. His very presence radiated dark power, inspiring enough fear to clear a path ahead of him. Naia jogged in his wake, at last closing the distance to walk at his side.

Darien didn't appear to notice her. His long, forceful strides propelled him toward the castle, while Naia had to jog to keep up. Seeing their approach, a group of Tanisars guarding the gates rushed forward. Darien stormed through their ranks without acknowledging them. He didn't slow until he reached the courtyard of the palace. Then he finally relented and looked at her.

"Do you have a plan?" he demanded, angling toward the steps.

"We'll use the Rothscard portal to transfer north to Orien's finger," she informed him, hurrying to keep up. "From there, we'll take the stairs into the warrens, just as we did before."

"What then?"

They entered the castle and crossed the foyer. "Then Kyel destroys the Well."

"And what about Renquist and Krane?"

Feeling a terrible, sinking ache, Naia halted in her tracks. Darien continued on a few steps before stopping to turn back. Choking on sorrow, Naia shrugged helplessly. "Quin never returned," she whispered. She had foreseen Quin's death in one variation of this future. They still had a chance of success. A chance that would have to be purchased with blood.

"Your plan isn't going to work," Darien grumbled. "Without the magic field, we're defenseless. But Renquist will still have the Hellpower."

Of course, he was right. She'd put so much faith in her vision, she hadn't thought of that.

"You're a darkmage," she said at last. "What do you suggest?"

Pacing slowly back and forth, Darien stared at the ground with a relentless scowl. "We need to distract them long enough for Kyel to reach the Well." Continuing to pace, he went silent for a long moment. Then he halted and said without looking at her, "I think I can manage that."

Naia felt a surge of hope. "How?"

Darien's expression collapsed into something that looked an awful lot like shame. He admitted, "Before you arrived, I agreed to help Renquist with a proposal."

"What proposal?" Naia asked warily.

He turned away. "I agreed to help him stabilize the magic field by absorbing enough power to release Xerys from the Netherworld. I was supposed to start with Kyel."

Naia stood speechless, staring at him in revulsion. "And you thought this was a good idea?" she finally managed. She felt throttled by disappointment. Like Kyel, she had allowed herself to hope Darien's soul might be salvageable. But his admission was a painful reminder of his nature. A reminder she dared not ignore.

He glowered at her. "At the time, yes. I thought it was a good idea, considering the alternatives."

"And have you changed your mind?" Naia pressed, angry now.

"I have. But Renquist doesn't know that. I'll tell him I killed Kyel and absorbed his gift. He will have no reason to doubt me, so he won't be guarding the Well. I'll keep his attention focused on me. That should give Kyel time to act."

Naia felt somewhat reassured. "Then this is the version I saw. We're on the right path with this plan."

"That's well and good." Darien's gaze drifted back down the hallway.

Just then, the magic field sprang taut, making the world teeter. Naia's stomach took a downward plunge. Her gaze shot to Darien.

"It's now or never," she warned.

He nodded. "I'll meet you down by the Citadel. There's something I have to do first."

He turned and strode away. Naia stood watching him go, daring to hope.

Darien retrieved the small bronze cylinder from the desk and, pocketing it, left the steward's office. He walked up the stairs to the guestrooms and found Sayeed's door. He entered without knocking.

Startled, the officer bolted out of his chair. He crossed the floor in three great strides, catching Darien up in a crushing embrace.

Darien stiffened. But then he relented, taking what comfort he could from the gesture. After a long moment, Sayeed let him go, and stepping back, regarded him with an expression of boundless sympathy.

Darien ignored the man's unspoken question.

Reaching down, he removed the two sheathed blades that hung from their belt-hoops at his waist. He unbuckled his war belt, the one he'd inherited from his ancestor, Braden Reis. The belt came off with a clatter of steel rings, heavy with the combined weights of the implements it bore. Very deliberately, Darien wound the leather strap around both scabbards. Then he offered the weapons and belt to Sayeed.

The officer's face went slack. He accepted the gift with great hesitance, opening his mouth to say something. But then he closed it again. He stood staring down at the jewel-encrusted hilts with a look of stricken awe.

"I want you to have them," Darien said, gazing down at *Valdivora*, the legendary sword of Khoresh Kateem, and its matching dagger. "They belong to the clans. I won't be needing them any longer."

Sayeed looked up with a frozen expression.

Darien continued, "The people of Malikar now have a land to call their own. And a capital to rule it from. Sayeed son of Alborz, when I became Warden, I named you First Among Many. Now I name you Sultan of the Malikari Empire."

Reaching into the pocket of his cloak, he retrieved the small bronze cylinder that was no bigger than his index finger. He handed it to Sayeed, watching the man's face as he opened the end of the tube and removed the thin scroll within. Sayeed's skin went pale as his eyes scanned over the curling parchment. When he reached the bottom of the page, he rolled the scroll back up and replaced it in its container, letting his hand drop limply to his side.

"Brother…" He shook his head, visibly groping for words. "I do not have the ability to express my gratitude. But only the Prime Warden has the authority to elevate me to such a high position."

Darien gestured dismissively. "After I kill Renquist, I will be Prime Warden. For a short while, at least."

Sayeed stared at him blankly for another minute. Then, very formally, he went to his knees. He took the hem of Darien's cloak and brought it up to his face, pressing the fabric to his lips. Darien frowned down at him, feeling repulsed by the gesture.

"Stand," he commanded.

Sayeed rose from the floor with grace and stood before him, his gaze lowered to the ground—another unwanted sign of deference. Darien reached up and firmly lifted the man's chin until he was forced to look him in the eyes.

"Never lower your gaze, Sayeed. And never kneel before another man again." Darien brushed past him, moving toward the hallway. Opening the door, he paused and turned back.

"Thank you for being my brother," he said.

And left.

Chapter Thirty-Nine
The Waking Storm

Rothscard, The Rhen

Naia stood in the courtyard, ringed by soldiers and horses. Overhead, dark clouds tumbled toward the horizon. Eerie colors erupted within their depths, spreading quickly across the sky. Jagged forks of lightning speared the ground, followed by rolling thunder that rattled the earth. All around them, the entire magic field lurched and writhed as if in pain.

The horse she was holding crabstepped, looking ready to bolt. Naia ran a hand over the gelding's quivering neck, attempting to sooth it. It did little good. The beast could sense her anxiety.

The ring of soldiers parted to admit a lone man into the ragged pool of torchlight: Kyel Archer. Naia sighed in relief. She had been beginning to fret he wouldn't show at all. Now they only waited on Darien. Looking up at the tortured sky, Naia silently willed him to hurry. They hadn't much time.

Kyel drew up in front of her, a scowl of irritation on his face. The silver weapon at his side shimmered with a kaleidoscope of colors reflected from the cloud-light.

"How is he?" Kyel asked, just loud enough to be heard over the whistling wind.

"As good as can be expected."

"Is he coming?"

"Oh, yes." Naia sighed. "He wants revenge. And he needs closure. This is the only way he'll get either."

She thought of the look on Darien's face when he'd cursed the image of her goddess. She couldn't blame him for his anger, though he had directed his wrath at the wrong deity.

"I hope he finds what he seeks," he said softly.

The magic field spasmed violently. Kyel winced, and Naia felt the shock of it all the way to her core. The Zakai around them appeared thoroughly unaffected. She glanced back apprehensively at the palace steps.

The magic field quieted, but still trembled on the far edge of normal. The night was cooling around them, and there was still no sign of Darien.

She turned to Kyel. "What about you? What do you seek?"

He stared at the ground. After a long moment, he responded, "I just want this to be over."

"That's all? No more?"

Kyel smiled regretfully. "I have eleven tiers of power in me."

Naia blinked in shock, feeling intense sympathy. She whispered, "I'm so sorry, Kyel."

He shrugged. "I'm already coming undone. You have no idea how close I came to killing Darien today. No idea."

"And what if you had?"

Kyel looked away. He stood in silence as the wind rolled over him, whipping his cloak. She waited for him to reply. Eventually, she realized he wasn't going to.

She asked, "Do you think me evil, Kyel? Because I killed in your defense?"

He looked at her, his eyes studying her face as if seeking there for the answer to her question. "No. Not evil. But you weren't in the right, either." He sighed heavily. "There must be some middle ground. I just don't know where it is or what it would look like."

"I think I know," Naia said. "And it has nothing to do with oaths, and everything to do with what's inside. Our decisions define us. Not our chains."

The ring of soldiers parted again, this time admitting Darien into their midst. He stalked toward them with the dangerous grace of a predator, his body emanating a penumbra of dark power. His black cloak rippled behind him in the wind, and his long, black hair lashed his face. When he reached them, he drew to a halt and stood staring into the distance.

Kyel shot a meaningful glance at Naia, one that seemed to question the man's sanity. To Darien, he said, "I'm very sorry about your wife."

The darkmage cast him a leaden stare and said nothing in reply.

"Where's your sword?" Naia asked, noting the blade's conspicuous absence.

Darien shrugged. "It was time to give it up."

A soldier led his horse forward. Another took Naia's reins and held her gelding for her to mount. She twisted in the saddle, waiting for Darien and Kyel, then clucked her horse forward.

Darien sent his stallion trotting after Naia's mare. The horses were skittish as they made their way across the palace grounds, perhaps sensing the tension in the air.

Ringed by a squad of Zakai, they turned onto the canal road. As it turned out, the escort was unnecessary. It was past the curfew the occupying military had imposed throughout the city. Rothscard's streets were eerily empty. During the long ride to the Lion's Gate, Darien saw very few people about, mostly soldiers. Many of the city's inhabitants had already fled, leaving their possessions behind. Signs of their passage were strewn everywhere in the streets: scraps of garments and shoes, housewares and children's toys. Stray dogs and rats rifled through the scattered garbage, emboldened by the absence of humans.

The wind had died down, though the clouds still roiled overhead. Their party rode in silence out the gate and into the thick of the Malikari encampment. Campfires marched toward the northern horizon in perfect, geometric patterns. Beyond them, Darien knew, stretched a struggling train of refugees filing down from the mountains to the north. They would find new homes and new lives, even new customs. It would be a very different society than the one they had left behind. But they would live. Darien felt no small amount of gratitude for that.

They rode for a long time in silence, past the encampment's long rows of tents bordered by lines of pickets and earthworks. Overhead, the lights within the clouds strobed in time to the pulse of the magic field. An erratic pulse, like a failing heartbeat.

Darien was surprised when Naia brought her horse abreast of his. He glanced over at her, unsure of her purpose. She rode for a moment in silence, her body moving with the slow rhythm of her horse's swaying strides.

"Tell me about your wife," she said at last. "Did she make you happy?"

The question caught Darien off-guard. He glanced down, fumbling for the right words to express his feelings. "She did. I didn't expect her to. She was the singular, most beautiful thing in my life. I ought to have told her that."

"I'm sure she knew what you felt for her," Naia said after a moment.

He shrugged. It wasn't a response. More of an attempt to dismiss her concern.

"Darien."

The way she said his name made him glance at her sharply.

"In my visions…I've seen what happens to you." She was looking at him with vast amounts of sympathy.

Darien shrugged again, letting her words slide off him. He had no interest in his future.

Naia said, "The most important part of my training as a Harbinger had to be skipped because we simply didn't have the time. I never learned how much of what I see is safe to reveal …and how much is best held back."

"Then don't tell me anything," he snapped, more sharply than he intended. He already knew what she was going to say, and truthfully didn't care.

"I think you need to know," she pressed, reining her mount closer to his. "There are now only two possible versions of the future left to us. And in both versions, Renquist spills your blood in sacrifice. In one version, your death is the catalyst that brings Xerys fully into this world. In the other, it is our only chance to prevail against him.

"But Darien," she paused, fixing him with a penetrating stare. "I feel certain it will be up to you—and only you—to determine which future comes to pass. All of us—and all the world—will be at the mercy of your decision. You *must* make the right choice."

Darien rode in silence for a time, head bowed against the occasional gusts of wind. Eventually, he asked, "So today's my last day in this world?"

"I believe so," Naia answered, her expression compassionate.

Darien allowed himself a dark and fleeting grin. "Good."

She stared at him flatly. It was a long time before she looked away.

The sound of the horses' hooves became muffled as they transitioned from the packed dirt of the road onto the spongy loam of the prairie. His stallion fought the reins, wanting to stretch its neck down to graze. He had to keep urging it forward. Kyel trailed behind them with the rest of the Zakai, either in a sulk or a gloom—Darien couldn't tell which.

"What about you?" he asked Naia after a long interval of silence. "Have you foreseen your own death?"

"I have seen my own death countless times. That doesn't bother me in the least. It's the loss of others I've cared about that saddens me."

"Quin," Darien guessed. He knew Naia and Quin had spent time together at the Crescent. He hadn't realized their relationship had progressed into something more. "I'm sorry, Naia. The gods are brutal, aren't they?"

"Don't blame the gods, Darien. That's too easy. And it minimizes our own responsibility."

He couldn't deny the logic of her words. He pulled back on the reins, drawing his horse to a halt. He let Kyel pass him by, then kicked his stallion after him. He followed at the end of their small column the rest of the way, flanked by two Zakai.

They rode in silence for hours.

Eventually, they came to a long line of serrated hills that marched in darkness toward the foothills of the Craghorns. They pulled their horses up just outside the opening of a large gash cut into a jagged hill. A small stream trickled out, feeding a willow grove downslope. There, they dismounted and, unloading their packs, handed their horses over to the Zakai. At Darien's directive, their silent guard bowed from their horses' backs and rode away, trailing the spare mounts behind.

"The transfer portal is this way," Naia said, indicating a deep fissure in the cliffs ahead.

Darien studied the cut warily. He'd been through these same foothills several times and couldn't remember seeing it before. He asked, "How did you know this was here?"

"I used it when Quin and I left Titherry." Naia shouldered her pack and set off toward it.

The crevasse slanted uphill at a sharp angle, bordered on both sides by fractured granite. Small, sharp rocks that had crumbled from the eroded cliffs provided an unstable footpath. Naia mounted the slope gamely, leaning forward under the weight of her pack. She was wearing a pair of men's breeches and a good pair of serviceable boots. Darien was surprised he hadn't noticed that before. She'd planned ahead.

At the top of the cleft, they came to a water-carved bow in the cliff face. There, Naia waved her hand and muttered a soft string of words. Instantly, the granite wall dissolved to reveal an opening. Darien followed behind Kyel into a dimly lit chamber carved into the cliff itself, taking note of the cross-vaulted arch perched in the center of the room.

"For a thousand years, no one remembered this was here," he commented wonderingly, shaking his head.

Without pausing for the others, Darien strode forward into the portal arch. Immediately, the world around him shivered and disappeared in a brilliant gush of light.

Orien's Finger, The Rhen

Darien stumbled out from under the arch, finding himself in a different chamber entirely. Gazing upward, he took in the sight of a dark ceiling riddled with tiny pinpricks of light. He recognized the place. He had been there before, with Azár. It had been the first time he'd ever held her hand.

There was another flash, and both Naia and Kyel appeared at

his side. Kyel gazed around, blinking, looking thoroughly disoriented.

This time, it was Darien's own whispered words that unlocked the doorway. He stepped out into a horseshoe-shaped canyon surrounded by charred cliffs that still bore the scars of his own insanity.

He strode out from the portal chamber then turned back to gaze up at the tall spire of Orien's Finger. It was from that high vantage he had summoned a fiery holocaust that had immolated Malikar's armies—men and women of the nation he would later come to defend. With a sigh, he turned his back on the monolith, too weary to confront its silent recrimination.

"This looks too familiar," Kyel grumbled.

Darien set off across the curved valley, outpacing the others by design. He remembered exactly where the entrance to the hidden stair was, beneath a spelled set of runic numerals. Fortunately, he knew the Word of Command that unlocked them. The numerals awakened, gleaming with an inner light. A dark opening appeared in the scorched rock beneath, revealing a set of dim stairs that climbed upward into darkness.

Darien looked back over his shoulder at the others. "Remember. Shield yourselves. We'll be walking into the vortex that surrounds Aerysius."

Naia dropped her pack on the ground, then knelt to rifle through it. She withdrew two short branches and a sealed earthen jug. Unstoppering the jug, she produced long, oil-soaked strips of cloth and began winding them around the ends of the shafts.

"This time, I thought to bring torches." She smiled up at him. The torch in her hand burst aflame.

Darien accepted the other torch with a feeling of appreciation. Too many times in his life, he had taken too many people for granted. Naia's name was at the top of his long list of regrets.

"You first," he said, moving behind her.

The Craghorns, The Rhen

The stairway was steep and brutal. Even with the torchlight, Darien found it hard to keep his footing. The pool of light they moved within extended only a short distance, enough to see the steps ahead, but not enough to see where they led. The stairs were broken intermittently by short landings, where their party halted to catch their breath. Over the edge was only a vast maw of emptiness. Darien had no idea what manner of death a fall would bring.

His mind wandered rampantly as he climbed. His thoughts turned to Azár, his beautiful wife. He tried picturing her in his mind. But, to his irritation, every image he summoned was out of focus, as though it had been years since he'd last looked upon her face. Perhaps it was just his mind's way of coping. If so, it was a cruel trick.

A ghastly roar shook the mountain beneath their feet, rattling the stair. Jagged fissures raced across their path, fracturing the steps. Kyel staggered and fell to his knees. He glanced up, eyes wide and startled.

"What was that?" he gasped.

Staring upward into darkness, Darien responded, "I think we're running out of time."

Chapter Forty
The Demon's Pawn

Naia tripped.

Darien reached out to catch her but was a fraction too slow. She hit the floor of the landing with a grunt and a splash. He reached down and helped her back to her feet, stabilizing her until she could find her balance.

"The floor is wet!" Naia exclaimed through chattering teeth.

Darien moved past her, his feet splashing through pools of water on the floor. The flame of his torch reflected in a distorted pattern off the surface of the water. Despite the light, he could see only a short distance ahead. But it was enough to make him feel certain they had finally come to the end of the stairs.

"We've reached the bottom of the warrens," he said.

"The Well's up three levels, isn't it?" Kyel asked. He mounted the last step and stopped beside Darien, his face a jagged dance of shadow in the flickering torchlight. At Darien's nod, he strode forward a few steps before turning back. "We have to keep moving. Can't you feel it?"

"I feel it," Darien growled.

He tossed his torch on the ground. The flame hissed out as it struck the water. In its place, he conjured a mist of magelight that trailed ahead of them, lighting their path with a silvery glow. Kyel stared at the magelight with a look of speculation on his face, then turned to glare back at Darien. He flung his own torch over the edge of the landing.

They followed Darien's magelight down a long tunnel. Naia trailed after him, while Kyel brought up the rear. Their feet splashed through water that pooled on the floor and wept like blood down the walls. The warrens were humid and cold, smelling sharply of loamy mildew. It wasn't long until they reached a series of adjoining chambers Darien remembered well.

They pressed on until they came to a winding stair that led precipitously upward.

Suddenly, the entire magic field wrenched and groaned, gasping like a dying thing. The field lines oscillated wildly, sending a sharp pain lancing through Darien's skull. He brought his arms up to cover his head, but the gesture did little good. It wasn't something that could be muffled or blocked out. It was more like something that was trapped within, clawing to escape.

Eventually it passed. But not without leaving Darien feeling shaken and fatigued.

He stopped for a moment, collecting himself, and then started forward again. The stairs ended in a long, mist-lit corridor that seemed to waver around them. Ahead, there was an intersection that looked familiar. Darien brought his hand up, signaling a halt. He groped along the slimy, spring-fed rock until he found a small button. He pushed it. The trap built into the wall gave a small click. Straightening, he turned and started forward—

—and jolted to a stop.

His magelight collapsed into darkness.

The air around him cooled to a glacial chill.

Utter blackness caved in on top of them, complete in its totality. Cold terror stabbed into Darien's gut like barbed crystals of ice. He didn't need to see to recognize the threat. Necrators. He could feel them there, lingering in the shadows. Waiting for their master's command.

From out of the chill emptiness, he heard the swishing sounds of footsteps. They paced slowly, relentlessly nearer, stopping just ahead. There was a long gap of silence. Then a malevolent voice pierced the darkness like a knife.

"I warned him not to trust you. He wouldn't listen to me. It took Alexa's death to convince him otherwise."

A sinister gleam of crimson magelight slithered toward them from out of the darkness. By its glow, Darien could make out the owner of the voice. Cyrus Krane strode forward to stand in front of him, gazing into Darien's face with a strange, mercurial expression that seemed stuck somewhere between contempt and regret. Krane's necrators glided smoothly forward, ringing them in like a shadow-woven cage.

Leaning closer, Krane asked in a taunting voice, "Has there ever been an oath you haven't broken?"

"No," Darien answered honestly.

Krane sneered. He turned away and, with a wave of his hand, beckoned them to follow. "Come. We haven't much time."

The ring of necrators constricted, herding them forward. Naia winced as one of the shadows reached out to touch her. Darien pulled her close against him, out of the demon's reach. With a hand on Naia's shoulder, he moved after Krane. The unnatural terror provoked by the necrators lessoned, slowly displaced by anger.

Chaperoned by their demonic guard, they had no choice but to follow the ancient darkmage up long flights of steps that wept running water in an unnatural cascade. As they neared the surface, the magic field wrenched atrociously, sending a shockwave through Darien that shook him all the way to his bones. He reached out and caught himself on the wall, his knees turning to jelly.

Krane glanced back at him and smirked.

Darien scowled his anger at Krane's back, but even that small token of resistance sapped his strength. A chill breeze fanned the magelight ahead. The crimson mist crept forward again only hesitantly. Ahead, the corridor ended at a steep flight of steps that angled through the roof of the tunnel. The stairs were illuminated by an awful green light that flickered and strobed, as if lit by a thousand jabs of lightning.

Another gust whipped Darien's hair and billowed his cloak. It brought with it a sharp, pungent odor, like the smell of clay after a heavy rain. He recognized the scent and knew the origin. The Gateway stood just above them, feeding the air with the Netherworld's taint.

They ascended through the roof of the warrens, buffeted by

gusts of wind. All around them, the magic field shuddered and winced. It was growing fainter, Darien realized, its struggles weak and exhausted. The rock walls strobed with a hellish light. Rumbling crackles of thunder shook the entire mountain to its core.

Darien paused at the top of the stairs, reluctant to take the last step. The empty terraces of dead Aerysius still haunted his memories. He had no desire to look upon them, to be reminded of the majesty of the city that had been his home and heritage. It took every last drop of resolve he had left to will his feet forward after Krane.

They emerged into a ghastly world of buffeting winds and tormented skies. Darien narrowed his eyes against the raging gale. His gaze was drawn upward to a towering pillar of green light that pierced the heavens high above. Surging clouds circulated the spire like a vortex. The sight of it, the smell of it, made his stomach clench in dread. It was an abomination, a malevolent lance that pierced the sky and impaled the earth. At his side, Naia issued a sharp gasp of horror.

"This way," Krane commanded, impelling them forward.

They had no choice but to obey. The ancient darkmage led them across the remains of the Grand Square's once-elaborate tiles, now broken and scattered. Ahead through the shrieking wind, Darien could make out a glowing orb of light where the enormous Hall of the Watchers had once stood. Now, only the bared footprint remained, jagged shards of broken stone jutting upward from the ground. The rubble of the hall had been cleared away, leaving behind only a half-buried foundation.

The ring of necrators constricted again, now little more than an arm span away. Darien could no longer ignore the fear inspired by their influence. It was too encompassing, eating away at his courage and resolve until very little remained. Staggering against the rage of the wind, he stumbled forward into the circle of light.

And stopped, frozen between strides.

He stood on the margin of Aerysius' Circle of Convergence. Its power had been quenched the night the city had fallen.

Somehow, impossibly, the Circle had been restored.

Silver light shone from its rock-hewn lines, bright enough to chase back the night. A liquid radiance delineated the Circle's rays, which converged to form an enormous eight-pointed star. The Circle hummed eagerly, already awakened and primed. Darien stared at it in awe, rocked by the sheer impossibility of what he was seeing. There was only one man who had the skill and knowledge to repair such an evolved artifact of magic.

Darien's stomach sank like a lead weight. He raised his eyes to look across the Circle of Convergence. What he saw confirmed his fear. Restrained by bonds of light, Quinlan Reis knelt, hunched in defeat, on the broken ground at Renquist's feet. The Prime Warden stood over him, wielding Quin's own sword in his hand. The sight was chilling.

Darien knew exactly what it meant.

He had failed utterly.

No. It was worse than that. He'd allowed himself to be manipulated from the very beginning. By Renquist's design, he had betrayed every person he'd ever loved. Every value he held sacred. Every cause he'd ever championed, every commitment he'd ever made. And he had done it all willingly, deluded into thinking he was in command of his own destiny. He had been Renquist's puppet all along, and too arrogant to recognize it.

The weight of that realization was crushing. It nearly drove him to his knees.

Beneath him, the Circle of Convergence throbbed in time to his own heartbeat.

Slowly, inexorably, Zavier Renquist crossed the pulsating Circle, leading Quin by a leash woven of magic. He drew to a halt before Darien, gazing upon him with the saddened face of a father sorely disappointed in a son. There was no air of triumph about him, and there should have been. Darien wondered at that. Summoning his courage, he lifted his eyes to meet Renquist's gaze. It was like looking into the depths of the abyss. There was nothing remotely human in that stare.

Zavier Renquist informed him, "It is time for you to complete your purpose, your final duty to our Master. Thank you, Darien, for your sacrifice."

He lifted the sword. At first, Darien thought he was going to strike him down. But instead, Renquist handed the blade to Cyrus Krane. Then he stepped back out of the Circle's pulsating light.

Krane stared down at the hilt of the sword in his hand as if unsure what to do with it. A slow smile formed on his lips. He turned to Quin, raising the blade. "I've waited a thousand years to gut you with this."

Quin stared at him blandly. "That's an awfully long time. You must be fantastically incompetent."

The blade jerked upward, slicing a cut across Quin's cheek.

"No!" Naia sprang forward, dodging a necrator.

Renquist waved his hand casually. With a startled scream, Naia staggered and collapsed. Instantly, Quin was in motion, throwing himself at Cyrus Krane.

He was knocked to the ground as if smacked by a god-sized hammer. He rolled over and groaned, coming to rest against Naia.

Krane swung his attention to Kyel. With a jerk of his head, he summoned the Sentinel forward. "We need your talisman."

Impelled by the threat of the necrators, Kyel had no choice but to do as directed. Darien finally realized Renquist's strategy: he was gathering them together in one place. He intended to kill them all, then use Krane as a conduit to store their combined power. For Renquist's plan to work, Krane would have to be touching all three of them when they died.

The way Darien saw it, they had only one chance.

"Stop," he commanded. Reaching into the pocket of his cloak, he withdrew the Soulstone. He held it up in front of him, swaying by the band, the red stone glowing brilliantly.

"With this, you'll only need one of us," he informed Krane. "I'm holding your thirty-two tiers of power in my hand. Quin fixed it. Now it draws vitrus right out of the magic field itself."

Staring at the medallion, Krane's eyes brightened for a fleeting second. But then he shook his head. "Even if you are correct, you can't know its capacity."

"I do," Quin growled. "I'm the one who created it. It can draw any amount of vitrus you need."

Darien glanced at Naia, remembering her warning. About the decision he would have to make, the one choice that would determine the world's destiny. He felt it in his gut: that decision was upon him. The most important choice he would ever make.

He looked back at Krane. "I'll be your conduit. If I can spare even one of them, I'll do it gladly."

Krane glanced at Renquist, who shrugged noncommittally. Then he looked at the medallion in Darien's hand, his eyes cool and considering. He nodded slightly.

Darien brought the necklace up and wrapped the silver bands of the collar around his neck. He closed his eyes and opened the clasp.

"Darien, don't!" Naia screamed, her voice shrill with panic.

But there was no other choice to make.

This was the one chance they had.

He filled his mind with a singular thought: *Thirty-two.*

Then he let the clasp spring closed.

The world went brilliantly, atrociously white. Then there was silence, complete and perfect, soon broken by a high-pitched ringing in his ears. From somewhere very distant, Darien was vaguely aware of pain. But the pain wasn't part of him. The world had stopped. Time had stopped. The motion of the universe had frozen to a standstill.

Then, all at once, it all came crashing back at a harrowing speed.

Darien screamed as all the vast agony in the world slammed into him.

Chapter Forty-One
Born in Blood

Aerysius, The Rhen

Quin sprang to his feet and wrenched Naia off the ground, hauling her after him toward the stairs. But she jerked her arm away, twisting out of his grasp.

"Get Kyel!" she cried and ran back toward where Darien lay writhing and screaming in an inferno of raging power.

Quin growled in frustration and fear. He turned back, searching frantically for Kyel. He found him at last, pinned by three necrators against a toppled column. Quin gasped, recognizing the danger: if the shades touched Kyel, they'd lose the talisman and their last hope of success. Quin knew he'd never reach him in time.

So he flung himself at Cyrus Krane instead.

He took the darkmage by surprise, knocking him off his feet and jarring the sword from his hand. Quin rolled, snatching the weapon off the ground. He brought the blade around in a sweeping arc, slashing Krane's neck.

Blood sprayed, and the demon slumped to the ground. Quin whirled, looking desperately for Naia. He didn't see her. Across the Circle, Darien lay still, most likely dead. Quin hoped, for all their sakes, he was.

Overhead, the magic field trembled. It shuddered violently, quaking the mountainside. Quin was knocked off his feet. He lost his grip on *Zanikar*. The sword flew from his hand and tumbled, skittering across the ground, sliding to a halt at Renquist's feet.

Across the glowing Circle, Kyel sidled out of the ring of necrators. The shadowy forms remained frozen in place, obeying the last command of their master.

"Hurry!" Quin shouted, spurring Kyel faster. He turned and looked frantically for Naia, but she was nowhere. He had no choice—they were out of time. He turned and dashed for the stairs.

Kyel caught up to him, and together they raced for the opening to the warrens. The Sentinel held his gleaming talisman in his hand, using its radiance to light their way. Quin followed him down the stairs and through a series of winding passages.

"Stop!" Kyel shouted.

Quin halted in his tracks.

Kyel pressed a button on the wall then stepped back, heaving a sigh. "The Well's just around that corner. I need you to guard the door."

Quin looked at him skeptically. "What exactly do you expect me to do?"

"Whatever you *can* do!" Hefting the talisman, Kyel strode away down the corridor. Quin traipsed after him, casting a frantic glance back over his shoulder.

He found himself in a dim passage filled with an appalling green light. The light poured from a doorway just ahead, streaming out in ghastly rays, brilliant and blinding. Kyel didn't hesitate. Gripping his weapon, he strode forward into the light. Quin stopped, holding his hand up to shield his eyes from the glare.

The magic field winced painfully. And then it died.

"Damn," Quin muttered, knowing exactly what that meant.

Clenching his jaw in determination, he followed Kyel through the opening.

And stopped, too paralyzed to move a step further.

The Well of Tears stood before them, a waist-high ring of granite stone. Around its circumference, sinister markings glowed malevolently. A violent column of energy erupted from the Well's bore, piercing the ceiling overhead. Quin knew where it went. It shot up through the rock, thrusting upward from the mountain to impale the sky.

Kyel stood staring at the crackling pillar of light, his cloak rippled by a wind of displaced air. He hesitated for a moment, unmoving. Then he raised the morning star over his head and brought it down with all his might, striking the Well's rim.

The weapon didn't impact. But the force of its magic did. Fragments of stone shot out, flying in all directions.

Somehow, the Well fought back.

Kyel was hurled backward, impacting with the wall behind him. Shaking his head as if dazed, he picked himself up off the ground. A thin stream of blood leaked from his nostrils. His face grimly resolute, he approached the Well and, raising the morning star over his head, brought it down with all the force in his body.

Naia knelt on the edge of the Circle of Convergence, constrained by bonds of light. But Zavier Renquist paid her no mind; his attention was focused on Darien.

Holding Quin's sword, Renquist strode across the Circle to where Darien lay on his back. Naia couldn't tell whether he was stunned or dead. Twenty-two tiers of power had slammed into him from the stone, on top of the ten he already had. Enough to kill him, she felt certain. She just didn't know how fast.

Renquist drew to a stop and lingered over Darien for a moment, gazing somberly down. Almost, Naia thought, the Prime Warden's face held an expression of regret. Gritting his teeth, he reversed his grip on *Zanikar's* hilt. Then he plunged the blade into Darien's chest.

As Naia looked on in horror, Darien's blood ran freely, spreading outward over the Circle of Convergence in an ever-enlarging pool.

Kyel howled in pain as jagged blocks of stone cracked and fell away from the Well's girth. Again, he was thrown back against the wall, this time sagging to his knees. Blood flowed in thick ropes from his nose, trickled from his ears. Like a drunken man, he hauled himself upright and lurched sideways. Then he lifted his weapon and threw himself at the Well again.

Stone rained. Kyel screamed. He brought the talisman up and slammed it down again and again, fracturing block after block. He reeled, stumbling backward, catching himself on the wall. He pushed himself off and staggered around the Well's circumference to attack the other side. Again and again, he brought the talisman down against the Well with all the strength he had, raining shards of granite all over the chamber.

Blood sprayed. Kyel dropped, moaning, to his knees. Thar'gon fell from his hands.

Quin looked on in horror. Without the magic field, there was nothing he could do. There was nothing to shield Kyel from the terrible force of the Well's backlash.

With a growl, Kyel grabbed the weapon off the ground and heaved himself back to his feet. He teetered and almost fell. Streams of blood rolled down his face, leaking like tears. The front of his shirt was saturated. The Well had been reduced to a pile of broken stone, only the blocks of its foundation yet remaining. But the portal was still full-open, the gush of energy still raging furiously upward from the bore.

Kyel heaved the weapon over his head and brought it down again with a furious shout. Chips of rock ricocheted off the walls, striking Quin in the face. Kyel screamed in agony, and Thar'gon flew from his hands. He wavered for a moment, off-balanced. Then he collapsed, falling forward toward the gaping bore of the Well of Tears.

"NO!" Quin shouted. He caught Kyel by the cloak and jerked him back. His momentum carried him to the floor, Kyel falling on top of him.

Quin rolled him over and sat up.

Kyel stared up at him with a loose, unfocused gaze, his face a glistening mask of blood. More blood ran from his nose in a viscous stream that drained down his cheeks.

Panicked, Quin glanced back at the ruin of the Well. There were still blocks remaining. Kyel needed to get up, needed to finish the job. Only he could wield the talisman.

Quin growled in desperation. He had to find a way to get Kyel back on his feet. Frantic, he grasped him by the shoulders, ready to try shaking him back to his senses. But then he stopped himself. It wouldn't do any good, he realized with a stab of desperation that felt like a gut punch.

Kyel wouldn't be getting up again.

Quin looked down at the glowing morning star that lay on the floor next to him. He glanced back at the Well. Then he looked down at Kyel. The Sentinel's lips were moving, struggling to form words Quin couldn't make out. He leaned closer, straining to hear.

"Take it," Kyel whispered in a gurgling breath. "Finish it."

Kyel's fingers groped for the silver talisman that lay just out of reach.

Drowning in uncertainty, Quin shook his head. "I can't. I can't lift it."

Kyel whispered, "You can if I'm dead."

Quin froze, gripped by cold revulsion as he realized what the Sentinel was asking. He shook his head in an attempt to deny him. But one glance back at the pillar of energy told him he didn't have a choice. He reached for his boot knife.

With a growl, Quin drove the knife as hard as he could between Kyel's ribs, burying it up to the hilt.

Kyel flinched. Then he blinked. And that was all.

Quin sagged back on his haunches, watching as waves of power gushed from Kyel's body in distorted waves, lost to the air. Quin threw his head back and screamed. Balling his fist, he smacked his hand against the ground in rage.

Across the room, the surge of energy yet surged from the Well's gaping bore.

Trembling, Quin reached for Thar'gon. But he stopped himself, suddenly mired in doubt. The talisman was designed to be wielded only by the Warden of Battlemages. And he wasn't a Battlemage.

But, then, Kyel hadn't been either.

With conviction, Quin closed his fingers around the weapon's haft and lifted the talisman from the floor. Immediately, warmth and solace flowed into him along with a newfound strength he'd never known. Filled with a blissful sense of euphoria, Quin rose from the ground.

He glanced back at Kyel and whispered his gratitude to the fallen Sentinel.

Then he raised the weapon over his head and, with all his might, brought the talisman smashing down.

The Well fought back.

Quin screamed.

The Gateway was still open. It shot upward into the sky, spearing the heavens.

Naia struggled against her bonds, trying desperately to escape the advancing demon. Across from her, sprawled in the center of the Circle of Convergence, Darien lay dying in an expanding pool of blood. It flowed into the gaps and crevices of the Circle's rays, outlining the marble tiles with heightened contrast. The blood continued to advance, as if seeking to saturate the entire Circle.

Zavier Renquist pushed Naia to her knees, positioning himself behind her. He drew the sword back over his shoulder, preparing to strike.

A thunderous clap of air sent him hurling backward. Naia looked up in terror, in hope, in desperation. She gasped in disbelief. Blood streaming down his face, Quin stalked toward her across the glowing Circle, the talisman Thar'gon glowing like a beacon in his hand.

"Run, Naia!"

Naia froze. Renquist was already pushing himself to his feet.

"Run!" Quin commanded again, raising the morning star.

He swung the weapon at Renquist, creating a concussive blast of air that knocked the Prime Warden back to the ground. Hefting the weapon, Quin advanced.

"No," Naia whispered, shaking her head. This was wrong. It was all terribly, terribly wrong.

"No, Quin!" she shrieked. *"Leave him! Help Darien!"*

Quin froze in the action of drawing the weapon back for another blow. He growled in frustration. Then he whirled and ran back across the Circle of Convergence.

He dropped to Darien's side and lay a hand on his chest. He closed his eyes, gripping the talisman. The silver artifact glowed, swelling with a powerful brilliance.

Darien gasped. Then he opened his eyes.

Behind Naia, Renquist was moving. He rose to his feet, eyes menacing pools of shadow. He raised his hand and struck out at her with the Onslaught. Naia was lifted from the ground and hurled through the air.

Her body impacted with the rock, cutting short her scream.

"Naia!" Quin bellowed.

He bolted toward her but halted as Zavier Renquist stepped between them.

Spreading his arms, Renquist began to glow with the vile light of the Gateway. It was then that Quin saw it: a streaking ribbon of energy arcing from the pillar to Renquist, as though he were drawing power from it.

Hellpower.

Quin realized that ribbon of corrupt energy was the reason why the portal hadn't collapsed. Renquist was drinking in the Onslaught, sustaining the Gateway by keeping the Hellpower flowing through it.

With a great, thunderous growl, Zavier Renquist changed. Before Quin's eyes, he swelled to enormous size, his arms growing and spreading into heinous, bat-like wings. Quin cried out, scrambling away from the twisted beast. Its head seemed all teeth, its eyes infinite pools of darkness. The demon gave a shrill screech, spread its leathery wings, and launched into the air.

Quin struggled to help Darien gain his feet. Darien wavered, his eyes sliding shut. Overhead, the demon emitted a piercing shriek. Quin looked up. His mouth fell open, his eyes going wide.

"Give it to me," Darien whispered.

It took Quin a moment to realize what he meant. He pressed

the morning star's haft into Darien's hand and squeezed his fingers closed around it. A bloom of silver radiance erupted from the talisman, overwhelming his vision. Quin whirled away, throwing his hands up to shield his eyes.

Recovering, he sprinted toward Naia. He ran off the Circle, falling down at her side and turning her over. She was unconscious. Blood ran from a wound over her eye, streaking her face. Without the magic field, he couldn't heal her. So he did the only thing he could do: he wrapped his arms around her and held her tight.

An explosive crackle of thunder rocked the mountain.

Quin looked back and squinted through the glare. Across the Circle, Darien was on his feet, surrounded by a sphere of dazzling light. Above him, the creature disgorged a stream of flame that gushed against Darien's brilliant shield, unable to penetrate. Darien danced back, raised his weapon, and swung it around in a great arc. A compressed wave of solid air slammed into the demon, knocking it from the sky and hurling it to the ground with a furious shriek.

The monster recovered quickly. It took to the air again then spun on wing, turning to retaliate. It opened its mouth and belched forth a roiling inferno of flames. Darien staggered, holding the talisman up defensively as a torrent of fire streamed over him. He fell to his knees, holding the glowing talisman over his head and straining with all his might to keep the shield of argent light in place.

The demon landed, spewing gouts of flame into the air. Its tail cracked into Darien, knocking him to the ground. He lost his grip on the morning star, and it flew away from him. He scrambled after it, snatching the talisman up and rolling onto his back just in time, as the demon landed on top of him. He used the weapon to bludgeon the monster's head, sending the creature cringing back in a showering spray of ink-dark blood. The demon flapped into the air with a cry of outrage, then banked sharply back toward the Circle, streaming fire in its wake.

The creature attacked, throwing itself against Darien's shield and sending him hurling backward. Overhead, the clouds thundered their fury. Bleeding and dazed, Darien fought his way back to his feet. But the argent brilliance of his weapon was dimming, his arms sagging to his sides.

The demon let out a hungering screech, then turned to attack. This time, it penetrated Darien's weakened defenses. The beast's mouth closed on his chest. Darien howled, flailing in the demon's grasp. Bringing the morning star up, he battered it against the monster's leathery hide.

The creature tossed him into the air, flinging him across the tiles of the square.

Darien rolled to a stop at the edge of the cliff. He pushed himself up and stood, swaying, his back against the cliff's harrowing edge.

The demon took flight, circling upward over the terrace. It opened its jaws, baring a mouthful of chiseled teeth.

Fire gushed from the creature's mouth. Darien threw himself sideways in an attempt to dodge. He wasn't fast enough.

The blast of flames swept Darien off his feet, hurling him over the cliff's edge.

"NO!" Quin screamed.

Overhead, the skies strobed and rumbled their fury.

The demon alighted on the terrace and, noticing Quin, stalked forward. Quin set Naia on the ground and rose, stepping between her and the monster. The demon opened its mouth, smoke trailing from its nostrils. Its sides expanded as it filled its bellows with a great chestful of air.

Quin threw his hands up.

There was a violent gush of wind, the crackling sound of flapping wings.

The demon shrieked as it was snatched into the air by a pair of enormous talons. It writhed and twisted, squirming to break free, finally dislodging itself from the dark-scaled creature that veered upward into the sky.

Quin threw himself to the ground.

Overhead, a tremendous dragon unfurled wings large enough to dominate the sky. It banked gracefully, circling the turbulent pillar of light. Its obsidian scales looked blacker than the abyss against the awful glow of the Gateway.

Quin gawked up at the sky, shaking his head in mute denial, jaw slack in disbelief.

Darien.

The dragon tucked its wings and plunged into a steep dive. With a deafening roar, it opened its mouth and flooded the Circle with flames. The demon was thrown across the ground, rolling to a stop. It lay still for a moment, singed and smoldering.

The dragon alighted on the Circle with a graceful backstroking of wings, the wind of its landing whipping Quin's hair like a gale. The beast advanced, stalking forward, head lowered and nostrils flaring. Cowering before it, the demon scrambled back. There was a brilliant flash of light.

The demon was gone.

In its place reared another dragon, larger than the first, its scales a dark emerald green. It took fluidly to the air, the obsidian dragon vaulting after it.

The sky thundered as the two beasts collided overhead, a writhing tangle of wings and talons and gushing streaks of flame. Both creatures screamed their rage, their claws raking scales, serrated teeth shredding wings. The ferocity of their battle trembled the clouds and shook the very roots of the mountain. Their dark blood fell from the sky like rain.

The monsters broke apart. The emerald dragon beat the air furiously to gain height, while the other soared low, favoring an injured wing. It banked over the terrace and angled sharply downward toward the valley.

The green dragon roared, wingtips parting the clouds, then threw itself into a plummeting dive. Its talons outstretched, it scooped its enemy out of the sky, dashing the black dragon hard against the cliff face.

Rock fractured. Part of the cliffside gave way, raining stone down onto the valley floor. Recovering, the black dragon roared a challenge. It pushed off from the cliff with a powerful thrust of its hindquarters, slithering after its adversary.

The beasts crashed together and locked in the air, a mass of spewing flames and clashing wings. Together, the dragons grappled with claws and teeth. Twined together in a deadly knot, each strove to rip the throat out of the other. Locked in a death-spiral, the two creatures plummeted down the face of the mountain, ragged wings outstretched, helpless to break their fall.

Quin sprang toward the cliff's edge, halting just in time to witness the dragons break apart. The black dragon tumbled away, coming to a rolling stop on the ground. The emerald dragon slammed against a rock outcrop then dropped, broken and lifeless, to the valley floor.

Above, a horrendous grating noise filled the night. The mountains lurched as if convulsed.

The spear of light erupted violently. The pillar shivered and distorted, caving in on itself. The green spire roiled like a frothing geyser, collapsing into the mountainside. The clouds above it slammed together with a shocking fury that showered the night with jagged streaks of lightning.

Shaking, Quin pushed himself back from the cliff's edge and stumbled back to Naia's side. He dropped down next to her and pulled her into his arms, clutching her tight.

"It's over," he assured her, stroking his fingers through her hair.

Chapter Forty-Two
Damned

Glen Farquist, The Rhen

D arien hadn't expected to wake.
He had a feeling he'd been floating somewhere between full sleep and full wakefulness for quite some time, like a man drowning in the ocean, groping for the surface. He cracked open his eyes, blinking against a riotous glare of light that stung his vision. He was shivering. Shaking. He couldn't control it. The air was stale. Cold. He burned from within. Beyond the light, the world was an obscure haze, as though he were looking out a window through a pane of mottled glass.

Something wet touched his face. A rag. It made him shiver harder.

"Where..." he whispered. It was all he could do to get that one syllable past his throat.

"You're in Glen Farquist. You've been unconscious for ten days."

He licked his parched lips. His eyelids felt too heavy to hold open any longer. He closed his eyes and drifted back under.

The next time he surfaced, he felt a bit better. He opened his eyes. He was still shivering, just not as violently as before. There was movement. And a voice. He tried to focus.

"Naia..."

"I'm here," she said. She was holding his hand. "Quin's here, too."

The room was so cold. So bright. A raging fire burned inside him, greater than he could ever endure.

"Try to stay awake," she urged.

He couldn't. It was too hard. He was too tired.

He drifted for a long time, floating on a tide of muddled dreams. The next time he awoke, he felt stronger. The room wasn't so bright, the air not so cold and stale. He'd stopped shivering. But the fire within him still raged.

He fought to sit up.

"Careful. You are still very weak."

Hands caught him and helped him upright. Someone stuffed a pillow behind his back. Darien looked around, squinting, at last recognizing where he was. In the Temple of Death. In the same room they'd lent him two years before.

"Here." Naia draped a blanket over him, her face tight with concern.

"What happened?" he asked in a raspy voice.

She glanced back over her shoulder. Looking past her, Darien saw Quin lingering in the doorway. Holding his hat in his hands, he approached the bed and sat down in a chair beside Naia. He kept his eyes averted and didn't say a word.

"Kyel and Quin destroyed the Well of Tears," Naia informed him gently. "You killed Zavier Renquist. The portal collapsed."

The flood of relief Darien felt almost washed him away. He closed his eyes. "Where's Kyel?"

"I'm sorry, Darien. He didn't survive."

That hurt. It hurt deeper than he'd thought it would. Darien took a deep breath, feeling a knot tighten in his throat. Kyel had been more than just his acolyte. He'd been someone Darien respected and admired, the most honorable man he'd ever known.

Naia patted his hand. "You need food. I'll bring you some."

Darien shook his head. "I'm not hungry."

"You must eat." she insisted. "You need to get your strength back."

"For what?"

Darien saw in her face that Naia didn't have an answer to that question. Neither did he. He could feel all thirty-two tiers of power raging inside him, burning him up from within. He couldn't survive that kind of assault, and she knew it. He saw the pity written in her eyes, and even Quin couldn't look at him. They both knew as well as he did that there was no point.

Naia said softly, "There might be something we can do."

"No." Darien shook his head. "Whatever it is, I don't want it."

Naia squeezed his hand. In the consoling tones of a priestess, she said, "It is your choice, of course, how you wish to die. I do understand the predicament you're in. It's not enviable. But you do have options."

Darien looked up at her uncertainly.

"You can stay here," she told him. "The priests of Death would care for you the rest of your days. They would be honored to do so, for the great service you rendered their goddess. Or you can come with Quin and me. We are going to Rothscard to build a school for mages. Nothing like Aerysius. But we could certainly use your knowledge and experience, as long as you are able to provide it."

It was a worthwhile endeavor, and it made Darien glad to hear. But he knew he wouldn't be around long enough to make a difference. He shook his head.

Quin blew out a heavy sigh, then finally turned to face him. "What are you going to do?" he asked in a dismal tone.

Darien shrugged. "I'm damned," he said, stating the obvious. "I don't want to go back to the Netherworld, and I'm denied the Atrament. My only recourse is Oblivion."

Naia bowed her head. Softly, she whispered, "Perhaps we can help with that."

Her words filled Darien with hope. Oblivion wasn't as simple a choice as it had once been. He'd lost his link with Xerys, the only god he knew who would be willing to cast his soul to the winds.

He whispered, "Tell me how."

Naia glanced down, looking hesitant. "Do you remember when you travelled with me into the Catacombs? We were separated. You wandered into a chamber where you were greeted by your dead. There, you met the shade of your father. He told you that you didn't belong there."

Darien nodded. He remembered that encounter well. It was one of the most painful moments of his life.

"Your father was right." Naia sighed. "You *don't* belong there. That hall is a very sacred place to the goddess. Damned as you are, Isap would shred your soul if you stepped foot back in there. There would be nothing left of you. You would be unmade."

Darien sagged back into the pillows, feeling the tension drain from his body. He closed his eyes and took a deep breath, savoring an intense feeling of relief.

"Then that's perfect."

"Are you very certain, Darien?" she asked.

He nodded wearily. "Aye. More certain than I've ever been of anything."

Naia leaned forward and kissed him on the forehead. Then, with a glance at Quin, she rose from her chair. "Wait here. Rest for a while. I'll go make arrangements."

Feeling content, Darien lay back into his pillows and closed his eyes.

When he awoke again, he felt stronger. Better. Hopeful. The fire still blazed within, consuming a bit more of him every moment. Darien felt glad he wouldn't have to linger, waiting for that fire to consume him utterly. He opened his eyes to find that Naia had returned to his side.

"Are you ready?" she asked.

Darien nodded without speaking.

Naia and Quin helped him out of bed. The act of standing took every last bit of strength he possessed. Once they had him dressed, Darien sagged back down on the bed and sat there, cradling his head in his hands. The room seemed unstable, rocking gently. The sensation made him queasy. Inside his head, the fire raged hotter.

"Wait here. I'll be right back," Naia said and left the room. He didn't ask why.

Quin sat down beside him, looking wretched. He was absent his hat, which Darien thought strange. Squinting against the motion of the world, Darien frowned up at him.

He asked, "What will you do, Quin? At the end? Do you want to go back?"

Quin shook his head. "Things are different for me. I struck the last blow that destroyed the Well of Tears. For some reason I'll never fathom, the goddess has forgiven me."

Darien was glad for him. Despite his propensity for disaster, Quin's heart was true.

A motion drew his attention to the doorway. Naia entered the room, a sympathetic smile on her face. She carried a white bundle in her hands, holding it before her reverently.

"The priests had this made for you," she said, offering the parcel to Darien. "They want you to wear it."

Darien started to reach for it. But then, realizing what it was, his hand froze. It was a white cloak, folded so that the Silver Star faced upward, glittering in the candlelight. Feeling a sudden gush of shame, Darien withdrew his hand.

"I can't wear that."

Naia's smile didn't falter. "You can. And you will."

Despite his protestations, they helped him to his feet and draped the thick cloak over his shoulders. Naia adjusted the lay of the fabric down his back, smoothing out the folds. Straightening, she took a step back and nodded her approval. "You look respectable."

Darien felt patently uncomfortable, knowing that his touch soiled the honor of that cloak. Before he could object further, Naia took his hand and led him out the door, Quin following behind. It felt strange to walk. His legs were weak, spongy. He leaned heavily on Naia, her strength keeping him upright. Keeping him moving. They turned a corner into a wide hallway.

Darien halted midstride.

The entire corridor was lined with priests and priestesses wearing stoles of various colors. Seeing him, they dropped to their knees in unison, bowing forward in the traditional obeisance reserved only for a Prime Warden. Darien caught his breath, stunned by the gesture. He groped for words.

"Why are they doing this?" he finally managed to gasp. "I led an army against them."

Naia turned to fix him with a proud smile. "Because they owe you their lives, Darien. If Renquist had succeeded, then every last temple would have been destroyed and the priests put to death. You saved not only their lives, but all their work and all their heritage."

It was too much. He didn't deserve it. Couldn't accept it. "Tell them to stop," he whispered.

Naia's smile only deepened. "If I did, they wouldn't listen to me."

Taking his hand, she guided him forward.

Chapter Forty-Three
Last of the Light

Glen Farquist, The Rhen

A diffuse glow filtered down from the ceiling. In the warmth of that surreal haze, the shrine of the Goddess of the Eternal Requiem seemed rendered from a dream, as though seen through the fog of awakening.

Naia clutched Quin's arm, watching Darien move ahead of them, his gaze wandering over the satin walls of the shrine. Naia's own attention was drawn to an alcove in the far corner. There, a life-size statue of her goddess awaited, one marble hand extended as though beckoning them near.

Darien appeared to be obeying her silent gesture. He gazed up into the goddess' face as he approached, pausing only when he stood at the statue's base. There, he reached out and touched her tapering fingers, caressing her stone skin.

Shoulders sagging, he let his hand drop to his side. He stood forlorn at the goddess' feet, bowing his head as if offering a prayer.

Or offering up his soul.

Whichever it was, Naia couldn't know, but the sight of him made her heart ache.

Quin released her hand and strode forward, his heavy footfalls disrupting the tension of the shrine. Reaching Darien, he clutched him in a tight embrace and kissed his cheek. Then he let him go.

Quin turned and hastened from the shrine, departing without a glance back. Naia knew he wouldn't return. She understood. And she knew Darien understood also. His eyes followed after

Quin, lingering on the doorway even after the man was gone.

Silence echoed.

Darien turned toward her. He still lingered at the feet of the goddess who had propelled his fate toward this end. And yet, he didn't appear to harbor resentment. Naia was grateful for that. Swallowing her feelings, she crossed the shrine toward him. She reached up and cupped his face in her hands.

"Are you ready?" she whispered.

Darien nodded. "I'm tired, Naia."

She took him by the hand. "Then come with me. I'll show you to a place where you can rest."

Gently, she guided him away from the statue's base. She led him across the shrine to a passage that opened into darkness. There, Naia paused and murmured a soft prayer. With a hesitant step, she crossed the threshold. For a moment, the world shivered, filling her with a sudden surge of vertigo. Then the darkness fell away and the floor steadied. The shadows parted to reveal a dim corridor lit by putrid green light.

Naia drew up, startled by the color. It took her a moment to realize its origin. Turning back, she took in the sight of the green aura that emanated from Darien's body, a ghastly symptom of his damnation. It had grown so much brighter than the last time she'd seen it. Looking at him, Naia felt her chest tighten. The aura was a dreadful reminder of the urgency of her task.

Darien gazed down at himself, studying the terrible light that rippled over him, his eyes darkened by shame. Naia felt a cold sense of resolve creep over her. She clutched Darien's hand and urged him forward, the awful glow of his aura illuminating their path.

The passage led to the doorway of a large chamber that stood cloaked in silence and shadow. Naia stopped at the opening, dreading what awaited within. She closed her eyes, summoning the last of her courage. It took everything she had to turn and face him.

"I hope you find what you're looking for," she said.

Darien nodded, gazing into her eyes with a sad smile. "I'll be fine. This is what I want, Naia. I won't miss this world."

"But this world will miss you," she whispered.

She took him into her arms and held him close one last time. It hurt to let him go. She remained behind as Darien strode alone into the darkness of the chamber. He didn't turn to say goodbye.

She watched from the doorway as he crossed to the center of the wide hall, drawn as if by a summons only he could hear. He gazed upward into the shadows of the ceiling, his attention captivated by something high above. Following his gaze, Naia saw a wrought-iron chandelier that hung from the ceiling. Six orbs hovered above it, glowing with a rich golden light.

As Darien neared, the dim light of the hall wavered and began to fade, diminishing into darkness. There was a great gap of silence, as if time itself had paused and stood waiting. Then, subtly, the orbs began to rotate. They spun slowly at first, then faster, picking up speed, the glows within them swelling to brilliance.

A tremendous deluge of light gushed from the chandelier, a torrent of radiance that consumed Darien entirely. The light savaged him, battering at his corrupted aura as if warring with it for mastery. The brutality of the light was appalling to behold. It was ferocious, a radiant inferno that ravaged his skin like searing flames. It clawed at him, burning away the Netherworld's taint and replacing it with an argent brilliance that streamed outward in glimmering rays.

High above, the orbs slowed and began to dim, losing the violence of their fury, eventually giving way to darkness.

Below in the shadows, Darien remained, the light of his presence fading to a soft azure glow. He turned toward her.

Naia gasped. Darien stood in front of her, just as he had before. But his flesh was gone, seared away by the goddess' grace. What remained was a luminous memory of the man she had known, glowing softly with the miracle of redemption.

Darien's shade raised his hands before his face, gazing at them, through them, as if confused by their significance. Naia looked on, her heart quietly breaking as she watched his eyes widen and fill with wonder. He shot a glance her way, his expression full of amazed disbelief.

From out of the darkness, delicate shapes began to emerge.

They crept silently forward, their pale glimmers closing in to surround him: dozens of fragile wights that shone with ethereal glows. Naia was filled with a terrified sense of awe, knowing that she gazed upon the dead of fallen Aerysius. All of the people Darien had ever known, had ever loved, had ever lost. There were so many faces Naia recognized, and so many she did not. Dozens. Perhaps hundreds. Their myriad glows saturated the hall.

The host surrounding Darien parted to admit a gentle shape that squeezed forward through the pressing crowd.

Naia gasped as she witnessed the joy on Azár's face as she swept forward into the arms of the husband who loved her.

More spirits emerged, filling the hall until their combined lights swelled into one all-consuming flame that defeated the shadows and then, eventually, diminished. Gradually, the host of wights drifted away, receding back into the walls from whence they came. One by one, their soft glows faded and winked out, until only Darien remained. He started after the others, but then paused. He turned back, fixing Naia with a look of heartfelt gratitude that lasted only a moment. Then he, too, was gone.

Naia stared after him with gladness in her heart.

The Last Sentinel of Aerysius had finally won his war.

Epilogue

A warm breeze sighed through the quiet of the morning, trailing leaves across the courtyard of Emmery Palace. Captured by a gust, the leaves tumbled along, carried upward and over the city walls. They lofted on an updraft, fluttering and spinning, before floating back down to scatter across the grasslands.

The wind swept briskly through the Malikari encampment, billowing the banners, flaring the cook fires, ruffling the horses' long manes. Gaining energy, the air sped over the plains, rippling the tall grasses, gusting past a long, winding column of refugees. The wind blew across the foothills, sweeping up the naked slopes of the Shadowspears.

The gusts howled and twisted, funneled through the ridges and canyons of the Pass of Lor-Gamorth, past the remains of two shattered strongholds that would soon be lost to memory. The wind raged across the black desert beyond, taking hold of a bank of flickering clouds and hurling them furiously at the horizon.

But then the impetus behind the wind lost its urgency.

At first, the change was subtle. The gusts faded to a breeze that slowly exhausted itself, dying peacefully somewhere in the dark hills above the desert. The tumbling cloudbank lost its inertia and slowed, coasting to a standstill. In the haunting stillness that followed, the vast entirety of the Black Lands seemed to pause in anticipation.

The black clouds lightened to gray, their soft edges brightening until they gleamed with a silvery glow. For long minutes, they held steady in defiance of the sun, as if determined to maintain their tyranny.

But they couldn't hold forever against the conquering dawn.

The skies opened, shedding brilliant rays that angled down to splatter the earth with sunlight.

In the east, dawn broke over the horizon, more welcome than any sunrise that had ever come before.

THE END

Preview of

Darkstorm

Prequel to The

Rhenwars Saga

A thousand years ago...

Prologue

Bryn Calazar, Caladorn

"Braden Reis."

He didn't look up at the sound of his own name being spoken from the doorway. Instead, he swallowed, squeezing his eyes shut as he ran his tongue across his parched lips. The sound of his own breath was a turbulent noise in his ears. He forced himself to concentrate on that sound, focusing his mind on every sharp hiss of air he sucked into his chest.

The sound of approaching footsteps made him flinch. Try as he might, he couldn't stop his hands from trembling.

"On your feet."

Braden ignored the command, knowing there would be a penalty for his defiance. He squeezed his hands into fists in anticipation of the pain. For heartbeats, he waited. When nothing happened, he allowed himself to relax a bit.

The pain hit with force.

Molten-silver lightning raged like a firestorm through his mind. He threw his head back, clenching his teeth. Slumping to the floor, Braden convulsed as liquid energies seared through his body. Bile rose in his throat, choking him as he writhed on the floor.

The pain lessened only gradually, taking a long time to completely go away. He lay on his back on the cold stone, staring upward, spent and gasping.

A different voice, soft and repulsively familiar, addressed him from the doorway. "Think very carefully, Ambassador Reis. There are many kinds of deaths, some much worse than others."

He shuddered at the sound of that voice. It was despicably seductive, stroking like soft velvet down the length of his nerves.

Braden kept his eyes squeezed closed, so loath was he to gaze upon that face.

He could feel her moving toward him across the cell. Her hands brushed his skin, a silken caress as she slid her arms around his torso. With gentle pressure she compelled him to his feet. He stood, swaying, naked from the waist up, arms chained behind his back. His breath still came in gasps.

"It doesn't have to be this way," she whispered gently in his ear as her soft fingertips stroked the skin of his back. "You can still choose to make a difference. Think of the lives you could save. It's the right thing to do."

His eyes shot open, glaring his contempt at her.

"Don't lecture me on morals, woman," he grated. "You have no idea what they are."

The smile that bloomed on her lovely face was only a dim reflection of the delight that filled her eyes. His response had pleased her. It sickened him, knowing that he had given her exactly what she'd wanted.

"I want you to die knowing that they chose me to inherit your legacy," she informed him with a grin. "One way or another, your gift will be put to the service of Xerys. With your power inside me, *I* will be the one destined for greatness. And you?" She looked at him sadly and scoffed with a shrug. "You'll just be dead."

Hearing her words, Braden Reis closed his eyes and bowed his head in acceptance of defeat. Never before in his life had he felt so utterly powerless.

The sound of her slippered footsteps moved away from him across the floor. Then hands were upon him, wrenching him forward. Braden allowed his guards to escort him out of the cell.

The despair that gripped him dulled his senses. It was as though he moved through a dim and murky haze, the world around him distant and strangely muted. They ushered him up many flights of stairs toward the floor of the Lyceum. The dance of magelight that churned at their feet only served to confound his senses all the more.

Braden gazed ahead with bleary eyes at the woman who strode

before him. She glided in a sway of blue silks, platinum curls spiraling to her waist. She moved with an easy grace, every motion poised, every step a deliberate, calculated seduction. Arden Hannah was just as alluring as she was vile. It was a powerful and frightening dichotomy. She gazed back at him and smiled, her wide eyes glistening in the magelight.

He dropped his stare back to the floor.

They reached the level of the Assembly. There, his guards wrenched back on Braden's arms, forcing him to a halt. The sound of a staff rapping thrice upon wood resounded throughout the hall. There was a pause. Then the knocks were answered in kind, echoing from the other side of the barred doorway.

The bars were thrown from the inside, the enormous double doors cast open, shuddering on their hinges with a throaty groan. Braden avoided Arden's eyes as his guards forced him forward. He could see very little, only shadowy silhouettes of people gathered above in the galleries. Within, the room was completely dark save for a single sphere of brilliant light in the center of the hall. It was toward that orb of light that he was made to walk.

Braden forced himself to hold his head up despite the chill fingers of dread that caressed his bare skin. Nervous sweat trickled down his brow. He couldn't help trembling as he stepped within that sphere of light. There he paused, hands bound behind him, completely blinded by the dazzling brilliance. That was the purpose of the light: to protect the anonymity of those gathered above in the galleries.

The doors slammed closed, sealing the chamber with a resounding *thud*. An awful, gaping silence struck the room. The silence lingered, long moments stretching on and on. Braden continued to stand, blinking against the glare, eyes groping desperately for the sight of just one face he could recognize. But he could make out nothing; the thick wall of light was dense and unyielding.

A deep and resonant voice addressed him:

"Braden Reis, you have been convicted, attainted, and condemned of high treason committed against the state of Caladorn and the Lyceum of Bryn Calazar. A sentence of death has been pronounced against you. May the gods have mercy on your soul."

Braden bowed his head under the sheer weight of the words. A paralyzing numbness overcame him. He stood there shaking, withered by the miserable knowledge that he had failed so utterly in his purpose.

Slithering ropes of energy twined around him, restraining him completely as they forced him roughly to his knees in the circle of light. He fought to draw breath, but succeeded only in producing a strangled wheeze.

The Prime Warden himself stepped forward into the wash of light to carry out his sentence. Panic seized Braden at the sight of the object displayed in Zavier Renquist's hands: a stone of many facets, lifeless, dull and black. It hung from the bands of a silver collar that shone like satin in the light.

The sight of the Soulstone was ghastly, terrifying.
Braden's eyes shot up, groping at Renquist's face. But in the gaze of his executioner, he found no trace of mercy.

Chapter One
Jumping at Shadows

Aerysius, The Rhen
Three weeks prior...

Rain pelted the dark streets of Aerysius as thunder rolled
expansively across the cloud-choked night. Merris Bryar
shivered as her feet splashed through growing rivulets in
the street, hugging her black cloak tightly against her body. She
was drenched, her toes almost numb in her wet slippers. It was
a terrible storm, the worst yet of the season. There was really no
good reason for anyone to be moving about the city streets on
such a night.

Which was exactly why Merris stalked the man who walked
ahead of her through the storm.

Of all the people in Aerysius, the person Merris followed had
the least excuse to be skulking through the shadows of the city.
Merris hung well back from him, relying on the cloak she wore
to obscure her features in the darkness. Her quest was dangerous, but that did little to daunt her. Rather, the thrill of the risk
she was taking urged her forward.

Merris was no stranger to the night. She knew perfectly well
how to navigate the city streets unseen. Her father had been a
cutpurse, her mother a sot and a swindler. Their combined examples had served Merris well in her youth. This was not the first
time she had tracked a mark through the city streets under the
cover of darkness.

It was just the first time she had done so since becoming an
acolyte mage.

And back when Merris had forged a living on the streets, she would never, ever, have considered selecting Cyrus Krane himself, the Prime Warden of Aerysius, as her quarry.

Merris moved as silently as she could, keeping at least a block's distance between herself and Cyrus Krane. She kept to the shadows, moving low, using the pillars of balconies and the arches of doorways as concealment. The rattle of the downpour covered any noise her slippered feet might have possibly made. Merris smiled slightly. She knew exactly what she was doing; she was in her element.

She watched as Krane turned and crossed the cobbled street toward the opening of an alleyway. Tonight, the Prime Warden wore just the thick, black cloak of a common mage rather than the white cloak with the Silver Star that was the emblem of his office.

As Krane disappeared around the corner, Merris dashed forward. She didn't dare take the chance of losing him in the darkness. Ducking down behind a large bin, she wedged her body behind it and peered around the edge of a building. By the light of a street lamp, she could barely make out Krane's shadowy figure. The Prime Warden had stopped, glancing around as he reached for the handle of a door. He cracked the door open. Into that opening Cyrus Krane quietly slipped, pulling the door closed after him.

Merris pulled back behind the bin, pressing up against the cold stone wall. She sat hugging her knees against her chest, shivering, wondering what she should do. She bit her lip, considering. She knew better than to follow her quarry inside the building. The right thing would be to turn back and return to the Hall of the Watchers. But she had no proof to validate her suspicions. Without proof, she would be sorely punished, most likely expelled from Aerysius for sure.

There really was no decision to be made. She rose from her hiding place behind the bin and slipped quietly into the alley. Here, the cobblestones ran with icy rainwater that flowed over the tops of her slippers. She splashed across the street through fast-moving rivulets, pausing beside the building Krane had disappeared into.

She stood there considering the door as the rain came down steadily, plastering her hair against her face. The wood was made of age-grayed pine, reinforced with iron bands. It looked like any other back-alley door in the heart of Aerysius.

Merris gripped the rusted metal handle. She started to pull it open but stopped herself, taking a deep breath and holding it in. Then, with gentle pressure, she pulled the door open just a fraction. Leaning forward, she glanced within then stole quietly inside.

She found herself in some type of storage cellar or undercroft. The room was very dim, lit only by two tapers that glowed from sconces on opposing walls. All around the room were stacked row upon row of wooden crates, the floor littered with straw. The only exit was another door at the far end.

The cellar appeared empty, but anyone could be hiding within those rows of crates. Merris strained to listen. All she could hear was the sound of pattering rain. She considered the door on the opposite wall. Krane must have gone through there ahead of her. Merris did not want to follow him into the guts of the building; she had pushed her luck already.

But she had come this far. Gathering her courage, she took a step forward into the cellar. Then another.

Merris reached the door and pressed an ear up against the wood, straining to listen. There were no sounds coming from the other side. Her hand trembled as she reached for the handle, depressing the latch. The door swung inward, revealing dark depths beyond.

The corridor ahead was lightless, narrow, and empty.

Merris moved forward into the shadows, pulling the door closed behind her. She lingered there for a moment, uncertain, trailing her hand along the cold wall. The stone was rough and uneven, carved by the harsh strokes of tools. This building was old, she surmised, possibly as old as Aerysius itself. So unlike the rest of the structures in the city, which had been seamlessly wrought by magecraft.

Merris stepped into the darkness, using her hands to grope along the walls to either side. She strained to hear the sound of footsteps that might be following. Her fingers traced the stone, searching for a doorway. Ten paces. Fifteen. Twenty. Still no sign of either door or passage leading off. The narrow corridor led straight ahead into the dark bowels of the ancient structure.

When her next footstep felt only air, Merris drew up short. She reached down ahead with her foot, finally encountering stone.

Stairs. Leading downward into blackness.

She shivered, knowing in her heart that she should turn around and go back. Merris forced herself to press forward anyway. It was imperative that she follow through with this plan, despite the risk.

She had discovered a letter in Cyrus Krane's office which professed his disappointment with her character and noted his intent to have Merris removed. Her entire existence in Aerysius depended on finding something she could use against him: some secret, some evidence of treachery. If she didn't, then the Prime Warden would proceed with her expulsion.

Merris was not about to let that happen; she couldn't go back to life on the streets. She had to find something, anything she could use as leverage. Some token, some bargaining chip that would persuade the Prime Warden to let her remain and pursue her studies.

He'd had no business testing her character in the first place. Krane had meddled where he didn't belong....

Merris followed the stairs cautiously as they curved around and down into darkness, arguing with herself at every step. She shouldn't be here—this was becoming too dangerous. She greatly feared what she would find at the bottom of those stairs. Or, worse, what would find her. In the darkness, Merris' imagination ran rampant. She wished for magelight or even a taper to light her path.

A loud, metallic *clank* resounded from far below.

Merris startled, flinching to a crouch. Another noise echoed up the stairwell. Trembling, she regained her feet and turned, ready to flee. From the depths below came the sound of voices.

Merris stopped in her tracks, straining to listen. The voices were distant, too indistinct to make out words. They did not seem to be coming any closer.

She bit her lip, trembling, glancing behind and ahead in desperate indecision. Her foot kept wanting to slide back up the stair behind her. She willed it forward instead. Courage nearly spent, Merris continued down the stairs in the direction of the voices.

She moved slowly, cautiously, creeping forward as silently as she could. There was another sharp, metallic groan. The sound of the voices ceased.

Then came another noise: that of approaching footsteps.

Merris turned and ran. Dizzy with fear, she was not at all careful about her retreat. She took the stairs two at a time, curving back upward in the direction she had come. She staggered and almost fell as she gained the top of the steps, catching herself on the rough stone of the passage. Then she was sprinting forward again on unstable legs down the corridor in the direction of the cellar.

She spilled through the cellar door, throwing it closed behind her and pulling it firmly shut. Wondrous light confronted her vision. She started toward the outer door, but brute stubbornness made her turn back.

Determined to glean some answers from this harrowing night, Merris dropped to her knees and squirmed herself into a corner between two stacks of wooden crates. She wriggled her body between them as far as she could, pressing herself tightly against them and pulling the cowl of her black cloak down to conceal her face. She fought for control over her panting breath, willing the speed of her heart to slow its frenzied pace.

Confident as she could be in her hiding spot, Merris waited as long moments dragged by. She strained to listen. Outside, there was the constant sound of the rain hitting the cobbled street. Inside the cellar, she could hear the faintest noise of soft, scurrying feet. Mice, or even rats, were about their business among the crates.

Abruptly, the cellar door creaked open.

Merris could see nothing; her eyes were veiled behind her cowl. The sound of voices only paces away made her flinch.

"All seems to be progressing well," echoed the familiar voice of Cyrus Krane. "Have Master Remzi keep working on the cipher. There's not much time; we have little more than a fortnight."

"All shall be made ready," responded the voice of another man. That voice Merris did not know. It was calmly authoritative, resonant and deep. Softly, Merris tried pulling back the lip of her cowl just enough to try to get a glimpse of the speaker. It was useless; the stack of crates in front of her blocked her view completely.

Merris realized that the air around her was starting to feel atrociously cold. The fear in her gut was like a tight knot that slowly writhed, working its way upward to choke her throat. She shivered, hugging her arms tightly about herself. The dread within her grew along with the cold, condensing into icy panic. The panic swelled, evolving gradually into terror.

Merris' eyes widened with realization: there was…something else…in the cellar. Something in there with them. Something *wrong*.

"I'm still working on the required payment," Krane's voice continued evenly, as if the Prime Warden himself sensed nothing at all out of sorts. "I have someone in mind, but nothing definitive as yet."

"Be certain there is no deviation from the covenant," the deep voice responded. "Failure is greatly misliked by our Master."

Merris chewed her lip on the edge of panic, the terrible feeling of dread becoming almost unbearable.

Movement stirred in front of her. Something streaked across her vision, coming to a rest on top of the stack of crates. A hand. A man's hand with thick fingers relaxed against the edge of the crate in front of her. A wide, silver band encircled the third finger. Merris shirked back away from the sight of that hand, her eyes welling with tears as she struggled to keep from crying out.

"There will be no failure," Krane's voice echoed, his tone full of dire promise.

Merris heard the sound of the outer door creaking open and then closing once again as the Prime Warden took his leave. The other man yet remained behind, his hand still resting on top of the crate.

The loss of Krane's familiar presence came almost as a blow to Merris. She resisted a powerful urge to bolt out of her hiding place and run for the door.

There was a rustle of fabric as the hand withdrew.

The sound of footsteps, walking away.

Then came the noise of the inner door shivering open and then closed.

Merris lingered, trembling violently, not daring yet to move. The awful fear within her refused to subside. Moments crept by, painfully slow. She strained to listen, hearing nothing. Even the scurrying of the rats had ceased.

Just then, a blur of dark motion streaked across the edge of her vision. The form of a man, all in black, faceless and in shadow.

To be continued...

Glossary

acolyte: apprentice mage who has passed the Trial of Consideration and sworn the acolyte's oath.

Acolyte's Oath: first vow taken by every acolyte of Aerysius to serve the land and its people, symbolized by a chain-like marking on the left wrist.

Aerysius: ancient city where the Masters of Aerysius once dwelt. Destroyed when Aiden Lauchlin unsealed the Well of Tears.

Akins, Tom: blacksmith from Farbrook.

Amani: daughter of Zavier Renquist and wife of Braden Reis who was executed for treason against the Assembly of the Lyceum. *(deceased)*

Amberlie: town in the Vale of Amberlie, where Darien Lauchlin was raised.

Anassis, Myria: ancient Querer of the Lyceum, now a Servant of Xerys.

Archer, Gilroy: son of Kyel and Amelia Archer.

Archer, Kyel: sixth tier grand master of the Order of Sentinels.

artifact: heirloom of power that has been imbued with magical characters or properties.

Arvel: Voice of the High Priest of Wisdom.

Asyaadi Clan: group of kinsfolk who live in the village of Qul in the Black Lands.

Athera: Goddess of Magic.

Athera's Crescent: Mysterious and ancient artifact on the Isle of Titherry.

Atrament: the realm of Death, ruled by the goddess Isap.

Auberdale: capital city of Chamsbrey.

Battlemage: ancient order of mages who accompanied armies into battle before the Oath of Harmony.

Black Lands: what was once Caladorn, now the desecrated home of the Enemy.

blademaster: title awarded to graduates of the School of Arms, or Arms Guild.

Black Solstice: The battle that ended the Fifth Invasion, when Darien Lauchlin destroyed the legions of the Enemy.

Bloodquest: ancient rite of vengeance condoned by the goddess Isap for righteous causes.

Bluecloaks: slang for the Rothscard City Guard.

Book of All Things: book in which the Everlasting Story is said to be scribed by the mightiest of all pens.

Bound: describes a mage who has sworn the Oath of Harmony.

Broden: Guild blademaster employed by the Mayor of Wolden.

Bryn Calazar: ancient capital of Caladorn.

Cadmus: Voice of the High Priest of Wisdom.

Caladorn: fallen nation to the north, now known as the Black Lands.

Catacombs: place of burial that exists partly in the Atrament.

Cerulean Plains: large grassland region in the North of the Rhen.

Chamsbrey: Northern kingdom ruled by Godfrey Faukravar.

Circles of Convergence: ancient foci of magic designed to draw on the vast power of a vortex.

clan: in the Black Lands, a kin-based group of close, interrelated families.

Connel, Byron: ancient Battlemage of the Lyceum, now a Servant of Xerys.

Craghorns: mountains that border the Vale of Amberlie.

Craig, Devlin: Force Commander of Greystone Keep.

Creek Hollow: town in the Vale of Amberlie.

Curse, the: term used to describe the darkening of the skies and earth of the Black Lands, as well as for the unusual weather patterns and electrical storms experienced in the region.

dampen: to shield a mage from sensing the magic field.

damper: an object that has the ability to dampen a mage from sensing the magic field.

darkmage: a mage who has abandoned moral principles.

Death's Passage: *see* **Catacombs**.

Desecration, the: the apocalyptic event that destroyed Caladorn by blackening the skies and the

Emmery: Northern kingdom of the Rhen.

Emmery Palace: the Queen's palace in Rothscard.

Enemy, the: collective name for the inhabitants of the Black Lands.

Everlasting Story: according to Harbingers, the ever-evolving story that chronicles all the events in the world.

eye: area at the heart of a vortex where the lines of the magic field run almost parallel.

Farbrook: town in the Vale of Amberlie.

field lines: currents of the magic field.

First Among Many: in the combined legions of Malikar, second-in-command to the Warden of Battlemages. The highest ranking officer who is not a mage.

First Sentinel, the: *see* **Braden Reis**.

Front, the: area bordering the Black Lands.

Gannet: town in the Vale below Aerysius.

Gateway: portal to the Netherworld.

Glen Farquist: holy city in the Valley of the Gods.

Goddess of the Eternal Requiem: statue of an aspect of the Goddess of Death; her face of Righteous Vengeance.

Grand Master: any Master of the forth tier or higher.

Great Schism: separation between the Assemblies of mages and the ruling bodies of the temples.

Greystone Keep: legendary fortress in the Pass of Lor-Gamorth that fell during the Fifth Invasion.

Hall of the Watchers: Fallen stronghold of the mages of Aerysius, where existed Aerysius' Circle of Convergence.

Hannah, Arden: ancient Querer and former Servant of Xerys. *(deceased)*

Hellpower: *see* **Onslaught**.

High Priest: title of the religious leader of one of the ten Holy Temples.

Isap: Goddess of Death.

Isle of Titherry: Isle off the coast of the Rhen where exists the artifact known as Athera's Crescent.

Jenn: nomadic people of the Cerulean Plains, remnants of an ancient Caladornian horse culture.

Kateem, Khoresh: infamous Emperor who united all of Caladorn under a singular rule before the Desecration.

Khazahar Desert: arid region in the Black Lands that was once an expansive grassland.

Krane, Cyrus: ancient Prime Warden of Aerysius, now a Servant of Xerys.

Larson, Traver: captain at Greystone Keep, friend of Kyel Archer.

Lauchlin, Aidan: firstborn son of Gerald and Emelda Lauchlin who unsealed the Well of Tears. Brother of Darien Lauchlin *(deceased)*.

Lauchlin, Azár: wife of Darien Lauchlin.

Lauchlin, Darien: former eighth-tier Sentinel and Prime Warden of Aerysius, now a Servant of Xerys.

Lauchlin, Emelda: former Prime Warden of Aerysius. *(deceased)*

Lauchlin, Gerald: father of Aidan and Darien Lauchlin, forth tier Grand Master of the Order of Sentinels. Executed by ritual immolation during the Battle of Meridan. *(deceased)*

Lightweaver: in the Black Lands, mages who have the ability to produce a color of magelight that mimics the full spectrum of the sun.

Lyceum: ancient stronghold of the Masters of Bryn Calazar.

Mage's Oath: *see* Oath of Harmony.

magelight: magical illumination that can be summoned by a mage that takes on the signature color of the mage's magical legacy.

magic field: source of magical energy that runs in lines of power over the earth.

Malikar: modern name of the nation that was once Caladorn.

Master: any mage; more specifically, a mage of the first through third tiers.

Meridan: *see* **Battle of Meridan**.

nach'tier: Venthic word for darkmage.

Natural Law: law that governs the workings of the universe that can be strained by the application of magic, but never broken.

necrator: demonic creature that renders a mage powerless in its presence.

Netherworld: realm of Xerys, God of Chaos

Newell, Alexa: woman met by Kyel Archer in the town of Creek Hollow.

Nexus: part of Athera's Crescent where the versions of the Everlasting Story are read by Harbingers.

Norengail, Romana: Queen of Emmery.

North, the: the Northern kingdoms of the Rhen, including Emmery, Chamsbrey and Lynnley.

Oath of Harmony: oath taken by every Master of Aerysius to do no harm, symbolized by a chain-like marking on the right wrist.

Oblivion: outcome for a soul who is denied entry into both the Atrament and the Netherworld, which results in the complete destruction of that soul and the denial of eternity.

Om: God of Wisdom.

Onslaught: the corrupt power of the Netherworld, also known as the Hellfire.

orders: different schools of magic among the Masters of Aerysius and the Lyceum of Bryn Calazar.

Orien's Finger: crag on the edge of the Cerulean Plains where Orien Oathbreaker made his stand and where Darien Lauchlin turned back the Fifth Invasion. Formerly known as Xerys' Pedestal.

Pass of Lor-Gamorth: pass through the Shadowspear Mountains that guards the border of the Black Lands.

Penthos, Luther: High Priest of the Temple of Death.

potential: the ability in a person to sense the magic field.

Pratson, Blake: Mayor of Wolden.

Prime Warden: leaders of the Assembly of the Hall of either Aerysius or the Lyceum.

Proctor, Garret: legendary Force Commander of Greystone Keep *(deceased)*.

Qadir, Sareen: ancient Querer and one the Eight Servants of

Xerys *(deceased)*.

Ranoch son of Tellat: warlord of the Jenn.

Regret, The: poorest quarter of Rothscard.

Reis, Braden: ancient Caladornian Battlemage who was executed for treason against the Assembly of the Lyceum. Founder of the Oath of Harmony and the Order of Sentinels. *(deceased)*

Reis, Quinlan: ancient Arcanist and brother of Braden Reis. One of the Eight Servants of Xerys.

Renquist, Zavier: ancient Prime Warden of the Lyceum, now a Servant of Xerys.

Rhen: name of the collective kingdoms south of the Black Lands.

Rhenic: common language spoken throughout the kingdoms of the Rhen.

rika: ceremonial beverage served by the people of the Khazahar during times of celebration or times of woe.

Rothscard: capital city of Emmery.

Sayeed son of Alborz: Zakai of the Tanisar corps at Tokashi Palace.

Seleni, Naia: former priestess of Death, now a third-tier Master of the Order of Querers.

sensitive: ability in some people to detect the emotions of others. Not dependent on the magic field, and not limited to mages.

Sentinels: order of mages chartered with the defense of the Rhen.

Servants of Xerys: darkmages sworn to the service of Xerys.

Shadowspears: mountains that separate the Black Lands from the Rhen.

saturation: Battlemage tactic of overloading with magical power in anticipation of creating an enormous discharge of force.

sharaq: ancient system of honor code of the Black Lands.

Silver Star: symbol of the Masters of Aerysius and the Lyceum, indicative of the focus lines of the Circles of Convergence.

Soulstone: ancient artifact created by Quinlan Reis as a storage receptacle for a dying mage's legacy.

South, the: Southern kingdoms of the Rhen, including Creston, Gandrish, and Farley.

Swain, Nigel: Prince Consort of Emmery, husband of Queen Romana and Guild blademaster.

Tanisar corps: legions of highly disciplined elite infantry units of the Khazahar.

temples: various sects of worship. Each temple is devoted to a particular deity of the pantheon.

thanacryst: demonic creature that feeds off a mage's legacy.

Thar'gon: magical talisman carried by Byron Connel that is the symbol of the Warden of Battlemages of the Lyceum.

tier: additive progression of levels of power among Masters. The higher a Master's tier, the greater that person's ability to strain the limits of Natural Law.

Tokashi Palace: fortress in the north of the Black Lands.

Torrence, Edric: third tier Master, also known as the Bird Man to the local peasants *(deceased)*.

transfer portal: ancient system of artifacts capable of transferring a person to various locations.

Transference: process by which an acolyte inherits the legacy of power from another mage, resulting in the death of the Master who gives up his or her ability.

Tsula daughter of Mundi: the last Harbinger.

Ul-Calazi, Masil: general of the army of Bryn Calazar.

Unbinding: the act of forswearing the Oath of Harmony.

***Valdivora*:** blade carried by Khoresh Kateem in the Battle of Harmudi, now in the possession of Darien Lauchlin.

Vale of Amberlie: long, narrow valley in the North of the Rhen.

Valley of the Gods: valley where exists the holy city of Glen Farquist.

versions: according to Harbingers, possibilities of the future, as read by Athera's Crescent.

Vintgar: ancient ice fortress and source of the River Nym.

vitrus: archaic term for the Gift passed from a dying mage to their successor.

vortex: cyclone of power where the lines of the magic field superimpose and become vastly intense.

Well of Tears: well that unlocks the gateway to the Nether-world.

Withersby, Meiran: Prime Warden of Aerysius.

Wolden: town in the Kingdom of Emmery.

Xerys: God of Chaos and Lord of the Netherworld.

Zakai: officers of the Tanisar corps that form their own distinctive social class.

Zanikar: magical sword and artifact created by Quinlan Reis.

Zephia: Goddess of the Winds.

The Orders of Mages

Order of Arcanists: order of mages chartered with the study and creation of artifacts and heirlooms of power.

Order of Architects: order of mages chartered with the construction of magical infrastructure.

Order of Battlemages: order of mages chartered with martial applications of the magic field.

Order of Chancellors: order of mages chartered with the governance of the Assembly.

Order of Empiricists: order of mages chartered with the theoretical study of the magic field, its laws and principles.

Order of Harbingers: order of mages chartered with maintaining watch over Athera's Crescent.

Order of Naturalists: order of mages chartered with the study of Natural Law.

Order of Querers: order of mages chartered with practical applications of the magic field.

Order of Sentinels: order of mages chartered with watching over and protecting the Rhen in a manner consistent with the Oath of Harmony.

Acknowledgements

I would like to thank Daniel Crabbe, Ashlynn Mudgett, Cameron Mudgett, and Paul Malcore for being the most incredible, supportive family a writer could ever ask for.

Connect
MLSpencerFiction.com
Facebook.com/MLSpencerAuthor
Twitter.com/MLSpencerAuthor